Awakened

Awakened A NOVEL

BY MARGARET ABRAMS

THE JEWISH PUBLICATION SOCIETY

OF AMERICA

PHILADELPHIA   5715·1954

TO HANNA AND RABBI . . .

*who lived in these years and preserved
for those less staunch of heart a
sense of the goodness of life.*

Awakened

Chapter 1

IN AUGUST, in the Rhineland, the summer is a ripeness, still and full; and children pick berries in the thickets along the roadside—but perhaps not in August 1941!

Ellen Rosen, who thought of the Rhineland, sat beside her husband in a train that had crept for hours through the vastness of the American midwest. They were nearing their destination at last. Ellen turned her eyes from the parched land that, itself, seemed to quiver with the vibration of the train.

"Is—*flach*—is not?" she said to her husband, making a leveling gesture with one expressive hand.

"Is flat," Kurt Rosen amended in his carefully articulated English.

Ellen nodded.

"It is also high, a high plain, 6,000 feet above sea level," he told her, and into his face came that special keenness for knowledge that she knew so well.

Ellen's dark eyes flashed him a look of mingled indulgence and exasperation. "I have no interest in sea level, *mein Goldeness.* Only that the land is—*flach*—and no—*Baum.*"

"No trees. Cannot the wife of the new rabbi speak English?" he chided her gently.

"*Nein!*" she tensed. "It is the rabbi, not his wife, who spent two years learning English."

"Say *this,*" he told her.

"Siss."

"No, put the tip of your tongue under the lower teeth, then the sound will be correct."

"This."

"Fine, now. Say *thank you.*"

"Sank you."

"Think of your tongue."

"Thank you."

"Right! You can do it!"

They laughed together. Whenever they laughed it was with the consciousness of laughter, for it was a thing they had had to

3

learn again; it was something they did with a sense of purpose, like eating or walking.

Beside the drab, yellow, railway station in Fall City, Sam Levinson, Benny Gold and Herman Morris waited as a welcoming committee to greet the new rabbi and his wife due to arrive on the train from New York.

Sam Levinson glanced at his watch repeatedly.

"What are you so nervous about, Sam?" Herman Morris asked, his thin face set in an expression of slightly malicious drollery.

"What'll we say to him?" Sam replied impatiently. "A German Jew! He probably won't even be able to speak Yiddish. We won't be able to understand his English. And I sure as hell can't speak German. With all the rabbis to pick from, why did we have to take a refugee?"

"Aw, come on Sam," Benny said, grinning. "You're one of the town's official welcomers, aren't you. You've welcomed everybody from FDR to the visiting firemen. Surely you're not going to get stage fright over welcoming your own rabbi!"

Sam Levinson shot Benny a cutting glance. He was thinking that a Jew who ran a pawnshop had a hell of a nerve talking to him like that.

The train ground slowly into the station. Ellen Rosen reached to the rack above the seat for the smallest of the bags, while her husband checked the rest of the luggage. Then she looked around for something else to do; she had the feeling that, as long as she could find something to do, she could delay the moment at hand.

"Come, Sweetheart!" Kurt took her arm. She wished that he had said *Liebchen*. It was a word that had the softness and endearment of having been worn long near the heart. She smiled at him.

They stepped down from the train on the stool the redcap placed for them, and the three men Ellen had glimpsed from the window moved toward them.

"Rabbi Rosen?"

"Yes—yes."

"Rabbi, I'm Sam Levinson—and this is Benny Gold—and Herman Morris."

"Indeed. I remember your letters. It is most kind of you to meet us."

With his spontaneous interest in people, Kurt Rosen forgot the special care he still must give to speaking, and the sounds that he uttered were German although the words were English.

4

He saw with regret that this distortion laid an embarrassing constraint upon his welcomers, and he felt a swift desire to put them at ease.

"Gentlemen, may I present my wife," he said, speaking with greater care. He caught Ellen's hand, and she moved closer beside him.

"How do you do," Ellen said, with hardly a trace of an accent.

The three men turned to her as one. Sam Levinson, despite his suavity of manner, had begun to sweat copiously. Now pleased surprise relaxed his face.

In that moment Kurt and Ellen Rosen, in a special glance, brought to each other a glint of humor in a situation that was almost humorless. What Sam Levinson mistook for Ellen's mastery of English was only a gift of inflection acquired through years of studying voice. She could have rendered a phrase in Siamese as artfully.

"Shalom—welcome to Fall City!" Sam Levinson said, a little self-conscious over his renewed attempt at heartiness.

Ellen flicked another meaningful glance at her husband.

"Sank you!" she said with solemn graciousness.

From the back seat of Sam Levinson's Cadillac, Kurt and Ellen Rosen caught a rapid glimpse of the town that would be their first American home. Their two years in New York had been a preparation for this moment, and now that it had arrived it seemed invested with unreality. There was about the town a midwestern plainness, squareness, straightness, flatness. The earth and what was built upon it seemed blended in a certain mood, and to Ellen it was a mood of strangeness—rigid and unbeautiful.

With great effort Ellen concentrated upon what the men in the front seat were saying—that they would go first for a look at the synagogue; then to the apartment that had been rented for the rabbi, next door; and then to a lake where the congregation was assembled to meet the Rosens.

"A lake—a *See?*" Ellen murmured incredulously, remembering the look of the countryside from the train window.

"A lake," Kurt assured her quietly.

Sam Levinson laughed. "Sure we have a lake. Antelope Lake. Man made, through the courtesy of WPA."

Ellen understood little of what he was saying—the Atlantic Ocean—Lake Michigan—Antelope Lake—the sense of the diminishing was frighteningly symbolic. Ellen slipped her hand in her husband's.

5

Sam Levinson stopped the car in front of a small tan brick building.

"Well, here we are Rabbi. This it it." Benny Gold said.

To Ellen it seemed that this building possessed a plainness and squareness that were of this place. Inscribed in the large cement arch above the door was the name, "Temple B'nai Emanuel." Two tall, cast-iron lamp posts rose on either side of a stairway that lead to double doors. They climbed the stairs and opened the door, and abruptly they were in the sanctuary of the small synagogue.

The very abruptness of the entrance startled up a host of memories for Ellen. She remembered a side entrance in the Duisburg synagogue where ivy once grew on the grey stone and where had hovered a quietness that would lay hold upon her gay and tempestuous spirit when she entered by that way.

The men paused to put on the *yarmulcas* that Herman Morris took from the drawer of a stand which contained the prayer books. The rabbi took one of the books in his hand. He walked slowly down the center aisle and the sharp sense of remembrance that had come to Ellen just inside the doorway came to Kurt Rosen as he stood before the ark of the new synagogue.

> *. . . the call in the night . . . "Rabbi! The Nazis! They're in the synagogue with picks and axes!" . . . that night Ellen waited beside a window in their apartment and watched the spire of a nearby cathedral stained blood red by the glow of the fire that consumed the synagogue . . . and Kurt Rosen stood in the street before the burning temple and saw the savagery that leapt from face to fire, from fire to face . . . and all across the land the synagogues were burning . . .*
> *"Shema Yisroel Adonoi Elohenu Adonoi Ehod!"*
> *"Hear O Israel, the Lord is our God, the Lord is One!"*

"Come Rabbi, let us show you the rest of the building." Sam Levinson was saying.

When they had finished their tour, they left the little building by the back entrance, and Sam Levinson glanced again at his watch.

"We'll have just enough time to see the apartment and leave your things. Then we'll have to start for the lake," he said briskly.

Ellen felt almost ill with the heat and weariness of the long trip. "Could we not . . ." she began, but she did not finish, and Kurt briefly pressed her hand in his. The Rosens started for the car again, but Sam Levinson called after them.

"No, here, next door! It will be convenient for you. Right next to the Temple and close to town."

Ellen turned with bewildered disbelief to contemplate the big, dreary house toward which Sam Levinson was leading them. In Germany her cleaning woman had lived in such a house, and once Ellen had given her new curtains to hide a little its look of dejection. Here, a little boy played, half naked, within the lazy shower of a sprinkler in the yard where grass grew only in tufts. And on one of the pillars of the wide porch was a placard which informed the public, "Rooms to Rent." Sam Levinson opened the screen door and moved ahead of them up a dim stairway. A door on the first floor opened and a woman, with a scrawny neck and wispy hair, poked her head out and then back in again and closed the door.

"Your landlady," Sam Levinson murmured, laughing as if there were some joke.

At the head of the stairs, he thrust open a door.

"I think we can fix it up so you'll be quite comfortable here," he said with faint distaste as if he were seeing the room for the first time. The air of the small, tight apartment was musty and oppressive. Sam raised a window, but it would not stay up. Benny looked around for something to prop it, and Herman hurriedly disappeared down the stairs to bring up the other bag.

"It will be fine," Kurt Rosen was saying.

Ellen Rosen stood still in the center of the room and tried to imagine herself in this setting—a faded rug, a lumpy couch, a bed in a curtained alcove, a tiny kitchen separated from the one large room by a half partition. Kurt's eyes met hers briefly. Without speaking, he went behind the partition to bring her a drink of water. He brought it in a glass that once had contained jelly, and for no apparent reason Ellen thought of the night that he had been made chief rabbi of the region of the lower Rhine.

Ellen felt the tears rising in her eyes. She turned away, toward the window that now was propped with a book. So this was home, and not even time to close the door! Sam Levinson was speaking again in his rapid, clipped English. Ellen felt the defensive impatience of the welcomers. The congregation waited at the lake.

To have traveled seventeen hundred miles in two days would have made almost any destination seem dear; but to be whisked away again, another thirty miles across a drought-scorched plain, to meet people who could just as well have stayed at home to be

7

greeted—Ellen knew that someday she might laugh about all of this; but not now. She closed her eyes and let the hot wind beat across her temples and into the edges of her black hair which she wore in a thick braid across her head. Eventually the lake etched itself across the horizon, a blue gray along the green gray of the land. It was a lake on a prairie, a flat expanse of water on a greater flat expanse of dry, parched earth. As Sam Levinson's Cadillac spewed up the dust along the road that skirted the shore, Ellen felt her nostrils assailed by the incongruous smell of dead fish. On a small shelf of land that jutted out above the lake stood a rustic western pavilion. And it was here that the congregation waited, and for Ellen Rosen there was a grim incongruity in this fact, too.

Sam Levinson was again girding himself with geniality. To Ellen, watching him, it seemed almost a physical gesture. A man stuck his head out of the door of the pavilion.

"They're here!" he called back to the others behind him. And as they entered the big, rustic room, a woman in a frumpy hat was trying to restore order by continuously tapping a knife handle against a glass; but no one paid any attention to her. Those nearest the door crowded around to meet the Rosens. There began a murmuring of names, a shaking of hands—a firm clasp, a limp one; bright eyes, dull eyes; the voices of Russia and Poland . . . and, above it all, the flashing nickelodeon in the corner, catching up the voices in a cacophony of sound.

In the press of people Ellen felt Kurt being drawn away from her side; she felt a wild impulse to reach out to him. But instead she clasped the hand that was extended to her, and smiled, and murmured the name that was spoken.

It seemed to Ellen that these people who crowded around her were caught in some fierce intimacy against which they secretly rebelled. Each person seemed to step forward with the estimate of the others defining his manner. There was in their very way of moving all the difference between Sam Levinson's "Paris Originals" and Sid Fineburg's second-hand suits on Fourth Street . . . all the difference between Dr. Ben Klein's crowded outer office and Jack Metz's lonely little Model A Ford in which he carried his knife-sharpening tools. Ellen didn't know the details, but the tenseness of emotion she could feel. And she began to feel that this tremendous pressure was being exerted against her, as well— that she was being forced into the mold of their preconceived idea of her . . . refugee . . . immigrant . . . foreigner!

8

Ellen cast a frantic glance at Kurt. His eyes had been awaiting hers, and they flashed her a look of teasing cajolery. And with a surge of familiar exasperated fondness, she stood still for a second and watched how Kurt already had learned the knack of making these people feel at home with him. Vigorous but gentle, alert but relaxed, he was, here among the Texas cattle brands and rustic benches, the same as he had been in Berlin or Duisburg or Koenigsberg or New York.

Ellen drew from the sight of Kurt confidence to ease the ache in her throat, and her eyes were even smiling a little as they turned back upon the crowd and came to rest on the small spry man who stood before her now. She had noticed him a few moments before, nibbling the fringes of his white mustache. And now he was pumping her hand excitedly, and his jaws were moving up and down although no sounds were coming from his lips. His pale-blue eyes were red-rimmed, so that he had the incongruous look of a white rabbit wearing a gray fedora.

"Mr. Friedman," she said, with inner laughter directed at herself instead of at him, "it was so nice you could come all this way to meet us. When we are at home, you must come to us for a cup of coffee."

"Would be better, maybe, a glass of tea mit lemon for me and mine wife," he replied, his mustache twitching.

"A glass of tea with lemon, then!" Ellen replied, and she shook his hand again, and in a happy daze he moved off into the crowd.

This moment released Ellen from the constricting sense of isolation and suddenly she knew the awkward, jerky, ineloquent words that were spoken to her for the welcome of hearts that live too closely with their own loneliness. And her own warmth reached out to the embarrassment and confusion of the others; for a little while she escaped the poignancy of her situation.

But then, across the floor came Benny Gold, leading by the hand his wife, Tita, red of hair and bright of eye, whose petulant face was skewered into a smile.

"It's wonderful you and the Rabbi could come to Fall City," Tita said when Benny had brusquely made the introductions. "I think you'll get to like us. Sometimes we're just a bunch of stinkers . . . but then, we're pretty nice, too!" She took Ellen's hand and Ellen tried to understand that her wish was to be friendly. She tried, but her head was beginning to ache.

Benny laughed loudly.

"Hey! Tita really said it!" he called over his shoulder to Herman Morris, the second member of the welcoming committee, who was standing now beside his wife, Esther, a tall young woman who carried her pregnancy with a certain regality.

"Tita says we're a bunch of stinkers, but we're pretty nice, too!" Benny elaborated.

Herman only smiled his bored smile, but the crudeness of the moment seemed to disturb his wife, and she reached out to clasp Ellen's hand with a nervous little gesture.

"Don't pay any attention to them!" she said, casting a reproving glance at Tita, who, in turn put an arm around her and hugged her briefly.

"See! . . . we don't like each other, but we do!" Tita exclaimed. Ellen smiled a little, not knowing how to enter into this brash heartiness.

But she was saved from the necessity of making any response because Sam Levinson approached her abruptly, his lip curled in distaste at the innocent vulgarity of the exchange he had just witnessed. He took her arm possessively. "Come with me, I want you to meet my wife," he said, shrugging off the others without a word.

Ellen followed him, but their progress across the floor was halted by a large woman who moved into their path obdurately.

"This is Mrs. Stein," Sam Levinson said impatiently, pausing because he could not proceed.

Ellen caught a fat hand in hers. She felt herself scrutinized by shrewd hazel eyes over which the lids seemed to breathe in a curious flexibility of motion.

"*Herlich Vilkommen*," Mrs. Stein said in her most ingratiating manner, heaving her pendulous bosom as she spoke.

"Thank you, how do you do," Ellen said.

"*Vee gefält es dich*," Mrs. Stein said.

The sounds were faintly like German, but not enough like German. "I'm sorry, Mrs. Stein, I don't speak Yiddish," Ellen replied.

"Don't speak Yiddish! A rabbi's wife and you don't speak Yiddish! Doesn't the Rabbi speak Yiddish either?"

Ellen shook her head.

"Jews and they don't speak Yiddish! What kind of Jews!" Mrs. Stein tossed up her hands and the flesh of her arms swayed with the gesture. She burst into nervous, conciliatory laughter, but there was neither warmth nor humor in the sound. Yet her eyes entreated Ellen to understand that she had not meant to hurt her, that she had not meant to say the wrong thing.

"I'm glad you don't speak Yiddish; that will make two of us!" someone said at Ellen's shoulder.

Ellen turned quickly and the face into which she looked was cool and beautiful and framed in straight black hair drawn tightly back. The woman who had come to stand beside Sam Levinson moved with a curious unrhythmic grace. As she held out her hand to Ellen, the silver bracelet on her wrist jangled pleasantly, and with the movement a faint scent of French perfume seemed to escape the folds of her simple, elegant, black dress. Her manner was brittle, but her handclasp was warm. She smiled at Ellen, and Ellen returned the smile gratefully.

"This is my wife, Myra . . . Mrs. Rosen," Sam Levinson said, the pride of possession heavy in his voice.

"I'm glad to meet you," Ellen said with slow sincerity, and then, before she could say more, she was caught again in the crush of strange names, strange faces, strange hands to shake.

Much later, when the younger members of the crowd had begun to dance to the tune of the nickelodeon, and when the others were splitting up into small groups around the rustic pine tables, Ellen was standing once more beside Kurt, her hand in his. A crochety, stooped old man in a quite debonaire sports jacket, came to them.

"Rabbi, I invite your wife for a cup of coffee," he said with a sort of whimsical gallantry.

"Good!" Kurt laughed. He shook hands with the man, and calling upon his prodigious memory, he said: "Ellen, this is Mr. Isador Jacobson . . . is not right?"

"That's right, Rabbi," Mr. Jacobson nodded. "We'll be in that corner over there, where it's quiet."

The blithe and spirited little old man led Ellen to a table which was back of the nickelodeon and away from the blare of music, the glare of lights. Two cups of coffee were waiting already, and a cheese sandwich on a paper plate for Ellen. Ellen felt oddly touched; she felt almost as if she would like to cry. Gratefully she bit into the dry sandwich, tasted the hot coffee.

"Is good!" she lied blandly. "You are a real friend."

"Friend in need is friend indeed, they say here," he answered. He splayed out the square fingers of his right hand to emphasize his point, and his bleak face lit up as he watched Ellen.

"I want only to tell you that so far you do all right. So far you make just one mistake."

"What is?" Ellen asked.

"Admitting that you can't speak Yiddish!"

"This is not something you must admit!" Ellen retorted laughing.

Mr. Jacobson laughed, too, for this was the answer he had desired.

"Is it so important . . . to speak Yiddish?" Ellen asked.

He nodded. "Here you have mostly East Juden," he said after a moment.

"And you?" Ellen teased gently, having detected already his strong Litvak accent.

He shrugged. "I was born in Kaunas," he said. "I remember what it was like to get up at 4 o'clock in the morning to read Torah at my father's side. I remember what it was like to wrap up in a *tallis* for warmth and not to forget what I put it on for in the first place."

"And the others?"

"When they came here . . . not most of these you see here tonight, but their fathers . . . and they were free in America and they could choose what to give up and what to keep out of the old life . . . what do you suppose they decided to give up?"

Ellen shook her head.

"The only precious thing they had in the first place . . . the love of learning. The other things they kept!"

Ellen looked out over the crowd of blurred faces. "I think I will like the people here," she said trying to make herself believe that it was true.

"Like them? Not like them? I like them all right. But they melted a little too much in the melting pot."

"Do they know you think so?" Ellen asked, teasing a little again, and relishing, at the same time, this odd small moment of rapport.

He shrugged again, and his gray eyes met hers levelly. "I only want that you not expect it to be different than it is. They're people. Not better, not worse than people anywhere. But I didn't want you to expect it to be different than it is."

Hours later, Sam Levinson drove Kurt and Ellen Rosen back to town, back to the small apartment. And with the closing of the door, they knew the first privacy, the first chance to reach out to each other, offering comfort and solace for the strangeness of this new life.

Kurt took Ellen into his arms and kissed her. He felt in her

12

body the tautness of her effort to accept whatever came as a matter of course. And their eyes met with the reluctance of fearing to reveal too much. Then suddenly they were laughing.

"It's not funny, I sink," Ellen said finally.

"Say *think!*" Kurt coaxed.

"No . . . *sink! O, lass mich in Ruh'!*"

"It would be funny if it were not happening to us," Kurt suggested.

"Kurt . . . how will it be . . . ?"

"Ellen it is always strange to begin a new life. But we can make it a good life. It is up to us."

"It has not always been up to us . . . making a good life," Ellen said.

"Here it will be up to us, you will see," Kurt told her.

"But Kurt . . . for you . . . to be a rabbi here! The people are so few . . . and they do not even seem to like each other. And that they should give you such a place to live! Here there is so little."

"Ellen that is good. To begin again a man must have something to build. To come where the building already is done—that is not a beginning, that is a refuge."

"Refuge . . . ?" Ellen seemed to search for her memory of this word.

"Refugee?" Kurt reminded her.

"Then you will not be a refugee, Kurtchen. You will build."

"Yes, Ellen, we will not be refugees."

Ellen looked about her at the small drab room where they sat. Gnats that had sieved through the window screen batted themselves drunkenly against the naked light bulb. Ellen tried very hard to see all of this as Kurt saw it, as a challenge to creative effort. Kurt watched her trying. He reached out a hand and brushed back from her forehead a strand of hair that had escaped her braid.

"It is so hot, Ellen," he said, "let's go walk for a little while."

Together they went back downstairs, to stand beneath the stars on the sidewalk in front of the darkened temple—to feel the coolness and the openness and the freedom of the night.

II

The roof of the big frame house held the heat pressed tight between its shingles. The barking of a dog, the sighing of air brakes on a truck that lumbered out on the highway a block away, entered the open window as hardly more than the illusion of sound. The room was still and Ellen Rosen slept the sleep of exhaustion.

Kurt Rosen knew when she slept, and he was glad to be yet awake. In waking hours he must never doubt her valiance, but when she slept he could cherish the vulnerability of her woman's soul. Now, when sleep would not come, Kurt thought of Ellen—and of Koenigsberg where he had met her—on a fall day—in 1924—the week he had come there as substitute rabbi during a leave of absence from the Theological Seminary of Berlin.

. . . In the street, Johannis Strasse in Koenigsberg, stood a tall graystone house with iron grilling; and outside pigeons pecked in the sidewalk crevices for seeds, and in the large bare room where Herr Professor Bach gave his voice lessons, the soft flutter of their wings could be heard now and again against the skylight. It was there that he had met Ellen—and he had come there quite by chance.

Jacob Klein, first cantor of the synagogue, had come into the educational building just as Kurt finished teaching a confirmation class. It was barely three o'clock, the sun was high, and the air coming in through the open window smelled of the salt of the sea.

"This is a good afternoon to spend over a cup of coffee in the Café am Artushof. Most of Koenigsberg will pass by there before dinner time. We might get a table on the sidewalk," Jacob suggested. He had a round, bland look and a teasing persuasiveness.

Kurt laughed. "My spare time is pledged to my thesis," he told him.

"Aha, I know better. I saw the tickets on your desk—to the opera—to the theater. Is that how you work on your thesis?"

"That is a different thing."

Jacob made a solemn face. "You know what it says in *The Duties of the Heart*—that on the Day of Judgment a man will be called upon to account for every innocent pleasure he has denied himself!—come!"

Kurt sighed resignedly. "All right. Just for a cup of coffee, then."

As they passed the graystone house on their way to town, Jacob remembered that he must deliver a message to Herr Bach.

"Only for a moment—and you must meet him anyway," he said.

The man who answered the door, when they had been ushered

14

upstairs to his studio, was tall, with a look of long-wristed angularity. And his clothes seemed oddly unsettled on his gaunt frame. But in his greeting when Jacob had made the introductions, there was an awkward warmth.

"Allow me to introduce Professor Bach, Herr Dr. Rosen," Jacob said.

"Come in, come in! Jacob, Herr Dr. Rosen."

"You're giving a lesson," Jacob said, "we'll stay only a moment."

It was then that Kurt looked beyond their host and noticed for the first time the young woman who stood beside the piano near the big windows that faced out on the street. The very blackness of her hair and eyes seemed to reproach the wooing brilliance of the sun that flooded the window behind her and laid a glow on her skin. She stood so still that Kurt suddenly wanted to laugh, but her very stillness intrigued him. It was the taut stillness of the vibrantly alive.

"Dr. Rosen, may I present my pupil, Miss Ellen Meier," Professor Bach said.

Some new quality in the teacher's voice brought Kurt's eyes back to him briefly. Then he turned again to Ellen Meier. The solemnity of her manner challenged him to provoke some gaiety. It was at that moment that he became aware of the pigeons that fluttered against the skylight.

"Do the pigeons come to hear you sing?" he asked her, his gray eyes taking on the depth of humor.

A flush rose in her face, as if she felt that he was making fun of her. She looked at him questioningly.

"Perhaps they do," she said.

Kurt was instantly aware that his attempt at levity had been misunderstood. But contrition seemed too somber a thing to be imposed upon his suddenly buoyant mood. The smile that came to his lips, instead of implying apology, invited her to join him in this bantering humor. But instead she glanced uncertainly at Herr Bach who was watching her reflectively. Kurt had suddenly the feeling that he had intruded upon a moment of rapport, and something combative in his nature was roused. His eyes were upon Ellen Meier and he felt oddly rewarded at the color that deepened in her face.

Unaware of the currents of emotion that crisscrossed the room, Jacob Klein was hurtling on in one of his breathless conversations. Reluctantly Herr Bach turned back to him, and Ellen, in an attempt to retire completely from this situation, took a dust-rag from the piano bench and began to dust the piano. She moved with a quick, almost angry grace, and Kurt Rosen's smile took on the faintest hint of insolence as he watched her.

"The piano is clean, Miss Meier, why do you dust?" he asked her.

Some exquisite complexity of response flickered in Ellen Meier's eyes. "It is not clean, I think," she said.

Herr Bach, continuing to give Jacob a cursory attention, seemed, at a deeper level of consciousness, to be acutely aware of what Ellen was feeling. He moved around the piano until he stood beside her. He took the dust-cloth from her hand and gave her a sheet of music in an oddly cognizant gesture. Although they moved no closer together, Ellen Meier seemed to retreat within the protectiveness of this gesture. Kurt noticed more discerningly this tall man with the wise eyes and gentle mouth, with the quickness of perception so unmatched to his languor of movement. And what Kurt had felt first as combativeness, became a quick resentment.

"I would like to hear you sing!" he said abruptly.

The girl's dark eyes met his squarely, at last, as if acknowledging the note of demand that had been in his voice. Slowly she shook her head, and it was a movement of firmness, not of shyness.

Herr Bach glanced at her. "Another time," he said quietly.

"Then we must go, we're disturbing your lesson," Jacob said, beginning the round of polite goodbys. When they were down on the street again, Kurt found that he had no patience for Jacob's garrulousness. The post office, looming morosely on the left of the street, suggested his means of escape.

"Jacob, you must excuse me! I completely forgot, I have two letters that must get off by the afternoon post. We'll have the cup of coffee another time."

Jacob laughed. "Sure old man. She'll pass right by here, I think. And it shouldn't be more than half an hour. Good luck!"

Kurt saw her coming and he walked nonchalantly down the broad steps of the post office building.

"Why hello! We meet again!" he said with feigned surprise, not entirely able to keep a straight face.

A smile flicked the nerve at the corner of her mouth without actually changing the expression of her lips. "So we do," she replied. And her sudden whim to indulge his pretense seemed to match her mood to his.

16

"Now that we've met again, perhaps we could take a walk," Kurt suggested. "You could show me the old fortifications of Koenigsberg."

Her eyes lit with amusement at his zestfulness. "I've never seen the old fortifications of Koenigsberg," she told him.

"You've lived here all your life and you've never seen them!" he replied with mock reproach. "Well, I've seem them already. I'll show them to you."

"How long have you been here?" she asked him.

"A week. I'm to substitute for the rabbi at the Temple till spring."

"I know."

"You go there?"

She cast him a quick glance. "Sometimes."

"Not often?"

She shook her head.

"I do know we'd better take a bus part of the way to the fort," she said.

Half an hour later, as they walked along the wet sand of the beach toward the looming fortifications, Kurt watched the panorama of what was happening as it reflected in Ellen's face. This face which had been so studiously composed when he saw her first, held now a caprice of mood, a mood compounded of sun and wind and sea-smell, taking to itself the piquance of a small girl squatting in the sand, the gentle melancholy of a bearded old man standing against the wharf, a mood taking into itself all that came within the gaze until it was the very essence of life. And Kurt wondered how he had known that this would be so.

It seemed to Kurt that the sight and sound and feel of life crowded in upon Ellen too intensely to be put aside, and this intense receptivity stirred and confounded him all the more for the fact that it seemed to have so little to do with himself. When they had climbed to the top of one of the ramifications of the fortress, they stood looking at the scene that spread away from them. A shy wantonness, a hint of a bright, wild ecstasy came into Ellen's eyes as she looked out at the sea. Kurt put a hand beneath her chin and turned her face from the sea. He looked for a moment into her face which was suddenly solemn and closed again into its provocative calmness. And then he kissed her lips. . . .

Beside Kurt Rosen his wife stirred, and then she slept once more—and the city of Koenigsberg was far, far away.

Chapter 2

THE NEXT morning Ellen Rosen awoke to the sound of a door closing, and with a start she realized that Kurt was no longer beside her. And then she heard him calling her name.

"Ellen, come! I have brought our breakfast!"

Ellen sat up on the side of the bed. A small sigh passed her lips, and she reached for her robe. "Kurtchen, why so early?" she called to him.

"It's eight o'clock!" he replied, coming now to catch her by the hand. "Come see what I bought. Is most wonderful supermarket at the corner!"

Ellen stumbled sleepily after him into the tiny kitchen. A carton of strawberries, in their pristine pinkness, sat on the cabinet.

"Most wonderful supermarket . . ." Ellen murmured philosophically. She was thinking that there had been luscious, ripe, red strawberries in the supermarkets of Manhattan when she and Kurt got off the boat, although it was a cold and dreary day in March. And now, in late August, strawberries in Texas. Where in America were the joys and sadness of season!

Ellen began to pinch off the little green crowns with quick nimble fingers.

And Kurt began to make the coffee in the battered coffee pot he found on the stove. It was his one culinary accomplishment and he performed it with his usual zest.

"Ellen, did you know that Alaska grows the largest strawberries in the world?" he asked companionably.

Ellen turned to him with a look of fond exasperation . . . but because he was so serious she had to laugh.

"No, *mein Goldeness,* I did not know it. How do you happen to know it!"

"Something I read to better my English," he replied blandly. "Are you not interested?"

"If I am interested you will tell me about the soil . . . and the climate!" Ellen retorted, her dark eyes teasing him.

18

Kurt laughed, a low, mellow, bouncing laugh.

"You are a naughty girl!" he said.

Ellen was pressing the loaf of bread in its bright cellophane wrapper, and watching her finger prints erase themselves. "Is like a loaf of air!" she said with wonder. "Was there no rye bread . . . no hard rolls!"

"The Americans like such bread," Kurt replied, defending his purchase stoutly.

"I am not so American on this point," Ellen retorted. She took out three slices and tried to decide what to do with them. She looked in the toaster of the stove and decided not to use it until it had been thoroughly scoured.

"We will eat it so," Kurt said, taking down a chipped saucer from the cabinet, and putting it into Ellen's hand. "Come now, the coffee's ready. And we have the strawberries with cream."

They sat together at the tiny table.

"What will you do now?" Ellen asked.

"I go to my office at the Temple. There are some books to unpack. And I must make my sermon."

Ellen nodded. "I stay here . . . and clean!"

When Kurt had gone to the synagogue, Ellen looked about her. The woodwork was begrimed, the windows were filmed, the floors had the pallor of dirty water scrubbings, the curtains were limp and dingy, the kitchen stove was caked with the grease of many fryings, and a cockroach wandered with idle unconcern along the cabinet.

Ellen dressed quickly and walked to the grocery store. She went directly to the counter where cleaning equipment was displayed and began to fill a basket—soap, steel wool, soap flakes, ammonia, a mop, a broom, wax, polish and starch. She had one five dollar bill in her purse, and with what was left of it she bought a loaf of rye bread, and then stopped at the meat counter.

"I would like to buy a little cheese," she said.

"Sure thing, lady!" The young man behind the counter lifted a round orange cheese out of the case and took a long thin knife out of the rack.

"A little swiss Gruyère," Ellen suggested, tentatively.

"Swiss what?"

"Swiss Gruyère," Ellen said with that feeling of going into an abyss which language difficulties always gave her.

"This here is long horn . . . American long horn," the young man said, as he began to run the knife along its cheesecloth covering.

19

"Long horn?" Ellen repeated doubtfully.

"Long horn, like in cows!" he began to whistle impatiently while he waited for her to decide.

"I take half a pound, please," she said with dignity.

Ellen took her bundles and walked back to the apartment. Immediately she set to work. She took down the curtains and put them to soak. She washed the windows; then the woodwork. She scrubbed the floor and waxed it. She finished washing the curtains and took them downstairs in the dishpan.

Ellen knocked at the door of her landlady's room, and immediately the wispy-haired woman opened the door.

"I'm Mrs. Rosen," Ellen began.

"Well, I declare, I was going to come up!"

Ellen held the dishpan in both hands. The scrawny hand that her landlady held out for her to shake bobbed back under her apron where it began nervously clasping its mate.

"Mr. Levinson said anything you wanted! He's a right nice man," she told Ellen. "My name's McCurdy—Belle McCurdy."

"How do you do," Ellen said gravely, "I wondered if I might use the clothesline."

"Well now, you certainly may. It's around in the back."

The little boy who had been playing in the sprinkler, the afternoon before, came to watch Ellen hang the curtains on the wobbly line that was stretched from the house wall to a tree.

"Are you a German?" he said.

"No. Not any more."

"Are you still a Jew?" he asked.

"Billy you come here!" a voice called from inside the house, but Billy made no response.

"The Jews go to church next door," he said.

"Yes."

"They go at night—on Friday!" he commented curiously.

Ellen observed him closely, there was no malice in his candid discourse. He watched her with guileless blue eyes.

"Here, hold the pins for me," Ellen suggested to divert his attention. He considered this proposal seriously.

"I'll have to go ask my mother if I can," he told her. And like a young rabbit he bounded away.

Ellen shrugged, she held the pins herself and hung the curtains to dry. When she went back upstairs she began to work on

20

the stove. To work so hard was a protest, the only protest she could make. And when the working was done the protesting would be done. Her hands were long in the soap and water, and the faint breeze of morning died away and the August sun was bright on the clear panes of the windows. And the sweat ran down Ellen's forehead into her eyes. It was sweat that burned her eyes, not tears. And she felt the fierce need to cover every inch, to cleanse every inch, to make ready for a new beginning, to make bearable, if not beautiful.

At nearly 2 o'clock Ellen sat down to rest. She wiped her brow with the back of her hand and considered whether she would iron the curtains now or wait until the cool of evening . . . it would be nice to have them up when Kurt came home. When she had rested for a few moments, she went downstairs to take them off the line.

As Ellen came back up the stairs, she saw that the door of her apartment was open and she heard voices from inside. She glanced over her shoulder and saw Esther Morris, Herman Morris' pregnant wife, carrying a large basket up the stairs.

Ellen turned back to her quickly. "Here, let me help you," she said, setting down her dishpan of dry curtains and taking the basket from Esther's reluctant hands.

"Surprise!" Esther said, her breath coming a little quickly. Ellen looked questioningly at her and at the basket which contained an assortment of groceries.

The people who spoke in the apartment had come to the door, and several more were entering the hall downstairs. They all seemed to be talking and laughing at once—to be exhorting Ellen to some response. With a sharp dismay she looked down at the basket of groceries in her hands. She took it into her own apartment and sat it down on the floor where there were two more baskets—baskets containing sacks of sugar and flour, and cans of vegetables and fruit. And on the unpainted kitchen table was an assortment of pies and cheese cake, and *taiglach,* and home made sweet-and-sour pickles.

"*Mazeltov!*" they were saying.

"Good luck . . . good luck!"

Ellen looked around at these women and tried to understand what they expected of her. A grocery shower—like this—was given for the poor at Purim. The tears that sprang to Ellen's eyes were tears of dismay; but the women, waiting a little anxiously, accepted them as adequate expression of surprise and gratitude.

21

They seemed to relax a little. At Ellen's invitation they found themselves places to sit. And they began to speak to each other with jerky, false heartiness because they could not think what to say to their new rabbi's wife who had come from a world they did not know.

"Mrs. Baer, how is Minnie's grandmother?" somebody asked.

"You have no idea how hard it is to get a tire," came a voice from another direction.

Ellen noticed that Esther Morris, who had carried the basket up the stairs, looked pale, and small beads of sweat lay along her upper lip.

"May I get you something? . . . a drink of water or some tea?" Ellen asked her solicitously.

Esther's dark unfathomable eyes revealed their inner fright to Ellen in the instant before her bright rouged lips formed their brittle smile, their flippant answer.

"Goodness, no! I'm fine!" She scoffed so brusquely that Ellen felt embarrassment for having shown concern.

Ellen glanced away and her eyes met the eyes of Myra Levinson who was watching her intently. And in Myra's eyes there was a concern like the concern which, a moment before, had prompted her to speak. And also there was a look of apology. It was too knowing, too aware a look to be met in such confusion, and Ellen only smiled a little and turned away again.

"It's just a shame how much it costs to get good kosher meat here," someone was saying. "It's no wonder hardly anybody keeps kosher."

Mrs. Stein, who was sitting in the chair with the sagging springs, leaned her ponderous weight forward so that the chair groaned.

"Do you know, Mrs. Rosen, we have to order our meat all the way from Kansas City! Think of it! . . . You do keep kosher, don't you, Mrs. Rosen?"

The deviousness of the question infuriated Ellen. "Yes, I do, for Rabbi. My own family is very liberal. But for Rabbi, I gladly do it!"

Mrs. Stein's eyes narrowed exactingly, but the younger women seemed pleased with Ellen's answer.

Tita Gold, her red hair framing her face coquettishly, began to laugh. "I'm afraid we're very mixed up, here. All the way from strictest orthodox to most liberal reform. We're a trial to any rabbi."

"Indeed, we are. In fact, we've had fifteen rabbis in eighteen

22

years—so don't get too used to things!" Mrs. Stein laughed heartily as if she had made a joke.

Ellen laughed, too; there was the dreadful need to laugh or to cry. "Please, let us cut one of the fine cakes, and I make tea," Ellen said.

"Cut my cheesecake!" Tita Gold suggested. "I made it this morning and it's very good. I practically had to smuggle it out of the house!"

Ellen, thankful for something to do, gave Tita a knife to cut the cake, and then she began to make the tea. And in a few moments the women drank from the cracked cups which they themselves had provided.

As they ate, Ellen saw that Myra Levinson was looking at the newly waxed floors, and in Ellen's own eyes were the achievement and the futility of having waxed them. And when their eyes met briefly once more, it was as if Myra shrank from the thought of having become a part of the hurt and bafflement that Ellen could not quite hide.

Myra stood up abruptly. "We should go," she said. "It's getting late."

Only she seemed to feel excruciatingly the inappropriateness of the gifts to the need of the one to whom they were given, only she seemed to feel a hot anger at the heedlessness of those who gave. She moved restlessly around the small room, and it was as if she wanted suddenly to run away from people and their ability to be carelessly cruel.

And Ellen saw all of this and it did not make the moment easier. She turned away from the sight of being understood.

Tita Gold was regarding Myra with quirked lips.

"Well, come on, if you want to go!" she said impatiently. "After all, it's your car!"

Mrs. Stein was heaving herself out of her chair.

"Be sure and save my pie plate for me," Minnie Wise was admonishing Ellen.

They began to file out, calling their goodbys back over their shoulders to Ellen, who stood in the doorway, watching them go. When the screen at the foot of the stairs banged shut, Ellen, her temples throbbing, stepped back inside her tiny apartment and silently closed the door.

Ellen was putting the last of the groceries into the cabinets when she heard Kurt's footsteps . . . his voice called from the doorway: "Sweetheart!"

23

"Here Kurtchen. The kitchen. Come."

"My . . . how clean everything is!" he stood in the doorway beaming at her.

Ellen stood up from where she had been kneeling at the lower cabinet. She brushed a wisp of hair from her forehead.

"Kurtchen, it seems we are the poor," she said wrily.

"I think we are very rich, we have each other!" he replied, his eyes moving with cajolery from her eyes to her lips. And he kissed her.

"Kurtchen. The women of your congregation . . . they came this afternoon and they brought baskets of groceries like we used to take to the poor."

Kurt opened the cabinets with their bulging load of canned goods. He opened the icebox and broke off a crumb of cheesecake, which he sampled speculatively.

"Ellen . . . we Jews are a very practical people. Here they can afford to pay their rabbi but little . . . but they do not want that his stomach suffers."

"But Kurt, it is not fair!" Ellen insisted, refusing to laugh. "I think only of you. They get themselves a rabbi who was known all over a nation. And because he comes to them empty-handed they show their esteem with . . . with sweet-and-sour pickles!"

"Ellen come! It will be different. They will know us better, and we'll know them better . . . Now, let us eat our supper, because tonight we must make a sick call."

"A sick call . . . I didn't know we knew anyone who is sick." A little of Kurt's humor had begun to penetrate Ellen's mood as she considered what of this bounty of food to select for a quick meal.

"You are an *Aeffchen!*" Kurt said. "We will visit Abe Kalman. They tell me he is a very fine man. And he has been quite ill."

"Go, Kurtchen. Wash your hands. I make it ready," Ellen replied.

Two hours later, Ellen looked into the blanched face of their host, and realized that she and Kurt had unwittingly intruded upon a very trying time for the Kalmans.

In the big brown clapboard house, the parlor shone, and the clock on the mantel seemed to tick with nervous intensity. Sara Kalman had served them tea and apple-strudel, and now she was taking the dishes back to the kitchen. The strudel had been baked for a special occasion. The Kalman's son, Maury, and his

24

family were due to arrive from Dallas at any moment. Maury, who had been away for five years, was coming home to manage the store for his father.

Ellen watched Abe Kalman as he responded to Kurt's zestful conversation with wry and humorous comments of his own. The pallor of illness was in his face, but warmth and brightness had not deserted his eyes, and it occurred to Ellen that the deep lines of his haggard face were not merely the imprint of past feeling, but rather the channels for the outflowing of current feelings. As his discerning gaze came back to her, Ellen said:

"Mr. Kalman, we must go. Your son will be coming soon. You will want to greet him alone."

Abe Kalman raised his hand as if admonishing her to silence. "Mrs. Rosen . . . I would be grateful if you and the Rabbi would stay," he said so earnestly that Ellen wondered at his meaning.

At that moment Sara Kalman came back into the room. Her graying dark hair was piled high on her head, and in her face were the traces of a once vivid prettiness. She wore a flowered print dress that all but obscured the shapeliness of her abundant figure, and in her jeweled hands she carried a shawl. For a large woman she was amazingly adept at fluttering. Abe Kalman felt the flutterings as Sara put the shawl about his shoulders, and he looked levelly at Ellen as if imploring her to notice and to understand.

"Is fine that your son can come home," Ellen said to Sara.

Sara shook her head. "Maybe it is not so good," she said.

"Sara, Maury is our son. Do you think of him as a stranger," Abe said gently.

"Rabbi, he is a stranger," Sara said suddenly. "For five years he has lived the life of a Gentile. He is a stranger."

"I wouldn't say he has lived the life of a Gentile," Abe admonished, catching his wife's hand as she still stood beside him.

"I'd say he has," Sara insisted, her eyes fiery. "He has lived with a Christian wife, away from his own people. They have no Jewish friends. I'd say they have no friends at all. Just the two of them . . . and the child . . . a child who isn't a Jew and isn't a Gentile. What kind of life? . . . What has Maury become!"

It was to Kurt that she had turned . . . from Kurt that she seemed to be imploring an answer; and Ellen knew that there was no answer, and her eyes leapt with concern to Abe Kalman's face. But his face was calm.

"Sara," Abe said, "Maury is still himself . . . what else could he be? And Lee? Lee is a fine girl. You could not help liking her."

"I don't like her, I don't not like her. I only say she is not the wife for our son. She grew up right here in the same town. Is her uncle a friend of yours?"

"Sara, if it is hard for us, think how hard it is for them?" Abe said.

Sara's eyes flashed a rebuttal, but as she started to speak again she became suddenly aware of the paleness that lay beneath her husband's skin.

"Abie, Abie. You, the sick one, and still you must be the strong one. Always I get excited. Rabbi, the doctor would send me away if he knew!" Sara came and put her arm around her husband. The scent of the lilac cologne that she used was warm and fragrant in the air like the vaporous ebb and flow of her volatile spirits.

"Mrs. Kalman, your husband is right. It will not be so bad as you think," Kurt told her, the vigor of real assurance in his voice.

Ellen had to smile . . . it will not be so bad as you think. . . . Always Kurt was assuring people that things would not be so bad as they expected . . . and he himself never expected things to be bad at all.

"The little boy . . . have you ever seen him?" Ellen asked.

Sara shook her head, the words brought quick tears to her eyes. But in that moment there was the sound of a car in the drive, and in that instant Sara was across the room.

As steps sounded on the porch, Sara Kalman reached the front door and thrust it open. Ellen saw in the light from the porch the tall, lean young man who stood there, and he took Sara Kalman into his arms and she clung to him. Maury Kalman's wife had come up behind him and she stood there a little hesitantly.

Sara pushed Maury away from the fierce possessiveness of her own embrace. "Where are your manners?" she demanded, "Do you leave your wife on the step alone . . . And the Baby! . . . Come!"

"He isn't a baby, Mom . . . he's four," Maury said. He reached back to his wife and drew her to his side. He took the little boy from her arms. The child twisted, closed his eyes against the light of the doorway. He buried his face in his father's neck, and the shape of their heads, so closely together, was comically identical.

"Here . . . here! Give him to me," Sara crooned. "The darling . . . the *Kleines Kind*. She took the little boy into her arms. He struggled briefly, but in his sleepiness he could not resist the softness of her body.

26

his feet, hobbling toward the door,

des he was beside him, shaking his

Maury, these are our guests . . . our
e Rosens."

aury's smile as he turned to greet
father's hand to shake hands, first
who complimented him on his
as grateful. He turned again and
fe, and he drew her forward to
blonde and blue-eyed, and her
f her hand was firm.

ing their grandchild, still.

in Fall City,
t as he crossed
e would spend

l, forming her lips lovingly over
sound had a strange mournful
d disturbed Lee Kalman, who
vere suddenly separated from
ls that had formed the lullaby
her hand.

bath candles as
ned the cabinet
a little as she
dles and bright,
dies were always
to meet a child
enthusiasm, he
astonished adult

ienced so recently a sense of
nd responsive sympathy for
s feeling in this room.

and then her eyes moved to
dson and laid a hand with
f his small head.

andelabrum and
ver candelabrum
beautiful mahog-
ed when life fell
. A few exquisite
Two small richly-
ut beside the bed
ver the most worn

ispered. "This is a moment
the others.

e. She struck the
ory, the touching
ching memory.

e bus along the summer-
h Kurt, and they swung

mselves much sadness,"

om asher kid'shonu

bbos.

g of the Universe,
nts and commanded

hope they learn to like

r there was no one
n to her mind, she
candles on the first
d.

sound was mellow in
e still held to his lips.
turns out!" he teased.

A T SEVEN o'clock, on their first Sabbath eve
Ellen stood at the window and watched Kur
the dry and dusty yard to the Temple, where h
an hour of quietness before the evening service.

Ellen turned from the window to light the Sab
the August sun moved low in the sky. She oper
drawer and took out two slender tapers, smiling
did it. Kurt was fond of buying both Sabbath can
cellophane-wrapped candies by the gross. The can
distributed in his pockets because he never liked
empty-handed and sometimes, in a moment of
even pressed the bright sweets upon some mildly
who had done him some small kindness.

Ellen took down the two-pronged silver c
fitted the candles into the sockets. . . . The si
. . . in Duisburg it had had a special place in a
any breakfront. Strange, the things that surviv
apart! Fragile china to be unpacked from crates
pieces of silver. Kurt's old German typewriter.
colored oriental rugs, one of which Ellen had p
in the alcove, and one beneath the table to co
spot in the big ugly carpet.

Ellen carried the candelabrum to the tabl
match. The flicker of flame enticed the men
of match to wick was a lonely gesture full of a

> *Boruch atto Adonoi Elohenu melech ho-o*
> *b'mitsvosov v'tsivonu l'hadlik ner shel sha*
> *Praised be thou, oh Lord our God, Kir*
> *who has sanctified us by His commandme*
> *us to kindle the lights of Sabbath.*

Ellen did not speak the blessing aloud, fo
to hear it; but as the words came unbidde
thought of the first time she lit the Sabbath
Friday night after she and Kurt were marrie

Abe Kalman was up on his feet, hobbling toward the door, and Maury saw him . . .

"Well, Dad!" In three strides he was beside him, shaking his hands up and down.

"Good to see you, son! . . . Maury, these are our guests . . . our new rabbi and his wife . . . the Rosens."

Ellen felt the warmth of Maury's smile as he turned to greet them, reluctantly letting go his father's hand to shake hands, first with her and then with Kurt, who complimented him on his family. Ellen saw that Maury was grateful. He turned again and put his arm around Lee his wife, and he drew her forward to introduce her. Lee Kalman was blonde and blue-eyed, and her eyes were aware, and the clasp of her hand was firm.

Sara had come up to Abe, holding their grandchild, still.

"Ooo-oo-oo-ooo-eee," she crooned, forming her lips lovingly over the roundness of the vowels. The sound had a strange mournful sweetness. Ellen saw that the sound disturbed Lee Kalman, who looked at her husband as if she were suddenly separated from him by the strangeness of the sounds that had formed the lullaby of his own babyhood. Maury caught her hand.

And Ellen Rosen, who had experienced so recently a sense of complete alienation, knew quick and responsive sympathy for the alienation which Lee Kalman was feeling in this room.

Ellen smiled at Lee, reassuringly, and then her eyes moved to Abe Kalman as he looked at his grandson and laid a hand with exquisite gentleness upon the curls of his small head.

"Kurtchen . . . we must go," she whispered. "This is a moment for families to share alone," she said to the others.

When they were out walking to the bus along the summer-scented street, Ellen caught hands with Kurt, and they swung hands between them.

"Kurtchen . . . people make for themselves much sadness," she said thoughtfully.

"Yes, Ellen. Much sadness indeed."

"Kurt, they're nice people . . . all. I hope they learn to like each other."

Suddenly Kurt was laughing and the sound was mellow in the summer night. He pressed the hand he still held to his lips. "Now you'll want to stay and see how it all turns out!" he teased.

Chapter 3

AT SEVEN o'clock, on their first Sabbath eve in Fall City, Ellen stood at the window and watched Kurt as he crossed the dry and dusty yard to the Temple, where he would spend an hour of quietness before the evening service.

Ellen turned from the window to light the Sabbath candles as the August sun moved low in the sky. She opened the cabinet drawer and took out two slender tapers, smiling a little as she did it. Kurt was fond of buying both Sabbath candles and bright, cellophane-wrapped candies by the gross. The candies were always distributed in his pockets because he never liked to meet a child empty-handed and sometimes, in a moment of enthusiasm, he even pressed the bright sweets upon some mildly astonished adult who had done him some small kindness.

Ellen took down the two-pronged silver candelabrum and fitted the candles into the sockets. . . . The silver candelabrum . . . in Duisburg it had had a special place in a beautiful mahogany breakfront. Strange, the things that survived when life fell apart! Fragile china to be unpacked from crates. A few exquisite pieces of silver. Kurt's old German typewriter. Two small richly-colored oriental rugs, one of which Ellen had put beside the bed in the alcove, and one beneath the table to cover the most worn spot in the big ugly carpet.

Ellen carried the candelabrum to the table. She struck the match. The flicker of flame enticed the memory, the touching of match to wick was a lonely gesture full of aching memory.

> *Boruch atto Adonoi Elohenu melech ho-olom asher kid'shonu b'mitsvosov v'tsivonu l'hadlik ner shel shabbos.*
> *Praised be thou, oh Lord our God, King of the Universe, who has sanctified us by His commandments and commanded us to kindle the lights of Sabbath.*

Ellen did not speak the blessing aloud, for there was no one to hear it; but as the words came unbidden to her mind, she thought of the first time she lit the Sabbath candles on the first Friday night after she and Kurt were married.

She had hesitated to tell Kurt that this was a ritual her parents no longer observed. And in her nervousness, she burned her fingers on the match.

"It is supposed to be a very beautiful gesture, *Liebchen,* not like taking a hot pan from the stove," Kurt told her, and suddenly they both were laughing. And the match went out, and when they were solemn again, Ellen took another and lit the candles, speaking the blessing as she did it.

Boruch atto Adonoi Elohenu melech ho-olom . . .

On that night Ellen had felt suddenly that she was entering upon a covenant that binds people together, and there was not in her that which likes to be bound. And for her it was a moment in which a meaning not personally felt awes the heart.

To Ellen it seemed that that first Sabbath as a rabbi's wife was strangely bound in mood to this first Sabbath in Fall City. She was gripped by the same tense anxiety; and now, her fingers shook a little as she finished dressing. Finally, she put on her hat, glanced briefly at her reflection in the mirror and went down the stairs and out the door and across the yard to the synagogue. As Ellen went through the sanctuary, noting details to see that everything was in order, she tried to think what the special Sabbath feeling was.

Ellen rapped lightly on the door of the study.

"Kurtchen . . ."

Kurt answered the door. He wore his prayer shawl and his *yarmulca,* and with them the dignity which they seemed to invest. But as his eyes moved with quick perceptive tenderness over Ellen's face, he saw in her dark eyes the shadow of the thoughts which the last hour had contained. And he took her hand, feeling its warmth and smoothness against his palm.

"You look beautiful, Sweetheart," he told her, touching his other hand to the braid of her hair.

"I am afraid it is not so, Kurtchen . . . only for you," she said.

"No one knows you so well as I," he answered, and he was thinking how it is to learn that beauty is the ache and love and joy of a woman's heart.

"Kurt, it's nearly time. They'll be coming soon."

"Yes . . . and you will welcome them."

"Kurt I have the feeling they think of this synagogue as only theirs, not mine. I feel as if I presume in welcoming them."

Kurt smiled at her. "Ellen, have you forgotten the first Friday night in Duisburg. You were so nervous over what was expected of you. It is the same now."

Ellen looked doubtful, and Kurt understood the difference all too well. The Duisburg synagogue had been a beautiful place in which solemnity dwelt in echoing splendor. There the special- ness and auspiciousness of the evening was reflected in Ellen's manner, so that, watching her, he had been amazed, and oddly stirred, and extremly proud.

"I think it is not the same, *mein Goldeness*," Ellen said finally. "There I had only to enter the mood of holiness, here I must create the mood. I want to do it for you. But I am not sure I know how."

"When the people begin to come it will be the same . . . you will see," Kurt told her. "Go now. Stand by the door."

"Kurtchen . . .?"

"Yes,"

"*Gut Shabbos!*"

"*Gut Shabbos* to you, sweetheart."

Kurt watched Ellen as she left him and went to the front of the synagogue. Through the opened front doors he glimpsed the lamps at the top of the cast-iron poles on either side of the wide steps, shedding their diffuse glow into the gray summer dusk. Kurt was thinking that this was the first time Temple B'nai Emanuel had been lit up all summer. And he felt something of Ellen's anxiety.

It was a little before eight o'clock, and Kurt saw that the people were beginning to arrive. But he could not bring himself to close the door of his study, because he could not bear the thought of shutting himself away from Ellen.

He stood quietly in the small unlighted room and he watched her. She stood now by the door and she was greeting the people as they came in . . . welcoming them to the house they had built for God to inhabit . . . and in her greeting there was the feeling that it was tenanted as was intended. He was not surprised, for he had known she would do it, and he felt in that moment only a deep and awesome gratitude for her life joined to his.

Kurt saw the Levinsons enter . . . and Maury Kalman and his young wife . . . and the Golds and the Morrises together . . . and Mr. Jacobson, hunched and crochety, and Mr. Joe Friedman and his plump little wife . . . and all the others, filling the seats. And there was in the air the uneven hum of people finding their places and speaking to each other.

Kurt glanced at his watch. It was eight o'clock. Quietly he entered the sanctuary and took his place behind the pulpit. He

30

stood for a moment looking out upon his congregation, out into the sea of faces—some attentive, some merely curious.

With a quiet gesture he opened the prayer book.

"We will begin our service with the reading of the first paragraph on page two," he said, and when the flutter of turning pages was done, he began to read:

> *How goodly are your tents O Jacob, your dwelling places, O Israel. O Lord, through Thine abundant kindness I come into Thy house and reverently I worship Thee in Thy holy sanctuary. I love the habitation of Thy house, and the place where Thy glory dwelleth . . ."*

. . . In Duisburg, towards the end, this glory had had no dwelling place but the hearts of the faithful. Sabbath candles were lit in the homes behind drawn shades, and Jews slept without ease. Kurt Rosen was thinking that to share their destiny was to know their hope . . . but to be cast off from their destiny was to know their hopelessness . . .

> *Ascribe unto the Lord, ye ministering angels,*
> *Ascribe unto the Lord glory and power . . .*

Kurt Rosen read.

> *Render unto the Lord the glory due unto His name.*
> *Worship the Lord in the beauty of holiness. . . .*

came the mingled voices of the congregants.

When the psalm was finished, Kurt called for the singing of the Sabbath song, "L'cho dodi . . . Come, my friend, to meet the bride, let us welcome the Sabbath . . ."

There was a pause when none seemed able to begin, but Kurt looked out over their heads with perfect serenity. And then Ellen, standing at the back of the Temple, began to sing. A ripple of surprise passed through the congregation at the beauty and magnificence of her voice, at the splendor of it singing the ancient and beautiful Hebrew words, at the throbbing sadness that was in the splendor of the voice that soared now above the wavering intonations of the faithful.

Kurt Rosen stood, unmoving, and listened. What this woman, and this voice, singing, meant to him! He knew there was none listening who could realize.

. . . to have been delivered and to have left behind the undelivered . . . to feel, imposed upon the thankfulness of the heart, their despair . . . to sing praises while bearing in the heart the despair of the living—this he must do. But to rejoice in deliverance, having left the undelivered behind . . . this Kurt Rosen could not do for himself . . . but for Ellen . . .

> *. . . city of holiness, filled are the years,*
> *Up from thine overflow, forth from thy fears.*
> *Long hast thou dwelt in the valley of tears,*
> *Now shall God's tenderness shepherd thy ways. . . .*
> *. . . God's tenderness shepherd thy ways. . .*

When Kurt had recited the *kiddush,* the silver goblet held high in his outstretched hand, he set the goblet down again on the pulpit and thoughtfully covered it. Moved, he surveyed his congregation. He closed the prayer book, and then he began to speak. "My friends," he said, "I thank you and your president for this confidence you have placed in me. I hope that this confidence will increase and become intensified. . . . To keep faith alive is one of the main tasks of a congregation and of its religious leader, the rabbi. Many people believe that religion is man's most intimate interest. It has its place in the innermost part of a man's heart. Therefore, so these people believe, a religious man shall live for himself and he himself will take care of his soul. Actually, we all are personalities and tend to develop the personalities of those around us. Our religion insists on human personality and on the right to its completest fulfillment. But no communal life is possible without some binding obligations on all, and without the collaboration of all. This congregation unites Jews who are orthodox, who are conservative, and who are liberal. Some might think it is much easier and simpler to work in an orthodox or in a conservative or in a reform congregation. But our religion always has recognized and respected individual freedom. If we are aware of this Jewish heritage, we shall be able to find a common basis for the different religious groups in our congregation, and we shall be able to enrich our communal Jewish life by our differences.

"We all come solitary into the world, we leave it as solitary souls. But during our lives we need fellowship. Everyone has to be elevated to the moral responsibility of his own will. Everyone of us must know that, whether he likes it or not, he represents the Jewish community to the outer world. How a woman treats her maid or a merchant his employee; how a woman walks down the street, whether her dress is simple or in bad taste; all this influences the attitude of other people toward us. Those who are not aware of this fact imperil the position of the Jew more than does Hitler. We say in private life that there is truth in the sentence of William Morris, the great poet, 'Fellowship is Heaven; and the lack of fellowship is hell.' This statement is true of our community life to a much greater extent. We must educate ourselves to the recognition of the fact that every one of us represents the Jewish community to the outer world; therefore, a Jewish congregation should sharpen the conscience of its members. Those of us who work for the community will soon find that our own lives have become enriched. A congregation should bring together those who are lonely. When people come together, they create a new situation, and a new life."

At first, Myra Levinson listened attentively to the rabbi, responding from some hidden depth to the quiet but profound feeling with which he read the psalms, and to the searching earnestness with which he began his sermon. But gradually she became aware of, and finally influenced by, her husband's restiveness. His attention was riveted upon his square-fingered immaculately manicured hands, and finally he made a fist and lifted his hand to gaze at his diamond and ebony ring as if it were an object of unique interest. Myra looked at Sam and saw displeasure buried deep in his eyes. She realized that she had lost herself a little, had slipped a little out of character, and had lost the trend of his feeling at the same time. Very carefully she composed her face into its habitual guise of sophistication as she turned her eyes back to Kurt Rosen. And at the same time she felt herself steeling her emotions against that in her husband which could be harsh and frighteningly cold.

Half way across the room, Lee Kalman sat beside her husband, Maury, her eyes fastened unwaveringly on Kurt Rosen's face. Before the service began she had asked Maury about the things that were strange to her, the ark with its beautifully embroidered drapery, the satin altar-cover adorned with the Star of David, the candelabra holding the lighted Sabbath candles, the Eternal Light suspended from the ceiling above the altar. All of these things had, in Lee Kalman's eyes, a mystic and symbolic look that stirred her imagination and kindled a receptive mood. And as the ritual unfolded Lee had felt herself strangely stirred; she had felt in her unknowing heart the beauty and the solemnity that Ellen Rosen had feared were left behind in a burned synagogue in Duisburg.

And Ellen Rosen, sitting almost at the back of the synagogue, saw that there were some who listened with rapt interest; but she saw too that there were others who were merely impatient because they found it difficult to follow the haltingly painful English of their new rabbi. And there was among these a restlessness and sometimes a shuffling of feet, and here and there old men nodded in their seats. Mr. Friedman, wearing his grey fedora and nibbling his white mustache nervously, had begun to make a curious rhythmic sighing sound. And even Mr. I. Jacobson, who had shown his friendship so openheartedly, was flipping the pages of his prayer book and humming a melancholy Hebrew melody under his breath.

With frantic concern Ellen's eyes were drawn again and again to Kurt's face . . . a face that was grave . . . and tired . . . and serene . . . a face that held an awful awareness among the unaware. And again and again her eyes went searching the worshipers for those who might understand his value and his worth. And there was, in her throat and in her chest, an awful ache that would not go away.

And finally, she tried to close out all the others . . . to see only Kurt . . . to hear only Kurt. And he was saying . . .

"It is a special privilege and gift which this great and free country bestows upon us. Here we have the right to have our own ideas and to speak them openly, so long as we do not harm others. There was a time in Europe when I, too, was as free as you all are now. Later I lost that freedom. Here I am free again; I know what that means. I am thankful to God who in His grace and by His providence saved my wife and me from Nazi barbarism. I am grateful to this country which enabled me to come, as we say in our prayer book *me-avdus l'cherus*—from slavery to liberty, and *mi-hoshech l'or*—from darkness to light.

"I love my fathers' faith with all my soul. I am convinced of its truth. Though our brethren in Europe have to suffer grievously, I believe in the future of the Jewish people. As I love my religion, so shall I try to create and preserve this love in the hearts of my congregation. May God give me strength to perform this task so that what I do serves the glory of the Almighty. Amen."

"We turn now to the Adoration, the congregation will please rise, and let us read together:

> *It is for us to praise the Lord of all, to proclaim the greatness of the Creator of the universe, who has not made us like the pagans of the world, nor placed us like the heathen tribes of the earth; He hath not made our destiny as theirs, not cast our lot with all their multitude . . .*

When the final blessing had been said, there was the filing out of the congregation, out into the cool night air, with the voicing

34

of many a *Gut Shabbos* to right and to left. And some, on the way to their cars, paused to speak and to compare their impressions of the new rabbi. The Kalmans spoke to Sam Levinson.

"I don't know," Sam shook his head. "I hope we haven't made a mistake."

"How so?" Maury asked, lighting a cigarette and watching its end glow in the darkness.

"He may be too orthodox for our blood; and, besides, he is damn hard to understand."

"Why didn't you try listening," Myra asked with carefully calculated raillery. But Sam ignored her.

"After all," Maury said, "he's been in the country just two years. What do you expect? I haven't been in town for five years and I don't know what you've been up against . . . but he's better than the last rabbi I remember."

"You hit the nail right on the head in the first place," Sam said. "Just two years in this country! I think we would have done better to get an American rabbi. I have a boy who'll be *bar mitzvah* in another year. He's ready for confirmation classes now. If even I can't understand the rabbi, how's he going to?"

"Don't worry about it Sam . . . I think he's going to be good!"

"Don't worry, he says!" Sam gave an eloquent shrug of his neatly tailored shoulders.

As the men talked, Lee Kalman standing beside Maury, listened and was unable to cast off the mood of the last hour. She had asked Maury to bring her to Kurt Rosen's first services in Fall City, because the Rosens had, simply by their presence, imbued her difficult homecoming with a real sense of welcome. But tonight she had understood their own need of welcome. And Sam Levinson was the man she would have counted upon to know what to say . . . what to do . . . to make them welcome. Listening, she did not know why he had failed them — or her. She knew only that on the next day she would send flowers to the Rosens.

When the last hand had been shaken, when the last car door had slammed and the last voices had been borne off in the night, when the big cast-iron entrance lamps cast their glow on an empty sidewalk, Kurt Rosen turned, with a weary smile, to his wife.

"How was?" he asked her.

"They are very lucky to have you . . . I only hope they know how lucky," Ellen said, a little fiercely. And Kurt laughed.

35

"Come, Sweetheart. Drink a glass of wine." He went back to the pulpit and filled two tiny crystal goblets from the *kiddush* cup.

It was a small and gracious gesture, and Ellen watched him. She took the glass he offered her, and he touched the rim of the glass to hers.

"*Le'Hayyim!*" he said.

"*Le'Hayyim!*" she answered him.

And the smile of his eyes was answered on her lips, and each carefully guarded from the other the valiance and the heartache of the moment.

Chapter 4

KURT ROSEN went early to his study the next morning. As he came up the back stairs, he glanced into the sanctuary and saw there Juan Batisto, the wizened little Mexican who served twice a week as janitor.

Juan, earnestly wielding a broom midway in the center aisle carpeting, moved with gnome-like agility, giving the broom a sort of frantic life of its own. On his head he wore a *yarmulka* like any pious Jew. It occurred to Kurt Rosen that here was a degree of affrontery that only innocence can achieve.

"Good morning, Juan!" Kurt called out.

The little man jerked with surprise, but at sight of the rabbi all the wrinkles of his face began to smile, and he came forward doffing his *yarmulka* as he might have doffed a battered felt hat. And Kurt smiled at that irrefutable dignity with which some small comic creatures invest themselves.

"You've made everything look fine, Juan," Kurt said, as he started toward his study.

"Si, si!" Juan replied with a pride that was entirely personal and not a little possessive. "A young man waits for you, Rabbi!" he called after Kurt.

The young man rose as the rabbi entered the room. He was chunky of build, and he had a face in which impertinence seemed to lurk in casual whimsicality. His confidence, however, was a little confounded by the rabbi.

"Rabbi Rosen?" he said earnestly.

Kurt nodded, extending his hand.

I'm Al Kahn . . . with the *Fall City Tribune*. I'd like to have an interview with you, if you could spare the time."

Kurt saw immediately that the young reporter was both eager and reluctant to acknowledge the bond of Jewishness between himself and the rabbi. His face was a little flushed with the importance of his assignment, his manner was brisk and impersonal.

"Sit down, Mr. Kahn," Kurt said, matching his formality to his caller's manner. "I will tell you anything I can."

37

"You were in a concentration camp, Rabbi?" Al Kahn said, balancing his notebook against his knee.

Kurt Rosen sat down behind his desk.

"Yes, in Dachau."

"How do you spell it, Rabbi?"

"Dachau, D-a-c-h-a-u."

"How did you escape?"

"It is almost impossible to escape from a concentration camp. The only possibility for release was for someone outside of Germany to guarantee immediate entry into another country. A rabbi in New York prepared the necessary affidavits for my release."

"How long were you imprisoned?"

"For twenty-two days—and during that time I lost twenty-one pounds."

"Rabbi, were you . . . could you tell me how it was?" the young reporter fumbled.

"How it was . . .?" Kurt Rosen repeated . . . How it was to be in a concentration camp? . . . . How it was to be a Jew in Germany under Hitler? . . . . How it was to be a man in a world where such things could happen? . . . . The rabbi considered Al Kahn's inept question which had released a flood of memories, living and dimensional.

I

How it was to be in a concentration camp . . . to be forced to stand at attention with back turned and hear a Jew die under Nazi whips . . . to be one of a whole line of Jews forced to stand . . . with back turned . . . and to hear . . .

"In Dachau there were fourteen to twenty-one deaths among the Jewish prisoners daily," Kurt Rosen began, "and for three consecutive days there were seventy-two deaths a day."

"How many?" Al Kahn asked, and Kurt repeated. He watched the young man writing it down.

"How did they die? Were they killed?"

"Strangely enough most of them died from natural causes," Kurt replied, remembering the final warnings that reprisals would be taken against his father if he presented the true picture of life in a concentration camp. "There was no medicine, and hardly enough food to stay alive," he told the reporter.

. . . how it was to come unexpectedly upon a man, who had been one of the leading judges of Germany, down on

*his hands and knees grubbing rotted fragments of food into
his mouth with the voraciousness of an animal, while peering with fear-glazed eyes from behind the garbage can lest he
be discovered . . . how it was to watch, then turn away for
fear of startling him . . .*

"Was there much sickness among the prisoners?" Al Kahn
asked.

"There was a great deal," Kurt answered. "Three times a
day, regardless of weather or state of health, the prisoners were
forced to assemble on the drill grounds. If a man failed to report in for roll call, several in his barracks might die. Those who
were too sick to walk were carried by their comrades. Prisoners
wore clothing like lightweight summer pajamas. We were forced
to stand at attention for hours in the cold mountain wind and
the rain and snow, and our clothing froze to our bodies, and later
we had to sleep on straw *in these same clothes.*"

> *. . . memory like sharp stones to bruise the mind. . . . A
> man lying on the straw, his flesh cut loose from his bones
> by a whip . . . because he remembered one simple homely
> thing and folded newspapers around his body to keep out the
> cold.*

"How many Jews were imprisoned at Dachau?" Al Kahn asked.

"How many Jews . . . ?" Kurt repeated. Al Kahn did not speak
the word as if he dwelt within its borders. He did not seem
to understand that Jews were not men without names, that
Nazis were not men without faces.

"Do you write about sports?" Kurt asked him suddenly.

Al Kahn glanced up from his notes, a flicker of interest crossing
his eyes. "Yes, sir, I cover the wrestling matches every Friday
night."

"You don't ever come to the synagogue?"

"No, sir, I have to work."

"How many Jews in the concentration camp . . . ?" Kurt repeated. "In the barracks where I stayed one thousand Jews were
crowded into space built for a hundred and fifty men. There
was not room for us to sleep on the floor, so they came and
built wooden shelves, extending out from the walls, and covered them with straw. One night a rotten board broke and a
Jewish boy fell through and ripped his chest on a nail as he
fell. There was a curfew and any Jew seen leaving a barracks
after sundown would be shot. . . ."

39

*. . . They stood in the doorway and called to the guards to
let them take Eli to the hospital. But the guards jeered and
stood with guns poised, ready to shoot the first men who
should step across the threshold with the wounded boy.*

*"Is there nothing you can do?" Kurt Rosen remembered
his own voice asking Louis Enelow, who had been a doctor
in his congregation, and who was now a prisoner too.*

*"In the hospital, with clamps and cat-gut, I might sew
up the artery. Here there is nothing."*

*Eli's brother, Joseph, hovered beside the doctor, his fright-
ened boy's eyes luminous in the darkness. "Doctor, Benjamin had thread and a needle . . ."*

*The doctor put a hand on the boy's shoulder. "Joseph,
you do not sew up people with thread and a needle, you do
not sew up people in the darkness."*

*"With a needle and thread you could try. You can't let
Eli die!" A small whimpering sound quivered in Joseph's
breath. He dropped on his knees and began to search with
his hands in the darkness, feeling along the rough floor,
fumbling at the straw, searching for a spool of thread and
a needle that Benjamin had lost.*

*And the throb of Eli's heart pumped the blood out through
the hole in his chest. And it stained the floor . . . and the
straw . . . and the hands of the doctor who tried to help
him . . .*

". . . They would not let us take him to the hospital. And in
the morning he was dead," Kurt Rosen finished lamely. He
felt again the wrath and the terrible helplessness.

Al Kahn wrote studiously, hardly raising his eyes from the
pad against his knee. What does all of this mean to him, Kurt
Rosen asked himself. He felt the sweat on his own brow, on
the palms of his own hands. He took his handkerchief and wiped
it away.

II

. . . How it was to be a Jew in Germany under Hitler . . .?

"What was the name of the town where you were rabbi?" Al
Kahn asked.

"Duisburg. It is a city in the lower Rhine, not far from
Holland . . . a city with factories, and fine stores . . . ."

*. . . It was a town like any other town, like this town,
with people who succeeded, and people who failed, and
people who wanted many different things: . . . a Jewish boy*

named Ralph Horowitz wanted to go to Holland to learn to
be a craftsman. . . . A young German named Hans Hefler
wanted to be a big man in the Nazi party some day . . .

"How many Jews lived in Duisburg?" Al Kahn asked.

"There were two synagogues in the city. In my congregation
were over 2,000 people," Kurt answered.

"How did they live after the Nazis came to power?"

"At first the pressure was economic and social. Jewish doctors could treat only Jewish patients. Jewish lawyers could represent only Jewish clients. Jewish businessmen were ruined,
and Aryan businessmen were afraid to hire Jews. We began
trying to get as many Jews as possible out of Germany, but it is
hard to tear up roots that have grown for centuries, even if the
plant above the ground is being trampled. . . ."

Kurt Rosen watched the young reporter arranging his notes.
Al Kahn's unheeding curiosity was youthfulness, Kurt thought—
but then Ralph Horowitz's bewilderment was youthfulness, and
Hans Hefler was young too.

Kurt tried to think of words with which he might tell Al Kahn
about Ralph Horowitz, about Hans Hefler . . .

*When Ralph Horowitz, sixteen years old, lost his ap-
prenticeship in Holland, he came home to Germany to his
parents . . . and he was arrested because of the secret edict
which ordered the arrest of Jews who returned to Germany
after having crossed its borders. Kurt remembered how
earnestly he had pleaded young Ralph's case with the Gestapo, and when he was able to guarantee that Ralph would
leave Germany again within eight days, the boy was released.
Kurt had waited outside the concentration camp to take
him home.*

*And Ralph Horowitz, bleeding from the mouth and from
the cuts on the body was shoved into a barn where horses
were kept and told to wash his wounds in water from a
slimy bucket. On pain of death he was warned not to look
around him at what the dank and fetid corners of the barn
might conceal in the rotting hay. As he bent over the bucket,
an unvoiced sob racked his shoulders, and an old Christian man tried to speak to him from the shadows, but the
old man was silenced, and the boy was taken again into
the sunlight. He was taken to the commandant and given
a paper to sign stating that he had not been mistreated, and
then he was released to the rabbi.*

*Ralph Horowitz was sixteen years old, and he was not
wanted by the land that had nurtured his young life, and*

it would take him the rest of his life to understand why this was so.

. . . And Hans Hefler? . . . Hans Hefler's story was a different kind of story. Hans, full of gusty, rowdy spirits, was one of the youngest storm troopers in the élite corps. But on the day when he was ordered to destroy the shop of a girl who would not become a Nazi, he was brought to full pause in the game of boy playing man. He shouted at his commanding officer that he would do such a thing to a man, but not to a girl he had danced with! And so he was arrested and sent to Dachau as a prisoner himself. And there Hans learned about survival, he learned what things were a question of survival, and when he was made a prisoner warden he knew what he was gaining in his desperate fight to regain favor. He had found an easy way. "Rabbi, Rabbi, why do you pray! There's no God. I know that Jacob Lazer hides a mezuzah beneath the straw in his box, and if I tell he will die. I will tell it! Would God let me tell it if he existed? Rabbi, there is no God!"

III

. . . How it was to be a man in a world where such things could happen . . .?

Kurt tried, wearily, to select words to tell the reporter a little about Ralph Horowitz, about Hans Hefler. But as he watched Al Kahn struggling feebly to comprehend life in terms of abject horror, he wanted suddenly to protest. It was not all like that; there were other things too: the way Ellen maintained that she cooked—as she sang—by inspiration; and the Sunday they came home from making sick calls to find the whole apartment filled with the acrid smell of slowly burning chicken: the New Year's Eve party that ended near dawn with ringing the doorbell at the home of an exceedingly pompous and exceedingly fat jurist, just to see what he looked like in his nightshirt: and members of the congregation—the way that Elimira Herschel, who weighed over 300 pounds, could eat two whole chickens or two pounds of whipped cream at a single meal, and how the crowds stood still to watch, that year at Carnival time, when she dressed as Carmen and went waltzing down the street as light as a powder puff . . . .

"Mr. Kahn," Kurt said, leaning forward a little in his earnestness, "there is something I would very much like to make you understand. You must remember, as you write this, anything that could be said of the plight of the Jew in Germany would be

42

a tragic understatement. But the more adequate the statement, the more surely it obscures the most significant fact of all. The most significant fact is not that these horrors exist, but that they have grown to fruition in a world of ordinary people doing ordinary things."

Al Kahn nodded his head solemnly, but he did not make a note of what the rabbi had just said.

"Why is it," Kurt asked, more of himself than of his interviewer, "that Americans seem to visualize Nazis as ogres that materialize out of nothing? . . . It is not so! They are men whose names you might know, whose voices you might recognize on the telephone. . . ."

> *. . . to call them on the telephone. . . . There is some special strain on the spirit, when the outward appearances of a give-and-take relationship were maintained between two men after one had become the pursuer, the other the pursued. . . . Kurt Rosen had called the Gestapo countless times, to protest, to appeal. He even recognized the voice of the member of the Gestapo to whom he talked the night they burned the synagogues. And what did the man tell him? . . . "There is nothing we can do, there are communist riots all over town tonight. Stay at home, Rabbi, and you will not be hurt." . . . To preserve even the evasions of a give-and-take relationship, in this there was a bitter irony.*

"Rabbi, how did you happen to be arrested in the first place?" Al Kahn asked.

"A seventeen-year-old Jewish boy assassinated a German consular official in Paris. As a part of the reprisals against the Jews still in Germany, the presidents of all Jewish organizations, the owners of businesses, and a quota of Jews from each district were imprisoned in concentration camps."

"When did it happen?"

"November 10, 1938—the day when they burned the synagogues."

"Did you know you would be arrested; did you have any warning?"

"We had not slept all night after they burned the synagogues. . . ."

> *Kurt Rosen had come home at last, the lines of fatigue deep in his face. And Ellen made coffee for him, she made him sit down and drink it.*
> *"Kurt, what is it they want of us—not only to ruin us, but to destroy us as well?"*

"It seems so." Kurt sipped the black coffee. And he watched his wife with a forced detachment, almost as if he watched only his memory of her, so treasured that its very glory was a sadness.

"Ellen," he said gently. "We must speak of it . . . if we should be parted . . ."

"It can happen, can it not?" she said as if she were actually facing the possibility for the first time. Her eyes met his directly.

"It can happen, any time."

Ellen did not speak, she put her hand against her face so that it covered her eyes.

"Ellen, if it should happen, you must try to leave Germany."

"Kurtchen, I could not! I could not!"

"You could not help me, Ellen, only by making it so that I need not worry over you . . . over what might become of you."

"I can't speak of it."

"Ellen, we must. There is never time at the last moment." Kurt felt the cherishing . . . the love and rage and passion and despair . . . and the profound gentleness . . . her dark hair, her dark eyes . . . a man does not unlearn the need of his heart simply because he knows he must.

"Kurtchen, we were so happy. It began so well for us. What happened to the world we live in?"

"Rabbi, you were saying . . .?"

"Yes, of course. At six o'clock the next morning the telephone began to ring. Members of my congregation were calling . . . to warn me, to see if the Gestapo had come for me."

"How long before they did come?"

"About two hours."

"Could you have escaped?"

"Perhaps. Holland was only thirty miles away. I thought about it."

"But you did not try?"

"No, I was afraid they might take my wife."

. . . How it was to be a man in a world where such things could happen? . . . For all his careful exactitude of answering, Kurt Rosen felt the young reporter's lack of comprehension, his sharp curiosity about the spectacular, his preoccupation with names and dates, his failure to understand, to grasp the meaning of what he heard. Al Kahn's bland confidence in his abilities as a reporter brought a weary despair to the rabbi, who suddenly saw himself through this

boy's eyes—a refugee, a man from a world too remote from this young man's world to have any bearing upon it.

"One more thing, Rabbi," Al Kahn said, folding up his paper. "When you were in the concentration camp, were you personally mistreated?"

"I cannot speak about these things, now. I shall speak about them when we are at war with Germany," Kurt said.

"What?" Al Kahn demanded, as if this were a supposition outside the realm of possibility.

"I hope not, but I am afraid it is inevitable," Kurt answered.

"Well, thanks, Rabbi, for the interview. Thanks for giving me so much time." Al Kahn stood up. He stuffed his pencil and paper in the pocket of his sports jacket.

When this young Jew had gone on his way, brisk and confident still, satisfied, for his part, with his job of interviewing the new rabbi, Kurt Rosen felt the challenge of this new life to be a more tremendous one than he had thought before, and he felt less equal to it. He felt again the need for prayer.

Chapter 5

THE next morning, Sam Levinson and his wife sat at the breakfast table, in the sunny east-room just off the kitchen. Although it was only eight o'clock, Myra Levinson's dark hair already was immaculately in place, and her lips were carefully made up. But her face, as yet without powder or rouge, was pale. Her wrists moved with a quick grace in and out the big open sleeves of her Chinese red-silk housecoat as she poured the coffee. But Sam Levinson did not notice. His attention was deeply engrossed in something he was reading in the morning paper. A little petulantly Myra lit a cigarette.

"Look at this!" Sam said finally.

"What?"

"In the paper . . . about the Rosens." But he did not relinquish the paper to her; he continued to read.

"What does it say?" she asked him again.

Sam made a quick impatient movement with his hand. "Persecution of the Jews . . . persecution of the Jews . . . persecution of the Jews. Every other breath, persecution of the Jews!"

Sam's own impatience was returned to him by Myra. "Sam, for goodness sake. The paper wanted an interview. And the Jews are being persecuted in Germany. What do you expect?"

Sam paid no attention to her reply. The lines of his face—the harder lines that underly the surface blandness—deepened as he continued to read.

"Good God! Listen to this. 'Rabbi Rosen, asked to elaborate on the treatment of Jews in Germany, replied, 'I will speak of these things when we are at war.' " Sam Levinson stood up and threw the paper on the floor. And the chair behind him toppled over with the suddenness of the movement.

"Sam what in the world are you so upset about?" Myra demanded. "A million times a day people say 'if there's a war.' How can you escape the thought, the way things are. Senators and congressmen and important people are saying it all the time. What makes it so different for him to say it?"

"He didn't say *if* . . . he said *when!*"

46

"Sam, for goodness sake. He knows what we're up against better than we know. Maybe he can see the handwriting on the wall."

"Handwriting on the wall! Ha! We get a new rabbi and already she's talking to me in biblical riddles."

"Sam, you're making a big *tsimas* about nothing!"

"It sure isn't nothing," Sam retorted, setting up the chair he had toppled over. His face was flushed as he straightened up again. "If you want to quote the rabbi, I'll quote him. He said himself everything a Jew does reflects on every other Jew. So he arrives in town one week and the next he's saying 'When we're at war!' That's just great. I can hear it now! The Jews are trying to get us into the war!"

Myra, who had been impatient, then angry, looked at Sam now curiously. "Sam, what in the world has gotten into you. Since when are you so touchy?"

Sam did not reply. He turned and stalked out of the room. Myra sat where she was; she folded one leg under her, as a small girl does, and leaned forward to reach the coffee pot. She poured herself another cup of coffee, and her hand shook a little. From where she was sitting she could see the paper sprawled on the floor and the black headline: "New Rabbi Tells of Persecution of Jews in Germany." Finally she went and picked up the paper; she straightened it and read the article. And when she had finished reading, her eyes were wet; and she did not want Sam to come back into the room and find her so.

But Sam did not go back into the room. As he got out his car and drove to town, he was already beginning to feel a little foolish, and his anger was reaching out beyond the story in the morning paper to include his own behavior with Myra.

Seldom did he let Myra suspect that he was not perfectly in control of a situation. Seldom did he try to engage her in conversation about issues that were vital or emotional. When he did, there were always two things that disturbed him. First, he secretly suspected that he had not changed Myra so much as he liked to believe. And second, he discovered that he had taught her just enough of cynicism to mock him.

Unaccountably Sam Levinson found himself remembering how he had first come to know Myra. It was fifteen years ago that he had joined with other merchants of Fall City to stage a stupendous Easter Style Show, and there had been the necessity of choosing models. The Junior League had furnished half a dozen young matrons ranging from the gaunt and angular to the plump and bouncy. The Women's Club had furnished four more. But of dozens interviewed only a handful had any aptitude for modeling, beyond the money required to buy the costumes after they had modeled them. As the project was about to flounder, someone suggested an audition for girls at the Fall City Junior College. Reluctantly, Sam had undertaken the job, and it was at this audition that he discovered Myra Levine, whom he had briefly met and quickly dismissed three months previously when she arrived from St. Louis to stay with her cousins, the Benjamins. Myra came to the audition wearing a baggy sweater and skirt and walking oxfords, and this irritated Sam because he suddenly discovered that she had the face and figure and grace of carriage to wear magnificent clothes. She was one of three co-eds whom he chose to model.

At the first rehearsal in the big Fall City Municipal Auditorium, Sam's eyes were much on Myra Levine. She handled the beautiful garments with such a loving touch, she was excited and oddly joyful, and she seemed to be taking the whole affair terribly seriously as she walked with grave, demure steps across the stage. The other young women, schooled in the blasé approach, regarded her a little curiously. Myra's ecstatic quiver of life among the ice-maidens had suddenly infuriated Sam . . . and somehow frightened him . . . and made him afraid for her . . . and filled him with rage that he should care, should feel concerned . . . that he should suddenly be possessed with the determination that she should be more beautiful than all . . . more beautiful even by their own standards of coldness.

That day, after the rehearsal, Myra Levine stayed behind after the others were gone. She came out from behind one of the stage props as Sam was gathering up the last of the dresses to take back to the store. She began, without speaking, to help him fold them.

"Mr. Levinson . . . was I all right? Is there anything I should do, differently?"

Her face, Sam suddenly realized, was always full of emotions tumbling over each other, clouding her beauty.

"Don't show so much in your face," he told her a little gruffly.

She laughed. "How do you keep things out of your face?" she asked him.

Sam considered. "Draw in . . . like breathing. Look . . . you draw a breath in and its life. You let it out again and it's gone in the air . . . nothing. It's the same with the things we feel.

48

You draw them into yourself and they're life. Let it all out . . . and it's gone . . . nothing!"

Myra Levine laughed again, but gently.

"Look . . ." Sam said suddenly. "Close your eyes and think of snow . . . just think of snow falling."

She did as he told her, and under the arc lights of the big empty stage, he looked upon the exquisite beauty of her face and found himself profoundly stirred. And she opened her eyes, and for an instant he looked into the depths of them, and she made no startled movement away from him.

"I thought so," he said finally. "Now begin to think of other things, but don't let your face change. Think of walking out on this stage before hundreds of people. Think of the saddest thing that ever happened to you."

She did not move, but her glance wandered away from him and she seemed to be concentrating very hard upon what he had said. Finally, she turned back to him and smiled.

"See. You can have a private life," he told her. "It doesn't all have to be right there in your face for any goddam fool to see!"

Once Sam Levinson had taught Myra to wear the mask of her own beauty, he could not escape her. And the mask had covered all the bright feeling which he knew existed . . . but which other people did not know . . . and this had been the measure of his own secret pleasure . . . and he had never been willing to let her emerge from behind that mask again.

As Sam parked his car, he was wondering how his thoughts had gone so far afield from their original concern. And he was aware that Myra's reaction had only deepened his sense of unease, instead of erasing it.

When Sam arrived at his office, he did not stay long. He had an irresistible urge to get out among people. As he came out the doorway, he saw Dory Winslow hurrying up the street.

"Hey, Dory."

Dory Winslow was in the furniture business, but he was always hurrying some place with a brief case under his arm, brisk and a little importunate. Now he turned, at Sam's call, and waved to him.

"Hi, Sam!"

Sam hurried a little to catch up with Dory Winslow. Some-

49

thing in Dory always discomforted him inwardly, but he never let himself admit it.

"Say, Dory, do you still have that Henry V *chaise longue* Myra was looking at a couple of months ago?" This was something that popped into his head to make conversation, but he was immediately glad he had thought of it. It was, he had the feeling, time that he did something nice for Myra.

Dory considered for a moment, trying to remember which *chaise longue*.

"Had the rose brocade on it?" he asked.

"That's it!"

"Tough luck, Sam. Sold it about a week ago."

"Here in town?"

"No, Valley View."

"Good . . . then maybe you could order it."

"Sure thing. Might be several months though. You know . . . things are getting pretty short these days."

"Boy, do I know! Just do the best you can."

They had come up abreast of the Grill and Sam was glad to be going in with Dory Winslow; he somehow had not wanted to go in alone. He and Dory sat down together at the counter. Charlie Grimes, head of the Public Service, was sitting in the next seat, a large, beetle-browed man with a florid, smiling face.

"Hi, Dory . . . Sam! What's new?"

"Not much," Sam said. "Coffee!" he told the waitress.

"Coffee," Dory said . . . "Same old 6's and 7's" he replied to Charlie Grimes.

"Say, Charlie . . . congratulations on being named head of the Community Chest," Sam said.

"Took it for just one reason, Sam. Knew I could count on fellows like you to help me put it over."

"Any time, Charlie. Just say the word."

"You know I will. Couldn't put over a drive without Sam Levinson."

Sam drank his coffee, smiling a little. He was beginning to feel expansive, good. They weren't evaluating him anew in terms of what they had read in the paper that morning. It was the same as always. Nothing was different.

Charlie Grimes reached for his check, swung around on his swivel stool so it creaked under his weight. "See you," he said.

He stood up, suddenly he seemed to think of something and he turned back.

"Say, Sam. Good article on your new rabbi in the paper this

morning. His observations seem very astute to me. Wonder if we could get him to talk for our Kiwanis meeting."

This was certainly not what Sam Levinson had expected. For a moment he was completely unable to draw his reactions into any recognizable shape. He drank down a large swallow of hot coffee. And his face was only a little red as he forced himself to meet Charlie Grimes' eyes.

"I'm sure he'd be honored . . . Charlie . . . any time. Heard him myself, Friday night. He's got a lot to say."

"I'll call him," Charlie Grimes said. He put on his straw hat and left them.

Dory Winslow made no comment and Sam was glad. He went on drinking his coffee.

"Sam, have they been to see you yet about starting a Better Business Bureau here?" Dory asked him after an uncomfortable little pause.

"Yeah. A fellow was around last week. I'm all for it."

"Good. I'd like to see it a going concern here," Dory said.

Sam picked up his check. "Got to get back to the store," he said. "See you around, Dory."

"Sure, Sam."

Even with Dory Winslow it had not been bad. When he considered it, Sam Levinson did not know quite what he had feared.

As Sam Levinson entered his store by the front way, he felt the familiar surge of pride at the sight of his window displays. "Levinson's" had class and dramatic vividness. Beside this store, its chief competitor, Harrison-Tremble, for all its studied gentility, was a little dowdy.

But even the sight of smart women shopping for smart clothes in the shop's mauve and gray interior, could not divert Sam Levinson from his ruminative mood.

Sam went immediately to his office on the second floor and closed the door behind him. He sat down behind his mahogany desk and began to check the proofs on advertising copy which his secretary had left for him during his absence. Sam realized that the words were passing in a jumble through his mind, making no sense. He leaned back in his chair and his eyes traveled restlessly around the room. On the wall hung a Rotary emblem, a Chamber of Commerce past-president's plaque and a black framed citation for outstanding service as chairman of the Community Chest drive. Sam, trying to understand his sudden restlessness, thought back over the pattern his life had taken.

It was right after World War I that Sam Levinson had come

to Fall City, then a raw, bumptious, striving little mid-western town half its present size. Something in the town's vigor had appealed to him. And what was intended to be a stop-over in his trip from a port of debarkation to his home in California lengthened day by day. He stayed; the town built, and he built with it.

When Sam Levinson came to Fall City there were less than half a dozen Jewish families in the region. There was Sid Goldberg, shrewd and parsimonious who had missed a train at the cow settlement of Fall City in the '80's and had remained to become one of the wealthiest men in the Southwest. There was Isador Stein who came to town as an itinerant printer at the turn of the century and stayed to raise six sons. There were Jacobson and Levitt who had owned the old J and L Theater, where vaudeville acts of the Orpheum circuit played weekly, bringing all the bawdy glamor and excitement of the "live" theater to this drab little town on the prairie. (Out on the prairie, west of town, there still stood the magnificent hulk of the old Levitt home which had been built as part of a real estate development that failed.) Then there was Abe Kalman, wise, kind and well loved, whose store had boasted the first electric-light bulb on Main Street. And finally there was Sol Meyers, who put himself in the junk business back in the '90's, by selling the buffalo bones which settlers gathered by the tons off the prairie to be shipped as return cargo on the wagon-trains that brought calico and window glass, sugar, flour and barbed wire to the new towns of the West.

Sam Levinson was of a different generation from these men, and he often felt a furious impatience with their "old-worldly" ways. He learned to live well, to get along well with non-Jews. His expansive nature won him friends, and in a half dozen years he became an integrated part of the community. Then, in the '20's, a land boom brought an influx of thousands of new people to Fall City, and the Jewish population jumped from six families to 50 families. Sam Levinson, standing somewhere between the old and new, became the link between these people and the other people of the town; he became the acknowledged leader of the Jewish community which built up inside the larger community. He was the principal worker and contributor for the building of a synagogue at the height of the boom in 1928. That was the same year he met and married Myra Levine.

He'd always been proud of being a Jew, Sam Levinson told himself fiercely; he'd never tried to run away from it. And what was troubling him now, he kept asking himself. It all seemed to have something to do with Davey . . . Davey whose small bright face was grinning at him now from the picture frame on his desk—a hinged picture frame which contained, also, a likeness of Myra's cool and beautiful face. Sam studied both pictures, but his eyes rested longest on Davey . . . Davey who could just say "Hey, Dad!" and make him glad to be alive.

Davey wasn't self-conscious—that was the most important thing. He never expected anybody to snub him, and nobody ever did. He went to all the parties, played on the teams, belonged to the clubs and made the honor societies at school.

In a way he was so damn much like Myra. He had her looks and her warm sympathetic nature. But, Sam assured himself, Davey had his ability to take hold, to organize and to lead.

Nothing in all the world mattered to him so much as that everything should be right for Davey, Sam Levinson admitted to himself, as he began again to shuffle the papers on his desk, trying to free himself from his reverie.

As Sam sat trying to focus his mind on the proof sheets that lay before him, Herman Morris opened the door of his office and stuck in his head.

"Go get a cup of coffee, Sam?"

Sam shook his head. "Come in, Herman."

Herman, long, lean and youthful, had a face whose look of sadness seemed unrelated to his droll disposition. His brown eyes smiled now without altering the moroseness of the face.

"What'sa matter, Sam? You look like a dog looks on a cat."

"I was thinking about Davey. In a couple of weeks I have to take him to the rabbi to begin his confirmation classes."

"So, is that bad?"

"You know, Herman, I wish to hell the rabbi wouldn't speak always of Germany. This isn't Europe; things are different here. He's making everybody so damn conscious of Jews as Jews. He's forcing us right back into the ghetto."

"Aw, Sam, it's not as bad as that," Herman said. It seemed to him that Sam Levinson was constantly trying to prove to himself that among his Gentile friends and associates the fact that he was a Jew did not matter. Herman could see that this was an attitude seriously out of balance with preparing a young son to be *bar mitzvah*. He looked at Sam with the reluctant pity that a stubborn and proud man sometimes evokes.

"You know, Herman," Sam leaned back in his chair and clasped his hands behind his head.

"What?"

"Sometimes it seems to me that my generation was caught in the transition. In the next generation—Davey's generation—things may be different."

Herman shrugged, optimism was not one of his attributes. "And the better things get, the more the small things rankle," he said pointedly.

This remark made Sam uneasy. He was still thinking of Davey. And sometimes the fact that Davey took things so much for granted amazed his father, and even frightened him a little.

"Oh, I don't know, Herman. After all, this is America. Sometimes I feel like the Jews of our generation have perpetuated the 'legend of differentness' by feeling it too much in their own blood. Maybe it's as much self-inspired as superimposed. Maybe Davey's generation, by not feeling it, can refute it."

Herman looked at Sam Levinson knowingly. "Why kid yourself, Sam? Look, if you can't go out for coffee, I've got to run. After all, the Mayfair isn't like Levinson's. I can't afford to be gone all day."

"I'll see you later," Sam said shortly. He picked up the papers on his desk in an impatient gesture before Herman was out of the room. Talking to Herman had only added to his sense of frustration that secret niggling fear which he so often and so fiercely suppressed—the fear that he was not fortifying his son to meet with dignity what life might hold for him, that he was leaving his son vulnerable. But no matter how he might wrestle with this problem there was one thing he knew for sure. The new rabbi, bearing the scars of European Jew-hatred, posed an insurmountable threat to the particular kind of unawareness he coveted for his son.

Chapter 6

ON THURSDAY afternoon, the first week of school, Davey Levinson stood at the corner waiting for his father to come for him. The hot September wind blew against Davey, pelting him with sand from the school yard where the sixth-grade boys were playing soft ball. Jimmy Holt slid to third base, then stood up, dusting his hands with satisfaction.

"Aw, come on Davey. You can play," Gary Williams called. Gary wasn't a good player himself, but he would rather see Davey score than Jimmy Holt.

"I can't," Davey answered, catching hold of the bus sign pole and swinging himself around it.

"Come on!"

"No, I can't!" Davey maintained. He was reluctant to tell them why he couldn't. They called Paul Thomas a sissy when he had to go to a music lesson. To have to go to confirmation class was infinitely worse. Davey stood there, stubbing the toe of his sneaker against the sign. He wished that his father would come. Finally he spotted the car two blocks away, and he ran to meet it.

Sam Levinson saw Davey coming. Davey's gustiness of imagination touched his movements, so that he seemed always to be wearing a figurative pair of seven-league boots. Sam stopped the car and waited, smiling, while his young son clambered in beside him.

"Hi, Davey!"

"Hi—wish I didn't have to go!" Davey said, as they passed the school yard again.

Sam saw the boys playing ball, it was a hard thing for him to take Davey away.

"You have to do it, son," he said without conviction. He seemed suddenly preoccupied, and Davey said no more. They stopped in front of the temple and entered by the door that lead into the vestry. The rabbi was waiting for them.

"Hello, Rabbi. Here's my boy I've been telling you about— Davey, this is Rabbi Rosen." Sam Levinson's manner was simultaneously brusque and hearty. Davey glanced at his father uncertainly, as if seeking some key to what his own manner should be. But almost immediately his attention was challenged by the personal force of the man he met.

"How do you do, Davey," Kurt Rosen said, extending his hand.

"Hi—Sir," Davey replied. Davey seemed to cast aside his boyish petulance at being deprived of play. He shook hands with the rabbi, responding to his father's introductions with a manliness of demeanor that not only surprised Sam Levinson, but vaguely irritated him.

"Well," Sam said, shortly, "I'll leave you two. I must go back to the store. Davey, you call your mother to come for you. Goodbye, Rabbi—See that he stays in line!" Sam's last words came back in his own ears as facetious and oddly unsuited to the dignified bearing of the two who watched his departure. Sam Levinson didn't understand what had come over Davey.

"All right, Davey, sit down. Perhaps today we should just get acquainted," Kurt Rosen said.

"All right—Sir," Davey replied. He was still in the chair except for banging his feet against its rungs.

For a moment man and boy sat looking at each other and in their first appraisal each found himself disposed to give the other the benefit of the doubt.

"Davey, do you have any idea what it means to be *bar mitzvah?*" Kurt asked him.

"You read out of the Torah in Hebrew, and then everybody eats," Davey answered blandly.

It seemed to Kurt that he caught a conscious irony of equal emphasis in Davey's statement; but perhaps, he thought, he was giving Davey credit for too much subtlety of perception. Kurt was encountering for the first time at close range that grandiose phenomenon, the twelve-year-old American male, and he did not know what to expect.

"And which do you think is the more important, Davey—the reading from the Torah, or the eating," he asked quickly.

"The reading from the Torah," Davey replied, but his bright brown eyes met the rabbi's thoughtful gray ones, and suddenly they both were laughing as if they knew something very funny about people which had to do with eating.

In a meeting of minds between these two—a twelve-year-old sixth-grader in the Fall City grade school and the man who had earned his doctorate after half a dozen years of study in the

56

best universities of Europe—there was something preposterous and, at the same time, irresistible to them both. At that moment Kurt Rosen and young Davey Levinson became friends.

"Davey, have you been going to Sunday School; do you know any of the history of the Children of Israel?" Kurt asked him.

"No, Sir. I went to Sunday School some when I was little, but I don't go anymore."

"When you were little?"

"When Rabbi Gold was here. I was seven."

"You know what the Torah is, don't you Davey?"

"It's the thing you keep behind the curtain—in the ark."

"But what is it?"

"It's all wrapped up in pretty material—in satin with fringe, and sort of jewels on it."

"Yes, Davey, but what's wrapped up?"

"The Bible?" Davey said doubtfully.

"The Five Books of Moses, the most sacred part of the Holy Writings," Kurt told him.

Davey nodded.

"Have you ever seen the Torah, Davey?"

"When Donny Epstein was *bar mitzvah* they took it out—and walked all around the Temple with it. And some of the people on the aisles kissed it as it was carried by. I thought that was kind of silly."

Kurt tactfully ignored Davey's commentary.

"But did you ever look at a copy of the Torah yourself?"

Davey shook his head.

"Then, come, we will go up into the sanctuary and I will show you."

Kurt took his own *yarmulka* from his hip pocket. As they entered the sanctuary he took one from the stand and gave it to Davey.

"Do I have to wear this, too?" Davey demanded, wrinkling his nose as if he had been asked to don a false face.

"Of course. We are entering the sanctuary and you are a Jew, are you not?"

"Yes."

"Do you know how it began, the wearing of *yarmulkas?*"

"No, sir."

"Do you know what the word *Israel* means in Hebrew?"

"No, sir."

"*Israel* means Fighter for God. It was the name that Jacob took. And after Jacob, Jews always have thought of themselves as fighters for God. Later they wanted some symbol of being fighters for God—and what do you think they chose?—what is something a soldier has that could be used for a symbol?"

"A gun?" Davey suggested.

"We do not fight with guns, Davey. What else?"

Davey looked skeptically at the *yarmulka*. "A helmet?" he asked uncertainly.

"Right!" They both laughed again. Davey Levinson was practically the first person Kurt Rosen had encountered in Fall City who had not approached him with the presupposed inability to understand. Davey's bland confidence in his ability to understand not only the Rabbi's words, but his meanings as well, and his naive responsiveness, were for Kurt a diverting and refreshing experience, lifting a little the pall of non-communication.

Davey was thoughtful for a moment. "My daddy doesn't wear a *yarmulka*," he said, "he just keeps on his hat."

"Some Jews just keep on their hats," Kurt agreed.

Kurt Rosen drew the curtain of the ark. He lifted out the first of the five scrolls and removed its satin case. He laid it on the pulpit and began to unroll it for Davey to see.

"Golly!" Davey said, "what's it written on?"

"It's written on goat or sheep skin such as is used to make the finest kid gloves. It will last hundreds of years."

"Who writes it?"

"Scholars. It takes a skilled scribe a year to make a single copy of the Torah."

"And what if he makes a mistake? What if he gets a word wrong?" Davey wanted to know.

"You see, the Torah is composed of sections. If the mistake is serious that section has to be replaced."

"Even if he makes a mistake on the last page?" Davey asked incredulously, fingering the blunt and much used eraser in his pants pocket.

"Even in the last verse," Kurt said, repressing the smile that came to his lips.

As Davey stood examining the Torah, there was a small flicker which made the sudden absence of a light more noticeable than its presence had been.

Kurt glanced up, and Davey's eyes followed his.

"The bulb in the *Ner Tamid* has gone out. Go, Davey, into the basement and ask Juan to bring the stepladder."

"What does it mean—*Ner Tamid?*" Davey asked.

"Eternal Light. Did you not know, Davey, that this small light burns always in a Jewish house of worship."

"Even when you're not here?"

"Even when I'm not here."

"Why?"

"It represents the light of our faith in God upon the earth, which must never be allowed to go out."

"Golly, how much electricity do you suppose that costs in a month?" Davey wondered.

"Go, Davey, bring Juan," Kurt said, drily.

Davey went.

Juan came carrying the stepladder, with Davey bouncing along beside him. Kurt brought a new bulb from his study.

Juan placed the ladder, very carefully, as if he were performing some mystic rite.

"May I screw it in?" Davey wanted to know.

"Yes, Davey. You may do that *mitzvah*."

"What is a *mitzvah*?" Davey asked.

"*Mitzvah* is a Hebrew word meaning 'commandment,' and since religion asks you to do only what is good, *mitzvah* also means 'good deed'."

Juan and the rabbi watched as Davey climbed the ladder and unscrewed the light covering which was shaped like a torch. He took out the old bulb and put in the new one and fastened the covering back into the brass holder. And the *Ner Tamid* burned again.

Juan watched this procedure with his shoulders hunched forward a little, his wrinkled brown face full of a curious awe. Learning English, Kurt Rosen had said "humbliness" for "humility," and it was a word the fitted Juan.

While Davey made the commonplace motions of replacing the red light bulb, he saw what was in Juan's face. When Juan had gone with the ladder, he said, "It doesn't seem to be such a holy thing—when you have to climb up a ladder and screw in a bulb."

"Even very holy things must be tended, Davey. Nothing can exist without being tended," Kurt Rosen told him, and he looked in Davey's eager bright young face to see if he understood.

"A human soul is the most holy thing of all, but the body that houses it must be fed and clothed and cared for in illness. Think of all the love and care your parents give to you."

Thoughtfully Davey Levinson nodded his head.

59

It was not the significance of the Eternal Light that had interested Davey Levinson, but the amount of electricity it took to burn it; it was not the Torah that impressed Davey, but the possibility of copying it without a mistake. When Davey had gone home, Kurt Rosen was in a thoughtful mood. Kurt thought of young Davey and it seemed to him that never in his life had he encountered a Jewish boy of 12 with so slight a sense of his Jewish identity.

. . . Jewish identity . . . *they said we* . . . Jewish identity . . . *they said we* . . .

These phrases that flicked through Kurt's thoughts enticed his mind, back, back, back. . . .

"Mama! Mama! They say we are murderers. They say we killed a little boy and used his blood to make Matzoh for Pesach!"

The sweat stood on Kurt's brow as he remembered. He had been twelve years old that year, just as Davey Levinson was now twelve. And his family had moved from the village of his childhood to Graudenz so he could go to high school.

That day, when Kurt came running in, Henrietta Rosen was in the big sunny kitchen, stretching out the dough for a *strudel* and the deftness went suddenly out of her fingers, and they were colder than the water in which she dipped them to smooth the warm pliant dough.

"Kurt, come!" she wiped her hand on her apron. She laid it on his head where the dark curls were damp against his forehead.

"I know it is a lie," Kurt said, speaking rapidly to explain away his own terror. "It is an awful lie. Our religion forbids us to eat any blood at all, and this is why you remove all the blood from our meat to make it kosher—you even forbade me to suck the blood when I cut my finger, though the other boys do it."

"Kurt, don't let them frighten you. You know it is a wicked and an ignorant thing they say." Henrietta told him.

"But why do they say it?" he demanded.

Henrietta Rosen stood looking into her son's face. How do you explain to a child what an adult cannot understand; how do you explain to a child that, while the truth must convince, hate need merely suggest.

Even now, thirty years later, Kurt Rosen recalled that day so vividly that all of his senses participated in the memory, recreating the exact sounds and sights, the taste and feel . . .

. . . the sun on the gray slate roof of the synagogue—the tantalizing, illusive, warm and vaporous odors in the big kitchen where Henrietta Rosen prepared the Passover food—the first time of going barefoot and the coolness and hardness of the spring wakening earth underfoot as he walked to Baker Roth's to get the Matzohs—and the sound of horses' hooves on the cobble stones, drumming behind the sexton's nasal voice, as he walked through the streets, calling "Burn your *hometz!* Burn your *hometz!*"

The chanted phrase had a strange, mournful, compelling sound which stirred Kurt's blood. He wondered how it would be to hear the words and not know what they meant, and his answer seemed to be provided by a small Christian boy who stood at the corner, his eyes wide, his feet poised for flight, listening in fascination as he watched the Jews begin to come out of their houses with the paper bags in their hands.

A man who had been standing in the shelter of a recessed doorway stepped suddenly into the street, almost at Kurt's side.

"What are those men doing?" he demanded.

Startled, Kurt wheeled around and found himself looking into the pale sharp eyes of Heinz, the knife sharpener, who daily made his way through the streets leaning on a heavy cane, his honing stone in a sack slung over his shoulder. Heinz had a wry, sly, nippy look, and the twisted peak of his cap was like the twisted smile on his lips.

"Well, speak up! What are they doing?" he said again. And Kurt felt, not so much impatience, as a certain raillery in his tone.

"They're taking their *hometz* out of their houses to burn it," he answered. Kurt had spent most of his life in a village where there were only two Jewish families. There, the Rosens had escaped the stigma of a minority and had enjoyed the prestige of absolute uniqueness, and Kurt had learned to answer questions with a sort of offhand authoritativeness.

"What's *hometz?*" the peddler asked.

"It's leaven—any bread that's made with leaven," Kurt told him. "Last night we had the ceremony of searching for leaven. My father carried a big wooden spoon and some goose feathers, and I carried the candle, and mama went along to show us where she hid the bread."

"If she knew, why were you searching?"

Kurt grinned. "Only so the proper prayers could be said. Mama has been cleaning for a week. She knew there wasn't a crumb in that house unless she put it there on purpose. So she showed Papa the crumbs and he swept them into the spoon with the feathers and said the prayers. And then he wrapped the spoon and the crumbs in a paper bag so that this morning he could burn it. With all the families it is the same.

"Why must they burn the bread?" Heinz asked suspiciously, hunching his weight over the knob head of his cane. Kurt began to fidget in his eagerness to be on his way.

"For Passover days we eat only unleavened bread, like the children of Israel had to eat when they were fleeing from Egypt. For the whole week we eat only matzohs."

"Matzohs!" the knife sharpener seemed mesmerized into some vicious mood by the word. His pale eyes piniones Kurt. "You make matzohs out of blood!" he accused.

Kurt looked at him in astonishment, and the flush of anger rose in his face.

"No, we don't! Matzohs are made out of flour and water. Jews can't even eat meat until all the blood is out."

"Don't lie! I wasn't talking about animal blood. You make matzohs with the blood of a Christian!" Without changing its shape the twisted smile on Heinz's face had become a horrible grimace.

"It isn't true! It isn't true!" Kurt said through clenched teeth.

"Yes, it is," Heinz said, swaying back and forth on his cane. "Yes, it is! One year we found a part of the body in the lake by the synagogue. The rest we found in the forest. In pieces. All cut up. A boy about your size—We would have killed all the Jews, but the Kaiser sent troops to protect them." The peddler spat in the sand at his feet.

"Then the Kaiser knew it was a lie. If he sent troops he knew it was a lie," Kurt insisted hoarsely. But Heinz paid no heed.

"This year we're ready for you," he said. "I hear the men talking. If anybody disappears this year, we're ready for you!"

The man spat again, and in the wind the spittle was a mist in Kurt's face. With both frantic hands he wiped his face, and the tears began to wash it, and with the tail of his shirt he smeared the tears on his face. And he began to run; through the street to his home, he ran.

Years later as a student of History and Religion, Kurt had learned how the ritual murder accusations had cropped up time and again to plague the Jews of Europe since the twelfth century. He could never understand why the accusations were connected with the Passover. His history teacher at the theological seminary shrugged his shoulders and suggested that because Christians thought there was no forgiveness of sins without the blood of Jesus, probably they were convinced that there existed some similar blood ritual in the Jewish religion. But this did not justify a connection with the Passover, Kurt thought; and later he, himself, discovered an explanation that satisfied him.

One day, home from the seminary at Passover, he observed an old Jewish custom. Several days before the festival began, all worn out Bibles and pages torn from prayer books which had been scrupulously saved during the year, were gathered from drawers in which they were kept and placed in a sack. The sexton, then, accompanied by two other members of the congregation, took the sack to the Jewish cemetery and buried it.

The connection leapt to Kurt's mind as he witnessed this ritual—three Jews carrying a sack to the cemetery to bury it— a sack that contained the worn-out Bibles and leaves from Sacred Books—but which might have contained a body. On that day, as a student, Kurt was excited by the possible historical significance of his hunch.

But on the night in Graudenz years before, he had known only the closeness of the terror, and he had begun to see how it is that people live with terror.

The memory of that night unfolded now . . .

When the family gathered around the white and candle-lit table for the Passover *seder,* young Kurt Rosen's eyes were constantly on his mother, confronting her with his dread. The candle light seemed to lay a serenity upon her face which he did not quite believe, and with a desperate anxiety he watched for a flicker of dread in her face, knowing that if he saw it, his own dread would engulf him.

When he came in off the street with this terrible thing to tell, his mother had quieted him, and soothed him, and helped him to dress to go with his father to the synagogue. And finally she had told him not to speak to the others of what had happened. But now, as he looked from one to the other, Kurt knew that his mother had told his father. And as the *seder* began, Kurt searched the solemn joy for the shuddering thought.

His father said the blessing on the wine; and then, when he had washed his hands in the silver basin his wife brought to him, he took the sprig of parsley and dipped it in the salt water, explaining solemnly to his family that the tender green parsley represented the new life which the spring quickened in the earth, and that it was dipped in salt water to remind Jews of the tears their ancestors shed under their oppressors in Egypt.

One by one the Passover symbols were explained as his father told the story of deliverance, following the text in the *Haggadah.*

And at the proper moment, Kurt, the youngest, stood beside his chair at his father's invitation and recited the four questions in Hebrew . . .

> *Why is this night different from all other nights?*
> *On all other nights we may eat either leavened bread or matzoh; but on this night only matzoh.*
> *On all other nights we eat all kinds of herbs; but on this night we eat bitter herbs.*
> *On all other nights we do not dip the vegetables even once; on this night we dip them twice.*
> *On all other nights we eat in either a sitting or a reclining position; on this night we all recline.*

As the *seder* moved at its dignified pace through a revelation of the deepest and most beautiful facets of Jewish life and faith, Kurt felt his fears subsiding. He remembered what the rabbi had said in the synagogue ". . . Few in numbers, with but seventy souls, went thy fathers down into Egypt, and now thy God has made thee as numerous as the stars. . . . Not one only sought to destroy us, but men in all generations; and the Holy One, Blessed be He, saves us from their hands."

As the climactic moment of the *seder* arrived, when the prayer would be said for the return of the prophet Elijah, when the door would be thrown open for his coming, Kurt looked at his mother and smiled. And she smiled in reply.

"Go, Kurt, the door!" she said, as his father poured the wine into the silver beaker that was reserved for the prophet's coming. And Kurt felt in his mother's voice only that curious gentleness in strength that belongs to the woman who knows that what she cannot protect she must cherish the more.

Kurt got down from his chair and with a feeling of specialness he went to draw the bolt of the door. And Henrietta Rosen did not breathe for a moment, and her white hand on the table did not move. And she knew what Kurt did not know, that on this holy night, when the Jews flung open their doors for the Prophet's coming, it had happened more than once that whole Jewish communities were seized and annihilated.

The big oak door swung wide under the pressure of Kurt's hands. The night's stillness seemed to push a little into the room. And the coolness of the night air was in Kurt's face. And he turned, quickly, to see if the Prophet's beaker might have been

64

lifted to the lips of an unseen Elijah. And still his mother smiled at him.

As Rabbi Kurt Rosen remembered his mother, he remembered the words he had used to tell her this awful thing.

Mama, they say we are murderers.

Kurt had said "we," although the accusations of which he spoke certainly had been raised before his birth and in a place where his family had never been. In that "we" young Kurt Rosen was voicing the oneness of Jews of all times and all places. It was a "we" that Davey Levinson did not understand.

Chapter 7

ELLEN answered the knock at the door, and found standing there a large man who, at sight of her, took off his hat and held it awkwardly in his hands. His eyes, bristly-browed and smiling, were fine and a little shy; and his manner was gravely courteous.

"Mrs. Rosen?" he inquired.

"Yes."

"Mrs. Rosen, I'm Charlie Grimes . . . I wanted to see the Rabbi."

"He gives a lesson now . . . in his study. I expect him any moment. You're most welcome to wait here . . . or you may go to him there."

"I'll just wait . . . if you don't mind."

"Please come in."

Charlie Grimes sat down in the chair that Ellen offered him, and she took his hat. Ellen sensed that, in spite of his shy deference with her, he was a man used to commanding, to taking hold, to stiffening the spines of lesser individuals. She smiled without realizing it, and he seemed delighted with the smile.

"Mrs. Rosen," he said, leaning forward in his chair, "I am glad to have this moment to speak to you! I am president of the Kiwanis Club, and I came here to ask your husband if he might speak to us. I read the story in the paper . . . and I know these things must be difficult for him to speak of . . . and if you think . . ."

"I think it is most kind of you to ask," Ellen reassured him, ". . . and here comes Rabbi now."

At the sound of Kurt's footsteps on the stairway, Ellen went to the door and called down to him. "Kurt, come. We have a guest. There is a gentleman who wishes to speak to you."

Kurt Rosen was holding his wife's hand as they came back into the room, and the warmth of the moment seemed to draw Charlie Grimes within its bounds.

66

"Mr. Grimes, may I present Rabbi Rosen . . ." Ellen said. "Kurt, Mr. Grimes wants that you speak for . . .?" with a graceful lift of her hand she beckoned Mr. Grimes to intercede.

"For the Kiwanis Club, Rabbi Rosen. We would consider it an honor if you would speak for us," Charlie Grimes told him.

"Thank you!" Kurt said, reaching out his hand to his guest. "About what do you wish that I speak?"

"Rabbi, I think we here in America should know more about conditions inside Germany. If you could tell us . . . any things you see fit."

Ellen's eyes were on her husband. She knew what it was that Charlie Grimes was asking; and the amazing thing was that he seemed to know, too.

"Mr. Grimes, this is a service, I gladly perform," Kurt promptly said. "I will tell you as much as I am able. There are some things I cannot tell you because our families live still in Germany. But I will tell you as much as I can."

"Thank you, Rabbi," Charlie Grimes extended his hand again to Kurt Rosen, and his smile to Ellen.

"I make coffee for us now," Ellen said simply. From the kitchen she glanced back into the room she had just left, observing the odd mixture of dignity and heartiness with which Kurt was making Charlie Grimes, born and bred on the Texas plains, feel at home in a transplanted atmosphere of European hospitality.

"Kurtchen . . . perhaps Mr. Grimes does not like the Swiss chocolates," Ellen called indulgently, as she watched with what pleasure Kurt broke open the box of sweets that had arrived that morning from friends in New York, and displayed the small bitter chocolates to their guest.

With large awkward fingers, Charlie Grimes lifted one of the candies from its nest. His eyes were twinkling as he did it, and his lips twisted a little as he tasted it.

"Mr. Grimes, it is so kind of you to come to us," Ellen spoke from the kitchen doorway.

"Mrs. Rosen . . . I am not quite through with my errand," he replied, "There is something else I wanted to ask if it would not be too much. It said in the article that you are a singer. I wonder . . . would you sing for us, too?"

Ellen was thinking that America was indeed a most incredible place. "I would gladly do it," she told him.

A few moments later the three of them were sitting around the small table that Ellen had set with linen, and Charlie Grimes was drinking his cup of coffee, and eating a piece of coffee cake with a bemused expression on his frank and friendly face as he tried to understand how it was that he had been made so welcome.

On the next Wednesday noon, Ellen sat beside Kurt at the long white-covered table in the banquet room of the Fall City Hotel, and while Kurt engaged in conversation with Charlie Grimes, on his right, her eyes traveled with searching concern over the faces of the assembled Kiwanians.

There were the sunburned, weathered faces of the ranchers and oil men, and the smoother, blander faces of the professional men, yet for the most part they were open, direct faces, quick to smile. It was their manner that filled Ellen with misgivings. Charlie Grimes had introduced them individually as they gathered, and they had offered a spontaneous, if sometimes shy welcome. But their manner among themselves was full of banter and rowdy comradeship and gusty spirits. In mood, they seemed utterly unprepared for the things that Kurt would tell them.

Kurt's mellow, bouncing laugh brought Ellen's eyes back to him, as he responded with quick humor to something that Charlie Grimes had said.

"Kurtchen . . ." Ellen whispered.

He only covered her hand with his where it lay on the table, and did not try to answer. And Charlie Grimes, sensing this by-play which was lost almost to sight or sound, leaned around Kurt and smiled at Ellen encouragingly, just as she had smiled encouragingly to him when they met in a setting that was hers.

The meal began with the inevitable fruit cup . . . and there was the clink of ice in glasses and the uneven grating of masculine voices, and finally the smell of cigar smoke as the dinner was ending.

At that moment the big double doors onto the mezzanine were opened, and a bright young blonde, wearing a brief red-fringed cowboy ensemble, came into the room followed by a young man who wore tight jeans and a bright silk shirt and carried a big banjo slung over his shoulder.

Charlie Grimes spoke quickly to Kurt again. "We have a show every year for Crippled Children and these young folks are among the performers.They asked if they might do a number here today to boost the ticket sales," he explained. "I think it would be best if we keep them until after your address," he said apologetically.

68

Kurt nodded in agreement.

The next moment Charlie Grimes was on his feet, introducing the rabbi. There was a scraping of chairs and a respectful clearing of throats as the Kiwanians prepared to listen. And Ellen felt Kurt rising beside her.

"My Friends," Kurt began, "you do me a great honor to ask me to speak to you, and I commend you upon wanting to hear what I have to say . . . for the facts that I must give are not easy to hear. I can only say that if there had been more people in Germany who showed the concern which you show today, in wanting to know what was happening, perhaps the worst things would not have happened at all. . . ."

Kurt began to try to make them understand exactly what had happened . . . exactly how it is that freedom is lost . . . how it is for men who have known freedom to discover that they are no longer free . . . that they cannot make themselves free again . . . and how their anguished spirits turn then to other free men, hoping against hope, that they will understand in time.

"I hear it said in America that an underground movement may yet overthrow Hitler's government. But here people do not seem to realize. An underground movement in Germany is not possible, and if it did exist it would be of no importance . . . for every man is set against his neighbor and even son against father. There is a paralysis of fear that strangles protest even where protest might arise. There is no help there for the persecuted . . . help must come from without."

Kurt's words rang sharp in the pool of silence that greeted them. The Kiwanians sat with kind and sympathetic and attentive faces turned to Kurt, and his words came echoing back from the ears of those who listened without knowing that they, personally, were challenged . . . and summoned . . . and implored.

And Ellen could not bear to look in Kurt's face at the lines of despair and futility etched there in a way that only she could see. He sat down beside her and the clapping welled up around him, warm and clamorous, a clapping that almost hysterically avowed, "We are glad that you . . . the Rosens . . . have escaped!" and by this simple declaration left the tens of thousands of others abandoned.

Ellen Rosen felt that she could not stand this moment. She felt that her voice would not leave her throat, when she heard Charlie Grimes speaking again, saying that she would sing. And briefly her eyes met the fine eyes beneath the beetle-brows of this warm-hearted Texan and she knew that he had understood. And for him she would sing.

". . . I think that I shall never see . . . a poem as lovely as a tree . . ." The words, clear and beautiful in song, winged their way from the world of stark reality and carried off with them spirits ill-at-ease and restive from their brush with unpleasantness. That their escape should be so easy, filled Ellen with rage and she could no longer look in their faces, could not accept the homage that they offered her. And while the last note still hung, exquisite and fragile in the air, she sat down beside Kurt, and slipped her hand in his.

There was a pause which contained no clear feeling of what might come after. Then Charlie Grimes stood up again. He glanced at Kurt and at Ellen, with a look meant only for them, and then he turned back to his fellow Kiwanians.

"We have only a few minutes left," he said, "and there are some young folks . . . who have come to entertain us. Miss Bebe Roland . . . and Johnny Wills."

The girl came into the center of the room, the fringe of her short skirt swaying above her shapely knees, her blonde curls bobbing around a pert and saucy face. For an instant her eyes met Ellen's and then she turned quickly away.

"First, I'll show you some trick roping. . . . Play for me, Johnnie!" she said huskily.

Johnny began to play the banjo, and Bebe Roland began to swing the rope in widening circles, and her lithe supple body became a part of the rope's slithering grace, and her lips were very red, and her face young. And the Kiwanians watched her and rescued themselves. They gave themselves into her keeping, away from any lurking hint of terror.

As the meeting ended and the men were shuffling to their feet, one young Kiwanian stood up and began passing out cigars a little sheepishly, and his fellow club members were shaking hands with him and patting him on the back. As he passed down the table he handed a cigar to Kurt, who accepted it with his usual dignity. All the men were examining the band on the cigar. Kurt glanced at it.

It's a Boy! the cigar band blatantly proclaimed. Kurt began to smile a little, he felt Ellen's eyes dark and somber on his face. He slipped the cigar band off the cigar and, like a ring, he solemnly slipped it onto her finger, bidding for her smile.

"Come, let's go," he said to her gently.

70

Kurt Rosen's lecture for the Kiwanis Club was only a beginning. This lecture, duly reported in the *Fall City Tribune,* called for a second lecture . . . and a third and a fourth. And in a matter of weeks Kurt Rosen was in great demand as a speaker, not only in Fall City, which was the hub of a large ranching area, but in the surrounding small towns as well. He spoke before business clubs and luncheon clubs, at church groups and at study clubs; at banquets and at box suppers. And always the people seemed most interested in hearing about survival in a concentration camp. Coupled with the awful need to put these things behind in order to mend a bruised spirit, Kurt Rosen was faced with the urgent necessity for reliving them each time he spoke in order to articulate them in a newly mastered tongue.

And Ellen sat by and watched him relive it each time, and knew the cost to him who spoke and the inconsequence to those who listened. And each time, when it was over, she was called upon to get up and to sing.

It seemed to Ellen that, while the barbed-wire fences encircled more of Europe, while the message that Kurt possessed became more and more worth the cost of repeating it, the people who heard apparently continued in their heedlessness, pursuing the more diligently the banalities of the American way of life while shunning its deeper concepts. And she and Kurt, comprehending with tragic insight the deeper concepts, were sometimes secretly appalled at the heedlessness and the banalities.

But the warmth of the people themselves Ellen could not resist. The gestures of welcome and of spontaneous love, which she so often encountered at the places where Kurt spoke and she sang, were offered with a baffling, endearing, childlike impulsiveness. Sometimes Ellen envied, almost, the naive unawareness of these people; sometimes for a moment she tried to pretend it herself. She would say, "This is what it feels like to be an American and to think that everyone in the world is free!" And then, when those moments had passed, she would feel even more keenly the demands that these people so innocently made upon Kurt, binding him somehow to his past; refusing somehow to let him escape it, though he had escaped it. And for Kurt her heart would ache.

On an early autumn day Ellen rode to town on the bus and went to Isador Jacobson's store on Main Street. She remembered so well his keen insight on the night of the welcoming party at the lake, and she had felt the perceptive warmth of his interest on Friday nights when he came to temple, sitting always near the back and tunelessly humming the prayers as Kurt read them. Now, she longed to see if he might understand, and make more understandable to her, just what it was that weighed so heavily upon her spirit.

As she entered the store, Mr. Jacobson was standing in the doorway, hunched and blinking, a little like a wise old turtle sunning himself. But he was as gaily clad—in plaid sports jacket and contrasting slacks—as ever. And he moved with quick liveliness to welcome her.

"Now, Mrs. Rosen, it's good to see you in my store. What can I do for you," he asked, almost as if he were teasing her a little.

"Mr. Jacobson, Rabbi and I have an anniversary soon. I would like to buy something for him," Ellen told him.

"Good! Good! What would you like," he waved his hand expansively as if he would like to make her a gift of the contents of the whole store.

"I don't know . . . exactly. Something very American, I think!" she said impulsively.

"Very American?" he mused. His discerning face shaped the idea, and Ellen saw that he would understand.

"Mr. Jacobson, they ask very often that he speak . . . and always about things that are hard to remember. The Americans have such a way to be happy in spite of everything. I want that he learns to be very American!"

Mr. Jacobson did not seem to find this strange, he smiled at her.

"How about . . . a very American tie?" he suggested gravely.

"Not quite." Ellen put a finger against her chin meditatively. Her eye was caught and held by a little boy who came swaggering into the store at the side of his father, flourishing his six guns and holsters and clad, from Stetson to boot, in Western cowboy garb.

Ellen laughed. "Something like that!" she said. "Something very Texas . . . even if it's very absurd!"

"Boots?" Mr. Jacobson queried skeptically.

"Boots, I think he could not walk in. Maybe a plaid shirt."

"Ya! Something comfortable and warm . . . and very Texas!" Mr. Jacobson agreed.

He began to take down plaid shirts from a rack . . . wildly colorful shirts in reds and blues and greens all jumping over each other.

"You promise not to let him out of the house in it?" Mr. Jacobson insisted drolly.

"I promise. It will be only to sit quietly in the house and make sermons in." She laughed. "But then, he is very easily disturbed to the ear. Even the drip of a faucet. If it is the same to the eye . . .?" Ellen laughed again. She picked up a shirt that was red plaid, and held it out at arm's length. "This, I think," she said.

"All right! To sit in the house and make sermons in," Mr. Jacobson reiterated. He wrapped the shirt and tied it with string. He handed it to Ellen. And in his face was a firm approval of her blitheness; and of her valiance, a mellow, unsentimental admiration which she saw and treasured.

The effects of Kurt Rosen's outside lectures upon the members of Temple B'nai Emanuel were calling forth varied reactions. The Jews, who had been skeptical of Kurt Rosen at first, nevertheless considered him their personal property and they began to be a little resentful that they were not called upon to foster and sponsor their "refugee rabbi." Some of them were all too willing to take their cue from Sam Levinson, who was inwardly tangled up in anxious embarrassment over what he called Kurt's "war mongering." When Kurt's lectures were quoted in *The Tribune* three times within the space of a week, Sam Levinson, as acknowledged leader of the congregation, felt impelled to pay the rabbi a visit. He came in the early afternoon to Kurt's study at the temple. He laid his expensive top coat on a chair and sat down with the air of a man who means business. Dispensing with introductory amenities, he plunged at once into the subject at hand, while Kurt regarded him with calm gray eyes from behind his battered but tidy desk.

"Rabbi," Sam began, "there's something we must talk about. You've been here with us only a short time, and it strikes me you haven't quite got the feel of the way we Jews in America fit into things."

"What gives you that impresssion, Mr. Levinson?" Kurt inquired, almost solicitously, as if he were inquiring about some infirmity of his caller.

"Rabbi . . . the thing I'm getting at . . . is all these talks.

73

So much about the Jews of Germany. . . ." Sam hesitated. "You're forcing us right back into the ghetto!" he declared, remembering the phrase he had used to Herman Morris.

"You are forgetting one thing, Mr. Levinson," Kurt Rosen told him, "The Jews of Germany did not live in a ghetto. They enjoyed as much prestige as you enjoy here in America. They were leading men in every field—government, science, art, finance."

Sam Levinson was getting red in the face. "That makes it even worse! It's as if you were always drawing a parallel for everyone to see . . . the Jews of Germany . . . the Jews of the United States!"

Kurt looked dispassionately upon the anger of his visitor. "Mr. Levinson, if there is . . . as you say . . . any parallel, it is only that people in America must be very zealous in guarding their liberty . . . that they must realize that the loss of one man's liberty is the loss of every man's liberty."

Sam Levinson stood up, he banged his fist down on the desk top. "Rabbi, you don't need to give me a sermon. Or maybe you do! Give me any sermon you like, but soft-pedal what you say to the *goyim!*"

Kurt stood up, too, but with complete self possession, as if he were merely concluding a routine interview, "Mr. Levinson," he said quietly, "in matters of congregational business I must, of course, heed your advice. In matters of personal judgment, I must follow the dictates of my own conscience. That, I am sure, you can understand."

Sam Levinson was picking up his coat. He settled himself into it as if it were a hair-shirt. Finally he turned back to Kurt.

"Rabbi, I'm not an insensible man. And I meant no offense. But, as I say, you are new here. We hope you can stay . . . can learn to fit in."

"Thank you, Mr. Levinson, for coming," Kurt said, seeing his bristling and disgruntled caller to the door.

The encounter with Sam Levinson had been disturbing, and Kurt did not feel like settling immediately to work on a new sermon. Instead, he glanced at his watch and saw that he would have time to go to Ellen for a little while before Davey's confirmation lesson. Later, as he sat watching her clean the silver, he found it quite impossible to evade her discerning eyes.

"Kurt, is something wrong?" she asked him.

74

"Sam Levinson thinks that I speak too much of Germany," Kurt told her.

Ellen did not immediately reply. She was thinking of all the kind and sympathetic and unheeding faces . . . and of all the times that she had heard the heart that cries out in the wilderness . . . of the many times she had then stood up to sing.

"Kurt, is it worthwhile? Do they even know what you're saying to them?"

"No, Ellen . . . they do not know."

Ellen felt a tremendous aching love for the man who sat beside her, bearing with humility and equanimity this hour's bitter futility. And again she felt the protest surging up in her.

"Kurt! How have we come to this . . . we who love life so much?"

And Kurt's face was lined and thoughtful, and he did not reply.

When Kurt had gone again to his study, Ellen sat alone and tried to visualize what tragic but unreal characters she and her husband seemed to be in other people's eyes . . . . *We, who loved life so much* . . . the words echoed disturbingly in her mind. And she began to think of the days when she and Kurt were life-loving . . . of the days in Koenigsberg when they wandered in moonlight by the sea . . . of the days when she had been blithely confident that choice controls life . . . and when she had made her choice to go with Kurt. Quiet . . . and alone . . . she began to remember . . .

. . . The second time that Kurt Rosen went to the studio of Herr Professor Bach in Koenigsberg was nearly a month after his first visit there. During that month he had seen Ellen Meier nearly every day. At first they had gone to the opera and to the theater. But Kurt's schedule of classes and organizational meetings was too tightly filled to allow many formal dates, and so they had begun to meet secretly whenever he had an hour of free time, at 9 o'clock at night, or in the first clear hours of morning, or in the bright sunny noon.

"I do not think your congregation would approve, if they knew their assistant rabbi was carrying on a secret romance," Ellen teased one day as they drank coffee in a small café.

"I do not think your mamma would approve if she knew we met so often without a chaperon," Kurt rejoined, and the smile leapt from her lips to his eyes.

75

"Surely an almost-rabbi should be qualified to be his own chaperon," Ellen laughed, but although the remark was flippant, Kurt recognized a perplexity that he had sensed before. Ellen seemed unable to reconcile the thought of romance with the thought of a minister. Always in moments such as this, Kurt thought of the voice teacher, and of the feeling of intruding upon a moment of rapport.

"You have your voice lesson today?" Kurt said.

"Yes."

"I want to come with you."

Ellen hesitated. "I don't think so."

"Yes. I want to hear you sing."

At two o'clock they went to the graystone house and to Professor Bach's studio on the second floor. Kurt was struck again by his first impression of this man, the unsettled look of his clothes, the quick perceptiveness springing unexpectedly from the languor of movement, the awkward warmth of greeting.

"Ellen—Dr. Rosen. Come in! It's good to see you again."

"Thank you! Ellen has been promising that I might hear her sing. I hope I won't disturb," Kurt said.

Ellen felt herself drawing strength from the consciousness of Kurt Rosen standing behind her. And at the same time she saw in Herr Bach's face that she should not have brought Kurt here. By bringing him here, she had made this a moment for decision. And she was not ready to decide. She felt her throat closing and in the palms of her hands there was a tingling dryness.

"You will not disturb at all. Ellen is ready for an audience, I think," Herr Bach replied, and he smiled at her as if he understood what she was feeling.

"Here, Dr. Rosen, sit down. Ellen, what do you want to sing?" He indicated the chair to Kurt, and then he stood beside the piano, shuffling through the sheet music that lay in the pile on its top.

Ellen went over and stood beside her teacher. Kurt Rosen's presence made the blood run faster in her veins, but Herr Bach exerted over her some tremendous power of response. She stood beside him now as a chastened child, awaiting reproach. But there was no reproach. He drew a song from the pile of sheet-music and put it into her hands.

The first love affair is only the touching of hands. Herr Bach had seemed to understand that it was for him to release the first raptures of a warmly loving heart, and he had not presumed upon this mission. But looking at him now, Ellen saw that he loved her as she did not love him.

Ellen glanced at Kurt. He was sitting in the chair with the curious arrogance of the life-loving. Ellen could have laughed, because he was able to make the stillness of sitting as positive and affirmative as motion. His gray eyes were expecting something of her.

"Do you like *Der Wanderer* by Schubert?" she asked him.

He nodded, "My favorite song." Herr Bach sat down at the piano and began to play the accompaniment. And Ellen began to sing . . .

> *"I come from the mountains, the vapors rise in the valley, the ocean roars. I walk silently along and am little happy— I am a stranger everywhere; where art thou my promised land, sought, imagined, but nowhere found—Oh land, where art thou? I walk silently, am little happy, and always ask, and sigh, where? In ghostlike breath it echoes back to me, where you are not, there is no happiness—"*

. . . to sing of wandering was an exquisite yearning—but to stand by the sea with Kurt, to feel his hands upon her arms, to hear him laugh against the sound of the sea—was a wild joy!

Ellen looked from Herr Bach to Kurt and back again as she sang. What Herr Bach offered her was the artist's unrequited yearning after life's illusions. But what Kurt Rosen seemed to be offering her was life itself.

And when the songs were finished, and the piano had murmured a plaintive ending, Ellen, looked again from one to the other and smiled. And both of them smiled in reply. And Herr Bach's smile released her, and Kurt Rosen's smile possessed her.

"That was beautiful," Kurt said. "I had no idea you had such a voice. It's wonderful."

"It is indeed," Herr Bach agreed. "And now, Ellen, that's all for today. I have an appointment I must keep in town—" he glanced from Ellen to Kurt and then hurriedly at the door. "Stay here if you like," he said, "but please excuse me."

Ellen stood looking after her teacher with troubled eyes; but Kurt Rosen seemed undisturbed by the abruptness of his departure. Kurt went to the piano and thumbed through the music until he found a simple melody. He played a few bars of it, and then he started at the first bar again, transposing it.

"Sing this for me," he said.

"Not in that key," Ellen answered.

"Try it in this key," Kurt insisted.

Ellen looked at him skeptically.

"Come. Sing!"

Ellen sang as he played. A new quality of richness and depth came into the tone. Ellen sensed this herself; she seemed almost to fight against it.

"I thought so," Kurt said. "It is a wonderful voice. But it isn't a soprano voice. How long have you been studying with Herr Bach?"

"Nearly three years."

"Ellen, this teacher will ruin your voice. You must come to Berlin where there are fine teachers!" Kurt's eyes were lighting to some new plan. The unconscious gesture of his hand took on the briskness of enthusiasm.

Ellen stood looking at him stubbornly, resisting his mood. So one in mood did she sometimes feel with Kurt that she naively had assumed he would share her enthusiasm over her teacher.

"Perhaps you mean I should go to Berlin because you'll be there," she flung back at him.

Kurt saw her anger, and laughed. "Only partly," he said. "I was thinking of the voice, too."

"Herr Bach is a very fine teacher," Ellen persisted. She had chosen Kurt, but having chosen him only increased her loyalty to the teacher who had so gently evoked her heart's awakening.

"Perhaps he makes you feel music, but he is not a fine teacher. He is trying to make you a soprano, and you are an alto," Kurt said.

Suddenly Ellen felt near to tears.

"I think he is a fine teacher. And I will stay here and study. And when you are able, you can come for me," she said, "and now, if you don't go to your classes they will discharge you and you will not be even an assistant rabbi!"

The following day Kurt called Ellen a little after noon. He sensed immediately that she was not as angry as he had feared, but he was baffled as to the exact quality of her mood. He told Ellen that he wanted to talk to her and suggested that they spend the afternoon at the beach.

The beach was crowded and they walked for a long while until they came at last to a tiny deserted fisherman's village. Nets, spread on the sand, rotted in the sun. And the hulk of a small boat rocked lonesomely against the wharf.

78

"I'm too tired to walk any more. Let's rest here," Ellen said. All the time they had walked Kurt had been unable to define her mood. They sat down, now, on the sand.

"You're not angry any more?" he said.

Ellen shook her head. "No—I've been thinking of something different."

"Was I wrong in assuming you'd decided yesterday?" Kurt asked her.

Her dark eyes met his, and then she looked away. "No. I had decided—but perhaps I decided wrong?"

"Why?"

"Kurt, Herr Bach understands what I'm like. I don't know if you do."

"I love you."

"It's not the same. You don't know me very well."

"What are you trying to say Ellen?"

Ellen did not answer immediately. She watched a seagull dip down to the wharf; she watched another alight on the sand; she watched the tracks it made.

"Kurt, perhaps the thing is that I don't know you very well." Her eyes searched his face solemnly. "I don't even know if you'd approve of the way you make me feel."

"Ellen, Ellen!" he laughed at her.

But Ellen did not laugh. "Kurt, I never thought of falling in love with a minister. With me, being in love isn't—it isn't something holy. It's wild and beautiful and fierce. I don't know if you understand that."

"Ellen, I understand it," Kurt told her gently.

"Kurt, religion plays such a big part in your life. But it doesn't in mine. Sometimes I go for days and don't even think about God. But you pray every morning, and every night. I'm not very religious, that's all."

"Ellen, to say you are not very religious is like saying you're not very hungry. The time comes when the spirit feels hunger, too. The hunger of the spirit is in all the joy you know."

"But Kurt . . . to be religious enough to be a rabbi—it's as if it held you tight . . . it's as if it wouldn't let you go at all . . . not to run in the sand and chase that wild bright feeling."

"Ellen, do you think it is possible to love God more by loving life less?" Kurt asked her.

"Yes. Yes, I guess that's what I think."

"Then let me show you it isn't so. Let me talk to your father.

79

Come to Berlin to study if he will let you. There's a wonderful student life there. And at least we could see each other. And as soon as I am ordained we can be married."

"All right, Kurt. I'll come. I'll let you show me."

The evening shadows were lengthening as Ellen drew herself from her reverie. As she got up and went into the tiny kitchen to begin preparing dinner, she was thinking of a time very different . . . she was thinking of the day after she and Kurt had landed in the United States, when they had gone alone to a small synagogue to pray. She remembered the psalm that Kurt had read that day. It was engraved in her heart . . . and the sound of his voice reading it . . .

> *If it had not been the Lord who was for us, let Israel now say; if it had not been the Lord who was for us, when men rose up against us; then the waters had overwhelmed us, the stream had gone over our soul; then the proud waters had gone over our soul. Blessed be the Lord who has not given us a prey to their teeth. Our soul is escaped as a bird out of the snare of the fowlers; the snare is broken, and we are escaped. Our help is in the name of the Lord who made Heaven and earth.*

On that day Ellen Rosen's heart had required some new legacy for its flight into the terror of the unknown. And this had been the legacy that Kurt claimed for her. . . .

> *Our soul is escaped as a bird out of the snare of the fowlers. The snare is broken, and we are escaped!*

Chapter 8

THE SISTERHOOD of Temple B'nai Emanuel was holding its annual fund-raising rummage sale, and Ellen had volunteered to help.

At nine o'clock on a sunny, windy October day, Tita Gold stopped by to pick her up, and with Tita giving Ellen a staccato description of what rummage sales were like, they drove through the early morning traffic to the second block on Northeast Tenth.

Tita parked her car at the corner, and gathered up her gloves, her coat, and a few scattered last pieces of rummage she had collected.

"Come on, we'll get the key to the store-room from Mr. Friedman," she told Ellen as they got out of the car.

On the window of the tiny store next to the dank and owlish Main Hotel, Ellen noted that the bright orange paint proclaimed; "Friedman's Second Hand Store." The door and window frames were painted a bright orange, too, so that the effect was a quixotic one. But Ellen felt reluctance tugging at her mood as she put her hand on the knob to open the door.

A bell jangled imperatively, as if Mr. Friedman might be anywhere except where he was—right behind the counter that contained the brightly polished, used, musical instruments, lovingly arranged on pieces of felt.

"Gut mornink, gut mornink! Mrs. Rosen . . . Mrs. Gold," Mr. Friedman called out, his white mustache twitching sociably. His shoulders sloped with a sort of wry dejection inside his coat, but he had already bounded around the counter to shake hands.

"Good morning, Mr. Friedman," Ellen greeted him warmly.

"Morning, Joe! Has anyone picked up the key?" Tita replied.

"No. I still have it," Mr. Friedman moved to the cash register and took out a key with a string on it. He handed it to Tita.

"A good day for your rummage sale you certainly got," he congratulated them. "Most of the greasers got paid on the fifth."

"Greasers?" the word had an ugly taste on Ellen's lips.

"The Mexicans! Would be better maybe I give you ladies a lesson on what are the facts on East Tenth Street," Mr. Friedman spoke with a weary, patient indulgence.

"We don't care about the facts . . . all we want is to sell the rummage," Tita countered.

Ellen glanced about her. The second-hand shoes were polished and lined in neat rows where they could be viewed from the window. Ellen's eyes lit unexpectedly upon a cage of parakeets hung on the orange windowframe. The tiny birds were enmeshing bills in ecstatic unawareness of any human presence. Ellen could not help smiling; she thought of the ancient, upright stove and the paintless baby-bed that cluttered the sidewalk in front of the second hand store next door.

"What do your competitors think of your orange paint?" she asked Mr. Friedman whimsically.

"They're not much for paint. For them is real *kopfvaitig!*" he told her, tapping his head. "Is better maybe you know they're not too much for rummage sales either. Come all the churches with rummage sales, too. And this they don't mind so much. This rummage comes out of the attic twenty years already. But the Jews is something different, they say. The rich Jews bring down the overstock from their husband's big stores on Main. Is not fair competition, they say," Mr. Friedman was now leaning over this counter earnestly. "Especially Mr. Bean, he says it!"

"Don't worry, Joe," Tita reproved him. "Don't worry a minute."

Mr. Friedman, his mustache now drooping dejectedly, straightened up as if he had, at least, done his duty.

"How is with Rabbi?" he asked Ellen solicitously.

"Fine, Mr. Friedman . . . busy as always."

"Is lots souls to mend," Mr. Friedman agreed sadly. Then he brightened. "Mrs. Rosen, me and mine wife is having anniversary of forty years . . . Mine wife would be thrilled if you and the Rabbi stopped in tonight . . . unexpected like!"He was suddenly delighted with the thought.

"We will, Mr. Friedman . . . we surely will. And *mazeltov!*" Ellen shook his hand again.

"Come on!" Tita was saying from the doorway. Let's get the place opened up! You know what the early bird gets!"

As they left Mr. Friedman's, Ellen saw that the three brass balls that hung over the entrance of the pawn shop they passed did not even catch the gleam of the bright morning sun, so grimed were they from the drifting train smoke that was wafted back along the street from the railroad station.

But midway of the drab block her eye was arrested by another bright spot—the marquee of the Roxy Theater, which currently regaled the public with flamboyant posters announcing an "adults only" movie.

"That's Marty Cohen's show house," Tita interrupted her chatter to inform Ellen. "You remember Marty . . . he was at the party!"

Ellen nodded. She remembered Marty. And she knew already that the Roxy was his source of income, exasperation, amusement and sometimes embarrassment.

Tita shrugged her shoulders disparagingly. "Pretty good, huh! Two Jews doing business in the 200 block of Northeast Tenth! Oi!"

Two . . . Jews . . . "Two Jews make a majority in a crowd of ten . . ." Ellen remembered the German commandant with the little squint eyes who had been so fond of making this statement. . . . She remembered . . . and she turned her thoughts from the memory. But did two Jews make a majority in the 200 block on Northeast Tenth, she wondered. And, however much she wished them not to be there, yet she felt an odd comfort in their presence, too.

"Here, take the key," Tita said, as they came to the store-room where the rummage sale would be held. Ellen fitted the key in the lock and opened up the big, dim room. Tita rushed on inside with her last armload of rummage. Ellen paused beside the doorway. Dust motes swam languidly in the sun's rays that obliquely penetrated the small windows. The old clothes had settled themselves in piles where they had been tossed until they looked as if they had been there forever. Ellen picked up a coat hanger from a folding chair. She slipped it into the neck of a crumpled black dress and hung it on a half-filled rack.

It was only moments later when the door clattered open and shut to admit the first customers. They hurried in, half a dozen at once, and went scurrying among the rummage. Tita went to help a tall, rawboned woman with bright red hair. And Ellen moved, more slowly, to see what she could do for three small, stooped, Mexican women who wore black mantillas drawn tightly about their heads. Ellen spoke to them, but they seemed oblivious of her presence. Tactfully, she stood a little back from them as they moved with small darting movement, plucking with furtive pink-palmed hands at this fabric and that.

Ellen, watching them, was struck by a poignance that began a flow of memory . . . and a sadness that moved in her veins. Here was something she had seen before. . . . Here were the stoop of shoulders . . . the clutch of hand . . . the obliqueness of eye . . . the form and figure of those adrift upon the face of the earth . . . the homeless, the bereft, the estranged, who must seek their sustenance from the very dregs of existence. Ellen drew herself up sharply, as one of the women grabbed up a bright, purple, silk blouse and approached with it, smiling toothlessly.

These women were not without homes, Ellen reminded herself. They had homes, homes in a midwestern town that believed staunchly in progress, and Christmas baskets, and moral turpitude.

Ellen smiled back at the wizened little creature who confronted her. She took the small coins that the woman offered her, and hated the feel of them in her hand. She watched the three little women scurrying off as they had come.

Ellen turned back to Tita who was finished with her customer and was busy sorting the last of the clothes. Without saying anything, Ellen began to help. Ten minutes later, Ellen and Tita looked up from their sorting as the door opened, and Myra Levinson moved briskly into the room, looking chic and cool as always.

"My God, Myra. Are we expecting the president's wife to tea?" Tita demanded, her gray eyes aware and mocking. Ellen, glancing at her in quick consternation, thought that Tita had the face of a minx, impertinent, inquisitive and exasperating.

Myra had long ago learned not to blush. Standing there flawless and immaculate, she slowly drew off her short gloves and tucked them into the deep pocket of her coat.

"You never know whom to expect nowadays," she said caustically.

Tita was unabashed. "Hide your coat," she warned. "Last year somebody sold Bessie Lewis' new coat from Saks Fifth Avenue along with the rummage."

"And they knew it perfectly well," Myra retorted.

Reluctantly, now, Myra let her glance meet Ellen's. And in her eyes was something like a mute apology for what her husband had said and done.

"Hello, Ellen," she said brightly.

"Hello, Myra," Ellen replied, feeling the inner uncertainty in Myra that seemed apparent only to her.

The front door clattered open again in its warped frame and a curious little pig of a man stood there, blinking at them.

Tita made a quick movement forward. "Can I help you?" she asked him.

He nodded his head in a vague, fuzzy way, as if terrified at finding himself alone with three women. "Shirts!" he croaked hoarsely. And resolutely Tita lead him to the shirts.

Myra watched them go. "He'll buy shirts," she said to Ellen with grim finality. "Just look at her . . . she's her own grandfather!"

Ellen saw that Myra hated Tita's acceptance of this place . . . this situation. It was something bitter and personal, as if the memory of such a place as this clung to her. As Ellen turned tactfully away, she caught sight of Myra's reflection in a smudged mirror that someone had put up for modeling old clothes, and she had the frightening feeling that if the sleek and exquisite surface of Myra Levinson's personality should crack . . . here . . . and now . . . she would not know how to mend it, she would not know how to put it together again.

"Myra," Ellen said hesitantly. "If you don't feel well, why do you not go home? Tita and I can manage. If we get busy, someone else gladly comes."

Myra stood up. "I'm all right!" she insisted briskly. "It's just . . . well . . . selling old clothes to poor people. It gives you a rotten feeling, that's all."

Ellen nodded. "Better you go home," she said.

Myra shook her head determinedly. Someone else was coming in . . . a tiny, flat-footed Mexican woman with two shiny-eyed little boys tagging behind her.

"I see what she wants." Ellen told Myra.

The little Mexican woman was overcome with shyness at Ellen's approach, but the smallest boy, clutching fondly at her skirt, volunteered staunchly.

"Mama mia wants a coat!"

The other little boy stood, still as a stone, his great dark eyes fastened imploringly upon Ellen Rosen's face in which existed a warm and haunting lovingness ready to embrace any living thing in need of it.

"We find her a coat then . . . a fine coat!" Ellen told the little boy, as if they had become conspirators.

And Mama mia herself, wearing a man's jacket with her pregnant stomach bursting forth beneath its one button, playfully cuffed her youngest son for his impertinence, then gathered him into the folds of her dress and stood nodding her head vigorously in the affirmative.

Ellen held her breath for fear she might somehow destroy the preciousness of this moment. She remembered how they had laughed at the last Sisterhood meeting when Myra Levinson had announced that she had brought a fur coat for the rummage sale —she even remembered the odd little quirk around Myra's mouth as if, in some curious sentimental way, she did not quite want to part with it. Now, she caught Myra's eye.

Ellen thumbed through the coats on the rack. "How would be with a fur coat?" she asked the little Mexican woman. And she took down the mouton which was worn only a little smooth in spots.

The Mexican woman formed her lips in a round Ohh! . . . but there was no sound. Her eyes began to dance much as did her little boys'. Instantly she was wiggling out of her husband's jacket. Ellen held the coat for her. She thrust her arms into the sleeves; she settled herself into it comfortably. The coat came near to her ankles. It amply covered the pregnant stomach.

"Is very nice," Ellen told her.

The littlest boy had begun to dance in delight. He caught his mother's hand and drew her toward the mirror, where he had, a moment before, been sticking out his tongue at himself. His mother stood before the mirror, her feet planted part, drinking in the sight of herself in a fur coat. The coat fit somewhat like the racoon coats that college boys once wore; but she was blissfully unmindful of this fact. And her eldest son, who had satisfied his misgivings with long and earnest gazing at Ellen, now had eyes only for his mother. Suddenly he let loose a cascade of Spanish.

His mother peeked up the sleeves, she fastened and fastened the buttons.

"How much?" she asked finally, in a rush of breath.

Ellen glanced again at Myra, who had quietly come a little closer, and in the instant that their eyes met, they understood each other.

"Seven dollars," Ellen said, although the coat was plainly marked for $12.

The little Mexican woman began to shed the coat. With one swooping movement she began to herd the little boys in front of her.

"I see if I can get the money," she said. And she could not hurry fast enough on her errand. She left Ellen standing there, holding the coat.

86

"She'll never get the money," Myra said to Ellen, some aching regret in her voice, when they had gone.

"Don't tell me Mrs. Levinson wishes she had given the coat away!" a voice said mockingly.

Startled, both Ellen and Myra looked up to see Marty Cohen, who apparently had been watching them for quite a while. Marty was a tweedy, clean-shaven man, who stamped when he walked and battered a chair when he sat down, and wore an habitual look of wry, startled effrontery. Marty sat down now, straddling a folding-chair.

"I see there are now two Cadillacs parked in the two-hundred-block on East Tenth," he declared sociably. Myra was making herself very busy, but Tita laughed, and Ellen watched the others trying to fit together the innuendos that defined their feelings for each other.

"Say, that reminds me; did you hear the joke about the three cars and St. Peter?" Marty demanded, addressing his remark pointedly to Myra's back.

"No, what?" Tita said.

"There was a Protestant preacher and he got to Heaven and they gave him a new Ford. Well, he was driving around and pretty soon he saw a priest who was driving a new Buick. So he went back to St. Peter and he says, 'How come the priest gets a Buick and I just get a Ford?' And St. Peter just shook his head sadly and says, 'But just think of all the things he gives up!' . . . So the preacher starts out in his Ford again, and pretty soon he sees a rabbi driving a Cadillac, and he goes bouncing back to St. Peter and says, 'Say, how come the rabbi's got a Cadillac . . . he didn't give up anything!' . . . And St. Peter shook his head sadly again, and said 'You know how it is. He's one of the family.' "

Tita began to laugh. Myra turned slowly from her preoccupation with the clothes rack. "Now, don't you want to tell the one about the Jews playing poker in the backroom of Heaven?" she demanded.

"And what is Mrs. Levinson so touchy about?" Marty asked with a shrug and an upward lift of the hand.

"What are you doing here, anyway?" Myra demanded.

Marty laughed. "A little drama I couldn't bring myself to miss. A rummage sale! A chance for the down-trodden to play out their resentments against the regular merchants who harass them with their debts. And this time they get a bonus—the hope of seeing the Jews get theirs."

"And what do you mean by that?" Myra inquired disdainfully.

Marty laughed again. "Mr. Bean, the kingpin of this motley block, doesn't like rummage sales . . . especially kosher rummage sales! Says the Jews bring down things like fur coats! And because it makes him so mad, his customers love to trade with you. Has something to do with the uncanny gift of the exploited for exploiting!" Marty was grinning sardonically at Myra as he concluded.

"Is not possible to bunch people together like that and say things about them," Ellen protested. "Look at the woman with the little boys who wanted to buy the fur coat."

"I looked at her," Marty said. "She grew up in a climate of dog eat dog, just like the rest of them," he told Ellen a little ruefully. He got up out of the chair, stretched. "Well, I got to go admit the adults-only to the movies. Don't you all take any wooden nickels!" With a bland, airy wave of the hand he was off.

Hour after hour Ellen waited for the little Mexican woman to come back for the fur coat, and the waiting was a pall on her spirit. Sometimes there was a face with a look of hidden courage, sometimes a flash of humor. But mostly there were red hands . . . or wrinkled hands . . . and often hands with dirty fingernails . . . searching . . . seeking . . . hesitating. And always the smell . . . the smell of poverty.

At twelve o'clock Tita went to lunch. At one o'clock Ellen went to lunch; but she could not eat, and she walked for a while in the October air and breathed it deeply and noted the turn of leaf to gold. And when she came back, Myra went to lunch.

It was a little after two o'clock when Mrs. Bundy, the madam herself, bustled her enormous bulk through the door. Tita went forward to help her, and Ellen came near to staring, for she could not believe her eyes. Mrs. Bundy had a face that looked as if it had been dabbed in wet clay, slack and unmolded. She brushed Tita aside and went straight to the rack where the coats and dresses were hanging. She pawed through them; turned in disgust. Then she spied the fur coat which Ellen had hung behind the mirror, and with a movement as swift as the dart of a snake's fang she had it in her hand.

"That coat is sold," Ellen said, her throat already dry with some curious foreboding.

Mrs. Bundy's pasty face was turned toward Ellen, but her eyes seemed to be focused above her head. "That other girl waits on me!" she said, tossing her head toward Tita.

She began to try on the coat. No confining garment modified

88

the grossness of her enormous cloddish body, crammed now, like so much putty, into Myra Levinson's fur coat.

Tita glanced at Ellen uncertainly. "Ellen, it's been six hours since the little Mexican woman was here . . . she isn't coming back," she whispered.

"Still she may come," Ellen said.

"Oh, Ellen . . . we've got this stuff down here to sell!" Tita insisted.

Ellen glanced at Mrs. Bundy and felt a revulsion and a wild regret. But in a way it hurt her even more to look in Tita Gold's unheeding face. Tita moved away from her, a little nearer to Mrs. Bundy, who was trying hard to stretch the fur coat around her enormous belly. She stood, preening in admiration, before the smoky mirror.

"I always wanted a fur coat!" she told Tita, her words ludicrously coy.

Tita glanced tentatively at Ellen. "The coat's already sold," she said without conviction.

"I pay you twice as much! . . . Anyway, there's not a scuttle-butted bitch in this end of town would touch the coat if they knew I wanted it."

She turned again before the mirror.

"How much?" she hissed.

This time Tita did not glance at Ellen, she liked to feel that she was being coerced. "Fifteen dollars!" she said quickly.

Mrs. Bundy opened her handbag with a snap that sent a chill through Ellen, who stood helplessly by, telling herself that, of course, it was true . . . the little Mexican woman wouldn't come back.

"I give you three dollars," Mrs. Bundy told Tita. "The rest I have to get back from Bean, I paid it to him for a coat with a fur collar only!" She laughed raucously, and in her eyes was the glint of her malice toward her fellow denizens of this block. She seemed to understand that she would be aggravating Mr. Bean unendurably, and the thought brought her only pleasure.

"I always wanted a fur coat!" she was saying again, as she began emptying herself out of the coat, emitting a foul smell as she did so.

"Put it up!" she said. And with that she left them.

Tita, not quite ready to face Ellen, slowly put the coat back on the hanger. She looked at the three dollar bills as if she did not know what to do with them. And she jumped, in a startled way, when the door opened. It was Myra returning from lunch.

"Guess what," Tita said brightly. "I sold your coat."

"What do you mean?" Myra demanded impatiently, "Ellen already sold it."

"The little Mexican woman didn't come back with the money. I sold the coat for $15," Tita told her, the color coming high in her cheeks.

Myra glanced at Ellen whose distress was so plain in her face.

"You can't," Myra said calmly to Tita. "The coat is mine, and I want the Mexican woman to have it . . . even if I have to find her and give it to her myself. I'll pay the fifteen dollars, if that's worrying you."

"That's very touching," Tita replied acidly, "but this is a rummage sale, and I took three dollars down on the coat!"

Ellen looked from one to the other, concern and regret deepening in her dark eyes.

With hardly contained fury, Myra turned from Tita. She went directly to the coat, took it from its hanger, and searched for an empty box to put it in. She found the box, folded the coat, and put it with her own coat away from the other things.

"Look, Myra," Tita said tentatively, not quite sure of her ground, not quite ready to give up. "There's no use being spiteful. Let's just say whoever gets here first with the money gets the coat."

"Nobody gets the coat . . . but the one Ellen promised it to," Myra replied with finality.

At that instant the door opened again, and a large, lumpy man came bounding through it, his short arms flailing about in an incredible way. He called out in a hoarse, rasping voice; "Who's in charge here? I'm going after the police!"

In the startled moment that followed Myra Levinson stepped forward.

"What can I do for you?" she said, and Ellen was amazed at the forbidding dignity that came so quickly to her manner.

"I'm Mr. Bean . . . and I want you out of here now!" he shouted. "It's not enough you take my customers! You send them to get their money back from me!"

The door was flung open again, and clattered shut behind the heaving, quivering mass that was Mrs. Bundy.

"You thief! You sneak!" she screamed, shaking her fat finger at Mr. Bean.

"Who calls the kettle black!" he screamed back at her, his voice traveling now to a wavering falsetto.

And when the door opened a third time it was Mr. Friedman

who crept in, his pale eyes large and staring, his mustache twitch-ing with agitation. He moved directly to Ellen with all the gal-antry of a sworn protector.

"It is as I told you," be began to mutter. He said it again and again, and his hands had the sound of dry parchment being wrung together.

"You don't have to worry about the coat," Myra said matter-of-factly to Mr. Bean. "It was already sold. It is we who will give her money back."

"Already sold!" Mrs. Bundy's massive form quivered with rage, and she turned now to Mr. Bean as if he were her confederate instead of her arch enemy. Her glance sought out Mr. Friedman witheringly. "They're all alike!" she screamed. "They take my money and then they tell me, 'We're sorry!' "

Myra took three dollars from the cash drawer. "Here. Take it." she said.

Mr. Bean's lip curled with contempt and reproach as he watched Mrs. Bundy snatch the three dollar bills. "You're not content to trade where you're treated right." His eyes slithered off in the direction of Mr. Friedman who wore his gray fedora pulled down on his head. "You have to come buy from the Jews!"

Mr. Bean turned on his heel and waddled off toward the door, and Mrs. Bundy hurried to follow him.

"I'll put an end to rummage sales once and for all! I'll go to the police. I'll get a restraining order. . . . They come down here and they . . ." The slamming door chopped off his words and left the room quivering with the echo of them. And Myra Levinson, as if suddenly weak in the knees, sat down on the nearest folding-chair.

"Wow!" Tita Gold whistled, as if her implication in this affair had been nothing at all. "Boy, baby, you really handled them o.k. But what's now?"

Mr. Friedman still twisted his hands. He seemed to have shrunk in size, and an old despair was wrung from his voice when he spoke; "It is as I told you. That man is a *farbissen hunt,* a mad dog."

Now that it was all over, only Ellen Rosen remained standing, still and erect, and they all turned to her as one, as if she might have the answer they needed.

"I think they will not go for the police . . ." Ellen said quietly, looking from one to the other. "After all . . . this is America . . . and we sell only old clothes."

And they all three looked at Ellen . . . Myra Levinson, and

91

Tita Gold, Joe Friedman . . . and each of them understood wha
she was saying to them, in a way that perhaps they had neve
understood before.

"Of course, it's silly," Myra said huskily, as if a little embar
rassed at having been wakened from a bad dream. "Things ar
really in a mess; let's straighten up," she said.

Joe Friedman, still muttering a little into the fringes of hi
mustache, went back to his own store, having come, spirituall
poorly equipped, on his errand of protection. And Myra and Elle
and Tita began to set things aright. As if an ill wind had blow
along the street, there was no sign of a customer. And the minute
ticked off slowly.

Hardly a half hour had passed when a tall blonde young ma
in a policeman's uniform opened the door. He hesitated for
moment, looking around him. His eyes lit on Myra, and suddenl
his lips moved uncertainly into a grin.

"Hi, Mrs. Levinson!" he said.

"Hello, Tom . . . what are you doing down here. I thought yo
were the school cop," Myra said, joshing him a little, her voice
taking on once more its tone of brittleness.

He laughed, a little embarrassed. "I got promoted," he said
"I'm on the downtown force now." He came up to Myra, and hi
blue eyes met hers for a moment and then he looked away. Hi
face was excruciatingly young. And he seemed still to be growin
too fast for his uniform.

"Mrs. Levinson, I hope you won't be mad," he said uncertainly
His glance moved out to include Tita and Ellen, and he smile
at them a little. "There's been some complaints about rummage
sales, and the judge promised to hold a hearing. . . . It hasn'
got anything to do with you folks . . . it's just that . . ."

"What have you got there, Tom?" Myra asked him almos
gently.

"A restraining order," he said, looking miserably at the paper
in his hand.

"You cannot help it." Ellen told him suddenly. She had been
watching him tautly, forcing herself to believe that he really had
come. And as she looked at him so hard, making herself believe
it, the painful, aching, lovable reality of his youth and gaucherie
were driven home to her.

"You do only your duty . . . you cannot help it. And, of course,
it will be all right tomorrow," Ellen told him, when Myra turned
her back and began to gather up her things.

He smiled gratefully at Ellen, but his troubled eyes followed

Myra Levinson who had so often waved to him in the mornings when she brought Davey to school.

"That's right, Mrs. Levinson. Just leave your things here," he said apologetically. "I'm pretty sure it'll all be settled by tomorrow. You can finish your sale tomorrow."

Myra could not quite turn back to look at him, she could not quite control the quiver of the little nerve at the corner of her mouth.

"All right, Tom . . . come on, let's go," she said to Tita and Ellen.

As the three of them left the building with the young patrolman, Tita locked the door and handed him the key. "For safe keeping," she said wrily.

And in that moment three figures came hurrying up the sidewalk, waving to them. It was the little Mexican woman with her two bright-eyed little boys still in tow.

"Mama mia has the money," the youngest called, breaking away from them, coming like a young donkey to nuzzle his head against Ellen's side.

The little Mexican woman held the bills in her hand, pressed out and folded together neatly. "It's here, you can count it!" she said triumphantly.

"Sorry," the young patrolman told her, a sort of droll look on his young face. "The place is closed for today."

The little Mexican woman saw Ellen. She turned to her imploringly, then back to the policeman. "She promised I could have the fur coat!" she told him earnestly.

"Not today," he smiled; he didn't understand how important it was.

The Mexican woman stood there and something seemed to wilt in her. And the pregnant stomach looked comically bizarre protruding from beneath the one button of the man's jacket she wore. She seemed about to cry.

Ellen only waited on the sidewalk with the others, looking at her. And suddenly she could stand it no longer; she turned quickly and got into Myra Levinson's car.

"The dirty Jews!" the little Mexican woman whispered. The ugly words contained all of her anguished sadness. She said it instead of crying. And in the eyes of her silent eldest son, fastened still upon Ellen Rosen, there was a monstrous reproach.

Chapter 9

THE SUN was low over the housetops and the autumn smell of smoke was in the air, as Myra Levinson let Ellen out of the car at the curb in front of her house. Ellen had hardly spoken on the drive across town from where the rummage sale had been held, and as she got out of the car, Myra seemed to feel that there was something she must say.

"Ellen, don't fret over it!" she said lightly. "There are some things you just can't help . . . and who wants to raise money with a rummage sale anyhow. There are easier ways," she laughed coaxingly. It was as if she had left behind on Northeast Tenth Street all the bitter, disturbing effects of the day.

"Thanks for bringing me home," Ellen replied. She could not say more. She waved her hand, as Myra drove away. And then she ran across the yard. Her feet could not carry her fast enough, so much did her spirit ache to be unburdened of the day's despair in Kurt's understanding presence.

As she came into the lower hall, an enchantment reached out to her and she stood still, breathless and enthralled as a child. Down the stairwell was wafted an exquisite strand of music . . . swelling . . . blending . . . throbbing with the heart's own knowledge of beauty and sadness.

The music was Brahms' F Minor Concerto . . . and Ellen had heard it on her wedding night. Suddenly she was running up the stairs.

She flung open the door of her apartment. And there in the chair with the broken spring, sat Kurt, smiling at her with the absurd calm of someone who has planned an amazing surprise. On the table was a small phonograph in its leather case, and with a soft little flutter a new record dropped into place, and the beautiful music was resumed.

Ellen stood looking from the phonograph to Kurt and back again.

"Kurtchen! How come! . . . Why . . .?"

"A man can give his wife an anniversary present, can he not?" Kurt demanded to know.

"But it is not until Saturday!" Ellen chided.

"And where in this apartment would you hide a phonograph . . . in the oven? . . . under your pillow?"

Kurt caught her hand and pulled her down on the arm of the chair where he sat, and she laid her cheek against his cheek, and then she kissed him.

"Kurtchen! This very thing they played on our wedding night. Remember! . . . you took me to the symphony on our wedding night?" Her laughing eyes confronted him with this fact ruefully, as they had so many times before.

"Don't act so reproachful. You were not anxious to go home, my blushing bride. After the symphony was over you wanted to go from night club to night club until almost dawn!"

Ellen laughed, a low throbbing sound, that seemed to draw its notes from the music itself. She laid her head now against Kurt's shoulder and was still. And the exquisite strains of music engulfed them, blending spirit with spirit and catching the sun's dying rays on the worn window sill behind them. Warm, living, fluent and breathless the music bound them.

Ellen sat up.

"Kurt . . ." she said, "I have something for you, too."

It was almost contrition that she felt, for in her own sight, her gift seemed to fall so short of Kurt's in penetrating the heart's true need.

"What is it?" Kurt asked her.

"Promise not to laugh."

Kurt solemnly nodded his head.

"Or better you promise *to* laugh," Ellen amended suddenly. "Promise!"

"Silly girl! Where is my present?"

Almost reluctantly Ellen brought out from her dresser drawer the bright plaid shirt she had bought from Mr. Jacobson. And Kurt did laugh, a mellow, bounding laugh. In Ellen's eyes he saw and knew exactly what her thought had been, and his laugh teased her a little because of it, so that this foolish little gesture was blessedly relieved of being important.

"Will you try it on?" she asked him.

"Later . . . when we are home. We must make a visit at the hospital. The Morrises have a baby girl."

"Oh dear, that reminds me. I promised Joe Friedman we would come to him tonight. He and his wife have anniversary today." There was piquant regret in Ellen's voice, but at the same time, she was wondering that it no longer seemed important to belabor Kurt with all of the minutiae of the day just past.

A little later, as Ellen and Kurt ate their bread and cheese and marmalade, Ellen found herself able to tell it all to Kurt, but almost whimsically, and without the bitterness she had felt earlier. She had only the uneasy feeling of wanting him to understand just why she had been so sure that the policeman would not come, and yet she did not want to make too much of a point of it.

"I think, Kurtchen, it is sometimes a little hard to discover America," she said ironically.

Kurt nodded, ignoring both the irony and the whimsey, and meeting directly the perplexity that underlay them.

"Ellen, it is not easy to be born again among people who have forgotten even how to grow," he told her.

Ellen looked at Kurt searchingly, and she understood a little better their special predicament. They found themselves in a new world, bursting with wonder, but they must dwell in it among people determinedly intent upon commonplaces. For them discovering America meant, as Kurt pointed out, rebirth as children into a brash new culture. And in this moment their eyes met, and each of them felt in the other the poignance of the fledgling finding itself in a strange nest.

Half an hour later, Kurt and Ellen walked through the still twilight to the corner to catch the bus, which came looming toward them, its headlights sweeping out into the dusk. They climbed aboard and Kurt dug into his pocket for the coins.

"Is a fine evening for driving!" he said to Jim Hicks, the tobacco-stained, scrawny-necked bus driver whose bleak face cracked into its unaccustomed smile.

"Rabbi, what time do you have down for sunset on Saturday?" he inquired, first casting a furtive glance over his shoulder.

"Sunset's at 7:22," Kurt told him, swaying a little as the bus began to move.

"It set on the dot tonight at 7:13 . . . four minutes later than last night. We'll just see if it sets at 7:22 on Saturday."

Kurt laughed, he tapped the man on the sleeve and passed on to where Ellen sat, three seats back, smiling to him indulgently.

"You've made a new man of him," Ellen whispered.

"Silly girl!" Kurt scoffed.

Ellen continued to smile. She was thinking of Jim Hicks, the dour and cranky bus driver, and of his sunsets. Jim Hicks had seemed to feel that sunsets were his own, personal, jealously hoarded secret, yet perversely it had added to his bitterness and sense of exclusiveness that people who boarded his bus evening after evening were oblivious to sunsets, and never stopped to marvel or to watch.

When Kurt had first noticed Jim Hicks timing a sunset with his stop watch and had recognized immediately what he was doing, the bus driver had been both disgruntled and wildly pleased. And when it developed that Kurt knew about sunsets, too, and even had the times written down in a book, he was simply overwhelmed. Ever since then he had been trying, with an earnest sort of pride, to outsmart the times written in Kurt's book.

But this was not the entire story of Jim Hicks, Ellen mused. The bus driver had found it utterly impossible to maintain his dour humor in the face of such warmth of greeting as Kurt always gave him when he boarded the bus for town or for sick calls. And it was as if the driver, deprived of his dourness, was deprived of his whole personality, and awkwardly he had begun to grow a new one more in keeping with what the rabbi seemed to think of him. Ellen knew that the other regular passengers of the bus had watched this phenomenon curiously, not able to believe it.

Ellen's idle reflection about the bus driver seemed, suddenly, to have some special meaning for this day which had been so difficult for her. She could not stand the feeling of being disappointed with America . . . she could not stand giving up her own dream of America. She began, as the bus lumbered into the downtown section with its frequent jerky stops and starts, deliberately to try to think of things on the positive side of the ledger to counter-balance this day's disillusionment. Anywhere in the world there were bound to be Mr. Beans and Mrs. Bundys. But they did not even begin to equate the others. Kurt was now busily engaged in conversation with a prim little old lady across the aisle, who had mustered great courage to tell him that she had heard him speak before her missionary circle. And Ellen was left to her reverie.

Perhaps this was the way to discover America . . . in the small kindnesses of small people, she thought . . . as she searched her daily life to prove her point. The dewy-eyed little soda jerk at the corner drug store, who wore saddle oxfords and bobby socks and a big canvas apron draped around her middle, could not cease to wonder that a man with the gallantry and old-world courtliness of Rabbi Rosen should take such naive delight in the more flamboyant flavors of ice cream sodas. Even after the management clamped down on maraschino cherries and restricted the use of whipped cream, she always put a full measure of cream and a cherry on the sodas she made for Kurt.

And there was the postman. He simply could not adjust himself to being so graciously thanked each time he brought the mail, Ellen thought, smiling to herself. And no matter how his feet hurt he always climbed the flight of stairs to the Rosen's door to deliver the letters personally because to be thanked like that made all the difference in the way an old man could feel about what he did; it gave back the humanness to an impersonal action, which a machine or an automaton could not do.

And each morning the milkman gave Ellen a full report on the symptoms of his wife's pregnancy and she always listened with grave concern. For the milkman it made the day all right, for he was young and a little frightened, and there weren't many people who had time to hear about this tremendous thing that was happening to him . . .

". . . Ellen . . ." Kurt said, and Ellen had the feeling that he had spoken her name before. She turned quickly from gazing out the window and smiled into his eyes that were smiling at her. In a quick little gesture she gave him her hand. And suddenly it seemed to Ellen as if the gentleness which both she and Kurt showed to strangers was somehow a part of their love for each other, and it accrued—not strangeness, but love—back to them. And as she and Kurt prepared to get off the bus at the hospital corner, Ellen felt no longer disillusioned, but heartened and reassured and warmed by the sense of a special quiet fondness existing in many places because of many paths casually crossed.

The street lights and the big entrance lamps on either side of the hospital doors were blinking on as Kurt and Ellen entered the hospital and rode the elevator to the maternity floor. Ellen paused by the nursery and a bustling, impersonal little nurse showed her the Morris baby while Kurt spoke for a moment to Herman who stood at the end of the hall smoking a cigarette. The baby's black hair grew down in well-oiled little spikes around its beautifully shaped head. Its eyes were tightly closed, and its lips puckered as if awaiting some elfin kiss. Ellen laughed softly in sheer delight, just looking, and was smiling still as she joined Kurt to go in and see Esther.

Esther Morris, her dark hair drawn loosely back by a ribbon, her eyes shadowed becomingly, smiled to them as they entered.

"Rabbi and Ellen . . . thank you for coming," she said, holding her hand out to them impulsively.

"Esther, she is a lovely baby!" Ellen told her.

For an instant something flickered in Esther Morris' young face —something like the awful yearning to be engulfed by the wonder she would not let herself acknowledge. And then she laughed her brittle little laugh.

"She looks like a little shriveled monkey! . . . All babies do!" she answered lightly.

Ellen thought of the day of the grocery shower . . . of the sense of a need to be met . . . and of the rebuff in meeting it. It was so hard to know what to say to Esther Morris.

"I think she's lovely . . so sweet!" Ellen said again simply.

And Kurt, sensing the curious drag of the moment stepped in with a story to tell, and renewed congratulations for the father, looking even more tall and droll than ever, who had now come in from the hallway to join them.

As Kurt and Ellen were waiting, twenty minutes later, for the bus that would take them to the Friedman's apartment, Ellen said: "Kurt, it seems that in America we must convince ourselves that little things matter a great deal and that big things don't matter at all!"

"Right!" Kurt said, "But perhaps it is only a symptom of young-ness," he said, remembering Esther Morris' face.

"In America everything is very young," Ellen mused quietly, as they boarded the bus again.

Kurt and Ellen found the Friedmans' small apartment located on a street of tired trees that murmured out their weariness in-to the quiet darkness. And a difficult hour later the visit to the Friedmans also was a thing of the past. The congratulations had been said. The glass of wine had been drunk; the *strudel* had been eaten and lavishly complimented. And Kurt, in rem-iniscent mood, had talked to them about how to stuff a goose, drawing a word picture which they, in turn, lavishly admired— while Ellen marveled at her husband's ability to find, always, some tiny island of mutual ground. And through it all, Joe Fried-man, achingly inarticulate, seemed still to brood on the earlier events of the day; and he had hovered about Ellen like a maligned starling who feels that in some way he must personally apologize to the lark for the ways of the world. His attempt was gentle, comical and touching. And his plump little wife just kept nodding her head.

On the long ride home Ellen spoke little and only listened quietly as Kurt spoke to her. The encounters with Esther Morris and with Joe Friedman once again seemed to have defined the boundaries of an immense loneliness. Ellen wanted desperately to recapture the mood that had been fleetingly borne on wings of song and of love early in the evening. But now it seemed beyond her reach.

When they were once again in their small room, Ellen, a little shudder jigging down her spine, drew down the shade quickly, as if trying to shut out the entire world. She turned off the overhead light and turned on a lamp. She lit the gas stove, and stood staring for a moment into the heart of the small blue flames. And then she took the records out of their cases and put them on the phonograph again. Finally, her hands empty of small chores, she turned to Kurt, who was standing in the center of the floor watching her.

For him she smiled. And Kurt accepted the smile, slowly, treasuring it, knowing, instinctively, its cost to her.

"Ellen . . ." he said quietly. He held out his hand to her, and together they sat down on the couch. And she laid her head against his shoulder, and for a while they only listened to the music. Finally he said, "Ellen . . . what is it?"

She sat up and looked with great perplexity into his eyes. "Kurt, it is so hard to find here in America a place where we belong. We always belonged so easily. We had so many friends. Why is it different here?"

Kurt, too, was thinking of the odd emptiness which this night's visits had brought, and of the emptiness that stretched back to the very first moment of their coming.

"Ellen, they mean it only well," he said.

"But, Kurtchen . . . why isn't there somewhere that we fit in?"

"Ellen . . . the only ones who really understand what it's like to try to get a footing in a new way of life are those who were immigrants themselves, twenty, thirty years ago."

"Like Joe Friedman, you mean. Kurt . . . it is very touching the way they do understand. But we cannot live from speaking always of a stuffed goose." Ellen almost smiled, but her mood would not quite release the smile.

"That's right." Kurt nodded. "And then there are the young American-born Jews. They seem to feel that nothing but strangeness exists outside the limits of the English language. Notice, Esther Morris watches us a little as if she expected to be startled."

"But the others, Kurt? They are not all young enough to be so naive. Why is it so hard to find a place?"

"Well . . ." Kurt mused, drawing Ellen's head down against his shoulder, stroking her hair. ". . . There are those who indulge their cultural pretenses at great expense. I ran into Benny Gold when I had just bought the phonograph. He couldn't stop laughing that I should find such a joy in spending only forty-five dollars for a phonograph. . . . Those people tend to classify their new rabbi by the $125 a month they pay him."

"We wouldn't like them anyway!" Ellen retorted indignantly.

She could feel that Kurt was beginning to smile. "And there is the poker-playing crowd," he added. "You at least have to give them credit for a sense of the fitness of things. They wouldn't feel quite right trying to include a rabbi in their gatherings."

"But the others?" Ellen insisted.

"Ellen, those who have lead ordinary, satisfying, uneventful lives . . . they don't understand the need . . . or the loneliness. Their lives were full before we came . . . and each one waits on the other."

In Kurt's voice there was not bitterness, only gentleness, and the compassion that is forged in crucibles of fire. Suddenly Ellen had the awareness of all he did not say . . . that those few who might have understood their need and their loneliness were too constrained by a deep sense of their own spiritual inadequacy to be drawn within the shadow of tragedy.

For a moment Ellen did not speak. And Kurt did not speak; he only sat, stroking her hair, holding her. And when she finally looked up into his face, the dim light of the lamp did not show the lines of weariness that were there. And his eyes met her questioning eyes.

"I was thinking only of the sermon I must prepare for Friday night . . . it's as if it were for us especially," he said.

"What, Kurt?"

"From the Torah we read this week about Abraham and how God called him to leave his own country, his homeland, and his father's house, and to go into a distant land that God would show him. And if he would give up everything this way, God promised him . . . not riches . . . or happiness . . . but that he would be a blessing."

Ellen sat up now, and looked into Kurt's face as he spoke, and he spoke to her very earnestly.

"Ellen, we have left our homeland and our families. We have come to this land of freedom while many perish. And what more could we ask than just that . . . that we should be a blessing?"

There were tears in Ellen's eyes and she did not answer. Kurt reached out his hand to her tenderly, and laid it against her wet cheek.

"Ellen, we can most especially be a blessing to each other," he said. "There are some very beautiful words in the Bible that say . . . 'I will give thanks unto Him for I am wondrously and fearfully made . . . and my soul knoweth it right well.' "

"Kurt, I know that. I couldn't live with you without knowing it." Ellen told him earnestly.

"Ellen, we've loved each other very much."

"Yes, Kurt."

"We've had such a richness, such an abundance . . . we've never really stopped to explore what human love is capable of."

"Kurtchen . . . I'm not sure I know what you're trying to say."

"Ellen, here . . . so alone by ourselves . . . we have the chance to find out truly how wondrously made we are. I think that if two people love enough they can learn to be all things to each other; they can learn to make all experience meaningful to each other. Two people with a great deal to offer can . . . loving enough . . . learn to offer it all to teach others."

Ellen knew that these words, as Kurt spoke them, had somehow become binding upon the two of them. And as she spoke again it was with the sense of moving, already, into a new era of experience. The need for terrible earnestness was past. She was smiling a little as she said:

"Kurtchen, I could not learn to be a scholar . . . to pore over your books with you!"

Kurt laughed. "We speak much of the Bible just now," he said, "but remember the proverbs that follow the *Kiddush* in the prayer book. 'She openeth her mouth with wisdom, and the law of kindness is on her tongue'."

" 'And Strength and Dignity are her clothing and she laugheth at the time to come,' " Ellen continued for him solemnly, her eyes dancing the while.

"Ellen . . . will you laugh at the time to come?" Kurt asked her.

"Kurtchen, I will try. With all my heart I will try."

Chapter 10

THE FALL CITY auditorium was a massive building whose vaulted, tin-domed roof was well known among celebrities of the one-night stands. The tin dome had rattled and moaned in a high wind on the night that Katharine Cornell played in Fall City, and even Paderewski had been no match for rain on that tin roof. Al Jolson had run down the wide cement aisles singing *California, Here I Come,* and Schumann-Heink's mighty voice had moved out into the hush that awaited it, reaching into the corners and crevices of the huge building.

But on an evening in October of 1941, the people came to see a different kind of spectacle. Fall City was holding its most gigantic Defense Bond rally.

When the stage curtain was drawn back with a portentous swish, four people occupied the big, bare stage with its bunting-draped rostrum. Two of these were Fall City's favorite sons, Congressman Luther Grogan and Henry Pritchard, assistant to the U. S. Attorney General, both of whom had flown in on the afternoon plane from Washington to be principal speakers at the bond rally. Phil Tilby, Fall City's tall, collapsible mayor, sat between them, looking primed and newly barbered. The fourth person on the stage was Ellen Rosen dressed simply, in black.

The brilliance of the spotlight which on the faces of the three men created a garishness and an ashy pallor, sparkled from Ellen's dark eyes and drew light from the depths of her dark hair. She sat unmoving; but the fluid grace of motion was in the taut lines of this stillness. Her eyes left those stage companions who had momentarily held her interest and searched expectantly among the pale blur of faces beyond the footlights.

Ellen Rosen had been invited to sing *God Bless America* at the rally. She caught her breath sharply in amazement at the size of the crowd; and, as her eyes searched for Kurt, the temper of the people—excited, expectant, demanding and eager—was communicated to her. Ellen felt a thrill rising in her own blood. She wanted to sing for these people, and even more she wanted to learn from them: she wanted to learn from them what America meant to Americans.

Mayor Phil Tilby moved stiffly to the center of the stage and leaned against the rostrum. Ellen's glance came back to him; he began to speak in a shallow, nasal voice, and she strained very hard to understand him.

"Ladies and Gentlemen," he said, "we're right lucky to have with us tonight at the same time, on the same stage, Fall City's two most illustrious claims to fame—two hometown boys who made good in Washington—Congress Luther Grogan and Assistant Attorney General Henry Pritchard. Y'know when these boys are up there in Washington saying howdy to the president and hobnobbing with cabinet members, I wonder if they ever remember how it was to grow up back here in Fall City. Why, Luther here, once burned up three sections of ripe wheat trying to set a fire with two pieces of flint. Luther always did accomplish what he set out to do, even getting to Congress. And Henry here—I do remember this—Henry could argue the spots right off a leopard. I guess the President knew what he was doin' appointing Henry in the Justice Department. I don't know how much Henry knows, but just to look at him you'd think he knew a heck of a lot."

Henry Pritchard smiled tolerantly and Luther Grogan laughed a deep-bellied laugh.

Ellen was a little confused by the meaning of all this; but the mayor seemed eminently pleased with his success.

"Ladies and Gentlemen," he continued, "we've come here tonight to talk about buying Defense Bonds. Well, I'm gonna let these other fellows do the selling, that's what we brought them home for. But I just want to say this much. It's a great country when a little insignificant town like Fall City can send two of its own up there to Washington to take an important part in our government. That's the kind of a country we've got and that's the kind we want to keep. Now, Luther, get up here and let the folks look at you!"

Luther Grogan stood up. He was a heavy-jowled man with bright inscrutable eyes. He moved quickly across the stage to the rostrum. Ellen watched him carefully; she waited eagerly for his words.

He took the microphone in his hand and sort of caressed it for a minute.

"Folks," he said, ". . . it's good to be home."

The crowd clapped for him and somebody whistled in the balcony.

"You know, I'm a sentimental man. I came down here with a fancy speech all made up; but when Phil Tilby got up and told about burning the wheat field—well, it's just not the kind of a speech I want to make to home folks. I'd rather just stand up here, and talk a little bit—about what it means to be an American."

Luther Grogan's voice had a burr and a croak in it. He made a small awkward gesture, now and then, which seemed to bring him right down off the stage into the midst of the people to whom he spoke. Ellen saw the way they listened to him, and she listened very hard herself.

Luther Grogan talked a long time. He talked about how it had been to be a farm boy, to do chores, to learn the value of money and work for an education. And when he used words like "privy" and "store-bought shoes," the crowd came alive with laughter as if he had said something very funny. Ellen had the feeling that she didn't understand, that she didn't understand a great deal more than the meaning of these particular words. And finally when he began to speak of buying bonds, he said that America was a country worth preserving because America was a place where any man could rise to the top by his own effort and will power and guts. And it seemed to Ellen that he still was not speaking of America, that he still was speaking of Luther Grogan.

When, at last, Luther Grogan sat down and Henry Pritchard walked to the rostrum, the applause of the crowd took on a slightly different note, more restrained and courteous.

Henry Pritchard began to speak of human dignity, of the great responsibility of Americans to preserve for themselves the right of human dignity. For a moment Ellen thought that Henry Pritchard would tell her what she wanted to know; but then, with a sense of chill, she realized that this handsome, cool and deliberate man was pleading his own case. He was not really pleading for human dignity, he was pleading for the right of the individual to his own estimate of himself. He was, in this moment, pleading for his own right to exist, unharried, behind the façade of attorneyship.

These two men, who had come here to speak of America, had spoken of themselves, and each had tried to argue for his way of

105

life as the American way of life. And when they spoke of America with words that stirred Ellen Rosen's blood, they gave these words no color or tone or dimension of life. When they said "free country," it was as if they said "rolling hills" or "sunny sky."

Ellen peered out into the blur of upturned faces. These were free people and they were naive about freedom. Suddenly, Ellen Rosen wanted to tell them what she had come hoping they might tell her. She had glimpsed what they had forgotten or what they never knew. It was burning in her heart and she must tell them. She must sing it to them, she must make them know that outside the free wind blew and they were free to walk in it.

The applause for Henry Pritchard was polite, emphatic, a little derisive by turns, and two cat-calls from the balcony flipped it to silence. People had had what they came for, they began crowding into the aisles, pushing ahead of each other. The heavy front doors banged together as the first few pushed out. With an apologetic glance at Ellen, the mayor hurried back to the rostrum.

"Just a minute, Ladies and Gentlemen—just a minute. We have here tonight as our special guest, Mrs. Kurt Rosen, wife of Fall City's new rabbi, who's going to sing *God Bless America* for us to conclude this program. . . ."

The audience seemed a little cross at him for trying to detain them. Some of them went and some of them stayed and there was the shuffle of feet again pushing back rows of seats.

"Everybody has time to hear *God Bless America,* that wonderful anthem of our wonderful country. Ladies and Gentlemen, be seated." The mayor continued to stand there, his arms outstretched, beseeching them to restore order.

Ellen felt the flush of humiliation rising in her throat, that he should stand there and beg them to stay to hear her sing! For a moment she lost the thing that had been wild and beautiful and joyous in her heart. She almost hated those people out there for their insensibility, for their heedlessness and careless unconcern. How could she love America and not love its people? . . . What was it she had loved for that wild beautiful moment? . . . The people were a part of it but not all of it, and it was a part of them but separate from all the rest. And when they let the bright essence of it slip from their lives, it did not desert them. It hovered there, all around them between earth and sky, in the very air they breathed. And they could have it back, by reaching out to it; they could have it back. It waited for them . . . it waited . . .

The mayor was nodding at Ellen, he was smiling at her encouragingly and she saw that his face was old and rather tired.

She stood and walked slowly to the center of the stage. The footlights were bright in her eyes and she could not see Kurt. She could only see dim, shadowy, restless outlines of masses of people.

Ellen nodded at the accompanist, whose face peered up at her from the cavern of the orchestra pit. The tinkle of the piano seemed to wash into the vastness of the auditorium, and only a wraith of it came to Ellen on the stage.

Ellen Rosen began to sing. The rich, full, magnificent tones moved out into the murmurous restlessness. And the people listened. A young mother put her finger gently against the lips of her child who twisted and fretted and she lifted him into her lap and held him close, and he was silent. An old woman, whose pulse was slow and soft, stopped fanning herself with the folded program and held it clasped tightly between her lumpy, vein-looped hands. A man with a sun-burnt skin and coarse clothes, who had held himself aloof from the importunings of the two speakers, allowed himself a moment of receptivity, and knew the weakness that a strong man can feel. A high-school teacher, who did not often smile, felt the wetness of tears on her cheeks. . . . And on the platform, the two men who had spoken did not meet each other's eyes.

The murmuring ceased and the moving ceased and there was a stillness in which each full note throbbed.

> *God Bless America,*
> *Land that I love,*
> *Stand beside her, and guide her,*
> *Through the night with a light from above.*
> *From the mountains to the prairies—to the oceans*
> *White with foam—*
> *God Bless America,*
> *My home sweet home—*

There are times when it does not seem to be the voice that sings, or the ears that listen, and what is beautiful leaves one's heart and enters the hearts of others, and before applause there is the breathless silence of knowing this was so.—But it does not happen often, and it is never forgotten—or ever quite remembered as it was.

After that night of singing Irving Berlin's *God Bless America,* Ellen Rosen had, for the first time, the sense of being an American. The next morning, while this feeling was new and hardly explored, Ellen answered the telephone, and it was Anna Meyers calling.

"Ellen, somebody said you send packages to your parents in Poland every month."

"Yes, I do."

"Well, listen, I have some things you could send, if you want to."

Ellen's quick gratitude reached out to ease the odd embarrassment of the offer.

"Thank you very much," she said. "They need things badly . . ." Ellen's voice faltered, she could think about them, but she couldn't speak about them.

"Well, O. K., I'll bring the things by," Anna was saying. "It may be tomorrow, but I'll see you."

As Ellen hung up the receiver, she was glad that Anna had called. Making a package would be a good thing to do on this day, feeling as she felt. Each month, as she began making the package to send to the Warsaw ghetto, there was the terrible need to feel that it would reach its destination confronting the practical certainty that it would not. But this time there could be a new fierce hope. It seemed to Ellen that she had discovered at last what the real heart of America was like, and she could not help feeling that surely this spirit would assert itself; that surely these people would rise up, finally, demanding rescue for the doomed who needed only a place to go to. Ellen knew that it was not an easy thing for the spirit of a people to move a government; but in America there was the chance that it could, if only it could in time.

These were the things that Ellen was thinking as she began to set out on the cabinet the canned goods she had been accumulating; and it was no longer so lonely a thing she was doing. She made a list of the staples—the sugar, flour, coffee, and rice—that she must get for the package; and then she put on her jacket and walked to the grocery store to buy them and to find a sturdy carton to take them half way across the world.

Half an hour later, when Ellen came back from the grocery store, she found Maury Kalman sitting on the steps of the rooming house.

"Why, Maury, hello," she said, some of the warmth of her mood reaching out to him.

"Hello, Mrs. Rosen. I stopped by to see Rabbi. When will he be back?"

"Not until late this afternoon, I think. Could I do something?"

"I just wanted to ask him to say a prayer for Dad. We took him to the hospital this morning. The doctor has decided to operate."

"Oh, Maury, I'm sorry!"

The determined hope, the insistent fear that Ellen had felt all morning she glimpsed briefly in Maury Kalman's face. But there was a difference. Maury knew more about hoping than about fearing. She reached out a hand and touched his sleeve.

"Maury, of course, Rabbi will pray for your father, and he'll gladly come to the hospital, too. When will the operation be?"

"In the morning, at eight o'clock—and Ellen—thanks." For an instant his worried eyes came to Ellen's, and then he waved a hand and crossed the yard to his car again.

Ellen stood there beside her carton and watched him go. He had called her Ellen, and he had thanked her. Did he thank her just for knowing how close human ties can be?

II

Kurt Rosen went to the hospital the next morning. It was just after mass, the nuns were moving silently up the halls, and hushed quietness seemed to ripple in their wake. But when they spoke, their voices were firm and cheerful. "Good morning, Rabbi. Good morning, Rabbi."

As Kurt left the elevator on the fifth floor, he saw Sara Kalman and Maury and Lee standing together at the end of the hall.

At eight o'clock, Abe Kalman, smiling at Sara as he passed her in the hall, was wheeled into the operating room. And the antiseptic whiteness seemed to Sara already to have isolated him from the warmth of her love. Her breath came in soft little flutters. Maury drew her within the circle of his arm, and stood holding her so, as Lee and Rabbi Rosen came and stood beside them. Forty-five minutes later, Abe Kalman was wheeled back to his hospital room, and a moment later Dr. George Barton, vigorous and blustery and full of the whims of good humor, came out of the operating room, his mask pushed over his forehead, his arms, bare to the elbow, newly scrubbed.

"Rabbi, when are your high holidays?" he said.

"The last of this month, they begin in the Fall, you know."

Dr. Barton put an arm around Sara Kalman's shoulder. "Sara," he said, "He'll be wanting the *gefilte fish*, but you must promise me—only the chicken soup!"

Sara began to laugh. She began to laugh and to cry at the same time. "Abie, Abie," she crooned, "could a heart so good stop beating!"

George Barton gave her arm a pat. "I'll see you later today," he said, "and, for God's sake, let the man rest, Sara. Don't start talking to him the minute he opens his eyes."

The next morning at seven o'clock, as the Rosens sat at their breakfast table, there was a knocking at the door. Ellen went to answer, and it was Lee Kalman who stood there, her face bleak and strained.

"Lee! . . . is it Mr. Kalman? . . . Kurt, come!"

"Yes . . . he is very, very sick. The danger is very great," Lee said.

"How could it be, the operation was a success?" Kurt asked her.

"It's hard even to say. He was given a sedative last night. But the medicine . . . it did something to his heart. Rabbi, Maury said for me to come, he said you would know what to do."

"There is only to pray, Lee," Kurt told her, and in his voice there was comfort, although he did not try to explain away sorrow. "I go now to the synagogue. . . . Stay here a little while. Let Ellen give you a cup of coffee."

Lee nodded.

"Of course, she will stay," Ellen said. "Go, Kurtchen. You must call the *minyan* for the prayer meeting before the men leave for work."

"Yes. Lee, I will come to the hospital immediately after the *minyan*," Kurt told her.

"Lee waits for you. She can take you to the hospital," Ellen said. "And now I will give her something to eat."

As Kurt left, Ellen was pouring the coffee. Lee came and sat down at the table.

"What is a *minyan*, Ellen?" she asked.

"When Jews pray together there must be at least ten men. It is called a *minyan*."

"Is that what Maury meant when he said that the Rabbi would know what to do?"

"I'm sure it is."

Lee was silent. She tried to sip the coffee, and Ellen buttered a roll and put it on her plate.

"Ellen, you didn't know Abe very well, did you?"

"Only a little. But I'm sure he is very kind. When we went to see him he did not act as if we were making a sick call upon him, but as if we were giving us an opportunity to welcome us."

The unconscious loneliness in Ellen's words released the tears Lee had held stubbornly in check. All things that were sad would be a part of the sadness of losing Abe—even Ellen Rosen's own sadness—and this was a thing Lee wished she might express, but she could not express it. She knew only that losing Abe would be like losing the key to understanding when there was so much yet to be understood.

Ellen went to the window and looked out on the street below. "They come already," she said.

Lee went and stood beside the window, too. Old man Jacobson, stooped and crochety of movement, got out of his car and hobbled across the yard. Benjy Stein drove up in his new Cadillac. Sam Levinson walked up the steps with the briskness that seemed to imply that now things could begin. A moment later, two more cars drove up. In witnessing this coming together, Lee felt something strange and moving. She could not quite turn from the window until the last had come.

"When there is sadness, they remember they are Jews," Ellen said quietly, more to herself than to Lee.

Lee turned to Ellen questioningly. She had the fleeting sense that Ellen Rosen understood many of the things about life that Abe Kalman understood, and which she herself despaired of understanding.

III

A little while after Kurt and Lee had gone to the hospital, the postman came, bringing a sheaf of congregational mail.

"There's one here with a foreign postmark," he commented to Ellen as he handed her the mail, and then went whistling down the stairs.

Ellen felt the taste of fear in her throat. One letter with a foreign postmark—Lublin, Poland—Frantically, Ellen's hands tore at the envelope, her eyes leapt to the signature—Mariam Leiber. Kurt had performed the marriage of Karl and Mariam Leiber; he had said a prayer for the naming of their baby daughter, Leah. Ellen sat down, with some awesome dread, her eyes scanned the pencil-written lines.

> *Dear Rabbi Rosen, I write to you to ask your help. When winter came we were transported from Duisburg to the Lublin ghetto. Owing to the way that the war is going we were packed like sardines in an open train, and when we arrived we had to walk several miles in the sleet. Karl and Leah and I were given a hut of one room to share with another family. The rain and the snow come in the cracks in the walls. Our only furniture is two benches taken from a synagogue that was burned. When we were deported we*

were allowed ten pounds of luggage each, and thirty pounds
of children's clothing for Leah. When we arrived at the
former German border, the S. S. took our baggage, promising
to forward it to us. But owing to the war conditions we have
not seen it yet, though it has been six months. We wish
only to ask you to send some little things for Leah as she
has only rags to cover her and is very ill and thin. You must
know that in the ghetto every rag counts, every scrap. It is,
of course, because of war conditions that these things are so.
                                                    Yours,
                                          Mariam Leiber.

Ellen folded the letter, but she did not put it down; it was as
if to put it down would be a gesture of abandonment. Mariam had
been very skillful in phrasing her plea so that the desperate message might pass the censors, might stand some chance of reaching the world outside, of bringing help . . . of bringing help . . . a
box with a few pieces of clothing in it? . . . What degree of help
was this?

A moment before, Ellen had been sitting beside the telephone,
the whole deep sympathy of her loving nature concentrated upon
Abe Kalman and those who loved him. But suddenly the tragedy
of one old, sick man dying quietly in a hospital bed was transcended by the tragedy of tens of thousands tortured, driven,
condemned and persecuted. And what was at one moment sympathy became in the next an intolerable grief, for among those
tortured and driven were her own. Ellen stood up; alone in the
room she felt as if she must run. She thought of walking to the
hospital, not to see the Kalmans, but to see Kurt. She needed Kurt
now, just as the Kalmans needed him.

While she stood there, uncertain what to do, the telephone
began to ring. A first call, a second, a third. From the dozen who
had attended the *minyan,* the word was spreading. Everyone
wanted to hear firsthand what had happened to Abe Kalman. No
matter how remote and withdrawn they had been in the months
past, they instinctively turned to the rabbi at a time such as this.
Ellen had been right; in sadness they remembered they were
Jews, and the rabbi was the core of their Jewishness. As the
morning wore on, it seemed that the mechanics of living had
stopped among the members of the congregation; it seemed that
they thought and spoke only of Abe Kalman. And as the telephone
rang endlessly, Ellen could not help feeling rebellious at this
intrusion upon her own grief. Here was a new lesson in Ameri-

canism. In America it was possible for a Jewish community to give itself wholly to grief and hope and fear for one. They did not seem to realize that as Jews they could not afford this extravagance of grief, for there were too many to grieve for.

Again and again Ellen related what had happened, mechanically at first. But gradually the armor of her own grief could not withstand the sincerity and concern in the voices of these people who called to ask about their friend, Abe Kalman. Gradually she could not resist the depth of sincerity in these voices. And even though, however much she needed it, she had no part in this sympathy and love, still she was glad to know that it existed. Almost she could have wept for having discovered the ability of these people to feel. And paradoxically, their ability to feel at all made the plight of those beyond the reach of their feeling less absolute in its terror and finality.

That afternoon, Anna Meyers brought the things she had promised Ellen. She came up first and knocked on the Rosens' door. Ellen answered.

"I can't stay a minute," Anna said, "I'm on my way to the hospital. But I thought, as long as I was passing, I'd bring these things by. Want to come help me carry them up?"

"Surely. I'm sorry that you have so much trouble," Ellen said.

"It's all right. The things are on the back seat," Anna said. She opened the car door and pulled out one of the cartons. It was hanging open and a little of the jumble of things inside was escaping out the top. Anna poked a stray sleeve back into the box. Ellen took the other carton, and together they carried them up the stairs.

"There!" Anna said, setting down her box in the middle of the floor. "If you can't use this junk, just throw it away. Most of it came out of the attic. Joe gets in the mood to clean out the attic about once in five years. And you know how it is—you hate to throw things away yourself. It's easier for someone else to. Anyway, I happened to think of those packages you send. If there's anything you can use you're welcome to it."

Ellen stood looking at Anna Meyers. "Thank you for thinking of us," she made herself say.

Anna considered her a little curiously, as if she had expected something more.

"Well, I would stay and visit a while, but I've got to get out to the hospital. Isn't it just too awful about Abe? To die from natural causes is one thing, but to die like that, because of a medicine— for no reason at all . . .!" She made a small, frightened, ineffectual gesture with one be-ringed hand. "Well, goodbye, Ellen. I'll see you soon."

"Goodbye," Ellen said.

Ellen stood still in the center of the room. To die for no cause? . . . How was the idea so new to them, were they not Jews? Ellen came and knelt beside the two cartons, and began to pull out the jumbled mess of sleeves and shirttails. She thought of the rummage sale and the tears were running down her cheeks. In eight careless, flippant words, Anna Meyers had invalidated the hope that was her very life—"If you can't use it, throw it away." Suddenly Ellen was remembering the way her mother had looked, her dark eyes smiling, her hair swept up, her shoulders white above the neckline of her satin gown, as she came slowly down the wide staircase of the house in Koenigsberg to greet her guests. And all eyes had turned to her mother; and Ellen, who was eight, had stood there, small and shy, half hidden in the velvet draperies, knowing in her ardent little heart that she might never see so beautiful a sight again.

Ellen tried not to remember. She pulled out a crushed and wrinkled woolen dress and held it up. A button was off, and the cut of the sleeves dated it; but the material was expensive and there was only a small triangular tear where it had been snagged. You would not deny warmth for the cold, just because of the memory of white shoulders above a satin gown.

For an hour Ellen sorted through the clothes in the two boxes. Some she laid aside to send to Mariam Leiber; the rest she would send to her parents. And Ellen knew that if it had not been for Mariam's phrase—"in the ghetto every rag counts" she would not have been able to send them at all. In the early afternoon, Ellen mended and replaced buttons. She pressed the clothes very carefully and folded them into the box.

For Ellen, to do this was to commit an outrage against all past memory. The love and the loyalty ached in her heart and became so intense that the pain was almost a physical one. When the task was done, Ellen realized that, however great the need of those she loved, to send them the cast-offs that someone wished only to throw away was a thing she could not have borne to do if she actually had thought that the things would reach them. And so,

114

the making of this package had become a gesture of hopelessness, not of hope.

Ellen felt now the frantic need to avow, to reaffirm the hope. She cast about for some way to reclaim it. Pressed and mended clothes you could send to anybody at all, and it was the same with cans of food. But there must be something in the world of possessions that could pass from loving hands to loving hands without conveying their meaning to any other. Ellen went to the dresser in the corner. From her own drawer she took a small and lovely handkerchief with a lace edge that she had bought one time in Switzerland, and from Kurt's drawer she took one of the linen handkerchiefs she had given him on his birthday. On the lace handkerchief she sprayed cologne from her atomizer, and the linen handkerchief she touched to the neck of the bottle that contained Kurt's lotion. And she put the two handkerchiefs into the package.

But even the handkerchiefs did not satisfy Ellen. She must think of something else to put in the package, something else that was not just for food or just for warmth, but which acknowledged that people had souls as well. It must be something that would take neither much of the space nor much of the money that could provide the stuff of life. But it must be something that you would not send to people who did not exist. Ellen put on her jacket and in the blustery afternoon she walked ten blocks to a tiny grocery store she had heard about, which handled only imported gourmet and fancy foods. Breathless from her walk, she entered the dim and quiet little store and moved thoughtfully among the shelves, looking at some of the foodstuffs she had not seen since she left Europe. Now and again she paused to read a label, to lift a jar and examine its contents—caviar—the jar was small, it would not take much room . . . she could hold it lightly in the palm of her hand. Ellen took the small jar of caviar to the front of the store where a birdlike little woman hovered behind an ancient cash register.

"This I would like. How much is?" Ellen asked.

"Caviar is hard to get now," the woman said a little apologetically, ringing up the figures without repeating them.

Ellen took two bills from her purse and laid them on the counter.

"You speak with a German accent?" the woman said tentatively.

"Yes," Ellen replied.

"The bastards!—but it's a beautiful country," the dour little woman remarked with a sigh.

"Yes," Ellen answered numbly.

She took the small jar of caviar and went out again into the sunny street. Caviar in the ghetto at Warsaw, where a person must have a blue card to get one pound of bread a week! Ellen's breath was coming fast. She felt as if she were committing some blasphemy. But it was not a blasphemy, it was a reavowal of hope, she told herself stubbornly. The people who would hold that jar in their hands would remember the same things she remembered holding it. It was not the caviar she sent them, but the memory. And anyway, caviar is something you would not send to people who did not exist.

Chapter 11

Then David took hold of his clothes and rent them, and likewise all the men that were with him. And they wailed and wept, and fasted until even, for Saul and for Jonathan, his son, and for the people of the Lord and for the house of Israel; because they were fallen by the sword.

II Samuel 1:11

IN THE gray dawn, while a chill autumn rain fell against the dimly lit hospital windows and made the leaves sodden in the gutters of the street below, a starched young nurse, just coming on duty, called a jocular greeting to the intern who stood poring over some charts; and in the room at the end of the hall Abe Kalman died.

When the last breath slipped out of Abe's body and another did not follow, there was a moment while Sara waited—as though a heart might only pause, then beat again. But when she knew that he could not hear her or be disturbed by her sorrow, she laid her head on her husband's chest and wept. And she took in her clenched fist the collar of her dress and yanked it, and the ripping was a small, stark sound in the room.

Lee saw the shadowy look of fatigue in Maury's face; she saw the pulse throb at his temple. Maury's own grief had been driven too deep to impassion an action; his dark eyes were on his mother with a look of compassion that was hurtful to see, and he did not turn his head as Lee took a quick step toward him. It was a tight, almost formal gesture that he made as he tore the lapel of his jacket.

"Maury!" Lee said, but the movement of the word upon her lips was almost soundless, and she did not move nearer to her husband. Lee felt some deep and mortifying sense of embarrassment, as if Maury's gesture had separated her from his grief. She felt the emptiness of her hands at her sides and their inability to give comfort.

Lee turned away toward the window. She suffered the anguish of disloyalty to Maury because her emotions had so fiercely denounced his act, and the almost hysterical fear that, having witnessed this symbolic action, an expression of Jewish grief, without understanding it, she had robbed it of its meaning. She wanted to turn back to Maury, but she could not. She pressed her hands against the cold sill of the window and quietly wept for her father-in-law . . . and for Maury . . . and for herself.

Lee heard the door open; a nurse entered and a moment later she heard the stretcher rolled into the room; she heard the whisper of its rubber tires on the asphalt floor. Other people were coming in, and someone was speaking to Sara.

Maury left his mother and came to stand beside Lee.

"Lee . . ." he said.

Slowly she turned and looked into his face with a constricting sense of fear that he might have assumed the strangeness she had consigned to him. But it was still the kind and gentle face that she loved, and sorrow had not changed it. She put her head against his shoulder and clung to him.

"Lee, we must go now," he said to her.

That night Maury and Lee and Julian stayed at the Kalmans' house. Maury and Lee went to bed in the big room they had occupied when they first returned from Dallas, before they found a home of their own. Unused in their absence, it seemed to retain some sense of their presence. One of Maury's ties still hung on the closet door, as Lee took down a hanger for his suit.

She settled the jacket on the hanger; she ran her finger over the torn place in the lapel. She had to speak of it to him.

"Maury, what did it mean when you tore your coat?" she asked.

"Jews do that when someone close to them dies," Maury said. He was taking off his shoes. His face was tired in a way that Lee had never seen before, and he seemed hardly to have heard her.

"But what does it mean?" Lee asked.

"Remember when the Bible talks about the rending of garments? Well, that's what it means. It's just a ritual . . . a symbol of sorrow."

Lee was thinking of Abe Kalman. The perplexity deepened in her face.

"What's the matter, Lee? Don't you understand it?" Maury asked.

"No. No, I don't! I think, to make a mere symbol of an action that was born in anguish is . . . is like making a travesty of it."

Maury looked at her in surprise, and she could have wept for what she had said to him.

"Maury, to repress the feeling and perform only the symbol of it . . . it's just something the spirit should not be required to do!"

118

Lee insisted. She was remembering how the pulse had throbbed in Maury's temple, how he had stood there, stiff and a little awkward, before he made the tear in his coat.

"Lee, it isn't like that . . ." he said.

"It was for you. You didn't want to do it."

"Lee, when you've gotten away from being close to your religion, those things don't come easy . . . but when the time comes for doing them, you do them just the same."

Lee had the terrifying sense of not understanding Maury, of not understanding the things that had formed him.

"But that's just it," she insisted. "It's as if to make a ritual of a thing takes away its reality. And what we all felt for your father was so real."

"Lee, Sweetheart," Maury came and put his arms around her and turned her to him. He felt the anxious tenseness in her shoulders beneath his hands. "It's such a little thing to upset you. All religions have their symbols and their rituals. You simply do them with a feeling for their meaning, not as if you were performing some mystic rite. They only seem strange if you haven't always known them."

"Maury, I'm sorry, I'm sorry! To bring up religion at a time like this . . . when . . ."

Maury sat down again on the side of the bed. His own face was troubled.

"When a person dies, that is one time you can't help bringing up religion," he said.

"Oh, Maury, I'm sorry, I'm sorry!" the note of hysteria in Lee's voice penetrated Maury's thoughtfulness. He was not sure what she was trying to tell him she was sorry about. He reached out and took her hand and drew her down beside him.

"Lee," he said gently, "please don't."

She began to cry, but the wild terror was not in her tears.

"Lie down," he told her. "I'll bring you warm milk, then you can sleep."

In the weeks after Abe Kalman died, it seemed to Lee that Maury retreated entirely into himself. It was no longer possible to walk into a room where he was, or recently had been, and to feel the bright varnish of his interest upon all the inanimate objects. It was no longer possible to sit across from him in a room, knowing that in a moment he would look up and smile at her.

Lee felt that she must go to Maury inside himself; and he

wanted her to come. Time and again, in moments of strangeness during the past week, he had reached out a hand to help her come to him. But she did not feel embraced by Maury's personality in the outer region that surrounded him. For the first time in their marriage she must go all the way, all the way to Maury, and she did not quite know how.

Each night of that first week, Lee Kalman sat in a room where ten or more Jews gathered so that Maury might say the *kaddish* for Abe Kalman, and each time she felt the strangeness of her presence there.

The room was not strange—it was the front room of the Kalman home. Numerous times Lee had dusted the furniture in the month she had lived there. The little shepherd in the bookcase was not strange—she had carefully glued it back together after Julian had knocked it off the shelf. And on the mantle, Abe Kalman's pipe rack still stood.

The faces were not strange. There were the three old men: Mr. Jacobson, who sat with his head hunched down in his neck, blinking like a sleepy turtle; and Sid Meyers, old, brittle and a little dapper in his snap-brim hat; and Mr. Goldberg, whose dark eyes brooded endlessly. And usually there were Sam Levinson and Herman Morris, Benny Gold and Milt Gilbert, Sammy Fine, Maury and Kurt Rosen.

The place was not strange and the faces were not strange, but the ritual was strange—ten Jews coming together to make a *minyan*, ten Jews coming together to pray. And her husband was one of them.

On the night of the last *minyan*, Lee sat in one of the chairs that had been brought in from the dining room and watched Maury talking to the rabbi. Sam Levinson arrived, making the tenth man, so the others settled down to begin. Maury came and sat beside Lee; he smiled at her and briefly enclosed her hand in his.

"This will be the last prayer meeting," Maury told her, as if her bewilderment reached through her answering smile.

"I'm glad we've had them, Maury. They've been very beautiful," Lee whispered.

The rabbi began the service with a reading from the Psalms.

> *. . . Keep me, O God; for I have taken refuge in Thee.*
> *I have said unto the Lord, "Thou art my Lord;*
> *I have no good but in Thee." . . .*

Lee listened, and now and then a phrase seemed to speak directly to her heart, easing a little the bewilderment and anxiety. These were the same Psalms that Lee had read in her childhood, but she had never quite understood that to read them was to pray. During the *minyans* Lee had begun to perceive a new kind of prayer—not the prayer of a person, but the prayer of a people through which the strength and comfort and holiness and beauty of the centuries is bequeathed to each individual in the hour of his need.

Now, as she listened to this different way of praying, Lee perceived for the first time the terrible loneliness of the sorrow that must create for itself its own idiom of expression, its own entreaty to God. Lee was remembering how her uncle had prayed on the night her grandmother died—an awkward, fumbling, apologetic prayer, filled with an aching inadequacy, a prayer that seemed to hobble and cripple the small words he could find for it. But with the Jews, it seemed to Lee, there was not this loneliness in death. By performing the same acts and reading the same beautiful prayers that had been performed and read through all the eons of their history, they bound themselves to the centuries, they vouchsafed themselves at least an eternity, if not an immortality.

> . . . *Therefore my heart is glad and my glory rejoiceth;*
> *My flesh also dwelleth in safety;*
> *For Thou wilt not abandon my soul to the nether-world,*
> *Neither wilt Thou suffer Thy godly one to see the pit.*
> *Thou makest me to know the path of life;*
> *In Thy presence is fullness of joy;*
> *In Thy right hand, bliss forevermore.*

"My friends," Kurt Rosen said, "in our synagogues this week we read the story of our forefather Abraham. When death overtook Sarah, the comrade of his life, it is said in the Bible that she was one-hundred and twenty-seven years old. The word 'year' was repeated after the hundred, after the twenty, and after the seven; or twice more than seems necessary. But we have been taught that there is not one superfluous word in the Bible, and so the rabbis have sought the meaning of this repetition. They have interpreted the passage to mean that at a hundred Sarah was as innocent as at seven and as beautiful as at twenty.

"The innocence of a child of seven is an unconscious thing, existing in the unawareness of evil. Sarah had seen the cultures and the lewdnesses of ancient Egypt and Babylon; her innocence was the innocence of a great soul, of a soul that remained untouched by the evil she saw in the outside world. It is the same with beauty. A face is marked by sorrow and disappointment and hardship, as must have been Sarah's in her wanderings at Abraham's side, deprived of the usual protections of life. But the inner beauty which is shown to the eye is a sign of the beauty of the soul, and persists at a hundred as at twenty.

"So it may be said of our friend, Abe Kalman: the characteristics that made him dear to us persisted regardless of what manner of fortune life brought; and so it is in this spirit that the mourners rise to join me in the final prayer, the *kaddish*."

Maury and Sara Kalman rose. Maury read the Hebrew words in a firm quiet voice, and with Maury's voice, his mother's voice and the rabbi's voice were joined. And in Kurt Rosen's face were a dignity and a compassion which seemed to hallow the words which came from the lips of those who understood only partly.

And Lee listened very hard, and tried to understand herself.

. . . *Yis-ga-dal v'yis-ka-dash shmay-ra-baw* . . .

Lee tried to divine the meaning of these words; she tried to imagine what comfort or hope or special promise they might offer the mourners to make them worth repeating again and again. The first night, when Maury and his mother had stood up to read the *kaddish*, Lee had recoiled fiercely from a practice that so relentlessly focused attention upon the mourners. The cloistering of sorrow was the only way she knew of meeting sorrow; and she had felt the constricting fear that Maury, called upon to stand before those assembled, might not even be able to find sound for his voice. But gradually Lee had felt herself impelled by what she did not understand.

At breakfast the next morning, Maury watched Lee pouring the coffee from the silver pot into the bright pottery cups, and the gesture seemed to await a touch of gaiety that did not come. The morning sun was meshed in her short blonde hair, but her face was pensive and her eyes cast down, intent upon the amber liquid that filled the cups. Maury regarded this gravity with a special delight, as one might regard the gravity of a child. When she put down the coffee cup, he caught her hand.

"What's the matter, Lee?"

"Nothing."

"Yes, there is."

Lee's eyes met his and he saw that the gravity was not the

evanescent mood of a child. This moment seemed bound to the perplexity of the night before. Maury had meant to speak to Lee when they got home, but instead he had held her in his arms and they had not spoken.

Maury put cream and sugar into his coffee and stirred it thoughtfully.

"Lee, is the trouble that you're seeing your husband as a Jew for the first time?" he asked her finally.

She drew her hand from beneath his. "Maury, please don't talk like that. It's just that for five years it never seemed to come up at all; and now, suddenly, everything revolves around it."

"Lee, we lived like two people alone in the world. It was a beautiful, long honeymoon . . . but it couldn't go on like that forever," Maury told her.

"Maury, if you knew it couldn't, why didn't we talk about it? You should have made me understand a little while we were still by ourselves."

Maury did not answer immediately. He felt the sharp bite of self-reproach, as if he had failed Lee in some way. He wanted to explain away this feeling of guilt.

"Lee, when you're a Jew, being a Jew is the whole thing that you are. It isn't something separate in yourself that you can hold up and explain," he said.

Lee's eyes searched his face for a moment. "Maury, I don't think it is like that for you. It's as if you just suddenly let it claim you without fighting for what you really are."

"What am I, really?" Maury asked, a smile almost reaching his lips.

"Just a person like any other person," Lee maintained seriously.

Now Maury did smile. "Lee, every person is just a person. But you can't whack off a finished personality from all the things that went to make it."

Lee got up from the table and moved restlessly around the room. Suddenly she came back and sat down again.

"Maury, we've got to be more honest with each other than this. We never even said the word—Jew—do you know it's hard for me to say the word. When you don't even talk about something, it gets so you can't even say it."

"It just never seemed to come up," Maury said, repeating her phrase.

"It didn't come up because we didn't let it!" Lee flung back at him. "Maury, maybe we don't know each other very well at all. I knew you so little that I didn't even realize how much a part of you these things are. And you knew me so little you were afraid of letting me try to understand."

Maury did not reply. He was searching his own mind to see if what Lee said was true.

Lee glanced at the clock above the stove.

"It's almost eight, you haven't much time," she said as if they had been talking of nothing in particular. She got up and went to the sink with her hands full of dishes. She stood there at the sink with her back to Maury.

He came and stood behind her. He put his hands on her shoulders, and his face against her hair.

"Lee," he said, "Do you have any idea how much I love you?"

She nodded, and he felt the softness of her hair moving against his cheek. He knew that if he turned her face around he would see that she was crying.

Later that morning, Lee's fingers pulled the red sweater down over Julian's dark curls, and his arms wiggled into the sleeves. Julian's brown eyes met Lee's blue ones with a look of mutual satisfaction. Both of them acknowledged that it was a victory of sorts to get Julian inside a sweater.

"Let's go!" Julian said, tugging at his mother's hand.

"Just a minute . . . the hat!" Lee said, making a grab for him before he bounded out of reach. She pulled the red-and-white wool cap down over his ears. "Now! Off you go."

Lee called goodbye to Amy who was ironing in the kitchen, then followed Julian who squatted now on the front doorstep, staring solemnly into the face of the kitten Maury had brought him.

"Well, come on. You were in such a hurry," Lee said. "'Would you like to go over to Aunt Myrtle's while I shop?"

Julian and the kitten exchanged a look of secret disgust.

"You haven't been there in a long time . . . Aunt Myrtle might have a cookie for you," Lee coaxed. "And I'd bring you a surprise from town," she finished lamely. She was thinking how her aunt had complained that she never saw anything "of the baby."

"I go with you," Julian informed her matter-of-factly.

"We'll both stop and visit Aunt Myrtle," Lee said. "Then you can stay if you want to."

"I go see Grandma," Julian suggested stubbornly, as Lee gave him a boost into the car.

"Aunt Myrtle is a little like a grandmother, too," Lee insisted, as she headed the car toward her aunt's house, "and she misses you."

Julian, occupied with trying to open the glove compartment, lost interest in the argument.

Thirty minutes later, after Lee had drunk a cup of coffee with her aunt, she persuaded Julian to stay while she went on to town. The next two hours she spent doing a variety of small errands which only partly occupied her mind, and there persisted the vague, uneasy feeling that neither her aunt nor her young son would profit by their opportunity to get better acquainted. When Lee returned, a little before noon, her aunt was waiting for her.

"Where's Julian?" Lee asked immediately.

"He's playing outside," her aunt told her, and through the window Lee glimpsed Julian's bright little cap bobbing beneath the bare branches of the lilac bush as he crawled on his knees pushing a small car in front of him. Lee smiled watching him. "What kind of time did you have?" she asked.

"All right," her Aunt Myrtle answered crisply, her smile tight-lipped and a little strained.

"Did anything happen?" Lee asked her.

"No. Not really. Lee, what exactly does *tochas* mean?"

"I don't know."

"Well, you'd better know. It's part of your son's vocabulary."

"What did he say?"

"Laura stopped by and brought her little Susie," Aunt Myrtle began. "Susie and Julian were playing, while Laura and I drank a cup of coffee in the kitchen. Julian came running in very excited to inform us that Susie . . . doesn't stand up . . . but—sits on her little *tochas* in the bathroom." Two bright spots of red appeared on Myrtle Morrow's cheeks as she spoke.

Lee laughed. She couldn't help it. "I think that ought to give you a pretty good idea of what it means," she said.

"It isn't funny, Lee! Things like that can be embarrassing enough . . . in English."

"Did you say anything to him?" Lee asked.

"I asked him who told him that word."

"Did you act as if it were a bad word?" Lee demanded.

"I just asked him who told him That Word," Myrtle repeated.

"And what did he say?"

"He said his grandma did. Really, Lee, you ought to speak to

Maury. The child will have a hard enough time without . . ."

"Without what?" Lee asked levelly.

"Now, Lee, don't act naive. Don't act as if you've been in wrappers all your life."

The back door slammed and Julian sidled into the room a little uncertainly. He wouldn't look at his Aunt Myrtle.

Myrtle Morrow glanced from Julian to his mother and was at a loss to understand how this moment had evolved until it seemed to be she who was in the wrong.

"I didn't scold him," she insisted pettishly.

Lee knelt down until her eyes were on a level with Julian's.

"I brought you a little wrecker to pull your cars," she told him. He began to jump up and down, and a tiny cup rattled in a tiny saucer on the hanging shelf, but Lee did not tell him to be still. "It's in the car . . . in the little sack," she told him, and he went bounding out of the house without a backward glance.

"Well, thanks, Aunt Myrtle, for keeping him," Lee said.

"Lee, for goodness sakes, I hope you're not angry!"

"I'm just sorry he embarrassed you," Lee said. "Come see us when you can." Lee stood at the doorway. She waved briefly to her aunt and went to the car with Julian.

Lee did not want to go home. They passed the park, and she said to Julian, "Want to swing a little while?"

He fingered the toy wrecker fondly. "I guess so," he said.

Lee stopped the car and, holding hands, they crossed to the swings. Julian climbed into the swing and Lee began to push him. His small sturdy body sailed through the air and came back to her hands, and he squealed with rich delight.

"Higher! Higher!" he called to her.

And she swung him higher, and his laughter was a small and lovely sound in the breeze. The emotions of people are so separate from their destinies, Lee thought. If Julian was destined to unhappiness he did not know it. He could laugh, laugh, laugh. She could make him laugh.

That night the moonlight moved slowly into the darkness, etching the branches of the willow tree across the west window. Lee lay still and waited for sleep that did not come.

Jew—Jew—Jew—I can hardly say the word. When you don't talk about something, it gets so you can hardly say the word. . . . What does it mean; what exactly does it mean?

Maury slept beside Lee; and in the lonely stillness of the night, her mind went searching back along the corridors of memory for some hint of meaning to ease her bafflement. She searched her memory for the sound of voices, familiar voices, familiar phrases. . . .

"If that don't just beat the Jews!" Aunt Abbie always said. . . . "I tried to Jew him down, but he wouldn't Jew." . . . "Take it from me, in my job it's always the Jews want something extra." . . . "And in Hollywood we ate in the restaurant where all the rich Jews go." . . .

Lee looked at Maury's face in the moonlight; she saw his face with all the awareness of her love. The urbanity and humor and resoluteness which were a part of Maury's waking self did not survive in sleep. In sleep his face was sensitive and gently beguiled, with the look of a boy who dreams. Maury stirred, he sighed and turned. Lee laid a hand on the smooth bare skin of his back and felt the even tempo of his breathing.

. . . "That's the Jews for you—fast cars and loud kids!" . . . "Who wants to see Coney Island, a bunch of fat Jews in bathing suits." . . . "Of course, you can be friendly with them, you can be friendly with your beauty-parlor operator or barber. That doesn't mean you make them your friends." . . .

Sharp pain in the palms of her hands made Lee know how tightly her hands were clenched. The brightness of the moon was everywhere in the room. Lee took the pillow and put it over her head. She stifled her own sobbing with the pillow against her lips; she pressed the pillow against her ears. But the voices she heard were remembered voices and they spoke inside herself.

They were not the voices of vicious people or of avowed anti-semites. They were the voices of her family, her friends, of people who believed in the Golden Rule and American Democracy, who laughed at small jokes, and cried over small sorrows, and who were wonderfully secure in their own good opinion of themselves.

And the words that they spoke were not attacks spoken in anger, but the idle words of idle moments.

This, then, was prejudice. If prejudice were deliberately taught it might be refuted, but when it came to you as the air you breathed . . . Lee sat up, she groped in the darkness for her slippers beside the bed. The most appalling thing of all was that unkindness could be so casual. Lee stood, she bent over and kissed Maury's forehead. He did not move. Silently, Lee left the bedroom and went to roam the rooms below in the company of the wretchedness of her thoughts.

Chapter 12

I

IN THE first days after Abe Kalman died only Ellen Rosen
understood Lee Kalman's grief and her loss—the loss of a
friend—and how she must suffer this loss alone and quietly because it was in no way like or commensurate with the loss of those
who were his own.

And as Ellen tried to reach out with understanding to Lee,
it seemed to her that Lee Kalman was confounded by the profundity of Maury's grief that took into account many things;
that became, not a grief over death, but over life; suffering, in
life's parting, all the poignancy of its denials. The dignity of this
grief Lee Kalman seemed to feel; the Jewishness of it she only
sensed, but did not comprehend.

And it was to the Rosens that she turned.

Together, one noon time, Kurt and Ellen and Lee sat down
around the small table to eat the cheese and rye bread, marmalade
and sweet butter that Ellen laid out.

"Here, eat! Let me pour you more coffee . . . and try the butter; it is very good," Ellen said to Lee.

Lee smiled in reply. Thoughtfully she buttered a piece of
bread, as if she were doing it just because she wanted to please
Ellen.

"Rabbi," Lee said hesitantly, "what does it mean . . . the
Hebrew prayer you say for the dead?"

"You speak of the *kaddish,* Lee, but it is not a prayer for the
dead," Kurt told her.

"But at the *minyans* . . . ?"

"It is a prayer that is said always by mourners, Lee, but death
is not even mentioned. The *kaddish* is a prayer praising God; it
is an adoration. It contains sentences like 'Great and Glorious is
his Holy Name.'"

"But when somebody dies . . . ?" Lee's face was troubled and
she made a small ineffectual gesture with her hand. Ellen, her
eyes dark with sympathy, saw that this was not the sort of comfort or promise that Lee had imagined. Ellen exchanged a quick,

perceptive glance with Kurt and their eyes silently acknowledged that Lee Kalman had no basis for understanding the answer she sought.

"Lee," Kurt told her, "when a Jew dies, his fellow Jews do not invalidate his faith and theirs by questioning the ways of God. Throughout our history Jews have died because they insisted upon remaining Jews. They literally have died for their faith. But no matter how many could have survived at the hands of others, they could not have survived as Jews at all, if they themselves had repudiated this faith by continually reproaching God."

Ellen, watching Kurt so earnestly framing his answer for Lee Kalman, was remembering suddenly the Passover service and with what tenderness it spoke again and again of "the stranger within our gates." It seemed to Ellen that this special tenderness was always in Kurt's manner when he spoke to those whose spirits were confronted with irreconcilables.

"But, Rabbi . . ." Lee was toying with a small bit of bread on her plate; she did not seem to know what words to find for her question. "Rabbi, I don't know if it can be that way for Maury. I don't know if Maury has that kind of faith. And what I must know is what it all means to Maury."

"Perhaps he is discovering the faith himself, Lee; perhaps he will make you understand it later on," Kurt told her. And she smiled at him, but her eyes were still troubled.

When Lee had gone, Ellen began to clear away the dishes, and Kurt sat at the table, still, peeling an apple and cutting it thoughtfully into slices.

"Kurtchen, I think Lee sees her husband for the first time as a Jew," Ellen said.

Kurt nodded. He was thinking of Lee . . . and of Maury whose perplexity was not less. "Ellen, people speak out so often against ministers, that they are narrow for arguing against mixed marriage. They do not seem to realize how even the best of such marriages accrue to themselves an almost intolerable burden of heartache."

"And the children . . ." Ellen said, thinking of young Julian Kalman, so much the image of his father, so schooled in his mother's ways.

"Yes . . . for the children a baffling legacy . . . sometimes a tragic legacy."

"Kurtchen, why is it that each young couple think that they can be an exception?"

Kurt smiled. He came around the table and kissed Ellen behind the ear, knowing her hands to be safely immersed in dish water. "Young people in love imagine themselves to be able to solve the insoluble . . . surmount the insurmountable!" he replied, kissing her again.

"Kurtchen, *hör' auf!*" she turned quickly, her smile flicking him ruefully. "One thing is sure," she told him, her eyes challenging him a little, "from the dire and solemn predictions of the ministers . . . rabbis included . . . these young people never gain the least idea what it is . . . in clearly human terms . . . that they face."

Kurt conceded the point, not jokingly, but with the keen thoughtfulness returning to his face. "It's true," he said, "but we only do the best we can."

Suddenly Ellen felt, in her love for Kurt, the compulsion of all love, and she tried to imagine how it might have been if such a problem had separated them. "Kurtchen," she said quietly, "if they can side-step all the reasons to hate . . . they may finally learn a great deal about human love in its . . . finest sense."

And this time, when Kurt kissed her, the playfulness had deserted his mood, which was touched now by Ellen's own profound gentleness.

In the weeks that followed Ellen and Kurt often answered their door to find Lee Kalman standing there, sometimes smiling, sometimes pensive, waiting always to be drawn into the warmth that seemed to inhabit the Rosens' small apartment. Lee never tried again to speak of the things that troubled her, but she seemed to feel that just to watch Kurt and Ellen would be to find out about life all that she needed so desperately to know.

One clear afternoon, Lee found Kurt pursuing the comic strips in the morning paper, while Ellen was writing a letter at the table.

"Rabbi, I'm disillusioned," Lee chided. "You're the last person in the world I thought I'd find reading the funnies."

"There are many things you can learn from the funnies!" Kurt retorted indignantly. "Like this . . . what does it mean, 'make whooppee.' Casper says 'Tonight we will make whoopee.' What does it mean?"

Lee smiled into Ellen's knowing face. "Let Ellen tell you," Lee said, "she knows."

"You tell me. What means . . . 'make whoopee'?"

"It means . . . well . . . go out on the town."

"Go out on the town?"

"Paint the town red!" Lee said, starting to grin.

Kurt shook his head.

"You tell him what it means, Ellen."

"It's no use," Ellen said, "We don't speak the same language any more. I learned English over the radio, and he learned English translating Durant's philosophy back and forth from the German."

"A word in the funny paper, and these two brilliant women can't tell me what it means," Kurt said resignedly.

"Auf'n Bummel gehen!" Ellen said finally.

"Aha!" Kurt said, "That's what I thought it meant. And now you owe me a dime for each German word. That's forty cents!"

When Kurt had gone to his study at the Temple, Ellen said, "The Levinsons moved last week into their new home."

Ellen felt a deep reluctance at the thought of making a courtesy visit alone; she looked at Lee tentatively.

"It must be very beautiful," Lee answered. "Maury said Sam Levinson told him he was going to make it the most damned house this side of Denver."

"Would you like that we make a visit?" Ellen asked.

"I think it would be nice," Lee said. "Let's go."

They drove in Lee's car through the traffic of Main Street and, as they turned into the wide boulevard that led East, Ellen said: "Would be good if we take bread and salt . . . it's an old custom to take bread and salt for the new house."

"All right. We can stop at Beeman's Bakery on the way out."

"Do you think she would like that we do it?" Ellen asked a little doubtfully.

"I would have liked it when I moved into my new house," Lee teased.

Ellen laughed. Her laughter had the rich warmth of her singing. "I would not have been sure," she said, "you might not have understood what it meant."

"I could imagine. Bread and salt—the most fundamental things of all— for the beginning of a new life."

"Ya! Something like that. To give the bread and the salt is to give the wish for the good things of life."

"It makes it all . . . sort of important," Lee said.

Ellen nodded.

"It seems as if . . . you . . . have customs like that for everything that happens," Lee said.

"Yes, but some Jews have only impatience for the customs."

"Why?"

"It seems we live in a very literal age. I do not imagine that Myra Levinson has any literal need for the loaf of bread or the salt." Ellen's dark eyes flashed with a perceptive humor.

"Let's take a chance on her. Let's take it," Lee said.

They stopped at the bakery and Ellen chose the bread—coarse, dark, rye bread, fresh and warm from the oven. And they went in the grocery store next door to buy a box of salt.

Moments later Lee drove the car into the wide, curving driveway that stretched out grandly from the mansion that Sam Levinson had built for himself.

"Not very elegant gifts for such an elegant house," Ellen remarked skeptically.

"Ah, but you're forgetting. The meaning is in what they represent," Lee said sternly. And they both were laughing a little as they rang the doorbell.

A black, little maid who seemed unrejuvenated by elegance, opened the door.

"Yes'm?" she demanded imperiously.

"We'd like to see Mrs. Levinson," Ellen replied.

"She's in the drawing room," the maid answered, opening the door. She eyed the loaf of bread and the box of salt darkly as if they were not standard equipment for formal calls.

"Elizabeth, who is it?" Myra Levinson called. The heels of her shoes tapped lightly on the polished tiles of the entry hall, and she stood there, chic, bright and radiant.

"Ellen, Lee! . . . It's nice of you to come. Come in."

"*Mazel tov,* Myra. Your house is lovely," Ellen said. "I brought bread and salt for you."

"Why, Ellen! . . ." Myra Levinson smiled with the quick pleasure of remembrance, and the smile, it seemed to Ellen, was oddly out of keeping with her bright, chic look. "Thank you. I wouldn't have thought of it."

And then Myra Levinson remembered something else. She glanced back over her shoulder and Ellen saw that she had another visitor, a plump, faded little woman with a small puckered mouth who was peering at them intently, sitting a little forward on her seat. She smiled quickly when Ellen's eyes met hers.

"Come on in," Myra said again, "You must meet Miss Bailey, Davey's history teacher. Miss Bailey, this is Mrs. Rosen—our rabbi's wife—and Mrs. Kalman."

Miss Bailey hopped up, she shook hands very eagerly, bobbing up and down a little as she did so. She seemed to feel that something special was required of her in acknowledging this introduction, but she did not know what.

"Hello, Miss Bailey," Lee said as the intense little woman pumped her hand.

"How do you do," Ellen said, with grave courtesy when Miss Bailey turned to her. Ellen still held the bread and salt.

Ellen glanced at Myra Levinson and saw that she was embarrassed. The moment seemed to have dreadful potentialities. Ellen had the feeling that if she put down the bread and the salt they would become small, pitiful objects amidst the grandeur of this Victorian room.

"Here, Ellen. Let me take those things." Myra was saying, and she received them from Ellen's hands. "I wouldn't have thought of it," she murmured again, not looking at Miss Bailey.

Ellen suffered intensely the reproach of Myra's embarrassment. With terrible dread she waited, in this moment of bruising contact, for the inevitable withdrawal of each person into herself. And she looked from face to face.

In that instant Ellen became aware of Myra Levinson's estrangement from herself in the personality her husband had created for her . . . of the little teacher's fluttery goodwill soaring and dipping above the vast desolation of a parched spirit . . . and of Lee Kalman's own vague awakening with vistas opening up. And through Ellen Rosen's sudden insight, human fallability became only the imperfection out of which human sympathy is born.

"It's a beautiful house, is not?" Ellen said softly to Miss Bailey, smiling at the same time into Myra Levinson's troubled eyes and reaching out her hand to Lee.

The little teacher bobbed her head up and down vehemently.

"I'd love to show it to you," Myra Levinson said, and Ellen felt in her voice the nearness of tears she would never shed. And Ellen knew that later each one, even she, might brood upon the implications of the moment just past; but as they lived it, through her example, not one had quite lost sight of the humanness of the others.

That afternoon the sun was slanting its rays low across the tops of houses, and through fences, and into nooks and crannies to warm surfaces of wood and brick, for a last hour before it was plunged below the flat rim of the earth. The afternoon was waning, and the late autumn was a haunting smoke smell in the air, as Lee took Ellen home. Lee stopped the car in front of the big old house next door to the synagogue and turned off the ignition key, and Ellen felt her need to speak.

"Ellen, do you know that somehow you change the way I have to feel about things?" she said abruptly.

"How?" Ellen asked, looking into Lee Kalman's young and earnest face turned to her now, almost imploringly.

"I don't know exactly. . . . It seems like most of the Jews I've known tried to ignore the fact that they were Jews, and were uneasy if other people didn't ignore it. But with you and Rabbi, people who don't know a thing about it get the feeling that it's something wonderful to be."

Ellen smiled, she knew that Lee was thinking of Miss Bailey and of Myra. She knew that to speak was not easy for Lee.

"Do you know something?" Lee said, "I'm ashamed to tell this even to Maury. I don't know how I can tell you. Until I knew you and Rabbi it never occurred to me that people could be proud to be Jews. When Julian was a baby, I used to think a lot about how we would explain to him about being Jewish so he wouldn't feel too badly about it. And do you know the explanation I thought of?"

Lee hesitated a moment. Ellen did not want her to go on. Her very spirit resisted what Lee might say, but she saw that Lee's need to bear the guilt of what she would tell . . . and to be absolved of this guilt . . . was too great. Ellen did not stop her, she sat very still.

"What explanation," she asked Lee gently.

"I thought of telling him that all people have some handicap to deal with in life. Lots of times it's something nobody else knows about. But sometimes it's something everybody knows about . . . like being a cripple . . . or being a Jew."

Ellen Rosen felt the inner flinching that no one might ever see, and Lee turned her face away, laying it against her hand on the steering wheel.

"Ellen, I feel so horrible when I think I might really have said that to him. But I didn't know there was any other way to feel."

"What about Maury? Is he not proud to be a Jew?" Ellen asked her quietly.

"We just never talked about it. Not even about what we might tell Julian. I didn't know how to ask him things. And he didn't know how to tell me. We just loved each other and didn't talk about it."

Ellen nodded. With her hand, she lifted Lee's face up so that their eyes met again. "And maybe you were happier that way?"

"I don't know," Lee answered. "It's as if Maury is just discovering that he's a Jew . . . it's as if he hardly knew it before."

"Maybe you should talk to Rabbi," Ellen suggested, "he explains things so beautifully."

"I can understand it better from you, even though you don't try to explain," Lee answered. "You're a woman, and I'm a woman, and I can look at you and know what it means to be a Jew—that it is a most splendid way to be a human being. And then I feel like I understand better than Maury does."

"Then why don't you tell him?"

"I can't. I can feel it, but I can't say it."

"You said it to me," Ellen reminded her.

"That's because you understand it already. I couldn't say it to anybody who didn't understand it already."

"Lee, you will make your little boy understand it," Ellen assured her. "Goodbye now . . . and thanks for going with me."

Ellen's hand was on the door handle, she opened it and got out of the car, and stood there at the curb to wave to Lee as she drove away.

A cripple . . . or a Jew. . . . A Most Splendid Way To Be A Human Being. . . . The pulses at Ellen Rosen's temples throbbed with the ache of centuries.

II

In the weeks after Abe Kalman's death, Sam Levinson came several times to see Maury and Lee, to offer condolences, or advice, or just to talk. He stopped by one evening several days after Lee and Ellen had been to see the new house. Lee and Sam sat down before the first log fire of the season, while Maury helped Julian with his bedtime bath.

"Your house is lovely, Sam," Lee said. "Myra decorated it beautifully. She told us she studied interior decorating."

Sam laughed. "Myra studied interior decorating all right. But just to be on the safe side, I hired an interior decorator to incubate a few of the ideas in her pretty little mind."

Lee smiled a little reluctantly, she felt that to laugh would be rank disloyalty to her own sex. Sam saw this, and laughed again.

"Anyway, it's lovely," Lee maintained.

"Thank you! . . . for God's sake, Lee, what was the idea of the bread and salt?" he demanded suddenly. "Why didn't you remind Ellen Rosen that this is America, 1941."

"I don't see what that has to do with it. I thought it was . . ."

"A quaint custom?" Sam interposed.

"No. A very beautiful custom."

"Well, Davey's teacher thought it was a quaint custom. Quaint, like the Eskimos or Fiji Islanders. The sixth grade is studying customs of many lands. Miss Bailey asked Davey to get up and explain the quaint Jewish custom of bringing bread and salt to a new house. It was sure as hell embarrassing."

"For Davey?" Lee asked pointedly. Her chin was up a little, and anger had darkened her blue eyes until it seemed that only the pupils showed.

Sam laughed again. He was one who could enjoy and ignore a flash of anger in a woman.

"Yes, for Davey," he replied knowingly. "You know how kids that age don't want to be different."

"What did Davey say?" Lee prodded.

"He didn't say anything. What was he to say? He didn't know what it meant. He had to come home and ask and report the next day. My God, we were practically freaks before it was all over."

"I think it is a beautiful custom," Lee said again.

Sam looked at her more keenly, he saw that her anger was more than a coquettish affectation. He saw that they had become antagonists. With his pudgy well manicured fingers, he mashed out his cigarette in the ash tray and turned a sardonic smile to her.

"Beautiful maybe for European peasants in their little thatched roof cottages. Or in a ghetto. In a ghetto they might have need of the bread and salt."

Maury came in from the hall, an oversized cup towel still draped around his middle. He looked from Lee's flushed face to Sam Levinson's sardonic one.

"Sayyyy . . ." he said in a conciliatory tone; he caught Lee's eye to coax back a smile.

"I'll make coffee," Lee said. She turned and left the room.

Lee began to make the coffee. She measured the grounds with a sort of fierce concentration. For quite a while now, Lee had felt restive in Sam Levinson's presence; she had felt hardly able to sit and talk to him, or quite to look him in the eye. His open opposition to the rabbi had begun the change in her friendliness to him. But now Lee realized that the intensity of her resentment against him had a purely personal implication.

Lee measured the water. She plugged the electric cord into the percolator. The laughter of men's voices came to her from the living room. She sat down in one of the kitchen chairs and tried to think.

Suddenly it seemed to Lee that Sam's bitter opposition to the rabbi threw new light on his early friendliness to her. She understood that she had meant to Sam Levinson exactly what he had meant to her—a refutation of the idea that the Jewish and non-Jewish worlds must remain separate and inviolate to each other. And the fact that she and Sam had mutually disguised this need of reassurance, in the pretense of offering and accepting genuine friendship, seemed to Lee, in retrospect, a shameful and cowardly thing to have done.

In a flash of perception Lee saw that, proportionate to Sam's first eagerness to accept her, was his reluctance to comprehend the plight of the European Jew as exemplified by his own rabbi. And in this reluctance Lee recognized an implacable and inescapable sense of shared destiny.

The coffee stopped perking. Lee poured it into the cups and cut pieces of fresh coffee cake. She opened the swinging door and carried the cups back into the living room.

"Here, let me help you," Maury said, jumping up.

"Just get the cake," Lee answered.

Sam watched them both, smiling. Lee didn't look at him, even when she handed him the cup and saucer. He put it down on the cocktail table and leaned forward a little.

"Lee, I'm sorry," he said.

Lee shook her head; her smile reached just a little beyond him, not touching him at all. "There's nothing to be sorry about," she answered. "Here, let me give you a napkin; the cake is very crumbly."

"Damn the cake! Look, Lee, I mean it. You can bring bread and salt to my house any time you want to. I'll even salt the bread and eat it. I'll even kindle the Sabbath candles if you want me to, though what the hell it means to your little Irish heart I'll never know."

Lee smiled. She looked at the unaccustomed expression of entreaty in Sam Levinson's confident face and she laughed a little. But inside she was not laughing; she was asking herself what was this sense of shared destiny that could be frightening enough to destroy kindness and sympathy in a man like Sam Levinson. And in the answer Lee feared to discover dreadful implications for herself.

Instinctively Lee turned toward Maury, and his eyes were on her with a softness and a gentleness that made her want to cry. It was to Maury that she went and she sat down on the arm of his chair. She looked back across the room at Sam Levinson.

"It's all right, Sam . . . really," she said.

"Then fine. And now I have to go. Myra will be wondering what the hell has become of me." He drained his cup and set it down again.

Maury and Lee went with him to the door.

"You two come over," Sam said a little imperiously.

"We will," Maury replied, and Lee nodded.

When they had closed the door, Lee started back into the living room, and Maury came up behind her and caught her in his arms and kissed the top of her head.

"What's that for?"

"Just like that!"

Lee glanced up over her shoulder into Maury's vaguely inscrutable face. His teeth were very white in his smile, and his black eyes both compelled her and teased her—shared destiny, Lee thought again. What was this shared destiny to which she had come voluntarily with such blithe unawareness, with such naive confidence in the basic goodness of human beings?

"What were you thinking about a while ago . . . when you were looking at me so . . ." Lee hesitated, searching for a word.

"Just that I love you very much," Maury replied earnestly, and for a moment longer his arms bound her to him. She retreated a little into the strength of his embrace.

Lee looked up into Maury's face again. It seemed to her that Maury shared this confidence in goodness, that out of some deep humanity he sheltered and nurtured the sense of it in her, perhaps as a bulwark against things which he knew and which she did not. She suddenly felt young by centuries in relation to him.

"Maury, don't let me go. Keep holding me," Lee said.

"Here in the entry hall?" Maury asked, grinning at her.

"You're making fun!"

"Of course. If a man can't make fun of his wife, whom can he make fun of?" He kissed her then, with a depth of gentleness he withheld from his voice. "Let's go listen to the radio," he said.

They went back into the front room, and Maury sat down beside the radio. Restlessly he flicked the dial back and forth from station to station, and distorted fragments of sound reverberated in the air.

Lee sat down on the couch. Once again she and Maury had come together very close to something that was vital to both of them. And they had not spoken of it. Lee felt a stifled, lonely yearning that seemed to press in her throat. She watched Maury's quick and oddly graceful movements which had become the rhythm of her blood. He did not turn to her need; he did not know that it is a profound and shaking experience for the yet unchallenged spirit to be drawn by love into the orbit of hate.

Lee picked up a pad of paper and drawing pencil off the table and began to sketch Maury in swift, sure strokes. The portrait was done in a few seconds. From memory she began to sketch other faces . . . faces . . . faces . . . faces—the faces of men she had known all her life—a teacher . . . a preacher . . . the grocer . . . the family doctor . . . her uncle . . . the father of her best friend—men whose humor and indulgence and kindness she had known. And Lee wondered if they were capable of hate. Hate. . . . Even the word was remote from her way of life. But tonight she had acknowledged at last that it was an actuality in the heritage that she must pass on to her son.

But even having acknowledged this fact, Lee did not understand hate. Her head ached with trying to comprehend it. Hate, she had no basis of comprehending. But simple unkindness— unkindness like that of Sam Levinson toward the new rabbi— was within her experience. It was a thing she could feel in her heart . . . and suffer.

"Maury," she said suddenly, "I wish Sam Levinson would like the Rosens."

Maury looked up at her and he made no quick or glib answer; and Lee saw that she was not so alone as she had thought. Maury knew what she felt, and, what was more, he cherished her ability to feel it.

Chapter 13

D AVEY LEVINSON sat at his desk during civics class, his eyes cast down, his face flushed. It was Friday afternoon, and Friday afternoons had become for Davey a special ordeal. At this time each week the members of the class filed to the front of the room, one by one, to read newspaper clippings which then were discussed.

These sessions had represented no problem to Davey until a month previously when a new boy named Willie Larsen had come into the class. Willie was larger than most of the boys. He had an underslung jaw and a shock of straw-colored hair that hung down to his eyes. Every week Willie read a current event about Jews . . . about Jews tortured and killed in Nazi Germany, about Jews herded like cattle through the streets of Vienna, about Jews in the ghetto at Warsaw. Willie Larsen read tonelessly, without expression in his face or voice, and then he sat down. He never even looked at Davey Levinson.

Davey read these things, too, and somehow they had become inseparable from the words he so laboriously read in the Temple:

> . . . Boruch atto Adonoi . . .
> Praised be thou o Lord . . .

and from the sight of the face, inexpressibly sad in repose, that he glimpsed through the door of the rabbi's study as he worked at his lessons . . . and from the rabbi's wife, who was beautiful and whose warm rich voice made him oddly glad to be alive, and who sometimes gave him chocolate or crackers and milk before he went home. And in a strange way these things had become inseparable from his own father, who was so confident and hearty, and from his mother, and even from himself.

When the door of the mind is opened a crack, it swings inexorably wider. Davey Levinson had begun to know who he was. And the things that he saw in the newspapers were never so terrifying and so personal as when he heard Willie Larsen tonelessly reading them.

On this Friday afternoon Willie read:

The following is an eye witness account by press corres-pondent Dean Callahan of London who hitched a ride to a secret rendezvous on the coast of France. Here is his story:

"Last night four men in a 40-foot launch 'invaded' the highly fortified coast of France to deliver a consignment of sulfa drugs to French resistance leaders.

"The dangerous mission was safely accomplished—but that is not the story I want to tell.

"As we headed back to England, I saw the burly skipper of our launch lift a dead child out of the duffle bag he had carried from the rendezvous. I saw the dumb, uncompre-hending look of anguish in his leathery face when the tiny boy would not move or speak.

"He could not understand it. Two hours before this rugged soldier of fortune had been persuaded by Jean Patau, French underground leader, to smuggle the child out of the country. He had seen the large frightened eyes peering at him over the rim of the bag before the strings were drawn shut. He had carried the child six miles on his back in the bag. And now he lifted him out, dead.

"The little boy's name was Saul.

"Scores of children like him have been hidden away by the French. But Saul was not easy to hide; he would not deny that he was Jewish.

"Jean Patau told Saul's story sketchily to the skipper.

"The child had seen his father shot in a doorway . . . and his mother shot even as she reached out to draw him into the protecting warmth of her body. And when he tried to creep into the haven of her being, he felt the warmth ebbing away. The storm troopers had left him there.

"Later . . . much later . . . weeks or months . . . as he lay huddled on a straw pallet in the corner of a cellar, com-forted by the chant of his grandfather praying in the light of a gutted candle, he saw the old man seized and dragged away. The concierge found Saul the next morning; a child of seven, his stunted body seemed hardly that of a four-year-old. She hid him and passed him unto the underground; but his protectors soon discovered that it would not be possi-ble for Saul to stay in France, and survive.

"Some fierce thing burned in this child. If anyone took him into the street he would stand, feet thrust apart, scream-ing: 'I'm a Jew! I'm a Jew!'

"Perhaps he saw denial of his Jewishness as the final irrevocable separation from parents he could no longer see or touch. Or perhaps it was some incredible perversion of the will to live. But he did not live.

"When we lifted Saul out onto the bottom of the boat,

the black curls were still soft at his temples. The clear light of the moon shone down on his small, pale face. The salty breeze of the sea wafted away the faint smell of death.

"The body of Saul was beautiful and unmarred. But the spirit of this Jewish child had fled from the treacherous caprice of our sympathy. He had descended without outcry into the pit of silence that has swallowed up his people.

"It is an agony-haunted silence that must lie heavily on the conscience of mankind when the relieving tedium of war's gross, impartial misery has cleared away.

"As we reached the coast of England, dawn was freshening in the east. I was glad. It would be easier to go back to a work-a-day war . . . than to think."

Davey Levinson sat very still in his seat. The hush of shame and embarrassment was in the room, making a silence to hold Willie's words. And each word was small and flat and dissoluble in the silence.

Willie finished reading; with a backward jerk of his head he tossed the hair out of his eyes and sat down.

Miss Bailey moved uneasily in her chair. Her small puckered mouth was drawn tightly together, and her forehead was puckered too, in a look of consternation. There was an awkward pause. She did not call for comments.

"That is why we should all be glad we live in America," she said a little breathlessly. "In America such things could not happen."

"Yeah! In America we got to tolerate niggers and Jews," Willie Larsen replied. He tossed back his hair again. His glance started off in Davey's direction, but wandered short of its destination.

In this strained, tense second Davey Levinson was on his feet. He was leaning forward a little so that the veins stood out in his neck.

"We don't want your damned old tolerance!" Davey shouted.

Miss Bailey jumped up. She did not know what to do, she glanced nervously around the room. She made a small conciliatory, protective, reproachful movement toward Davey who was one of her favorites.

"Davey, tolerance is what makes it possible for all of us to live together," she gasped out.

"It isn't! Tolerance is a hateful thing. People have got to respect each other, not just tolerate each other . . . the Rabbi says so," Davey finished lamely. He was near to tears now. Suddenly too exhausted to stand, he slumped back into his seat.

One of the bigger boys near the back of the room snickered.

The small horrible sound released the spring of tension, and suddenly they were all laughing. The boys and girls of the sixth grade were laughing as if Davey had made a joke.

And then the bell rang, and they could not believe it; they could not believe that, after all, they were to be allowed to escape from this awful moment. In haste they gathered their books and went shuffling out of the room.

Davey Levinson sat at his seat until they were gone. He rubbed his fingers together and felt the chalk dust between them. He sat there, waiting until they would all be gone.

The last to go was Willie Larsen.

"Hi, Rabbi!" he called back to Davey when the teacher had moved out of earshot down the hall.

Thirty twelve-year-olds took home the story of the dramatic incident in civics class. And the next morning Davey Levinson's outburst was being discussed up and down Main Street. For most who told it or heard it, it was merely an anecdote to liven the coffee hour.

But Davey Levinson had not told of the incident at home. He had come home just at supper time, and he had eaten his supper in an unusually pensive mood, his dark head bent low over his plate. And because his eyes were so bright, Myra had given him an aspirin and hot tea at bed time to ward off a cold.

It was downtown that Sam Levinson learned what had happened to his son.

Herman Morris, lank and morose, was standing in the doorway of the small chain-store he managed down the block from Levinson's. He saw Sam walking along the sidewalk toward the Grill for his morning coffee.

"Say, Sam!"

"Hi, Herman."

"It's rough about Davey!"

"What about Davey?" Sam was aware of the bristly feeling of the hair at the nape of his neck. He did not know what he expected to hear.

"God, Sam, I thought you knew. All the *goyim* are talking about it. Didn't Davey say anything at home?"

"Anything about what?" Sam demanded violently.

"Davey got in a tangle with a kid at school yesterday. The old story. Gentiles and Jews. But instead of waiting till he got out on the playground and giving the kid a black eye, Davey got up before the whole class and made a speech—quoted the rabbi!"

Sam glanced sharply at Herman Morris. It seemed to him that Herman relished this situation. He did not reply to him.

"Sam, I'm sorry as hell. I never dreamed Davey didn't say anything."

Still Sam did not reply. He turned and walked off and left Herman standing there.

Sam went on to the Grill just as he did every morning. He was bent upon convincing himself that Herman had been exaggerating. He stopped at the cigar counter and bought three cigars. He lit one and put the other two in his pocket. He spoke to John Stanley, the insurance man, and Noble Carter, the public service executive. They spoke to him in exactly the same way they spoke to him every morning.

Sam sat down at the counter.

"Hi, Sam!" Norman Gibbs called to him on the way out. Sam waved a well manicured hand. He did not feel reassured. If what Herman told him were only a little bit true there should be some sign of it in these faces. To encounter only impersonal cordiality when affirmation is so desperately sought can be more shattering to the sensibilities than hostility. Sam felt as if he couldn't breathe. He felt as if there were some active conspiracy to wall him in with his own gnawing dread.

"Sam, you coming to Rotary today?" Bob Manville called from the front booth.

Sam only nodded.

"Want me to warm it up, Mr. Levinson?" the waitress asked. She filled his coffee cup. She smiled at him in her usual not quite coquettish way.

"Thanks, Jennie," he said. He didn't drink his second cup of coffee. He got up and went back to his office. And on the way he thought of Davey. He thought of Davey with his head bent so low over the bowl of soup—"Davey, can't you sit up at the table?" —"Yes, Sir."

Sam went into his office and closed the door. His rage, his bitterness and fury were terrible things. . . . That this should happen to his son . . . his son! Sam felt a sharp dismay that Davey should have so flaunted the unwritten rule of feigned indifference, that he should have made himself vulnerable by speaking out—"he didn't give the kid a black eye, he made a speech and quoted the rabbi" Herman had said.

The rabbi—for all that had happened Sam Levinson blamed the rabbi. The very thought incensed him further. His fury must be directed somewhere; it was too fierce to be expended upon the generality of social injustice. Illogically it was directed at Kurt Rosen.

"Damn him! . . . Damn the bastard!" Sam Levinson murmured.

Lee Kalman finished piling the meringue on top of the pie and stood for a moment looking at it, as if its frothy top were somehow an affront to the perplexities of life. She put the pie in the oven and took a table cloth from the drawer.

Julian came up on the back porch. He had a muddy wooden spoon in his hand, and there was a smear of mud across the bib of his new corduroys.

"My pie's done," he said with satisfaction.

"That's fine."

"I made a lot of pies, in fact," he told her.

"Where are you baking them?" Lee asked, suddenly suspicious.

"On the front step," Julian confided with a manner of grand unconcern, as if he hadn't been told time and again about baking his mud-pies on the front step.

"Julian, with a back yard a mile wide, it does look like . . ." Lee began impatiently. Julian looked at her with a sweet and patient reason in his wide brown eyes.

"You have to bake where the oven is," he said logically.

Lee felt like scolding him, but suddenly she could have laughed at a small boy's complete confidence in his ability to outmaneuver his mother. Lee went out the backdoor and took one grimy small hand in hers.

"Come on," she said, "if the pies are done maybe we could wash them off the step before daddy comes home and steps in them."

"I have to ride my tricycle," Julian said reluctantly, as if he really hated leaving her with the cleaning up to do. "I have to," he repeated earnestly.

Lee let him go; it was better than having him get wet in the water from the hose. She turned the water on the step and watched the neatly arranged mud-pies begin to dwindle and to trickle off into the flower beds. And she thought about Davey Levinson.

That morning Sara Kalman had told Lee about Davey. All day Lee had thought about it. She couldn't stop thinking about it. It seemed to Lee that she had been on the point of resolving much of her own conflict. In the last weeks she had made herself

145

able to accept, without that instinctive surge of protest, her husband's more affirmative Jewishness. And in her conscious effort to do this, Lee had begun to experience a strange thing in her relation to her husband. Sometimes it seemed to Lee as if she were falling in love again, falling in love with the substance of a shadow. It was as if, at last, she came into the world, loving, instead of existing in the fantasy of "loving, we are a world unto ourselves." And little by little Lee had felt the joy, the keenness, the singing alertness, and the tautness of falling in love.

That a feeling which began as renunciation should have emerged as joy, left Lee unprepared for the impact of what had happened to Davey Levinson. She felt a sharp parallel between Davey and her own young son, and her keen sense of identification with what had happened to Davey was the more appalling because it was new to her. She felt Davey's hurt as if it had happened to Julian. And compelled by a mother's protectiveness, she was once again thrust into frantic flight from all she had thought herself ready to accept.

Lee went back in the house and set the table. Maury came in with Julian riding on his shoulders. They ate their supper and Lee put Julian to bed. She came back downstairs to where Maury sat reading the evening paper.

"Maury?"

"Hmmm?"

"Did you hear about Davey?"

"Uh huh."

"Maury, did anything like that ever happen to you?"

"Sure, Lee, it always does, sooner or later."

"Always?"

"Just about."

"Isn't there any way you can prepare a child?"

"Maybe. But some things don't get easy to take no matter how you're prepared."

"Maury, how did it happen to you."

"What's the use of talking about it?"

"I want to know."

"It was at Christmas time . . . when I was eight. In those days they had big community Christmas trees for all the kids in school. The trees had candles on them and they touched the ceiling, and there was always a Santa Claus with a pillow in his middle. There weren't more than six Jewish kids in school here then. For us it had all the excitement of the wonderful and forbidden. A little

Jew can yearn over Christmas plenty, I guess you know . . ." he mused wrily.

"And what happened?"

"They always had red mesh stockings with candy and fruit and nuts for every child in school. And Santa Claus passed them out himself the day before vacation. . . . Well, that year, when I was eight, my teacher sent me to the bookroom to get a new speller. And two of the teachers were in there filling the stockings. One of them was the band master . . . he had a harelip, and I never could watch him speak."

"And he said something. What did he say?"

Maury shrugged. Lee saw that it was hard for him to tell it even now.

"He didn't see me. I don't think he saw me. He was talking to the other teacher. He said 'Do we have to fix stockings for the damned little kikes along with the rest of the kids?' "

"Oh, Maury," She turned her face so he couldn't see her eyes.

"See, Lee. There wasn't any use talking about it."

"We have to talk about it. I have to understand for Julian's sake, can't you see that? Why does it have to happen to children? If it just happened to grown people, it would be bad enough. . . . Maury, how did you grow up to be like you are? How did you not grow up to hate people?"

"You learn to be a person, Lee. You learn that life isn't a matter of approval from outside."

"Maury, do you know something, when I was little I always felt approved of. Always."

"I know, Lee."

"Maury when I was falling in love with you, sometimes you wished I wouldn't."

"For God's sake, Lee. What makes you say that?"

"I can see how it would be . . . not to want to be loved by somebody who didn't know what it was all about . . . who didn't know at all . . ."

"Stop it, Lee. Stop it now!"

His hands were on her shoulders, his fingers were biting into the soft flesh of her arms. In his eyes was a look she had never seen there before. And his mouth came down on hers with a fierce hunger which sucked the breath which was her life. And he kissed her until the frantic need to flee deserted her, until she lay in his arms, unresisting, unmoving.

"Don't ever talk like that again," he said to her.

Lee did not speak. She suffered the need to flee, as despair—

the special despair of loving . . . her husband, her son . . . and the different things which these loves seemed to demand—took hold of her.

Davey Levinson pulled up the zipper of his jacket; the wind blew and he shivered. There was another half hour recess to endure. Most of the boys from his room were playing volley ball. Davey stood over near the fence and pretended not to watch them.

Out of the corner of his eye Davey could see Jeanie Robins. Jeanie was playing with the girls, but, when she ran, she ran toward where he was standing. When she ran, her soft blonde hair flew out behind her. In classroom or hall when their glance met, Jeanie's eyes moved quickly away, but once or twice Davey had surprised in them some aching awareness. Davey had the feeling that Jeanie wanted to come to him now. But she did not come. The girls moved away, and Jeanie went with them.

Davey Levinson, the boy who had moved with confidence and assurance among his contemporaries, was alone. No one felt quite at ease trying to be his friend. Davey had cast himself off from them and there was not one who reached out a hand to draw him back. It seemed to Davey that they stood a little apart, watching him curiously to see what he would do.

The bell rang. Davey wanted to be one of the last to go in. He played with the zipper on his jacket. He pretended it was hung. He yanked and yanked at it.

The game had broken up: the boys were going back into the school. They were chasing each other. When the game ended it was Willie Larsen who had the ball. He bounced it in front of him as he went running up the walk. He saw Davey and stopped running, but kept bouncing the ball.

"Hi, Rabbi!" he sang out to Davey. "How is the Jew-boy today?"

Two of the bigger boys ran up beside Willie. They laughed at the dismay in Davey's face. Davey rubbed the back of his hand across his mouth because he had the awful feeling that his lips might tremble. He looked around. There were some who had heard, but those who were his friends receded farther and farther into the distance, and he could only glimpse their faces, cool and impersonal, bearing the traces of hostility.

Slowly Davey turned and walked toward the school.

There had been a time when Davey Levinson was so completely divorced from any real sense of his Jewish identity that he had reacted no more strongly to being ridiculed as a Jew than to another taunt that young boys fling at each other in a savage give-and-take of learning to live together. But now when they called him "Jew," Davey knew that it was a taunt not interchangeable with any other taunt, that it was a taunt especially for him.

Kurt Rosen waited at the temple for Davey to come for his confirmation lession. Kurt had heard the story of Davey's difficulties at school from half a dozen members of the congregation. Everyone was inclined to make much of the fact that Davey had met his downfall quoting the rabbi. Kurt Rosen himself could not have expressed his pride in Davey. He thought about Davey, and he thought about the white gloves. Now suddenly, because he was remembering how it was to be twelve years old, he remembered Max Weil and the white gloves.

. . . All the people in Graudenz had talked about Rabbi Weil's white gloves, and wondered why he wore them. He had dozens of pairs of white gloves, all meticulously clean. He officiated in them; he ate in them; he wore them always.

When the Rosen family moved to Graudenz the white gloves were an unexhausted source of curiosity, and Kurt had heard, with a twelve-year-old's untarnished interest, all the speculations concerning them. The rabbi wasn't married; he never went to parties; he only rarely accepted invitations to dinner. All of these things seemed a part of the strangeness of the white gloves.

It was to Rabbi Max Weil that young Kurt went for his *bar mitzvah* classes. This rabbi who wore the white gloves was a coldly aesthetic man, aloof and remote, and his square black beard was as shiny as his oddly luminous dark eyes. But when he spoke, people could not help but listen; and Kurt could not help but listen.

This association, which was to affect Kurt Rosen's life more deeply than any other, achieved its first significance in a moment of the profoundest humiliation for them both.

One afternoon, Max Weil was discussing afflictions with a class of half a dozen twelve-year-old boys. The discussion veered to the subject of disfiguring eczemas.

Impelled by a sudden flash of insight, young Kurt was on his feet.

"Is that why you wear the white gloves?" he demanded, excitedly.

The white gloves! . . . To have flung the truth out carelessly, a thing quivering with life and shame and its own nakedness! Thirty years later, Kurt Rosen could remember and feel a hot flush rise in his face.

But that day Kurt Rosen had felt his first deep sympathy for human beings grow from his own heedlessness. Because a child, with a careless word, had found in a man, who was proud and courageous and lonely and brilliant, the vulnerability of all human beings, he came to the feeling that somehow people should be taught not to hurt each other.

And now, as he sat at his desk in the Fall City synagogue, half a world and a quarter of a century away from that day, he tried to remember what it was, exactly, that Max Weil had offered him. Certainly it was not a philosophy which might resolve itself into pleasing homilies, but rather an example of how the human spirit can hold in abeyance the crushing realities of life. And now he tried to think what it was, exactly, that he had to offer Davey Levinson. . . . How does a man teach a boy? . . . How does a man make a boy wish to become a man? . . . How does a man offer comfort for the stringencies of the lessons?

Kurt heard Davey's footsteps coming up the stairs; Davey came in, his hair a little rumpled, his face flushed.

"Hi, Rabbi," Davey said.

"Hello, Davey." Kurt spoke quietly. His gray eyes invited Davey's confidence, without pressing for it. "Shall we begin with the *Shema?*" he asked after a moment. Davey opened his Hebrew book, but he did not begin to read.

"Rabbi, did you hear about what happened at school?" he asked suddenly.

"Yes, Davey. I heard about it."

"Rabbi, what should I have said to them? I didn't know what to say."

"Davey, the next time you have this trouble, tell them you are proud of being a Jew. Say to them, 'Without Jews, you would not have your own Christianity; we gave you the Old Testament which is three-fourths of your Bible. And we Jews gave you Jesus; he was a Jew. So if you say again that you have to tolerate Jews, you forget that without Jews there would be no Christians.' . . . That is the answer you can give, Davey."

Davey nodded. "Rabbi, there is something else," he said, "What you were saying, that people have to respect each other . . . what good does it do us to know that, if other people don't know it, if they don't want to know it."

"Davey, if a problem looks too big, there's just one thing you can do—make it small enough that you can handle it."

"I don't know what you mean."

"There's nothing you can do to make all Gentiles respect all Jews. But there's a lot you can do to make the Gentiles you know respect Davey Levinson."

"But that's just it! They used to like me. Until I got up in class and said that about people respecting each other . . . and now they don't like me any more."

"Davey," Kurt said quietly, "Do you wish you hadn't said it?"

"I don't know. . . . I only know they used to like me."

"You feel badly about them, Davey, about the other people. But about what you did . . . do you feel right about that?"

"I don't know."

"If it all happened the same way again, would you still feel like saying what you said?"

Davey hesitated. He thought about Willie Larsen—*in America we gotta tolerate niggers and Jews*—

"Yes sir," Davey said, and the words had hardly any sound in them.

Kurt looked at the boy.

"Davey," he said, "if the problem is still too big, we can make it smaller still."

"How?"

"We can narrow it down to one. . . . We were talking about respect—how do you feel about Davey Levinson? Do you respect him for taking a stand on what he believed? After all, Davey, everything begins and ends with one. Respect begins and ends with self-respect."

Davey nodded. He sat there thinking for a moment.

"I guess I'd say it again," he said.

Kurt smiled a little. "Then that's about as much as any man can ask Davey—to feel inside that he hasn't been afraid to do the right thing."

Davey smiled a little, too. He nodded his head again. But his face was still deeply thoughtful, there was something he still wanted to ask.

"What is it, Davey?" Kurt said.

"I don't know. It just seems like people wouldn't want to hurt each other so much," Davey said.

The words carried Kurt back again, back to the day when his own feeling had begun that somehow there must be a way to teach people not to hurt each other. Perhaps this, then, was the crux of growing up, the point of understanding at which a boy begins to become a man.

When his class was over, Davey hated to go home. There was such an awful tightness around his mother's lips, and her eyes were so bright and moved so quickly from thing to thing. And she kept jumping up to do things for him as if he had been sick.

And his father! Davey was aware that, in addition to what he had done to himself, he had done some dreadful thing to his father. Although he had not been able to formulate the thought, it was as if he had destroyed some pretense which his father had carefully established, believing in it himself. And there was shame in this unformed thought which seemed to belong more to his father than to him.

When Davey came in from his confirmation lesson, his father was already at home. Davey glimpsed him in the den, talking on the telephone, as he hurried down the hall to his own room. Davey closed the door behind him. He was breathing fast. He had the closing-in feeling that his father would try to talk to him. He went over to his desk, put down his books and switched on the lamp. He was still standing there a moment later when the knock came at the door.

"Come in," Davey said, as his father opened the door.

"Hi, son," Sam Levinson said. He came into the room a little awkwardly, as if he felt like a trespasser there.

Davey tried to remember how, exactly, it was that he and his father had been so close. It hurt him to try to remember.

"Hi," he said.

Sam sat down on the window seat, he seemed too big for it.

"Davey, I hear you had a little trouble at school a couple of days ago," he blurted out, awkwardly, brusquely, and with too much feeling.

"I guess so," Davey replied, restive and non-committal in his father's presence.

Sam Levinson felt the bitterness of knowing his son lost to him, and buried deep in his consciousness was the added bitterness of knowing that he had lost even his own estimate of himself.

"Would you like to talk about it?" Sam asked clumsily, feeling the answer before he spoke. He had been enduring on an adult plane much the same thing that Davey had been enduring on a childish plane. 'When they see me now, they don't think *Sam Levinson*, they think *Jew!*' Sam told himself. But the parallel

152

experience had not drawn father and son closer together; they looked at each other as strangers.

Davey shrugged. He picked up a pencil and put it down. Reluctantly his eyes met his father's.

"There's nothing to talk about," he said.

Sam Levinson's eyes were the first to waver. He recognized that his son had grown in stature . . . and without his help . . . and in a way that was anathema to him.

Sam got up, he started for the door.

"Did you speak to the rabbi?" he asked.

Davey nodded.

Sam Levinson walked out the door and down the hall. In his bitter heart he knew that he would use all of his influence, that he would do anything within his power, to see that Kurt Rosen was not elected as rabbi of the congregation for another year.

Chapter 14

THE NOONTIME sun made only a pale disc in a damp grey sky, and a Sunday quietness lay over Fall City. Kurt sat at the table with an atlas and two dictionaries in front of him. And Ellen sat in the chair with the broken spring, knitting a sweater for the Red Cross, the tip of her tongue caught between her teeth with the intensity of the effort.

Kurt closed the dictionary with finality.

"Ellen, did you know that in English there are sounded and parallel unsounded consonants? Z is sounded; S is unsounded; B is sounded; P is unsounded!"

"No, Kurtchen, I did not know it. Do I have to know it?"

"The librarian did not even know it!" Kurt replied triumphantly.

"Then how do you know it?" Ellen asked, the gleam of humor coming to her dark eyes.

"It's part of the rule for pronunciation of *ed* and *s*. The librarian said you must remember for each word. I knew there must be a rule, and I found it here," he patted the dictionary fondly.

"Kurt, it seems that Americans don't often stop to examine what comes to them by birth . . . even their language," Ellen said thoughtfully. For a moment she concentrated very hard on a dropped stitch, and when she had it safely on her needle again, she watched Kurt, now pursuing the atlas with keen interest.

"There is something else. The people here are so informal . . . the way they say 'you' to each other," she continued.

Kurt laughed. "In Germany they would have the answer, 'I didn't lie with you in the gutter!' "

"Why do they speak so?" Ellen asked.

"It is the difference in language It is not so in English that 'thou' is said to family and intimate friends."

"Kurtchen, do you remember . . . how Else sat behind us at the opera in Berlin and wrote home that we must be secretly engaged because Ellen said *Du* to Dr. Rosen! The Americans would laugh!"

"Yes . . . they would laugh."

"Ellen, in America, you could get lost," Kurt said, still poring over the atlas, imprinting in his mind the size and shape and place of the forty-eight states.

"Because it is so big?" Ellen asked, gently taking Kurt's books away to set the table for lunch.

"No, another reason," Kurt answered. "In America you do not have to tell the police when you come to a place and you do not have to tell the police when you leave a place. In America you can be any place you want."

"Perhaps we should take a trip, Kurtchen . . . See America First!"

"Pardon?"

"See America First! . . . It is a thing they say!"

Later, as they sat together eating, Ellen was still intrigued with the comparative tone of their conversation.

"Kurtchen, the way they eat here! They cut up their meat so!" She illustrated with an exaggerated criss-crossing of knife and fork. And Kurt began to laugh.

"Do you know what I read? In Germany they recognized an American agent, not because of his accent, but because of the way he used his knife and fork. We must learn to eat like Americans." Kurt studiously made an effort at what seemed to him an awkward business.

Now Ellen began to laugh. "One thing I know! They don't eat enough! A coke they give you all evening. The next time we are invited we will eat a bar of chocolate first."

"You best bring along your bar of chocolate . . . and we'll see a little of America First . . . right now! We have to make a call on the Benjamins . . . and we may as well walk!" Kurt told her.

"Kurtchen, could we not spend one afternoon at home!'

"Come, to walk is good," Kurt coaxed, and he took her hand.

They started out, holding hands, into the damp, forbidding afternoon. The sky was a leaden gray, and the bare branches of the trees were brittle in their stirring.

It occurred to Ellen that she and Kurt made a gay and a carefree picture, swing hands between them; and the thought suggested the mood.

"Kurt, I wish we could go somewhere," she said.

"Where?" his gray eyes teased her, even before she answered.

"Oh, I don't know . . . a trip. Most any place. Just the two of us."

"It is late for a honeymoon . . . and we have work to do," Kurt answered very solemnly, his eyes still laughing.

A car was moving toward them down the street. It moved erratically, slowing from a fast speed to make a wide slow arc toward them. A bareheaded man stuck his head out the window.

"The Japs just bombed Pearl Harbor!" he hollered, and the car sped away.

Kurt and Ellen stood looking after him in amazement.

"Kurt, I do not think that it is true!" Ellen said, and even as she spoke she had the awful premonition that it was true. When her eyes met Kurt's eyes she knew that it was true. The wind was chill, and she and Kurt were alone in the street. The people were all in their houses; and the houses stared with blank eyes. And from somewhere a radio blared and was silenced.

Kurt and Ellen Rosen stood still at the curb and silently acknowledged the reality of a war their spirits had fought for so long a time.

All the rest of that bleak Sunday, and all of the next day, in which an icy wind swept down upon Fall City, Kurt and Ellen Rosen stayed close beside their radio. And the brittle voices droned on and on, and at noon on Monday came the voice that they, and millions of Americans waited to hear.

". . . . Gentlemen, the President of the United States . . ."

Ellen Rosen waited, hardly breathing, for the voice that to her sounded, always, the clarion notes of hope. And Franklin Delano Roosevelt began to speak:

"Yesterday, December 7, 1941, a date which will live in infamy, the United States of America was suddenly and deliberately attacked by the naval and air forces of the Empire of Japan. The attack yesterday on the Hawaiian Islands has caused severe damage to American Naval and Military Forces, and I regret to tell you that very many American lives were lost. . . ."

Ellen listened to the words spoken by the President of the United States, and in a way that she could not have told her heart reached out to him.

"Kurtchen, they are so surprised," she said to Kurt.

Kurt nodded, acknowledging the wonder in her voice.

That afternoon Kurt and Ellen rode to town on the bus; they walked down the street together, they went to the grocery store. They looked into the faces of their fellow Americans, faces that were angry and baffled and hurt and bewildered. And their hearts ached with compassion for the innocence of people who had not understood the spreading, creeping malignance of war.

Late that afternoon when they returned home, Ellen opened

156

up the evening paper on the table, and the black headlines seemed to leap up at her.

> *U.S. Declares War on Germany and Italy . . . Congress unceremoniously declared war on Germany and Italy today. Both houses quickly took steps to make this nation a full and formal participant in the world fight against Axis Domination. President Roosevelt had asked for the declaration immediately after learning that Germany and Italy had declared war on the U.S.*

And then the text of Roosevelt's message:

"The sudden criminal attack, perpetrated by the Japanese in the Pacific, provides the climax to a decade of international immorality. Powerful and resourceful gangsters have banded together to make war upon the whole human race. Their challenge has now been flung at the Unitd States of America."

Ellen wept, reading, and Kurt came to her. He took the paper and turned up her face and kissed her lips that were wet with the salt of tears.

"Kurt, I weep only for all the years that America was not our own . . . it is only for that, I weep."

War immediately made itself felt within the congregation B'nai Emanuel. The first to receive his country's call was Maury Kalman, who held the rank of captain in a National Guard outfit. In less than a month from the date of Pearl Harbor, his unit was mobilized. Three days before he was to leave, Kurt and Ellen Rosen came to pay their farewell call.

In the waning day, they walked from the bus stop to the Kalman's gray clapboard house, midway of a tree-lined block. And Ellen felt oddly stirred and restless, moving in the tranquility of the early evening.

"Kurtchen, I never know what to say . . . what is there to say?" she asked.

"You make people feel better . . . it's a gift you have," Kurt reassured her, catching her hand. He knocked on the door, and it was Lee Kalman who answered.

"Rabbi, Ellen! Come in! We were going to stop by to see you before Maury leaves . . . but it's so nice to have you here."

Lee, laughing a little, turned back to Maury who was down on his hands and knees in the middle of the rug with young Julian astride his back.

157

"That's all old-timer," Maury said, beginning to get up. And Julian howled furiously, clinging to his father's collar so that the horseback ride became a piggy-back ride. And Maury, breathless, touseled, and a little embarrassed, came forward, holding out his hand to Kurt.

"Is good that you get in training!" Kurt commented laughingly, as he felt in his pockets for the inevitable small bright candy for Julian. Julian, sliding down off his father's back, accepted it gravely.

"Come in, come in!" Maury said. He shook hands with Ellen, and she saw in his eyes the look of gratitude she had glimpsed there once before. Kurt and Ellen took the chairs that Lee offered them, and young Julian began to prance and caper around Kurt's knee.

"Look, cowpoke, you stay with Amy now," Maury told him, "I'll fix it up with her so you can dry dishes . . . and there's a nickel in it for you, if you do a good job," he told his young son earnestly, taking him by the hand. Julian, reluctantly, allowed himself to be led away.

Ellen noticed that Lee Kalman, standing a little apart, was watching her husband and son with an intensity that was almost hurtful to see. How, Ellen wondered, does the language of commonplaces become a ritual to contain the anguish of the heart. And how does a man go to war . . . and how does a woman stay behind . . . and how does a heart let go a little when it must, yet cling the more?

"He looks like you," Ellen said, when Maury came back, and Maury grinned at her.

"Heaven help him!" he said.

Maury sat down, and Lee came and sat on the arm of his chair.

"The picture of his father . . ." she said. "Maury! We should have had a family portrait made. But there was so little time."

Maury winked at Ellen. "The sentimental creatures that women are!"

"No, really, I wish we had," Lee insisted.

"You have a picture of me," Maury scoffed.

"Oh sure! Class of 1933! Rah! Rah! Rah!"

"Tell her, Rabbi. That's the way a man likes to be thought of. Young and handsome and full of pep," Maury teased.

"Rabbi, you be my witness," Lee countered. "Maury, when you get to camp promise you'll have a really good picture made for me. Promise!"

"Of course, he promises," Ellen said. She felt the underlying

158

current of fear and longing mounting under the casual words. She smiled at Lee, coaxing her back from the cascading fears.

And Maury seemed to know . . . and once again to be grateful.

"Rabbi, you and Ellen will have to take care of Lee. She's taken quite a liking to you," he said.

"Indeed we will. It will be our pleasure," Kurt assured him.

"Don't be silly, Maury. I'm a big girl now. I can take care of myself," Lee chided.

Briefly, Lee Kalman's eyes met those of her husband, and the glance seemed to demand too much of them both; and she turned her eyes away, back to Kurt, and she began talking to him in a babble of words that were about nothing at all.

Ellen's eyes lingered discerningly on Maury Kalman who watched his wife as if he had been drawn, already, beyond the point of reaching back to her. It occured to Ellen that in the parting of a husband and wife there is a dimension with undefined boundaries circumscribing the sensitivity of each to the spiritual existence of the other. And when there has been some special problem, this physical region is inhabited by some special poignance. Ellen had the awful feeling that Lee and Maury Kalman still would not talk of things that needed to be put into words; that now, under the terrible pressure of time, they would not discuss anything that could not be disposed of in half a dozen sentences.

Kurt had begun to speak to Maury about where his unit might be sent. And they spoke earnestly as one man to another and their faces were grave. Julian crept back into the room, and hung now against his father's knee.

Almost automatically Maury glanced at his watch and flicked on the radio for the newscast.

"Jap bombers . . . Luzon . . . war . . ."

Maury ran his fingers back through his hair. "The bastards. The dirty damn bastards!" he said, as if he could not help himself.

Julian Kalman watched his father with wide and questioning eyes. Some awesome excitement seemed to be communicated to him by the voice that moved out of the radio and into the room like a living presence.

"What's a baster?" Julian said. He began to jump up and down in a frenzy of excitement. "Baster! Baster!" he shouted in a shrill little voice.

Maury grabbed Julian up and held him. Julian kicked because he did not want to be held.

And Ellen saw that Lee Kalman wanted to reach out for her

child, that she wanted to snatch him away. Ellen saw that in Lee's innermost heart she thought of Julian as hers. And in Maury's fierce protective action it was obvious that in his innermost heart he thought of Julian as his. And Ellen felt for each of them the aloneness instead of the togetherness of this moment.

Kurt Rosen was invited to serve on the Advisory Committee, as Fall City prepared to set up its organization for Civic Defense, and he spent long hours conferring with civic leaders. Ellen Rosen was one of the first volunteers when an Emergency Red Cross Drive was announced. She spent one week sitting at an improvised booth in the post office, and the next week she took a district and went from house to house knocking on doors and asking for contributions.

Everywhere she was greeted by the stunned faces of people awakening from what had seemed to be a terrible nightmare to discover that it was painful reality. And there was always the odd little shock of seeing people doing usual, ordinary things with this look on their faces.

"Kurtchen, how could they have been so surprised . . . how could they?" Ellen asked again and again. "How did they imagine that it would never happen to them?"

And Kurt had no answer.

Ellen Rosen suffered in her soul, not only because Americans had not known, but that these wonderful light-hearted ones must come to know. With deep concern she searched their faces: on the bus, in the stores, on the street, when she knocked at their doors. The anguish that was new in these faces was old in her heart, and in a thousand small and futile ways—by the glance of eye or touch of hand or spoken word—she tried to draw from them into her own accustomed heart the pain of this anguish newly born. And she waited for them to know it fully.

This was war. . . . But war was at least a fighting back, a chance to fight back . . . a chance not to be taken. This, she waited for them to understand.

Knowing the precautions which must be taken by a nation at war, Kurt Rosen had much upon his mind what steps America might take to safeguard herself against the nationals of enemy countries within her borders. He did not mention his fears to Ellen, but he breathed a breath of profound relief when Congress amended the Alien Act, under which he and Ellen already were registered, only to the extent of requiring of enemy aliens that they obtain special permits for travel.

One morning, a week later, Kurt answered a knock at their door to discover Joe Friedman standing there nervously, a newspaper clipping in his hand.

"Mr. Friedman, good morning, come in!" Kurt said. "Ellen makes coffee. You drink with us."

"Rabbi, I think it is that I am in bad trouble," he whispered.

"What kind of trouble, Mr. Friedman?" Kurt asked soothingly.

Mr. Friedman held out the newspaper clipping which was about the treatment of enemy aliens.

"Rabbi, two years ago I should have registered as an alien. Now I am become an enemy alien, and still I am not registered. If I go now they ask why did I not come before?"

"That's true . . . they will ask it? Why did you not, Mr. Friedman?"

Mr. Friedman nibbled his mustache nervously. "I just didn't," he said like a stubborn child.

"Here, Mr. Friedman, drink the coffee I make for you. We come with you to talk to the man," Ellen interposed sympathetically. "Rabbi knows the man well. He makes it all right." Ellen was soothing the ruffled little old man; she smiled companionably at Kurt.

Kurt returned the smile knowingly. He was well aware that Ellen had recognized this as a moment for being stern with Mr. Friedman's lapse of responsibility; but with a woman's prerogative in such things, she had lifted the moment sweetly out of his hands.

"We come with you," he said resignedly. And he sat down with Mr. Friedman to drink the coffee.

When the three of them arrived an hour later at the Federal Courthouse, they found the clerk of the court preparing to begin a session of instruction for a citizenship class. Kurt was amazed to encounter in this room two more of his congregation who had lived in America well over thirty years and who, themselves, had applied for citizenship only when they were required to register as aliens the year before. There was Mrs. Stein who greeted them warmly, waving her fat arms and calling out to them across the room. And there was Mr. Benjamin, a fragile, little wraith of a man who stood numbly by a radiator that kept popping and thumping out vague alarms.

Kurt Rosen spoke briefly to the young court clerk whom he had made his enthusiastic friend at the time he and Ellen applied for their second citizenship papers. He explained about Mr. Friedman, who stood fidgeting to one side, until the clerk summoned him with the lift of a finger.

During the routine formalities Ellen had been watching Mr. Friedman, and some curious thing seemed to come over him as he scrutinized the "non-Americans" who filled the benches and chairs of the musty little courtroom. There was new starch in his step as he came forward to confront the clerk, and his gray fedora seemed not to sit so heavily upon his ears.

The clerk took down his name on a form sheet.

"Mr. Joseph Friedman. . . . You are not an American citizen?" the young clerk asked.

"I am," Mr. Friedman avowed heartily.

The clerk glanced up quizzically at Kurt and back to Mr. Friedman, as if he were prepared for anything at all.

"You have citizenship papers?" he inquired.

Mr. Friedman drew a determined breath. "I live in America thirty-eight years now. I love America. I raise three sons in America. I buy a cemetery plot in America from a young man who comes to collect seventy-five cents a week. In Poland, I belong to the *Hevra Kadisha,* the burial society, where Jews bury their own. In America I own a plot in the cemetery. Is the only land I have ever owned, but is in America."

Mr. Friedman's white mustache was beginning to quiver alarmingly. The young clerk leaned forward patiently.

Mrs. Stein, who was fond of exhibiting a certain disdain toward Joe Friedman, had, in spite of herself, crept closer and closer. Suddenly she was wildly partisan to his cause.

"Since when is paper making Americans?" she demanded to know from the young clerk.

An Austrian woman with red hands and a kerchief over her head, felt impelled now to enter the argument. She also moved closer, with expressive clickings of tongue. And a tall, stooped man, with a carpenter's level sticking out his overall pocket, stood near-by solemnly nodding his head. Joe Friedman was encouraged, but the clerk ignored the interruptions.

"But papers, Mr. Friedman, what about citizenship papers?" He said. "There is such a thing as citizenship. Didn't you ever want to vote?"

Mr. Friedman sighed, as if to cope with the crassness of youth was an impossible thing.

"Young man," he said, "I am a simple man. Do I know who is

good, who is bad? Am I acquainted with Mr. Roosevelt? Did I have the pleasure with Mr. Wilkie? I pay only my taxes so the good government is running. Can I do more?"

"But no papers?" the clerk persisted.

"My heart is American. Nowhere on paper am I American," Mr. Friedman finally admitted.

The clerk turned to Kurt imploringly. The situation was about to get out of hand, the tides of patriotism were threatening him. He glanced back at all the reproachful faces that were turned to him.

Kurt stepped quietly to Joe Friedman's side. His eyes moved also from face to face.

"That we come here today is only another proof of how wonderful America is," he told them. "It is proof that America is strong enough, and good enough, and big enough in spirit, to see how unfair it would be to intern those very ones who have reason to love her most. There is only a card to sign. There are no internment camps waiting."

The big carpenter swallowed and his Adam's apple moved up and down. Mrs. Stein sighed and the little Austrian woman moved quietly back to her seat.

Now the grateful clerk began to ask Joe Friedman the routine questions; and Mr. Friedman, his show of spirits spent, answered meekly. He nibbled his mustache miserably as he was finger-printed, and his shoulders hunched together, and his grey fedora seemed to slip down again against his ears. To him, finger-printing was a mark of shame that put him on a par with criminals . . . with men who robbed gas stations and stole from banks.

When the clerk handed him the little card, he turned away numbly and looked for Kurt and Ellen. Kurt moved in front of them briskly, vigorously illustrating the proper way to feel about the whole thing. But Ellen laid a hand on Joe Friedman's arm. She understood how he felt. Outside on the street . . . even in these very corridors . . . was America, and in her pocket also, a card that bore her name was stamped "Enemy Alien!"

The afternoon paper quoted a remark that Kurt Rosen had made to a young reporter who sat beside him while he waited for Mr. Friedman.

"Rabbi Kurt Rosen, refugee from Nazi Germany, pointed out the greatness of the American Congress in recognizing the inhumanity of an Enemy Alien Act that would intern the victims of persecution with their persecutors. He hailed as a shining example of American justice the new policy toward enemy aliens which, for the first time in history, allows nationals of enemy nations to maintain their freedom in a country at war."

Sam Levinson read this account on the front page of his afternoon newspaper before he left the office. He also had been treated to a full account of Joe Friedman's appearance before the Federal clerk earlier in the day. When he got into his car to drive home he was in a rare temper. And as he blustered into his own house, Myra's cool imperturbability only angered him further. He picked up the copy of the paper on the living room couch, and threw it down again.

"I guess you saw, your friend the rabbi has blossomed into print again!" he said.

Myra gathered up the paper and folded it and laid it on the table. She did not reply.

Sam started pacing, up and down, pausing to light a cigarette, and, on his return, to straighten the cigarette box on the lacquered table.

"Can't you sit down!"

At this remark, Sam turned on his wife indignantly. He did sit down, with the weary movement of a man tried beyond endurance.

"You think I'm unreasonable," he accused. "Try to consider this . . . how it would sound . . . to read in the paper that the First Methodist Church welcomed their enemy alien minister! Can you imagine any church in town letting themselves be faced with a situation like that?"

"Sam . . . Really!"

"I mean it! Here they've got us saddled with a German Jew. And everybody knows goddam well that there's nobody so German as a German Jew. Their *Kultur* . . . a hell of a lot of good it's doing them now!"

"Maybe it's doing them more good than you know!" Myra countered.

Sam ignored her. "It makes me sick!" he said. "They say 'I'm a German Jew' like they might say 'I'm a Jesus Christ!' . . . and I for one am just about as much impressed."

Myra got up, stretched, as if she were bored with the conversation, "I must say you're in a very nasty mood," she commented.

"Don't try to act so goddam sophisticated," Sam flung back at her. "If you don't care how we look in the eyes of the rest of

164

the community, I care. And you could damn well care too. You've got a son coming along, you know. You've already had a little idea of that."

Myra's head was flung up. Her face paled, and she did not speak. Her husband could not quite look at her. His voice sought now to placate her without abandoning his stand.

"Look, Myra," he said reasonably, "all I'm saying is this—once a German Jew always a German Jew. Their war isn't against Germany. It's only against Hitler. They're as much German as they ever were. So what does that make us?"

"Shut up, Sam! That doesn't sound good coming from you! How can you identify the persecuted with the persecutors!"

"Oh, so you did read the paper, after all. Quote . . . Rabbi Rosen!" A sardonic smile just reached Sam Levinson's eyes, now unrelentingly on his wife.

Without another word, she turned her back on him and started angrily from the room. And in that instant they both became aware of Davey standing in the doorway, his young face white with the look of having been there all along. He saw his mother coming, and he turned around and ran to his room.

Myra glanced back over her shoulder at her husband standing in the center of the room, his arms hung limply at his sides. She did not know what to do; she fought against waiting for him to tell her.

The next afternoon, Davey Levinson started out from school for the synagogue for his twice-weekly Hebrew lesson. He dangled his books at the end of a leather strap, swinging them expertly so they didn't slip out. He walked very slowly, and he kept kidding himself that at some corner he would turn in a different direction, and not go to his Hebrew lesson after all. There was some illusive margin of safety in the feeling that if, at the last minute, he simply could not face up to the lesson, then he did not have to go.

Davey passed the suburban fire station and the fireman's pet dog came out and barked at him as usual. He passed Danny Newman's house, and there was only one block left to go. Davey was thinking of the rabbi. The love and admiration and respect that he felt for Kurt Rosen had become difficult things for Davey to contain in himself—because they could not quite fit in the aching hollow that had contained the love and admiration and respect he could no longer feel for his own father. Sam

Levinson had been the sort of father who inspires a young son's ardent hero worship, but Davey had not been able to ignore or explain away his father's vicious and petty attacks against the rabbi. And sometimes, in a strange hurtful way, Davey almost hated the rabbi for being the cause of bringing this littleness and pettiness to light.

Davey came to the synagogue. He climbed the outside stairs and tried the door. It was locked; the rabbi was not yet there. Davey sat down on the top step, he sat with his chin in the palm of his hand. He sat there, thinking very hard.

Davey did not see Kurt as he got off the bus and hurried across the yard. He saw him first as he started up the stairway.

"Hello, Davey. Sorry to be late," Kurt said, smiling. "Were you thinking so hard about your Hebrew lesson?"

"No sir," Davey said, picking up his books. "I was thinking about something else."

"Well, then you'd best switch over to thinking about the Hebrew right away, we're getting a late start," Kurt said, unlocking the door of the Temple.

"Rabbi, I don't think I'm coming any more. I don't think I want to be confirmed," Davey blurted out.

Kurt was walking ahead of Davey, down the aisle to his study. And he did not glance back at the boy who followed his footsteps.

"We'll talk about that, Davey," Kurt said. He was aware of Davey's excruciating embarrassment over his father's attitude, and the last weeks had not been easy for either teacher or pupil. Often Davey had been withdrawn and uncommunicative and sometimes he had failed to come to class altogether. But Kurt could not forget the yearning that was beneath the sullenness, or the eagerness that was beneath the restraint.

"Sit down, Davey," Kurt said. "Now, why do you not want to be confirmed?"

Davey didn't look at Kurt Rosen. "Well . . ." he said hesitantly, "there's a war on and things like Hebrew lessons just don't seem very important, that's all!"

"Davey, when men must fight for what they believe, it is very important that they know what they believe," Kurt answered quietly. Davey still did not look at him. "Is there something else that troubles you," Kurt asked.

"Well, I just don't . . . I just can't see why you'd even want me to be confirmed!" Davey said. Something almost twisted in the boy's face—almost, but not quite.

166

"But I do want you to, Davey," Kurt said. "I want you to be very much."

They sat for a moment looking at each other. And Davey Levinson was able to ease his heart of a little of what troubled him, without actually putting it into words. And Kurt Rosen was wondering how he could help this boy to feel a sense of his own identity and his own obligation to himself apart from anyone else, even his parents, without discrediting them.

"Davey," Kurt said, "did you know that in Hebrew, the language in which our Holy Sriptures were written, there is no word with the exact meaning of 'sin'—the Hebrew word most often used for 'sin' means 'Missing the mark'—understanding what your heritage requires of you, and then not doing it."

"But what about the way some other people act? . . . it's their heritage, too," Davey countered stubbornly.

"Yes, it's their heritage, too, Davey," Kurt replied, "But people must understand a thing, their own relations to it, before they can know that they have failed it."—Kurt was thinking of the way that young Davey's mind leapt to a new concept, of the way his mind turned an idea carefully, savoring its quality, comprehending its nuances. In unfolding the concepts of Judaism for Davey, Kurt had seen that this boy was capable of making these concepts a means of self-discovery, that he would be capable of expanding them into a means of self-evaluation.

Davey wasn't looking at the rabbi, he was trying to press the eraser out of the top of a pencil with his thumb.

"I don't see how I could understand better than . . . well, better than people who are grown," Davey insisted.

"Davey, many people have worked hard all their lives and have never had the time or the chance that you have to reach an understanding. You, Davey, must be responsible to the limit of your own understanding, not anybody else's."

Davey still played with the pencil.

"Shall we begin now?" Kurt asked him.

Davey reached for his book without looking up, he opened it to his lesson for the day.

"I read it first to you in English," Kurt said of the psalm that Davey was learning in Hebrew. And Kurt Rosen began to read:

> Behold how good and how pleasant it is for brethren to
>   dwell together in unity.
> For these the Lord commanded the blessing, even life for
>   ever.

Except the Lord build the house, they labor in vain that
    built it.

Except the Lord keep the city, the watchman waketh but
    in vain.

Better is a dry morsel and quietness therewith, than a house
    full of feasting with strife.

Better is little with the fear of the Lord, than great treasure
    and turmoil therewith.

Lord, my heart is not haughty, nor mine eyes lofty; neither
    do I exercise myself in things too great, or in things too
    wonderful for me.

I wait for the Lord, my soul doth wait, and in His word do
    I hope.

My soul waiteth for the Lord, more than the watchman for
    the morning . . .

Chapter 15

THE WINTER darkness had come stealthily and soon and now was pressed black against the windows of the Temple as the time neared for the Friday night services to begin. Mr. Jacobson, feeling even more crochety than usual, stepped in from the cold darkness, exchanged his hat for a *yarmulka* and took a seat near the back of the sanctuary. He thumbed through his prayer book and tunelessly hummed a Hebrew melody.

At ten minutes to eight, Ellen Rosen came through the door of the rabbi's study and, when she saw Mr. Jacobson, a look of welcome and pleasure kindled in her face. She came to him and shook hands. She asked about his rheumatism, about his daughter, Gussie, in Kansas City, and she chided him for not wearing a scarf against the winter cold.

When Ellen went to stand beside the door to welcome the congregants who were now assembling, Mr. Jacobson continued to watch her out of the corner of his eye. He hummed a little louder because he knew she would recognize what he was humming. He was thinking how much heart it is possible to put into a thing without anybody else seeming to know or care. Only Ellen Rosen had ever seemed to understand what an ache of long abandoned hope was borne, still, in the tuneless humming. And sometimes, when Ellen Rosen sang, he thought of his youth in far-off, icy Latvia and of how he had longed to be a cantor.

When Rabbi Rosen began the service, Mr. Jacobson continued to hum, more quietly now, and only intermittently, as he waited for his spirit to be touched. And it was drawn, irresistibly, by the voice that spoke resoundingly, but with a quiet profundity, a quiet solemnity, a quiet, almost inaudible, compassion. Little by little, Mr. Jacobson lent his spirit to this moment, little by little he released his spirit to it.

Finally, still and silent, he listened to the voice that read:

> *Grant that we lie down in peace,*
> *Secure in thy protecting love,*
> *And shelter us beneath thy wings*

To keep us safe throughout the night.
On the morrow raise us up
In perfect peace to life, O God,
To face each task with faith in Thee,
Our zeal renewed and strength restored.
Save us for Thine own name's sake
And guard us from all lurking foes.
Remove all sorrow, hatred, strife,
And turn thy children's hearts to Thee.
Spread thy tent of peace, O Lord,
Above Jerusalem we pray.
And shield thy people Israel
Dispersed abroad in every land.
Praised be Thou, our Lord and King,
Whose sheltering love spreads over us,
Enfolding all who seek Thy peace,
Who find their hope and Strength in Thee . . . Amen. . . .

Amen! . . . As these syllables escaped his own lips . . . a long, lonely and audible sigh . . . old Mr. Jacobson realized how far into the limitless, boundaryless plains of eternity he had been drawn by Kurt Rosen's reading of this prayer . . . how far away from the now of black headlines at the supper table . . . and the ache of Jewish hearts in the still of night. It took a special kind of courage to read that prayer, Mr. Jacobson was thinking, a kind of courage that such people as Sam Levinson wouldn't know anything about. "And shield thy people Israel, dispersed abroad in every land. . . ." What would Sam Levinson know about that. Mr. Jacobson let his eyes seek out Sam Levinson, who, sure enough, was nodding in his seat.

During the silent prayer, Mr. Jacobson began to hum again; it was the only way he could even begin to keep his mind off Sam Levinson's outrageous behavior. He even began to sway back and forth. He gave the impression of a man deep in his prayers. But in spite of himself he was thinking of people . . . he was wondering if it is ever possible for people to make up to each other for unkindness unfairly suffered. It was an interesting thought; it seemed to have implications as far reaching as the prayer he was reading. And when he sat down again he was in the grip of a furious urge to do something for the Rosens to make up for Sam Levinson. Something, but what?

While he was grappling with this question, Ellen Rosen began to sing. He did not turn his head; he only listened with his heart. And he hardly breathed, lest his breath quiver in the air upon which these magnificent tones moved out. He was swept back by a nostalgia too great. In her singing were captured all of the inestimable sadness, all of the inestimable courage. For a man to have courage was one thing; for a woman, it was something else. Suddenly, as the last clear note throbbed and lingered in the air, old Mr. Jacobson knew what he would do.

Monday morning Ellen brought in the mail and sat down with Kurt to open it before he went to the Temple. She handed him the envelope with the hardly legible scrawl. He tore it open, and to Ellen he read aloud:

> *Dear Rabbi Rosen, For a long time now I have wanted to give a gift to the Temple in honor of my late wife. Last night it came to me that I would like to give an organ. I ask only that you entrust the Rebbitzen with the job of picking it out. Most sincerely,*
> *Mr. Isador Jacobson.*

For an instant Kurt and Ellen looked at each other in complete amazement.

"An organ . . . Kurt, how wonderful!" The hint of an old bright joy flickered in Ellen's eyes, its shadow moved exquisitely in her solemn face. "Kurt, whatever do you suppose made him do it!"

Kurt almost smiled. "I think, *Liebchen*, that your voice made him do it," he said wrily.

"Oh, You!"

"Ellen . . . don't be too glad . . . yet," Kurt said tentatively.

Ellen sighed. She picked up the letter, glanced at it, put it down again. "I know," she said, "the orthodox members won't like it."

"Sweetheart . . . after all . . . the unity of the congregation is more important than an organ. Maybe we'll have it. I hope we'll have it. But it isn't something we can count on."

"I know." She opened the next letter in the stack of mail, which was a solicitation for funds; and the next letter which was an invitation for Kurt to lecture. She handed it to him, and she noticed then that he was sitting there without moving, an oddly attentive and bemused expression on his face.

"Kurtchen, what is?" Ellen asked him curiously.

"Nothing."

Her perceptive eyes studied his face for a moment, noting the taut line of his lips, the keenness in his gray eyes.

"You think there'll be trouble . . . and you act almost as if you are glad," she chided him.

Kurt laughed. "At least they'll become a little more aware of their heritage . . . if they have to argue about it!" Kurt told her, still laughing. And when he got up from the table and walked across the room there was the vigor of anticipation in his step.

Ellen shook her head. In her eyes was the look of fond and weary indulgence. She threw away the envelopes and gathered up the letters. The one from Mr. Jacobson, she saved for the scrapbook.

When Kurt had gone, Ellen thought about the organ with a sense, almost, of having been betrayed by her first wild impulse of happiness. With an odd little emptiness she thought of Kurt's excitement that was so separate from the organ itself. And she could almost have wept, not for the organ, but for this poignant insight into how eagerly Kurt welcomed even the thunder that might conceivably bring the rain that would raise for his careful tending the first bloom in a great and trackless spiritual desert.

The first hint of conflict came from the source that Kurt least expected, and from one that doubtless would have amazed Mr. Jacobson.

On Monday morning Sam Levinson paid a visit to the rabbi in his study. He came in with the thought of his last visit already rankling in his mind. He took the chair Kurt offered him, fidgeted irritably while Kurt answered the telephone and solicitously recommended rest in bed for Susie Finegold's cold. As soon as this conversation was concluded and Kurt had apologized for the delay, Sam Levinson stated his business abruptly.

"Rabbi, I hear Mr. Jacobson wants to give an organ to the Temple. I think you ought to persuade him to give new seats for the sanctuary . . . or a new air conditioner, instead."

"Are you personally against the organ, Mr. Levinson?" Kurt inquired.

"I am."

"Mr. Levinson, I was under the impression that you considered yourself reform."

Sam Levinson fidgeted; he had the vague, angry feeling that he had come poorly prepared. "In most things I am," he agreed.

"You are aware, of course, that all reform congregations and many conservative congregations do have an organ?"

Suddenly Sam Levinson retreated into an old tactic. Leaning forward a little, he interlocked his stodgy, well-manicured hands together determinedly. "Rabbi, that may be. But if we here in Fall City want to adhere a little more closely to our Jewish tradition, surely that is our privilege."

Kurt Rosen had not actually applied himself to the question of music in the synagogue since his student days, but as he sat now, looking into Sam Levinson's faintly mocking face, he thought of how many men of sincerity and integrity had grappled with this problem honestly. To these men the question had been vital and alive with imagination and the thirst for understanding. And suddenly Kurt Rosen felt a hardly-to-be-contained anger at Sam Levinson's preposterous falseness.

"Mr. Levinson," Kurt said, "I am well aware of the intricacy of the question we face, and of the many shades of feeling which may honestly be held regarding it. I was prepared that in our congregation opinion would be sharply divided. I will admit, however, that I am surprised to find you among those who oppose the organ."

Sam Levinson felt oddly rebuked. The experience was galling to him. "Well, I do oppose it!" he said huffily. "We are all aware of Mrs. Rosen's fine voice, and of Mr. Jacobson's appreciation of Mrs. Rosen's fine voice. But, after all, this is a synagogue!"

"It is, indeed," Kurt answered with dignity. He stood up to indicate that the interview was over.

Sam Levinson sensed that he had gone too far. "Look, Rabbi," he said, his tone almost obsequious. "All I'm saying is that whether or not we have an organ is a question for the congregation, not for Mr. Jacobson, to decide."

"The congregation will be consulted . . . before I accept Mr. Jacobson's offer," Kurt assured him. He did not extend his hand. Sam Levinson glanced at his watch.

"That's fine, Rabbi. That's fine!" he said. He was suddenly consumed with the urgency of his business elsewhere. The synagogue door banged loudly as he let himself out.

The late afternoon sunlight lay in bright swatches on the kitchen table, as Kurt, eating an early supper, told Ellen about his conversation with Sam Levinson. He spoke as off-handedly as he could, studiously buttering a roll all the while.

"Kurt, it isn't fair. He makes trouble only because he doesn't like us," Ellen answered.

"That's true."

"He's a fine one to complain. Nothing is reform enough.

Nothing is liberal enough. And now he doesn't want an organ!"

"Right again. And nothing is so contemptible as a man who falsely uses religious principle to cover up personal antagonisms. But Ellen . . ." Kurt waited until her eyes, a little reluctantly, met his, "Ellen, however that may be, we both know that he raises a legitimate question. And it must be debated."

"Kurt," Ellen said thoughtfully, "when you came here, you thought it was such a challenge—to bring reform and conservative and orthodox Jews all together under one roof. And now this comes up to cause trouble. Even to me an organ isn't worth it."

"Ellen, when I'd been here only a little while I discovered another challenge even greater than bringing everyone together under one roof."

"What is that?"

"Ellen, we've been in their homes. We've lived with them for months now. Can you see much difference in the day-by-day lives of those who insist that they're orthodox and those who call themselves reform?"

Ellen shook her head. She seemed a little less than attentive, and in her face was a wistfulness that Kurt knew he must somehow resist. He covered her hand with his own where it lay, palm down, on the table. He knew that somehow he must make her understand.

"Ellen, the real challenge is to awaken some essence of true religious perception in them all. You can't feel that you've accomplished much in achieving 'unity' if unity is just indifference. Now a situation has been created in which they must actually . . . grapple . . . with a problem that concerns preserving their heritage. This is the first opportunity really to achieve unity."

"Kurtchen," Ellen had almost begun to smile. "I am not so much a philosopher," she said. Suddenly she laughed, only a small little laugh, but it was genuine and warm.

"Why do you laugh?" he asked.

"I was thinking . . . if you hadn't just happened to stop by a music studio in Koenigsberg that day . . . I might have had all the organs in the world. And you might have had all the problems to yourself!"

Her eyes were teasing him, the more so when she saw by the faintly quizzical look on his face that with typical male ego, he considered the possibility of regrets on her part hardly worthy of a moment's dalliance.

"Kurtchen," she said wrily, "sometimes I think I am not cut out to be a *rebbitzen*. But if you feel you must achieve unity at the expense of my organ, you go right ahead."

Kurt looked at her closely; he saw that she made it all right to smile. He came around the table and kissed her soundly.

"You are a naughty girl!" he said.

The next day had not passed before Kurt had heard a great deal of discussion concerning Mr. Jacobson's gift of an organ to the Temple. There was, Kurt noted with regret, a quality of gloating in the enthusiasm expressed by reform members of the congregation, who kept his telephone ringing with congratulations most of the day.

By late afternoon Kurt decided that the time had come for action. After making a call on Mr. Jacobson and explaining the situation to him, Kurt telephoned the four most orthodox members of the congregation and asked that they meet him in his study that evening.

A little after eight the four gathered, and Kurt seated them in folding chairs around his desk in the small study. There were Joe Friedman and old Mr. Benjamin. There was Asa Weber, a self-made millionaire whose favority story began, "When I got off the boat, I had but seventy-five cents in my pocket. . . ." And there was Harry Greenglass, a graying, impassive man, who sighed occasionally with a monstrous boredom.

Kurt felt in the air something forbidding and hostile, as if he had already come out in favor of the organ. He searched his mind hurriedly for some anecdote to clear the air and at the same time to set the stage for them.

"Gentlemen, in our congregation here we have a great many different kinds of Jews . . . and I for one am glad . . . it only illustrates how blessed we are with a freedom of choice."

Kurt hesitated over the last words so that their silent echo might penetrate reluctant ears. Then he began, slowly, to smile. "Did I ever tell you anything about the history of my former congregation? It is very interesting. When the Duke of Rarensburg conquered Duisburg, he allowed for the first time that Jews settle there . . . but it was his whim that, aside from their rabbi and the employees of the congregation, only Jews who were butchers might live in Duisburg. When my predecessor took office in 1904, there were ninety Jewish butchers in town. When I came in 1927, there still were forty Jewish butchers. But by that time, there were professional men and industrialists and merchants as well. And the Jewish butchers were the first to welcome the variety." Kurt's eyes were twinkling as he finished, and he searched face after face to see who might have followed his trend of thought. Then, suddenly turning aside, as if the story had been a mere irrelevance, he said:

"I am sure that all of you are aware that Mr. Jacobson wishes to give an organ to the synagogue."

The protesting voices lept up to him in unison, and Kurt held up his hands for order. "Gentlemen, one at a time, please. Each will be heard. Mr. Weber, what is your feeling?"

Mr. Weber sat back in his chair. He spoke softly, smiling a little. "Rabbi, I give much money to the Temple. It is not so rich a Temple it could do without this money."

"You mean, Mr. Weber, you would withdraw your support if the organ were placed in the synagogue?"

"Rabbi, you are a man of principle. Could I belong to a synagogue that departed from my beliefs?"

Mr. Weber seemed stubbornly unconvinced. Kurt smiled a little, he said:

"Our great teacher Hillel tells us 'Separate not yourself from the congregation.' . . . An example was given us by Moses. When the Israelites made the Golden Calf, Moses was asked by God to separate himself from them so that they might be destroyed. But Moses refused. He remained faithful to his people. . . . Surely, Mr. Weber, you will agree that having an organ is not such a crime as turning to pagan worship immediately after the Revelation at Sinai?"

The subtleties of Kurt's reproach vaguely disturbed Mr. Weber and he seemed to be trying to grasp them. Kurt turned quickly to Mr. Greenglass, sparing Mr. Weber the embarrassment of a rebuttal.

"And Mr. Greenglass, how do you feel on the subject of the organ?" he inquired amiably.

Mr. Greenglass shrugged, sighed one of his bored sighs. "Rabbi, I am an orthodox man; I come of an orthodox family. Do you want that I take off my hat? Do you want that I eat *traif*? Is there a place to begin, a place to stop? An organ, yet, in the synagogue!"

"Mr. Greenglass," Kurt said, "it is a wise question you ask . . . where is a place to begin and where is a place to stop. But when you balk at the organ, I like only to show you that you choose arbitrarily a place to stop. The place to begin you yourself chose long ago."

176

Mr. Greenglass was leaning forward to protest, but Kurt held up his hand for silence.

"Mr. Greenglass, do you not go to business on Saturday? Do you not ride on the *Shabbas*. And you keep *kosher* at home, Mr. Greenglass, but it is not a vegetable plate I see you eating at the Grill for lunch."

Mr. Greenglass was beginning to splutter self-righteously. "Rabbi, am I worse than others? A man has to adapt himself . . ."

"True! I want only to show you one thing. There are deeper reasons for adapting than a man's own personal convenience. Mr. Greenglass, when your father died, you were concerned over how long you should let your beard grow and whether you should burn candles seven days or thirty days. . . . But in the first week you asked that the time of a *minyan* be changed so that you could attend a wrestling match. Is it not so?"

Mr. Greenglass sighed again. "My father, I had not seen since I was a lad of twelve. I no longer knew him," he said, his apology a flat and lifeless thing in the air.

Kurt hesitated. "I bring up these matters not to embarrass you. I do not say that to have the organ is right or wrong. I say only that the time has come for us to examine our religious motives. How much is sentiment? . . . How much is habit? . . . How much is genuine? . . . Mr. Friedman, what would you like to say about the organ?"

Joe Friedman stood up as if he had been called upon in school. "Rabbi," he said, "Is true everything you say. But I am not so big a man and I don't understand it. I care nothing for the reform members. To me they are as the *goyim*. One thing only I care about, one thing only makes me sad . . . and that is the *rebbitzen*. For her I would build an organ with my own two hands. But with me is a matter of a long time. In the Talmud it says that we must grieve without music for the Temple that was destroyed in Jerusalem. . . . Benny Gold says to me 'Is not two thousand years long enough to grieve?' . . . but maybe is not. . . . It says in the psalms, 'A thousand years in Thy sight are but as a day that is past, and as a watch in the night.' . . . Perhaps it is only that we too much hurry God."

There was an odd little silence as Joe Friedman finished speaking. He sat down suddenly, and his mustache seemed to go all awry with the nervous twitching of his lips. His eyes had the blurry look of unshed tears. And he was ashamed.

"Mr. Friedman," Kurt said quietly, "I think you have said what these other gentlemen wish they had said. I, for one, thank you. . . . And now, Mr. Benjamin, is there something you would add?" Kurt asked, turning to the little wraith of a man who had listened to them all without murmuring.

"With me is the same as with Mr. Friedman . . . but that I don't speak it so well," he said shyly.

Kurt nodded his head. "Gentlemen," he said, "I will present your views at a meeting of the board, which you yourselves are invited to attend if you wish. When all is said and done, I am sure that we will abide by the decision of the majority . . . and now, thank you for coming tonight."

When the four men had departed, Kurt sat alone at his desk. The conversations of the evening had confronted him with a deep perplexity. Ringing in his thoughts were the simple, almost anguished words of Joe Friedman, "One thing only makes me sad . . . and that is the *rebbitzen!*"

Feeling so keenly his responsibility as the spiritual leader of a group of people, Kurt had determinedly refused to consider the matter of the organ in personal terms. And now, although he might not allow himself to be swayed by these considerations, he knew that he could outdistance them no longer. And sitting alone at his desk he allowed himself to reexperience those first moments Mr. Jacobson's letter had come.

Now, in retrospect, he let himself see with the heart's own eyes the look of joy and quick bright happiness that had come to Ellen's face as he read her the letter. And now, he allowed to penetrate his consciousness that special quality of rapture that had first . . . so long ago . . . baffled and intrigued and challenged and inspired him. He remembered the first time he had ever seen Ellen, standing beside a magnificent piano with that special taut stillness of the vibrantly alive, while the very blackness of her hair and eyes seemed to reproach the wooing brilliance of the sun that flooded the window behind her and laid a glow upon her skin. . . . He remembered the shy wantonness, the hint of bright ecstasy that came into Ellen's eyes on a day they stood on top of the old fortifications and looked out to the sea. . . . He remembered the day that she had sat upon the sand and watched the seagulls and said to him, finally, "But Kurt, to be religious enough to be a rabbi . . . it's as if it would hold you tight . . . it's as if it wouldn't let you go at all . . . not to run on the sand and chase that wild, bright feeling."

And what had he answered . . . Kurt tried to remember . . . "The hunger of the spirit is in all the joy you know."

Kurt sighed and began to set his desk straight. With the organ, as with so many things, it seemed, the idealistic and the human were hopelessly pitted against each other. Kurt thought of Ellen, of what the organ would mean to her in human, loving terms. And he tried to consider what would be violated, both theoretically and actually, in allowing the organ to take its place in the synagogue. Kurt knew that, having heard strong opinions expressed by both factions, he could neither accept nor reject the organ on his own. But he knew that he must, in his own heart at least, know where he stood.

As he sat, deep in thought, Kurt heard the door of the sanctuary swing shut again, and he glanced through the doorway of his study to see Ellen coming toward him, her coat hugged around her, a scarf tying back her hair.

"Kurt!"

"Here . . . Sweetheart!"

Kurt saw that Ellen's color was high from the outside cold as she came into the warmth and brightness of the tiny study.

"Kurtchen, I saw the others leave . . . so long ago. What was?"

"Just as you might expect," he told her.

"They won't have the organ."

"You can hardly say that . . ." Kurt told her, smiling. "They don't want the organ."

"Then don't have it," Ellen said wearily, not quite looking at Kurt.

"It isn't so easy as that. The reform members are just as determined that we shall have it." The wryness of Kurt's answer coaxed her to smile; she did, a little.

"Kurtchen, all over the world people are dying for such little things . . . and for such big things . . . and we make a big *tsimas* over an organ."

Kurt was no longer smiling. "It is not always possible to tell which are the little things," he said.

Kurt called the board meeting for the following night. He asked Mr. Jacobson to come a little earlier, and they sat down together on two of the straight chairs in the vestry before the others began to arrive.

Mr. Jacobson sat there, pyramiding his fingers thoughtfully, blinking his eyes.

"Mr. Jacobson," Kurt said. "One thing I want you to know . . . how much Ellen and I appreciate what you've wanted to do."

"I know that, Rabbi. I think we understand each other," Mr. Jacobson said.

Old Mr. Jacobson said "Rabbi" as if he were addressing himself with respect to a title nobly worn through the centuries. But as Kurt looked into Mr. Jacobson's deeply lined face, fleetingly, he saw his true self reflected in the thoughtful gray eyes. And he was startled when he saw there, not the personage or rabbinical dignity whom Mr. Jacobson seemed to be addressing, but the reflection of a young man who is striving valiantly along ways that have found approval in a wise old heart. Realizing, suddenly, how tired he was, Kurt felt this brief insight easing, a little, the loneliness of responsibility, transforming it once again from a burden to a challenge.

"I have felt all along that we understand each other," Kurt answered, and the depth of his gratitude was mellow in his voice.

Mr. Jacobson sensed Kurt's gratitude. "Rabbi," he said, "you are the leader. It's up to you to keep the unity. I made the gift. You accepted it. Between us it is the same even if the organ never leaves the factory. Now, here the others are coming."

The door was thrust open, and Benny Gold and Herman Morris came blustering in out of the cold. Benny stood stamping his feet on the floor, and Herman rubbed his hands together.

"Too cold out for man or beast," Benny complained.

"This night they'll all be here, wait and see," Mr. Jacobson predicted.

"Mr. Jake . . . it's pretty swell about the organ," Benny said.

Mr. Jacobson smiled.

The door opened again and Sam Levinson came in. Close on his heels were Dr. Ben Klein and Sol Lewis, the jeweler. Within the next ten minutes the last three members had reported, and Kurt called the meeting to order.

"Gentlemen," Kurt said, "I have called a special meeting of the board to consider a question of importance. As all of you know, our good friend, Mr. Isador Jacobson, has very generously offered to donate an organ to our synagogue. However, as we are all shades of Judaism worshipping together under one roof, we must have the approval of the board before accepting this fine offer. Mr. Jacobson, being one of our most steadfast members, heartily agrees, and he will not be offended by those of you who do not agree that we should have an organ. And so now, I would like to hear discussion."

This invitation was greeted by a babel of voices, and Benny

Gold went and got the gavel that belonged to the B'nai Brith and banged for order. Having restored a moderate quiet, he seemed to consider it his privilege to speak.

"I say there's not even any question," he croaked in his raspy voice. "We oughta be giving hurrahs for Mr. Jake. Liven up the service a little bit . . . an organ!"

For Benny this had been a major speech, he sat down grinning.

Old Mr. Jacobson regarded Benny with a smile. He looked slowly around the table from face to face, and it was Sam Levinson who spoke next.

His face was sardonic, his fingers drummed briskly on the table. "Mr. Gold is right, but only in that there is NO question," he said blandly. "Regardless of how individual members consider themselves, this is not a reform congregation. And there's no place in our synagogue for an organ."

Old man Jacobson's face blanched, Benny Gold's face reddened. And Herman Morris abruptly stopped doodling. All of this Sam Levinson saw. It gave him a sense of power.

And in that interval, when the whole question was momentarily thrown off balance, Asa Weber and Harry Greenglass came in. Ponderously they took off their heavy coats, and they drew chairs to the circle and sat down.

By this time Benny Gold had recovered. "Since when are you so orthodox?" Benny demanded in his raspy voice.

"What I personally do is of no concern here . . . any more than what you personally do is of concern here," Sam Levinson replied with broad insinuation. "The question concerns the congregation. We started out as an orthodox congregation."

"Well, we're not an orthodox congregation anymore! There are three times as many reform members. Just take a count." Benny shouted.

"Then why did we hire a conservative rabbi?" Sam Levinson demanded.

Kurt took the gavel that Benny had brought and rapped for order.

"Gentlemen," Kurt said, "We have worked hard to achieve cooperation and we must maintain it. Here we are few, and disunity which caused our congregation to fall apart would deprive all of us of a chance to worship together. I have just one request to make—that we discuss this question without anger or stubbornness on either side. Now, let's proceed."

Sam Levinson sat down. Mr. Weber and Mr. Greenglass were grinning broadly.

"Dr. Klein, what is your opinion," Kurt asked.

The doctor was a mellow, dispassionate man. He shrugged his shoulders slightly, smiling at the rancor of his fellow board members.

"Rabbi, how would it be if we had the organ for Friday night services. And not for the high holidays?" he asked.

"Yeah, why not?" Benny was ready to concede.

"That's a good idea," Herman Morris called out.

Kurt shook his head. "It seems there are only liberal rabbis and no liberal Jews," he said indulgently. "If you agree to that you are sentimentally orthodox. The question is not decided in such a way, it is merely evaded."

"Rabbi's right. It's all the way or not at all." It was Sol Lewis, the jeweler, who spoke.

"No organ!" Mr. Weber felt called upon to declare.

"Look who's so orthodox . . . that goes to the movies on Friday night!" Benny whispered, loudly.

"After all," Sol Lewis continued, "We read always in the prayer book about worshipping God in the beauty of holiness. Well, if an organ isn't the beauty of holiness, what is?"

Sam Levinson let his glance rest momentarily upon old man Jacobson who was eyeing him grimly. "We didn't come here to discuss the merits of organ music. We came here to discuss the merits of Jews," Sam replied with maddening sarcasm.

And once again the house was in uproar.

"Look, Sam, cool off!" It was Dr. Ben Klein who spoke. "Rabbi's right. Here we are few and we have only to do the best we can. A boy baby is born and there's no *mohel*. So a Jewish doctor does the circumcision, and a plain rabbi reads the prayers. Are the orthodox members of the congregation going to complain that he isn't as good a Jew as the next one? We simply have to do the best we can."

Once more Sam Levinson smiled sardonically. "It's true," he sadi. "We have to compromise where necessity is concerned. But that doesn't give us license to compromise for the sake of pleasure . . . for the sake of livening up the service . . . as Benny says. We are Jews, and as Jews we have been given certain rules to follow. If we don't always follow them in private life . . . at least we can follow them in the synagogue."

Ben Klein turned from Sam Levinson to the rabbi. "Rabbi, I'm like a lot of the fellows here, if they'd admit it. I don't know as much as I ought to. Actually, what's all the fuss about an organ? Is there anything in the Bible against it?"

"No, the organ was unknown in biblical times. In Psalm 150 we are told of the many instruments that were used in the Temple service. The orthodox basis for rejecting the organ is a passage in the Talmud describing how we must mourn for the destroyed Temple in Jerusalem. But such modern rabbinic authorities as Rabbi Aaron Chorin, Rabbi of Arad at the beginning of the 19th century, Moses Kunitz of Ofen, who was born in 1818, and two Italian talmudic scholars all went on record as saying that music in the synagogue is not against Jewish law."

"Then why all the big *tsimas* about an organ in the first place?" Herman Morris demanded.

"Sometimes tradition is stronger than law," Kurt replied, his eyes twinkling.

"Reform! Reform! Reform!" Greenglass scoffed. "If they're not careful they'll let the baby go down the drain with the bath water!"

Kurt cast him a reproving look.

"Do we no longer grieve that the Jews are homeless?" Mr. Weber demanded, coming to the aid of his friend.

"You have a good home, don't you?" Benny Gold shot back at him.

"Gentlemen," Kurt said, "In Micah we are told that all six hundred and thirteen Jewish laws may be reduced to three: that we do justly, love mercy, and walk humbly with our God. It does not seem that we can obey even the three, let alone the many others . . . for no one can say that we are displaying much of humility here tonight."

There was a little embarrassed laughter to meet Kurt's mildly spoken reproach, and in a more relaxed atmosphere, Herman Morris began to doodle again.

"All right, so we're right back where we started. What's against having the organ?" Dr. Ben Klein inquired.

"We're against it!" Harry Greenglass called back. And once again challenge had been flung out and accepted, and no single voice made itself heard in the multiplicity of voices that lept up.

Kurt's head ached with the ugly raucousness of voice contending against voice. Fleetingly he thought that, if Jews could divide themselves so violently on such a question when their whole survival as a people had been threatened, then surely they must already have lost the very spiritual heritage which they clamored to preserve.

Wearily Kurt stood on his feet again. Gradually the clamor of voices became quiet. His face was gravely thoughtful as he began to speak.

"Gentlemen," he said, "I come so recently from a world in which a Jew was a Jew and it was a matter of life or death . . . it still seems strange to find myself in a world where Jews may enjoy the privilege of perpetuating their differences."

Kurt paused. These words laid a certain restraint upon the members of the board. Mr. Jacobson sat there, hunched forward a little, looking like an old, old man. Sam Levinson examined his ring, and then the faces of his fellow board members, with an unrelenting intensity.

Kurt Rosen's eyes were on Sam Levinson. And in his eyes was something both more and less than contempt; in his eyes there was a profound awareness of the irony of what he himself was about to do.

"So far in our discussions, we have decided nothing," Kurt said. "There is . . . at this point . . . just one thought that I would like to give to you. As a minority people, we have a special obligation in the way that we treat our own minority. There are more reform than orthodox members in our congregation. They could easily vote the organ into our synagogue today. But this one thing I ask you to consider. Those of us . . . myself included . . . who want an organ, want it because it is a thing of beauty, which will add beauty and dignity and solemnity to our religious service. But most of those who do not want the organ, do not want it because it actually violates what is to them an inviolate religious principle. For my part, I am willing to sacrifice my pleasure to their conviction. This I ask you, also, to consider when you vote. Now; I think that we should take a brief recess, before we vote."

There was a scraping of chairs . . . a loosening of collars . . . a lighting of cigarettes . . . a pushing up of sleeves . . . and more agitated conversation in groups of twos and threes. Kurt spent the recess talking to Mr. Jacobson, each of them trying in a fumbling, inept way to console the other for the thought of Ellen. At the end of ten minutes Kurt called the meeting to order again and asked for a written vote. Herman Morris shredded a piece of paper into small slips, and Benny Gold passed out the pencils that he found in the cabinet. And eleven men hurriedly wrote down their votes.

"Mr. Levinson, will you count the votes," Kurt said.

Sam Levinson looked a little startled. He gathered up the votes that the men handed to him. And aloud he began to call them out:

"For . . . for . . . against . . . for . . . against . . . against . . .

184

against . . . for . . . against . . . against . . . for. That's five for . . . and six against." Sam Levinson spoke with a voice of authority, and there was a glint of victory in his tones; but something, else, too . . . a slight bafflement at the strangely bitter taste of victory.

Kurt did not look at Sam Levinson. His eyes swept the faces that were turned to him, and came to rest on Isador Jacobson's face.

"It was a fine thing you wanted to do, Mr. Jake," he said, "And I'm sure that even those who could not accept the gift . . . appreciate the wonderful gesture . . . of the giver."

The two of them shook hands . . . Old Mr. Jacobson and Kurt Rosen. And the rest of the men in the room seemed, for the first time, oddly embarrassed and constrained, as if they had failed, in the hour that was past, to grasp something important.

When Kurt had turned out the lights at the Temple and locked the doors, he slowly climbed the stairs to that small haven where Ellen awaited him. Ellen. His throat ached. He felt too tired to stand up straight. She heard him coming and she opened the door.

"Kurt?" the sound as she spoke it was small and dear.

"Sweetheart." Kurt came into the room and closed the door.

Ellen's discerning dark eyes were on him. "Don't speak of it, Kurtchen. What is there to say? . . . Come only and drink the coffee I made for you. I waited for you . . . a long time."

Chapter 16

ON MONDAY night of the next week, Ellen waited with supper for over an hour. Outside, the late winter dusk seemed to draw its last remaining light away from the windows, and inside the small tight apartment the gloom deepened. Ellen turned on the light, and outlines that had been blurred and soft leapt to a garishness, a harshness. She turned the light off again and lit the candles on the table.

Ellen heard Kurt's step in the hallway; she ran to the door.

"Kurtchen! You're so late. I thought . . ." Ellen did not finish what she thought.

"Hi, Sweetheart!" Kurt said with the warm vigor of greeting that made each small reunion a little special. Ellen smiled; it seemed to her that the American idiom fit a little strangely upon her husband's tongue.

"Oh, you! . . . What's now?" she said, taking his coat to hang in the curtained alcove.

"Nothing new. Mr. Stein suffered severe indigestion because of Mrs. Stein's fondness for cooking, and she required the comfort of the rabbi. And Bennie Goldstein, home on furlough, has thrown his entire family into a state of turmoil by admitting that he is dating a Gentile girl in St. Louis. They thought the rabbi should talk to Bennie."

"So he did?"

"So he did."

"What else?"

"Nothing else. I'm hungry."

"Come, let's eat. I'll put things on the table while you wash your hands."

Kurt came to the table and the meal began with the prayer and the breaking of bread. Their hands touched as Kurt gave Ellen the piece of bread, and he held her hand for a moment.

"Sweetheart!" he said.

They smiled at each other in the candlelight, and Ellen knew the warm feeling of being cherished. And in this moment of close-

186

ness she felt an uncontrollable urge to speak to Kurt of the things that so troubled her—of Sam Levinson—of what might lie ahead.

"Did he say anything, Kurtchen . . . Sam?"

"He still thinks he would like a different rabbi," Kurt said matter-of-factly. From the large serving dish he spooned the meat and the vegetables into the plates.

"Kurt, could we not ask for another assignment?" Ellen said fiercely. "If we would write to the Rabbinical Organization they would send us some place else."

Kurt sat looking at her for a moment, he reached out a hand and brushed back a strand of hair from her forehead in a small caress that was an answer to the urgency in her voice.

"Ellen, there is something we must think of besides ourselves. I was one of the first refugee rabbis assigned. If we fail, we make it just that much harder for those who come after us even to have the chance to try."

"But how could we have tried any harder . . ."

"Ellen, Sam Levinson is only one man."

"But I think there are many who blow out of the same horn."

"I don't think they do. . . . It's very hard here, but . . ."

"Why should it be so hard?"

"Maybe our approach has been wrong," Kurt said.

"How could it be wrong? What could we have done that we haven't done. . . . It won't be any different than it is."

"Perhaps not with the older ones. It's true they have little spirituality. But think of this—many of them began as emigrant peddlers. They worked very hard, they thought only of making money, of making a place for themselves. But now they've made the money and their children will have time for the books. In the next generation, the culture and the spirituality are coming back. I can see it already." There was a real eagerness in his voice. Ellen looked at him questioningly.

"Kurtchen, you speak of generations, and we have only years," she said finally.

"Ellen, in Europe we were the fortunate ones. In Europe I would not have thought of accepting a call to a congregation so small as this. . . . Perhaps we have come all this way to learn humility."

Ellen started to answer, but she did not answer. Suddenly she felt a sharp regret for having spoken at all; for in Kurt's face she saw the weariness and fatigue of a long day spent in heeding the small and varied demands of his recalcitrant congregation. And as he spoke, Ellen had glimpsed his keen sense of the need of these people, and his earnest desire to minister to this need; and beyond that, his imperviousness to the hostility, and his confidence that it could be overcome. But Ellen was not confident that the hostility could be overcome, and to have him worried was a thing she felt she could not bear. She looked at him across the table, and she could not smile when he smiled.

The meal was hardly done, when the telephone rang and Kurt was called again to the bedside of a sick child. Ellen Rosen was left alone once more, to deal in some way with the dismay of this hour.

For most people life is built upon the illusion of permanence. But once this illusion is shattered, it seems beyond the power of will to recreate it.

For Ellen, the illusion had been broken; for her there no longer existed the secure sense of permanence. And in her heart there was a great hunger for this sense of belonging, and a great reluctance at the thought of allowing herself to be enticed into new vulnerability by its promise of ease.

Not once in the months they had been in Fall City had she allowed herself to feel that this was more than a respite, a pause in wanderings that were to be endless.

To Ellen it seemed that life must ever after be episodic. For her husband's sake she would not deny life's joy, but she would not trust it. However much the soul yearned, she would not allow herself to begin knitting the thread of continuity into the events that occurred in their lives. And this disjointedness was, itself, a kind of forgetfulness, a passionate and bitter and hopeful forgetfulness in which reality was denied to all things.

It was even possible sometimes—by trying hard enough—to imbue past experience with this detached episodic quality, so that some small memory might, for a moment, contain only its own elements of joy or sorrow without portent of things to come.

On this night, when Kurt had gone, Ellen did not read or listen to the radio or play records. She was alone, and she remembered. . . . She remembered another life: in Koenigsberg . . . and Berlin . . . and Duisburg. . . .

I

. . . In Koenigsberg . . . the year she was eight . . . the year her mother gave her the beautiful doll for her birthday . . . the beautiful doll . . .

It was her father who came up to see her when she was ready for bed that night. He rapped lightly on the door, and then he came in. Ellen sat up in bed, hugging her knees, as he sat down beside her.

He picked up the doll from the foot of the bed and looked at it thoughtfully, then he looked at her.

"Ellen, don't you think you could like the dolly just a little . . . for Mama's sake?"

Ellen shook her head, her dark eyes were full of self-reproach; but still she shook her head.

"Why not, she's a very pretty doll."

"She isn't real."

"You can make believe. You like to hear stories; you make believe about stories."

"That's different," Ellen answered very seriously. "Then you make it up altogether. You can't make believe it's a baby if it's cold when you touch it. . . . And anyway, it doesn't look like a baby." She took one of the doll's kid-gloved hands in her hand; almost apologetically, she touched a ruffle of her exquisite hand-stitched taffeta skirt.

"No, she looks like a fine lady, doesn't she? A lady going to the opera. That's how ladies look who sit in the boxes at the opera, did you know that, Ellen? Some night I will take you. . . . Let's see, her name is Frau Oppenheimer. . . . Frau Oppenheimer, may I show you to your box, please?" He picked up the doll, he held her as if she put one gloved hand on his arm; he escorted her to a seat on the nursery window-box.

"And now, Miss Ellen Meier will sing for us. . . . What will Miss Meier sing for us?" he asked, as if he did not quite recollect.

"Unter den Linden," Ellen said shyly, and very gravely.

"Unter den Linden," her father repeated, smiling and nodding at Frau Oppenheimer. He went over to the toy piano and knelt down on his knees instead of sitting on the bench. He began to tinkle the tiny keys. Ellen stood up in the center of her bed, her pink toes peeking out from beneath the lace edging of her billowy, beribboned, flannel gown.

"You begin," she said finally.

Her father turned back to Frau Oppenheimer with mock consternation. "A duet," he said, "Miss Ellen Meier and her father."

He tinkled the keys some more and then he began to sing.

"Ach, Du lieber Augustine . . ."

On the third bar, Ellen joined, her treble riding the crest of his rich baritone like a humming bird hovering on ecstatic wings over the crest of a river.

"Bravo! Bravo!" her father said when they were through. "May I kiss the prima donna? . . . And now, hop in bed and cover up." He bent over and kissed her again, brushing the soft hair back from her brow.

At the doorway, he turned back for a moment, "Tomorrow could you tell Mama that you like Frau Oppenheimer?" he said. ". . . but don't tell anybody her name. That's a secret just between us."

II

. . . Berlin . . . Berlin . . . and the first music lesson with Madame Renée who once had been Enrico Caruso's teacher . . . and beyond the window the city with its spires and steeples . . . and it's challenge.

In an old and dimly lit building on Prager Platz, a plodding, inept young man ushered Ellen into a studio to await an audience with Madame Renée. The walls were hung with pictures of the great and famous that the teacher had known, and there was in the room the sort of blowsy, gusty, temperamental disorder which had strewn music to many corners and stacked books in uneven piles.

Left alone, Ellen went immediately to the window to see if she could see Kurt, who had left her a moment before, moving in the crowd below. He stood at the corner of the square, his eyes trained on the window, and with a spontaneous zest of movement he lifted an arm and waved to her. And the gesture could have been born in her heart so well did she know it. She raised her hand and waved, and her own gesture was small and slight with the wistful grace of the thought that does not know how to be spoken. Kurt turned then, and went striding off into the crowd, and she watched him go.

When Ellen moved from the window, so receptively alive did she feel that the exact shape and color of a rose pictured on a piece of sheet music became imprinted in her memory forever. At that instant the door opened and a gust of wind blew the music to the floor. Ellen stooped to pick it up and arose to confront a personage so formidably overwhelming that the stooping seemed, in retrospect, almost to have been a gesture of obeisance.

"You're Ellen Meier," the woman said. Her dark hair was wildly streaked with white. Her eyes were black and penetrating in a face that was lined and watchful and intent.

Ellen nodded.

"I'm Madame Renée," she said, moving swiftly and a little grandly into the room.

Ellen nodded again, a reply would have seemed almost an affront.

Madame Renée turned from gathering up a handful of music and regarded her keenly. She saw in the girl who stood numbly before her that profoundly stirring rarity, a beauty which is not static but creative, as variable as light on the sea, becoming an exquisite reflection of all life.

"You sing. Can you not speak?" the older woman asked a little brusquely.

Ellen felt in that instant the poignant kindness of an austere personality. She smiled a little.

"Please forgive me," she said, "You must understand, Madame Renée, for me this is an overwhelming experience."

Madame Renee laughed. She sat down at the piano.

"What is your range," she asked.

"Mezzo soprano," Ellen told her.

The teacher lifted one expressive brow in interest, "Let us hear the notes in the lower register," she said, and she began to sound the chords.

Ellen moved around the piano until she stood once more beside the window. She took a deep breath and the very air seemed to sing in her lungs. She felt some wild and joyous excitement, mounting, mounting, until it must be borne out in sound.

As she sang Ellen looked out the window. Kurt was no longer to be seen in the square below. But beyond the square lay the city with sunlight on its domes and steeples. And Ellen felt the challenge of the city . . . and she felt an awe and an expectancy that sang in the nerves of her body. This moment was a threshold and a reaching out.

But in this moment was contained the memory of another moment—a train . . . a train from Koenigsberg to Berlin . . . and how a meeting is planned that must appear accidental . . . the German-Polish border and the dusk and coldness, and the grim weary faces of strangers . . . and the tired look of old luggage piled on the platform . . . and suddenly Kurt coming toward her . . . Kurt moving down the platform where before there had been only strangers and strangeness . . . Kurt who moved with vigor and zest . . . Kurt who wooed the excitement of life from a scene upon which others looked with dull and apathetic eyes . . . Kurt, Kurt! . . . At that moment, on a train that stood at the border between two countries, Ellen experienced an overpowering sense of the fusing of destinies which bound them, not to time or to place, but to each other.

Ellen sang for Madame Renée; she sang with some glorious exultation and knew in her heart that this was a moment she had waited for all of her life. But she sang with the joy that contains its own sadness; for with the chance to do what always she had wanted most there came the small aching sadness of not wanting it most any more.

III

. . . In Duisburg—in Duisburg as a bride, the wife of the new rabbi.

One afternoon Ellen looked into the eyes of the imposing dowager who had come to call and tried to see herself there. But she did not see herself, she saw someone who did not exist, but had the look of Ellen Rosen. Kurt came home just as this pompous and opinionated visitor was departing, and they passed each other on the stairs.

Kurt came into the apartment which Ellen tended with such pride and found her simply standing in the center of the floor.

"I see you've had visitors," he said, his eyes flecked with humor. Ellen only nodded; she seemed to have retreated far away from this moment.

"How does it feel to be a *rebbitzen?*" he asked her, his voice teasing a little. But she turned to him with such seriousness in her face that he wanted to laugh aloud and to hold her close.

"Kurt, I feel married to you, but I don't feel like a rabbi's wife."

"How should a rabbi's wife feel?" he asked.

"I don't know . . . pious?" she said, beginning to smile a little, too.

"And how do you feel?"

"Sometimes wild and joyous and gay and sad. I feel like I want life so much. That's it. I want it . . . all of it. And in life there is so much that is not pious. In Berlin it was different . . . the hours we could have together . . . they were just between us . . . and everything that is possible in life was possible in them."

"And now?"

"They know exactly what they expect of you . . . and of me,

too. I feel . . . tied down by small imaginations. Do you know what it is to want to soar?"

He smiled. "Is that all that's troubling you?"

"Not exactly. I feel a little like I'm trespassing on God's domain. You know I told you I'm not very well acquainted with God . . . but suddenly I feel like he's watching all the time. And all the things I feel inside me, I don't know for sure which ones he might disapprove of."

Kurt Rosen looked at his young wife, the mild perplexity so pretty on her face, and he laughed. Kurt understood the myriad facets of emotional response newly opened to a warm and passionate nature, and he gently cherished her perplexity.

"You don't suppose God has a small imagination, do you?" he said. "Don't you think maybe God is a little weary sometimes of the way people stifle the wonderful capacities for feeling He gave them. You know how it is to give a gift you think is wonderful, and see it hidden away in a closet and never used."

"Kurt, are you laughing at me a little?"

"Only a little."

"Why?"

"Does it worry you that it may be wicked for the rabbi to kiss the *rebbitzen* with such vigor?"

"Maybe . . . a little?"

"I think it will not worry you long," he said, and he took her in his arms and kissed her lips.

IV

. . . Duisburg—twelve years later—the day of Kurt's arrest by the Gestapo.

At dawn they had drunk coffee together and had spoken of the burned synagogue. And then the telephone began to ring with frantic voices exhorting Kurt to flee. The telephone kept ringing when only moments were left to them.

Ellen watched Kurt go again to the telephone, she listened to him speak to some member of his congregation. His voice, calm and reassuring, seemed to move in her body like a physical sensation. Catastrophe should be swift, Ellen thought. To stand like this, at its brink, was a thing the spirit should not be required to do.

Kurt turned from the telephone, he saw in her face the shadowy lines of an anguish that has not yet grooved itself deeply into the expression of a face.

"Ellen . . ." he said to her, and into his voice came the

exquisite tenderness in which the fleeting of time has become the essence. He held out his hands to her, and she came and put her hands in his. And in the warmth of this physical touch, it was not comfort that Ellen knew, but the first sharp sense of how tenuous and indefensible are the bonds by which a caress may bind.

Kurt reached behind him and took the telephone off the hook.

"Come, sit down!" he said. He sat on the couch and drew her down beside him. Ellen leaned her head back against his shoulder so that he did not look into her face, but with one finger he gently traced its outline.

Ellen caught the finger in her hand as it paused against her lips.

"Kurt, where will they send you?" she asked him, her voice small and strangled.

"I don't know . . . possibly to Dachau."

"Kurt, you've helped so many, surely there will be someone who can help you."

"You must write the letters as I told you, Ellen, but be very careful of what you say. Say only what I told you."

Ellen did not speak again. There was left to her only to sit beside him and to be held a little while yet in his arms.

The knock came at the door . . .

Kurt got up and went to answer. Two members of the Gestapo stood there; uninvited they moved into the room.

"Dr. Kurt Rosen?" the older one asked.

It seemed to Ellen that her very spirit snatched the words from his lips, that her very soul resisted the passing of that name across those lips. She looked at the two men and felt a numb wonder that they should look like human beings . . . that one should be young and pimply-faced, that the other should be glum and morose with a cold in the head.

"I am Dr. Rosen," Kurt replied.

"You are under arrest," the first man said.

Kurt glanced at Ellen. Ellen only stood there. When action cannot match the dreadful, shattering urgency of a moment, it is a thing that must be suffered in the heart. There was nothing that Ellen could do but stand there.

"Come with us," the younger man said, making a jerky forward movement. He put a hand on Kurt's arm in a sort of token gesture of coercion. Ellen looked into this face whose brutality was only an insensible glumness and hated it with a bitterness that was blinding to the eye, scalding to the throat.

"Would it be permissible for me to take anything with me?" Kurt asked.

"You won't need a thing," the officer replied, smiling mockingly. "Come!"

Kurt's eyes met Ellen's and they both knew that to let these barbarians glimpse their anguish was a thing they could spare each other.

"Goodbye, Ellen," Kurt said quietly, as if he would be gone only a little while.

Ellen could not speak. She swallowed, and the small flutter of motion in her beautiful throat was his answer. He touched her hand, and she raised the hand and waved to him goodbye.

She watched him go, then, taking nothing which was his own, not even his hat.

With that last touching of hands Ellen Rosen knew a moment when life seems a thing no longer to be contained in the living bodies that may be wrenched apart; when the spirit feels some transcending compulsion to flee the confines of its bodily abode! To know such a moment was to know how awful can be the need of human beings to escape their humanity.

v

A train sounded in the distance, its mournful whistle moved out through the cold stillness of the night . . . seeking haven . . .

Ellen heard. It was the first sound she had consciously heard in over an hour. She tried to stir from her reverie. But she was caught between worlds in which reality had deserted the present and fled to the past.

The knock at the door . . .

The knock at the door had been a cleavage of time. And of all of life that proceeded that bitter hour, nothing remained but their love for each other . . . nothing at all, not even the ability to remember without pain.

And how does a heart that has been wracked by such extremes of love and hate concern itself again with small affections? How does such a heart begin again to trust itself a little to the whims of others? How does such a heart seek a new home?

On this night alone, in Fall City, Ellen Rosen knew that if Kurt had begun to find the answers, then she must find them, too. And if she could not find them, then she must want for his sake what she could not want for herself. She could try for his sake what she would not try for herself—to win these people . . . to win their love and affection . . . for his sake.

Chapter 17

A SICK child slumbered in the night. The small, shaded light burned on the table, and a vigil was kept near the bed. The fever deserted the child, melting the formless shape of fear in the room. And the child's brow was cool, and his breath was even and he slept.

At eleven o'clock Rabbi Rosen left the bedside of the little boy to catch the last bus home. He stood on the corner beneath the single street lamp which cast an arc of warmth on the brick paving, small and immediate and heartening beneath the remote brightness of the stars in a vast, cold sky.

The bus came rumbling up the street, its windows lighted and empty, the driver a strangely lonely figure at the wheel. It stopped for Kurt at the corner. His nickel, ricocheting into the money box, made a sharp clink in the night stillness. He went half way down the aisle and sat on one of the imitation-leather seats which was cold and sticky to the touch. The window pane gave back only his own reflection, while vague, dark shapes moved behind it. Kurt Rosen closed his eyes and drifted back into that morass of thought which only fleetingly had relinquished him.

Leaving Ellen on this night Kurt had felt, as keenly as did she, the significance of their suppertime conversation. And for the dismay that he saw in her face there had been hardly a moment for offering comfort. He had felt a deep reluctance at leaving her alone with this dismay, knowing as he did how hard a thing it would be for her to follow the lead he had indicated in allowing her to sense how much it meant to him to be able to stay in Fall City.

And now there was something that he must ask himself. Why did it mean so much to him to stay? He considered this question with a deep and curious interest. Thoughtfully he examined the events of the day just passed for some hint of their meaning, but in the tedium of this typical day there was little to explain his strong desire to stay in this place, among these people. There was little in Mr. Stein's indigestion or Benny Goldstein's romantic problems to inspire this sense of creative energy, and he was at a loss to understand his own feelings. It seemed to him a strange paradox that, after ministering to two thousand Jews in the hate-infested Rhineland, he should be able to feel so great a challenge here among ninety Jews enjoying the freedom and lack of persecution of the American midwest. And yet he did feel the challenge.

With Kurt Rosen it was not as it was with Ellen. He did not feel so keenly the serverance, the cleavage of time. To him it seemed as if each event, as it followed, had been contained in the event that had passed, even to the present moment. And how, he asked himself, was this so?

Kurt had been ten years old when he decided he wanted to become a rabbi. And what had he seen of life until then that might bear upon such a decision? He had seen already the extremes of love and hate that exist between people who are unlike . . . as a small boy he had seen them . . .

In the village in East Prussia where Kurt Rosen was born there had lived only three Jewish families in a population of two thousand Polish Catholics. There was always a bad time for the Jews when a fanatical priest would come to town, but the Rosens personally were almost free of animosity. The Bishop of the province was a friend of Kurt's mother, and he always stayed with the Rosens in their home instead of with his constituents when he came to the village.

The first such visit that Kurt remembered had occurred when he was seven. The tall, dark-clad man with the round white collar who was visiting in his home seemed to him no different from any other person who might come to visit.

But when he went out in the village Kurt began to sense the difference. Grown people who never noticed him at all spoke to him. And he had the feeling that other people, who were not usually so careful of his feelings, were speaking behind his back instead of to his face. And it was not a comfortable way to feel.

On the way to deliver a note for his mother, young Kurt passed the Cathedral where a wedding was being celebrated. It was a large wedding and many of the villagers who could not crowd inside the chapel were kneeling on the steps outside. Many of them had no soles on their shoes, only rags tied around their feet. Kurt paused for a moment and, with a child's irrefutable logic, he wondered how people who did not have shoes could allow themselves the luxury of scorn. Quickly he moved away from the gathering. He could feel in the air the anger of the people, although their faces smiled. For no reason that he could have told, he suddenly began to run. When he was out of breath he sat down on a large stone by the roadside.

Kurt understood that in some way he had taken on added stature, and he wondered. There was more than one way of acquiring prestige, he had discovered. The world had been changed somewhat by the advent of the chocolate-covered marshmallow bars. Because his father owned the store that sold them, Kurt was the only boy in town who could have a chocolate bar any time he wanted it, and he had learned the magic of trading chocolate bars for favors. This was a prestige that could be counted upon, that could be measured in terms of value received. It was an impersonal thing which required nothing of him but the ability to deliver. But this new prestige that had to do with the visitor was complex and a little frightening. In it was all mixed up the way that people felt. In it was mixed scorn with envy, disdain with jealousy. In the bartering for this kind of prestige there was no measuring value received; it was a prestige of granting concessions, of compromising pride on both sides.

When Kurt had rested for a while on the stone, he got up and walked home, forgetting the note that his mother had sent him to deliver. When he got home it was nearly dusk; it was a busy time of day and his mother and father were both in the store. Kurt slipped, unnoticed, up the back stairs. The visitor was sitting by the table, reading by lamplight. Kurt regarded him curiously for an instant, then went to wash his hands without disturbing him. He came back into the room, and the bishop still was reading there alone. He looked up at Kurt with a sort of quizzical amusement in his gaunt and craggy face.

Kurt kept thinking of the whispered comments he'd heard in the village.

"Why do you stay with us?" he said without meaning to. "The people don't like it."

"Your parents are my friends," the bishop answered. He had the look of someone surrounded by distance, yet Kurt felt like coming close to him. He moved up against the table and leaned his elbows on it.

"Aren't the village people your friends? They think they own you."

The man laughed. "They are not exactly my friends," he said.

"People become friends only after they have shared something that is their very own."

"What did you share with my parents?" Kurt asked. He had the feeling that his parents would not approve of this conversation, but he did not care.

"Your mother taught me to read," the Bishop told him. "When I was a boy your size, your mother was a very beautiful young lady. She was my sister's friend, and when I asked her, she taught me to read."

"Why didn't your father teach you?" Kurt asked.

"He didn't know how himself," the bishop answered simply.

Kurt felt a swelling of pride. "My mother and father are the only people in the village who can read, except for the German officers. When anyone gets a letter he must bring it to my mother and father to be read. My mother and father know what happens to everybody!" Kurt added with a small boy's puckish, sly smile.

The bishop laughed.

"And sometimes the villagers bring animal hides, or a basket of eggs . . . in hopes that they won't tell?" he answered.

Kurt looked at this man with new regard, he had not expected his humor to be relished and embellished in the other's thoughts.

"How did you know?" he asked curiously.

"It is the same in most of the villages where I go. Usually, it is only the Jewish innkeepers who know how to read and write. Your people love learning, Kurt. It is a real part of their love of God." Kurt sensed some profound wistfulness in this statement.

"Are you lonely because your people don't know how to read?" he asked.

Just then Kurt heard his mother's steps on the stairway; and he heard her voice, too; she was humming a little. She had a bowl of fruit in her hands and she came and set it on the table before them.

"Thank you, Henrietta," the bishop said with a grave courtesy which seemed, paradoxically, to demand a laughing reply.

"Eat it in health!" Kurt's mother said, and she was smiling. Her eyes had in them some light of a hidden humor as they lingered briefly on the face of their guest.

Kurt had the feeling that he did not understand what was being said, between these two people who were grown and who lived in a world of strange dimensions. But he was somehow relieved to see that his mother did not act as if this man were doing them a favor by being there, though other people seemed to feel that he was.

Henrietta Rosen looked into her son's thoughtful face and sensed a discernment upon which she almost would have congratulated him. But instead she ran slender fingers through his thick dark hair.

"Did you take the note to the baker?" she asked him, and Kurt suddenly recognized this question for its deviousness, such as grown-up people indulged in among themselves.

Kurt only shook his head, and he was not even surprised that his mother did not scold him, for he knew that she had not been thinking of the note at all.

Now Kurt heard his father on the stairs. Jacob Rosen came into the room, gingerly carrying a large napkin-wrapped pie in his two hands.

"Frau Glomsky brings a pie; I think she would like to be invited," he said, a little ruefully.

"How many pies now?" the bishop asked.

"Seven!" Henrietta answered.

And it seemed to Kurt that some special quality of humor, that had flickered briefly in his mother's eyes and in the bishop's craggy face, reached a full fruition in his father's warm, deep, bouncing laugh. It was a humor that mutually embraced the shortcomings and the fallibilities of humankind as a part of the love that individuals may bear for each other. Kurt Rosen stood a little outside this awareness and sensed it only with the sureness of a child's heart. He knew only that, a moment before, the warmth of human love and friendship had seemed so fragile and delicate a thing to be maintained in a climate of hostile, unrelenting pressure from without. But now he began to understand the tensile strength that withstands the buffeting storm.

It was that same year—the year he was seven—that Kurt Rosen first observed the opposite extreme, the extreme of hate between people who are unlike.

All through the East Prussia of that day, in almost every village, there were general stores called inns, which were owned by Jews. These stores sold supplies to farmers: dry goods, seeds, flowers, coffee, beans, groceries, petrol for the lamps, cut wood for the stoves.

In the village of Czersk, one such inn was owned by the Rosens, and another was owned by a Jew named Hirsch, who was assisted by a wife and three timid, unattractive daughters.

Hirsch was a large, bulbous man, whose waistcoat and pants never quite seemed to meet, and whose fat neck bulged over his collar. It was his way to pay back contempt with contempt, or even to anticipate contempt with contempt. He looked out upon the world with small, roving, bitter eyes, from behind his cash drawer where he sat, hour upon hour, atop a high stool.

Hirsch had no compassion; in the winter when people starved or huddled freezing in the streets, he would give no credit. And more than once he had had people arrested for their debts.

Jacob Rosen, on the other hand, could never deny an honest need, and this trait kept him almost constantly embroiled in matters of conscience and finance. The inn was, of course, not open for business on the Sabbath. But the Rosens lived upstairs, and were always at home to a knock on the door. Nor would Jacob turn away a villager who needed oil for his lamp, wood for his stove, or food for his table. But, being a conscientious Jew, Jacob could not accept money or write on the Sabbath. And so the Sabbath debts were debts of honor between him and the customers, who soon learned to take advantage of him unmercifully. There were times when the unwritten and often uncollectable Sabbath debts equalled more than three days' ordinary business.

Hirsch looked upon this practice of his competitor with scorn that more than equalled that which he felt for the *goyim.*

"You do them a favor and they take advantage of you!" he would scoff at Jacob Rosen who was becoming poor while he became wealthy.

"Better to eat herring and dry bread than to deny one, honest need," Jacob would answer imperturbably.

Jacob Rosen despised Hirsch as much as any *goyim* despised him; but there was a difference—Jacob despised him as a man; the *goyim* despised him as a Jew.

On a summer day, the village of Czersk was alive with good humor. A German official, who had been unbelievably harsh upon the population for a period of six years, was recalled to Berlin and the people attended his departure with as much jubilance, as much ribald and heckling humor as they dared in the presence of his successor. When the departing official had been waved down the railroad track, the appetite for vengeance was unappeased, and they cast about for some new victim. The celebrants began to coagulate into a roving mob.

"Get Hirsch!" was an idle shout that soon became a frenzied demand. Suddenly everyone was remembering how Hirsch had been an informer to the German officer, who had, in turn, upheld him in his own ruthlessness.

"Get Hirsch! Get Hirsch!"

The mob grew, and through the street they went to the inn that was owned by Hirsch. But the door was padlocked from outside, and the windows were locked down tight. And no amount of shouts and threats and rock throwing elicited any sign of life from within.

"He's gone! He knew you'd come—he left during the night!" a shrewish-looking woman shouted from the window of the house next door.

That its wrath had been anticipated piqued the mob even further. A great hulking man began to heave his shoulder against the oak door. And more rocks were hurled at the windows. With sticks men began to try to break the glass out of the windows. Intent upon looting, they tried every possibility to break in.

"It won't do you any good," the sharp faced woman cackled. "He didn't leave nothin'. It's all packed in a freight car at the railroad station."

With a curious mass instinct the crowd abandoned its vandalism and headed off to the railroad station. As they tramped through the streets they sang Polish songs, waving their arms and shouting to each other.

Almost in the center of the town two crowds met. The second, made up mostly of children and women, had been berry-picking in the thickets beyond town. In their hands they carried buckets of full ripe blueberries. Young Kurt Rosen was with this second crowd, both hands weighted with this rich harvest, his shirt-tail out, his mouth stained blue, his dark curls falling unheeded down across his forehead. Kurt hitched up his pants by digging his elbows into his waist, and stood still to watch what happened.

The two crowds began to fuse. Men saw their wives among the berry pickers and drew them to their sides. They found their children among the blue-mouthed urchins and heaved them to their shoulders. The two crowds became one, and the early mood of jubilation returned; but neither purpose nor destination was abandoned, though the errand became one of vicious merry-making. On to the railroad station they went. And Kurt, unaware of their purpose, trudged along in their wake, reluctant to be parted from so excited and jubilant a throng.

At the railroad station they converged on the box car that stood on a siding, awaiting the next freight train. With picks and axes the mob began to splinter the wooden door. The door gave way; it was bashed in entirely. And out into the impatient mob was hurled an overstuffed chair. The men began to function like stevedores. Down from the car came tables and chairs and beds and boxes, and crates and trunks and chests of linen. Onto the brick platform they were piled in wild disorder. Children cavorted around them. And now and again someone would burst into song.

Kurt Rosen watched what was happening with a look of dismay in his small earnest face. The excitement and gaiety and gusty spirits of the crowd seemed so at variance with what they were doing. Here were human beings bent on destruction and, in a way that his blood knew, he was defenseless. He shivered; goose flesh was rising along his arms. He was almost afraid of calling attention to himself by running away. Kurt was standing a little apart from the others beneath a big oak tree. Because he did not know what else to do, he climbed the tree, leaving his two buckets of berries at its foot. He hid himself in the branches and peered out to see what was happening.

The celebrating crowd was, for the most part, empty-handed. When Hirsch's belongings had been dumped out, they had only their bare hands as tools of their wrath to finish the job of destruction. With some diabolical whimsey, Johann Klepack, the blacksmith, grabbed up a bucket of blue berries, and with a mighty heave sent its contents showering over a brocaded sofa. The bruised berries bled their juice grudgingly in small blue stains that spread no larger than a coin. Johann lifted up the first little boy he could catch, and dumped him down on the berry-covered couch. The child began to prance with a frantic glee, squashing the berries between his bare toes.

The crowd watched with admiring fascination. And suddenly they were all doing it. Bucket after bucket of ripe berries rained down upon the belongings of Hirsch, the innkeeper, and the children climbed and clambered over the furniture and linens and clothes, dancing and cavorting like mad wine-makers. And the grown people joined the orgy, pressing out the juice of the berries, squeezing it out, smearing it.

And in a tree not twenty feet away, young Kurt Rosen watched in horror.

"Hirsch! Hirsch, the Jew! . . . We'll show him!"

He heard them shouting. And all the gaiety and jubilance was gone, and there was left malice and excitement, and a viciousness that seemed to shriek in their movements. It was a viciousness that transcended its immediate expression. And they were smeared with the juice of berries as they might have been smeared with blood.

Kurt felt as if he would be sick. He clung to the branch of the tree with both hands, he pressed his face against the branch of the tree, he gripped it with his knees until the rough bark cut into his flesh. Below him on the ground were two more buckets of berries—his berries. He had picked berries with them and had been the same as all the others. But now there was a difference. His berries, below him on the ground, marked the place of his hiding, and his vulnerability, and his defenselessness. Their berries had become the effigy of a smoldering hate.

Both of these incidents—the bishop's visit, the villagers' revenge—Kurt remembered always as seen through the eyes of a seven-year-old boy. But not until many years later, in the vile and infamous concentration camp, Dachau, did the portent of these events seem fully realized in the ordeal of a Christian architect inhumanly punished for slipping coffee to Jewish prisoners who, without food or drink for twenty-four hours, had been kept standing at rigid attention for eight hours in a cold rain.

Kurt could close his eyes and remembered the despair of that day. He could remember the hunger . . . and the thirst . . . and the feel of the rain freezing the clothes to his body. He could remember the wet gray side of a barracks on which the eyes were focused endlessly, and the way the rain bounced a little on the frozen earth when once his head drooped forward on his chest. He could remember how it was to wish to be dead . . . and how the body goes on feeling after the mind has willed it not to feel . . . and how the mind must, by its very nature, continue in its efforts long after it can no longer endure what is to be assayed.

And he could remember the smell of the forbidden coffee, the feel of the steam in his face, the feel of the cup in his frozen hands, the scald of the liquid in his throat. But most of all he could remember the face of the man who brought the coffee . . . the face of a man who had not lost his humanness, who had not allowed his humanness to be swallowed up in terror . . . the face of a man, gaunt and lined in the light of a lamp . . . reaching out his hand . . . into the abyss . . .

The Christian architect who had ministered to the suffering Jews was apprehended by the prison guards as he took the empty cups back to the camp kitchen. And many days later those he had helped learned what had happened to him. This man, who in years past had done more than any other to eliminate slums from the leading cities of Germany, refused to promise the Nazi guards that he would not help the Jewish prisoners again.

And so the Nazis tied a heavy stone to his feet, they tied his hands behind him, and then they raised and lowered him from the branches of a tree until he fainted.

Twice they threw water in his face to revive him, and twice they demanded to know why he would help the prisoners.

And twice he gave them his answer . . . twice he told them . . .

"Because the Lord said: *Thou shalt love thy neighbor as thyself!*"

. . . *as thyself* . . . *as thyself*—this last phrase echoed again and again in Kurt Rosen's mind, seeming to imply the neglected key to the real meaning of this exhortation.

Could a man who loved himself so much have endured so much for others?

This question could only be answered with another question.

Could a man be really aware of the worth of other human beings unless he were excruciatingly aware of his own worth as a human being?

Kurt thought of his martyred benefactor and wondered in his own soul what this cruelly-gained understanding could portend.

What of now? . . . Kurt knew that in some way all of these things must become related to the present, to the handful of people who had come under his care, in this place, where he found himself.

Kurt got off the bus three blocks from home and walked in the clear, cold night, trying to find his answer before going home to Ellen again. What real significance could all of these things have for ninety Jews living free and unmolested in a country that fiercely maintained the right of all to strive for and to pursue happiness? And in this atmosphere of freedom, what was withheld from them that made their need seem almost greater than that of Jews who lived and many of whom persished in a climate of hate?

Suddenly, as he stood at his own doorstep, Kurt understood. To have arrived here, where people, teaching themselves not to hate, were teaching themselves not to feel; to have arrived here where the love was as strenuously denied as the hate; that was the missing portion of the challenge.

Chapter 18

A S the taxi drew up in front of the big rooming-house next door to the synagogue, Kurt Rosen looked at the "Rooms to Let" sign with a fine disdain he had never really indulged in before.

Kurt paid the driver, and then hurried up the walk and up the stairs to tell Ellen his good news. As he neared the top of the stairs, he was startled by Ellen's voice behind him.

"Where are you going, kind sir, kind sir?" she said, smiling at his haste.

Kurt came back down the stairs and took the grocery sack from her hands.

"Fine thing," he said indignantly. "A woman should be properly waiting for her husband at home, not slipping up behind him when he comes bringing glad tidings!"

"What glad tidings?" Ellen's dark eyes laughed, as Kurt pushed open the door of their room.

"How would you like to leave this miserable abode?" he asked grandly.

"Kurt, tell me!"

"A gentleman we don't even know has offered to rent us a three-room apartment for the same rental that is being paid here. What do you say to that?"

"Kurt, why? Who is he?"

"He is the gentleman who asked for the lecture today—the president of the Lions Club. He had heard me speak twice before."

"And he thinks you're wonderful, as you are!"

"I wouldn't say that!" Kurt was laughing at her jubilance. The lilt was back in her voice, moving into an unacknowledged void in his heart. The bright radiant joy of this moment brought to him sharply the poignance of a more typical joy that was not born of the heart, but created of the will—her offering to him. And he treasured in a way she could not have known this small fleeting joy of the heart.

"Kurtchen, I do not even care about the apartment . . . only that somebody here begins to understand how wonderful you are!" Ellen said.

"Ah, she doesn't care about the apartment!" he teased. "Ellen, you will be able to take a deep breath, a really deep breath! You will be able to move!"

The urgent need to reach out to happiness seemed to quiver in the air. And Ellen moved quickly beyond this moment, which contained the pulsing awareness of often unrealized dreams and hopes, before it should engulf them both.

"When can we see it, Kurtchen? Can we not see it now?" she asked him, smiling.

"We could walk past it at least!" Kurt said, and he caught her hand.

In the sunny afternoon, Kurt and Ellen walked the three blocks to the address that Kurt had written on a card. Lawn sprinklers wet the grass on the lawns of the houses they passed, and the wetness was a sweet, fresh scent in the spring air.

"It is not too far from the synagogue, we could walk even in the worst weather," Kurt was saying.

"Yes, Kurt, and it will be nice to have a little more room when we want to take people home with us on Friday nights. Soon there will be so many soldier boys, it will be nice to have a place to bring them to that is more like home."

Ellen smiled a little, she was thinking of the few pieces of linen and the china and the fine old silver, those incongruous and deeply cherished survivors of her other life, which in their pride had never acquiesced to their surroundings. It was only her own pride that had been so mortally upset; it had taken an excruciating humility, that had been unknown to her blood, to invite a guest to the place where she lived, in the dismal, drab and cabbage-smelling house next door to the synagogue.

"It will be nice to live in an apartment house—not a rooming house!" she added finally, her nose wrinkling a little in distaste at the last word; and Kurt squeezed her hand.

"This is it," he said, as they came in sight of a three-story, tan-brick building which stood on the corner. Its windows had little protruding ledges, and there was iron grill-work on the front door. Ivy climbed the north wall, the small square lawn was neat, the hedges were low and trim, and evergreen shrubs grew in clumps at the entrance.

Kurt and Ellen stood for a moment, just looking.

"Shall we go in?" Kurt asked her.

"The apartment is not yet empty?" Ellen asked.

"Not yet."

"Then only as far as the doorway," Ellen laughed in reply. The heavy door sighed discreetly as it closed behind them. Just inside the entrance hall was a brass panel of mail boxes, with the name cards neatly inserted in the small slots.

"Would look nice here—Rabbi and Mrs. Rosen!" Kurt said.

Ellen laughed. "Come, Kurtchen, before someone wonders why we stand here in the hall!"

As they walked again along the way they had come, a bemused silence seemed to catch Ellen in its thrall. Suddenly she was able to look back on the last months as on an era that is past . . .

True to her resolve on that night she had sat alone waiting for Kurt, Ellen had set out to win the people of her congregation. At first there had been the not knowing how, and the deep, deep sensitivity that made it so hard a thing even to contemplate taking the initiative in approaching those who had been hostile or indifferent. A tremendous effort had been required for the first encounters.

With unrelenting determination Ellen tried to see herself as these people seemed to see her, and it occurred to her that many of them had never seen her smile. To smile—that was a warm and simple thing . . . a beginning. And from that beginning Ellen tried with intense effort to allow them glimpses of a woman whose heart once had sung for joy. But most of the people were merely confused. They seemed to prefer their conception of the refugee woman harboring an insoluble sadness; they seemed unable or unwilling to merge the two. They wanted a smile, yes, but they seemed to prefer a hollow smile to one that lay too lightly upon the throbbing, unhealed heart.

The effort was too great, the response too disappointing. So Ellen tried another way. She cut her hair. The dark hair, that had wound into a thick, smooth braid across her head, sprang into soft, short curls under the snip of scissors. Ellen looked into the mirror the delighted beauty parlor operator gave her and suffered pangs for the irretrievable. That afternoon she was a long time deciding to go home. She was already standing on the corner, waiting for a bus, when the last buoyance of a planned surprise deserted her. She went into a drugstore phone booth and dialed the study at the synagogue.

"Kurt, I have something to tell you—I cut my hair!" and suddenly she felt like crying, not because of the vanquished tresses, but because they represented a concession to what seemed hardly worth the conceding.

But at least this had been a new way to begin, a new way to try. Ellen began to use cosmetics the way American women used them. She experimented with lipstick, once tried eye shadow, debated over the shade of nail polish, and in a weak moment allowed a door-to-door cosmetics salesman to sell her eight dollars worth of fancy creams and lotions. Kurt regarded the studiousness of these endeavors with an amused indulgence.

"Why do you act as if you just discovered cosmetics?" he teased. "Don't you know that in the twelfth century there was a law in some Jewish communities in Europe that the women must be provided with cosmetics?"

"That isn't your story, Kurtchen, you took it from Rabbi Golden," Ellen chided, remembering the frail little wraith of an octogenarian who had been one of Kurt's history teachers in Berlin.

"Nobody's story . . . a plain historical fact," Kurt contended blandly.

"I doubt the historical fact; but you remember the rest of the story don't you?"

"What rest?" Kurt inquired innocently.

"To quote Rabbi Golden 'It was a simple measure of self preservation . . . so the men wouldn't fall in love with the *shikses.*' "

Ellen concentrated more intensely upon grasping the American idiom of speech, and learned to say "Oh Brother!" with just the proper inflection. She learned to qualify for a fourth in bridge. And finally, when she had learned strictly to observe all the tenets of superficiality, these people relented a little; they began to seem pleased with her.

Was this success, Ellen wondered? Was this the beginning of acceptance?

Ellen had looked about her, and there was little comfort in the realization that what the people denied her was not greater than what they denied each other—the simple warmth of human kindness. And in this final realization there was both an awful hope and an awful hopelessness for the future. . . .

Now, as Kurt and Ellen returned from their visit to the apartment house, as they came again into the room where they had lived for the past year, Ellen closed the door and stood just inside it, looking about her with a feeling of remoteness and detachment which denied any claim of this place upon her heart.

Her eyes moved slowly from chair to table to lamp, and slowly to Kurt's face, where they wavered.

"Ellen, why are you so quiet? What are you thinking?"

Ellen looked into Kurt's thoughtful, questioning gray eyes, and felt for him a rush of love and tenderness that ached in her throat so that, for a moment, she could not speak.

"Kurtchen, I was thinking, that in all the months we have lived in Fall City—in America—the new apartment is the first thing that comes to us entirely as our own!"

"Ellen! . . ." Kurt said gently; his eyes were on her in full awareness, but his voice coaxed her back, back to the warm bright mood that had enthralled them, back from the anguish and bitterness that lay so close beneath its surface.

Ellen shook her head.

"Kurtchen, I did not mind the room so much . . . only that they should have offered you such a place to live. And now, I'm so glad it is somebody who is not even a Jew who offers us the apartment, somebody who simply understands your worth. I'm so glad that it comes to us like this . . . as something that is our own . . . our very own."

II

The Rosens were not the only ones who were contemplating a move. On a March day, the house that had plagued Lee Kalman so relentlessly with Maury's absence suddenly became intolerable; and the determination to move away from it came to Lee with such force that it sparked immediate action.

The first step was to tell somebody. Lee picked up the car keys from the hall table. She would go tell Sara Kalman. Lee's solution to her problem might suggest to Sara a similar solution—that she might either go back to Minnesota where she had relatives, or find a smaller place to live by herself.

Lee stopped the car in the driveway of the big, brown house. She found Sara in the parlor engrossed in doing needle point.

"You'll ruin your eyes!" Lee chided from the doorway.

Sara glanced up a little crossly. "You startled me," she said. "Come on in. Where's my boy?"

"Amy has him at the park," Lee replied. She came in and sat down on the big, old-fashioned sofa.

"Guess what I've decided to do," she said, and the words

sounded so gauche that she was amazed at having uttered them.

Sara's dark eyes studied her speculatively, before she began re-threading the needle. "I don't know."

"I'm going to rent the house . . . and get an apartment for Julian and me."

Sara quit trying to thread the needle. Her fancy work slipped unnoticed off her lap, her hands fluttered a little.

"Rent the house!" she gasped, as if this thought invalidated the last hope of Maury's existence.

"It's so lonesome without Maury. I want to try to stay as cheerful as I can," Lee answered, almost as if she were arguing. She felt a miserable ineffectivenes which Sara sometimes evoked in her.

Sara did not answer for a moment, she picked up the needle point and threaded the needle. Lee saw that she was thinking very hard.

"Why don't you and Julian come here to live?" Sara said matter-of-factly, as if the question were settled. Lee looked at her in astonishment.

"We couldn't do that . . ." she began.

"Why not? There's plenty of room. Too much room. You could have your privacy. I could take care of Julian for you. You could get rid of that ridiculous maid—Amy." Sara was rushing on, her eyes were snapping with a bright new interest. The idea was getting a grip on her that she could not throw off, and Lee wanted to shout at her to stop.

But she didn't shout. "I just couldn't," Lee said. "I'm too used to having a place of my own. I couldn't have it any other way . . . and be happy."

"Nonsense. We're both alone. Do you think I'm not lonely? And the house is large. Why should you spend money for an apartment when you could come here?" This time, as Sara spoke, she was neither imperious or wheedling. And the simple unpresupposing directness of her appeal suddenly freed Lee from the terrible tensions of their involvement. She looked at Sara Kalman with complete detachment. She saw a woman in whose face and figure there remained the vestiges of a warm, rich life-embracing beauty. She saw also a woman who had been forced back upon her own resources after half a lifetime of pampering love. Abe Kalman had loved this woman with a depth of devotion that Lee had never entirely fathomed; yet she would have trusted his human perceptiveness above that of anyone she had ever known. And Maury—Maury's young life had been molded and enriched by this woman. What, Lee wondered with a gnawing self-reproach did she fear from her mother-in-law? She did not know, she knew only that she felt herself resisting as she had never resisted before.

"It wouldn't work out . . ." Lee said again lamely.

"And why not? Think of the baby. An apartment you'd take him to? When here he could have the whole big yard to play, the whole house to romp in?"

"I am thinking of Julian," Lee said trenchantly. "I'm thinking that it's not good for any little boy to have two mothers."

"And if his own mother is so busy it's better he has a Negro maid than a grandmother?" Sara demanded.

"He loves Amy, and loves to stay with her!" Lee countered hotly.

"And he should not love his grandmother, I guess. You want that he should not love his grandmother?"

"Oh please, Mrs. Kalman. I didn't mean that at all. It's just that . . ." Lee looked into Sara's hurt and lonely face and felt a rise of sympathy that all but quelled her resistance. "Let's talk about it another time," Lee said. "It's such a new idea. And I'm not sure myself what I want to do."

Sara only nodded, and her eyes did not meet Lee's; and Lee, remembered with aching confusion what Maury had said to her.

When Lee was alone again, she felt the awful need to think. She headed the car out the highway, driving fast, so that the wind blew back her hair and sang in her ears. The way was clear, and for a moment she felt that she might keep going forever. But there were things that she must think about; she must think about Sara Kalman.

So reconciled was Lee to the vague antagonism and wariness that always had existed between her and Sara that she was completely unprepared for the fact that Sara, being a partner to it, could so insistently ignore it. Instinct warned Lee that for them to try to live under the same roof would be disastrous; yet she must try to understand what desperation had prompted the offer.

Julian—it all seemed to revolve around Julian. To Sara Kalman, distraught and frighteningly lonely, her grandson represented her only link with her dead husband, her soldier son. Lee had felt and resisted in her the frantic need to claim him, to cling to him. With an insight borne of love for her husband, Lee suddenly understood how Sara Kalman must feel—that if she did not hold this child close, he, too, would slip away from her, back into the world from which his mother had come, forever beyond her reach. This insight inspired in Lee a compassion, where before there had been only a tense wariness; and her sympathy brought her close to the natural liking she might have felt for her mother-in-law if their paths had crossed in any other way. Yet the closer she came to understanding, the more fiercely Lee felt the will to resist. However much she felt on the brink of discovering Sara Kalman as a person, her mind stubbornly balked at the thought of going into her home to live. To Lee it seemed that her very personal identity would be challenged in such an arrangement, an identity which she had yet to define to herself. In spite of her loneliness, this need for aloneness was a profound one. And she could not bring herself to relinquish it.

Lee was afraid to face Sara Kalman's determination again, until she had made definite plans herself. The only answer she knew to her problem was to find an apartment and be ready to move into it before speaking of the matter again. There was one person who could help her—her own Uncle Bill. Lee turned the car back toward town; she would go to him without delay.

Lee stopped at the drugstore on the outskirts of town and called her uncle at his office. Since he was not there, she called him at home and told him that she would like to come by and speak to him.

Lee arrived twenty minutes later to find both her uncle and aunt waiting for her. Her Aunt Myrtle had made tea and laid it out very neatly on her finely polished table. The old family silver, with its elegant monogram, seemed in some insistent way to reproach Lee, as she lifted a spoon and turned it idly in her fingers.

"Sit down, Lee, I thought you might be thirsty," Myrtle said. She took the silver tea pot into the kitchen to fill it. Lee sat looking at her Uncle Bill. He had taken off his coat and his vest seemed almost to be bursting its buttons over a genial robustness. He was smiling at her now with a sort of bungling and exuberant fondness.

"Doggone it, Lee! We've seen damn little of you lately. Sure nice to have you around," he said.

Myrtle came back and removed the paper which he had put down on the table, spoiling its carefully contrived grace.

"What did you want to talk about, Lee?" Myrtle said, filling her tea cup and passing the sand tarts to her in a small formal gesture.

"I want to rent my house," she said. "Uncle Bill, I thought being in touch with the real estate business you might help me find an apartment."

"Well now, that sounds like a good idea," Bill Morrow said tentatively, and Lee felt that the idea was not a new one to him. Myrtle Morrow exchanged a significant glance with her husband.

"Tell her what we thought of, Bill," she prompted him.

Bill Morrow stirred his tea, sloshing it a little over the side of the cup. He seemed concerned over his own awkwardness, fumbling with the napkin ineffectually.

"Leave it, just tell her," Myrtle said impatiently.

"Look, Lee," Uncle Bill began a little plaintively, "We were thinking . . . maybe you might want to go back to Dallas, start a home there again."

"But why . . .?"

Bill Morrow took only a cursory glance at his wife's tense face, and then launched determinedly into the discussion.

"Lee," he said, "I'm going to speak plainly, for there's no other way to speak. It has grieved us to see you getting so out of touch with your own kind of people. Now don't get me wrong, I'm not saying it hasn't been fine of you to make friends with Maury's friends, but . . ."

"Fine! Uncle Bill you talk as if I had been doing Maury a favor. As if I had been humoring him. It makes me sick inside for you to say that."

"Now, Lee, you know I like Maury," her uncle said in a conciliatory tone, "and I wouldn't hurt you for anything . . . and it's a damn shame the way people feel about Jews. I don't feel that way myself, but most people do. And you can't change it . . .you can't buck it."

"Lee, Bill's right!" Myrtle Morrow avowed; and then she seemed, without actually moving, to scuttle away, unable to face Lee's steady, incredulous gaze. Lee turned back to her uncle.

"Uncle Bill, you seem to be forgetting. . . . My name is Kalman . . . my husband's name is Kalman . . . and my son's name is Kalman. And I intend for him to be proud of his name!"

"Lee, I can't say I quite understand you, considering how you were raised," Myrtle interposed again, pettishly.

"Hush, Myrtle!" Bill Morrow said shortly. "Lee, you know how people feel about Jews. You knew it when you married Maury. If you wanted to let yourself in for it, that's one thing. But you owe it to your child to save him from as much of it as you can."

214

"I'm the one who doesn't understand, Uncle Bill. I don't understand at all what you're trying to say to me." Lee looked at him with dark, unwavering eyes. For her the hurt of this moment had gone beyond the depths of anger into a region of feeling she had not known before. She stood up from the table pushing the chair back behind her; she stood there waiting for him to go on.

Bill Morrow was miserable; he wiped his brow with his napkin and then got up, too.

"Look, Lee. All I want is to make you a proposition. Go back to Dallas. I'll pay for everything. Start a home there; so when Maury comes back, that's where he'll come. In Dallas, Maury wasn't with Jews. People hardly thought of him as a Jew. And you both were happy there. He could sell the store, or let somebody else run it. As I see it, right now you've got a God-given chance to get back on the right side of the fence."

For a moment Lee only stood there. Then she walked to the couch and picked up her sweater; she walked out of the house and the screen door slammed shut behind her; she got into the car and drove away.

It was five o'clock; it was time to go home. Suddenly she was swept with guilt for having been away so long; she was possessed with the need to get home . . . home to Julian . . . home!

She drove the car into the drive; with a terrible sense of haste, she went running up the walk, calling,

"Julian, Julian! Come! Mommy's home!"

Late that night, when Julian slept and the house was still and brooding, Lee went downstairs and sat alone in the darkened living room. She raised the blinds to let in the moonlight and sat looking out into the shadowy tree-peopled yard and the quiet moon-paved street beyond.

Until this night Lee Kalman had thought of antisemites as people without faces, people with brutal hands and bitter hearts. She had not thought of an antisemite as a man who would bring home a puppy for a little girl, or sit in slippers beside a fire reading baseball scores, or plant tulips, and sign report cards, and pay too much for a first party dress, grumbling amiably all the while. She had not thought of antisemites as people who were able to love and be loved. And so, this night, Lee Kalman explored that new region of desperation that lies below the level of anger in the stillnesses of the soul.

To hate her uncle! . . . Lee had walked out of his house without speaking to him; she had walked out of his house with the intention never to return.

But it is not easy to hate someone whose past kindnesses have been known. And somehow a guilt that has been shared in innocence cannot be as bitterly and finally denounced as one that has never come within the experience at all. Lee thought of her uncle and searched her own heart. If the one emotion stronger than hate had not come into her life with its revealing light, would she not have allowed the group to enforce its mores upon her as strongly as they were enforced upon her uncle? And even if she grew beyond their concepts, would she have spoken out against them?

Even now, she had not really spoken out. Where before indifference or unconcern might have kept her silent, this day hopelessness and despair had kept her silent. But somewhere the voices must be raised, and they must be voices impassioned by personal experience; for how else could they be heard or heeded? Yet she had not spoken, not even for the sake of her son, not even to the uncle whom she had loved. And she had found that it is not easy to speak of injustice too tremendous for the conscience to bear.

But hate? How do you hate a man who is not consciously guilty of his own hate? How can you do more than weep for him, and for yourself? . . . and for all the ages of men who have hallowed hate? What ancient fear was his heart susceptible to, and how is it that a man in shackles thinks of himself as free. Lee, in this moment, reached the real and terrible crux of her problem. The world was inhabited by men like her uncle, by people who did not personally consider themselves prejudiced, but who were willing to make any and all concessions to what they considered to be the monstrous prejudice of others. Perhaps, then, it was a world in which the shadow far exceeded the substance; but how was the light to cast out the shadow?

Once again Lee thought of Sara Kalman. She thought of the hunger of the heart she had seen in that tired and vulnerable face, and she felt the greater compassion that insight brings. It seemed to Lee that, having thought these things through, she should be able to go to her mother-in-law. It seemed to her that if, in her own heart, she was sincere, she should be able to change her feelings. And yet this frantic, urgent need to preserve a sense of personal identity was too great to be ignored. And Lee Kalman

216

could not reconcile her attitude. She did not know what she must do.

She tried to think of Maury; she tried to think what he would say. But she didn't know . . . they had never really talked about it.

And there was no way now that she could ask him. Maury's last letter, weeks before, had come from a Port of Debarkation, and she waited now for that undefined signpost in a soldier's destiny—an A. P. O. number to which she might address her letters.

Captain Maury Kalman . . . Somewhere . . . This World . . .

III

Ellen Rosen heard what they were saying about Lee Kalman. She heard it over a bridge game, at a sisterhood meeting, in half a dozen telephone conversations.

Sara Kalman's friends were outraged, they were indignant— "That poor Sara should have such an ungrateful daughter-in-law. Wasn't it enough she should lose her husband and see her only son go to war? Must she also have her only son's wife reject her when his back was hardly turned? Had this *shikse* no compassion, no humanity, that she should deny poor Sara the comfort of her only grandson when she was doubly bereaved? And Sara so kind and generous, too, offering her home and asking nothing in return. But that's what came of a Jew marrying a Gentile. What could you expect? Poor Sara!"

This trend of conversation had been gathering momentum at an amazing rate since the afternoon when Sara Kalman had confided to three of her closest friends that Lee was going to rent her house and she did hope she could persuade Lee to come and live with her.

Ellen, observing how the tone of the gossips became more and more vindictive, well remembered Lee's deep and genuine affection for Maury's father. And that Sara should forget it, or ignore it, allowing the ugly implications of prejudice to go unchallenged, outraged Ellen's sense of fairness.

Ellen watched Sara Kalman. However genuine Sara's grief and tribulation, still, for her it was an invigorating experience to become a tragic heroine, lavishly consoled. To Sara, this excessive sympathy was balm to the spirit. She accepted it eagerly;

she encouraged it endlessly. She simply had no thought for what she was doing to the wife of her son.

Ellen glimpsed Lee, walking across the street to the post-office. Lee walked swiftly, her arms held close to her sides, her eyes large and dark and directed straight ahead. It was the way of walking of those who are new to ridicule, and Ellen's heart was touched. She thought of Sara Kalman basking in sympathy, and she thought of Lee Kalman walking in solitude. It was to Lee Kalman that Ellen went.

Ellen knocked at the door of the little, gray, clapboard house and waited. A moment later Lee opened the door, and her face lit with surprised pleasure when she saw who was there.

"Ellen! Come in. I have to show you what I've just finished for Maury."

Ellen followed Lee onto the sun porch where the big round table was strewn with a dozen small pen and ink sketches.

"Look!—a sequence entitled Julian Kalman's Day!" Lee gathered the sketches up and shuffled them into order. "All the big events, from orange juice in the morning until story book before bed."

"Why, Lee, they're wonderful!" Ellen told her as she thumbed through the pages; then spread them out again on the table. In these small, wry pictures was caught the unwary enchantment, the recalcitrance, the pixie mischievousness, and the vagrant whimsey of a small boy's long and timeless day.

"Maury will love them," Ellen said.

"They're better than I could do in a letter," Lee answered, a little wistfully.

"What do you hear from Maury?" Ellen asked her.

"Not much. The A. P. O. number is on the West Coast, so I guess that means the Pacific. I've had just one letter from overseas and he said the mail would be slow coming through. I think he's homesick," she laughed a little, and the laughter was a small sound in the room.

"Sit down, Ellen. I'm so glad you've come."

"I haven't seen you in a long time," Ellen said, sitting down on the rattan sofa by the window where the sun streamed in.

"I'm not very popular with your congregation right now. I didn't want to put you in an embarrassing position," Lee said.

"Be not silly!" Ellen told her.

Lee sat down on the big hassock, hands on knees, the way a

small girl sits. But the strain of the last weeks showed plainly in her face.

"Ellen," Lee said, a little tentatively, "I know what they're saying, but it isn't true. It isn't true that I want to shun it . . . it's that I have to find it . . . to seek it out . . . what it means to be a Jew. I've only glimpsed it now and then, in you and Rabbi, and in Maury's father, and this may sound funny, but even a little in Davey Levinson. In people who are Jews with their souls. . . . But it's not that way with Maury's mother. She's only a Jew in her habits."

Ellen laughed. Lee laughed, too; but then immediately she was serious again.

"No, really I mean it," Lee said. "Ellen, I know it isn't fair for me to try to make you partisan to my cause, but if I could just make even one person understand why I can't go and live with her. I meant that about habits. It's as if they were too ancient to be broken. It's almost as if they were her religion in themselves. And when people feel that way about things, you don't contend or contest over them for trifling reasons. It's as if she has the centuries on her side and I have only twenty-eight years on mine. And the person who is Lee Kalman would be awed right out of existence."

Although there was a wry smile on Lee's lips as she finished speaking, there was no mistaking the earnestness of her wish to be understood.

"Lee, if you know what you want to do, the thing is to act quickly so that there's no longer anything to argue," Ellen said gently. And Lee saw that Ellen did understand better even than she had imagined she could.

Lee smiled her appreciation.

"Ellen, let me get us something to drink," she said. "I didn't mean to dump it all in your lap so suddenly, but I've worried about it so much."

Ellen felt some curious tenderness for Lee's perplexity. When Lee had gone into the kitchen to make coffee, Ellen sat alone in the sunny room and thought about Lee . . . and Sara Kalman . . . and she perceived the eons that separated them. In a way it was true that Sara belonged to antiquity. In her blood there was memory, her emotions were steeped in memory that had lost its form but retained its essence—rich and tragic and full of glory. And back through the morass of folkway and superstition, her mind yearned after the illusive source of this memory.

But in Lee Kalman's blood there was no memory, only an alchemy of unlike things. And her emotions searched their present surroundings for their challenge, and her mind was clear and ready for a fresh imprint. Lee Kalman belonged to the future, and Ellen had seen her take the first timid, groping steps toward an understanding of Judaism . . . toward a Judaism that was more than Sara's *gefilte fish* and *challa* . . . toward a Judaism that was remembered in Sara's blood, but not in her conscious mind.

Restlessly Ellen stood up, she went to the window and looked out into the windy sun-strewn yard. Julian Kalman was playing on a rope swing that hung in the branches of a pear tree. He lay across the board on his stomach, balancing his weight in a wobbly way, while his feet occasionally scuffed in the dirt giving himself a push. Suddenly he abandoned this lackadaisical pastime and went running around the yard with some quick bright joy. Ellen waved at him, he saw her and waved back, jumping up and down as he waved. His kitten, grown into a lean, long cat, came to him, and he scooped it up with a rush of love and joy. He held it, staring rapturously into its sphinx-like face, while its long thin tail flicked back and forth hanging down below his knees.

Lee came back with a tray which she set down on the table. She came and stood beside Ellen and watched her son for a moment, too.

"He's a nice little child," Ellen said.

Lee nodded. "It's all so important because of him." She hesitated for a moment. "It's all so confusing, Ellen, because most of the time I seem to be acting just the opposite of the way I feel."

"How do you mean?"

"Well, I say that I want so much for Julian to be proud of the fact that his father is a Jew and to understand what it means. And it seems as though, if I really felt that way, I could go to his grandmother without a question because she knows and could teach him. But I have the most fierce feeling of wanting to teach him myself. And that's so ridiculous because how could I, a Christian, teach him what it really means to be a Jew?"

"Perhaps you could teach it better. Did she teach it to Maury so well?" Ellen asked, knowing that this was a thing she should not say.

"But how can I teach him?" Lee said, a little hopelessly.

"Lee, it doesn't take a musician to love music, or an artist to love beauty. And it doesn't take a Jew to comprehend the wisdom

220

and the beauty of Judaism. . . . It just takes someone with a heart, and a soul."

Lee was silent, the intensity of her thoughts was in her face. Ellen felt a deep awareness that Lee Kalman, by understanding Judaism, by loving it perhaps, could make it the more meaningful and beautiful and deeply cherished by her husband. And as for her son, it was hard enough that profound differences should be contained within a family; but for a little boy, who must contain them within his own soul, there could be no greater source of comfort and strength than to know that all things contained in himself were lovable in the eyes of his mother.

"Come, drink the coffee you made, it's getting cold," Ellen said finally, coaxing Lee from her perplexing reverie. Lee poured the coffee; she held out the plate of small rolls to Ellen. She smiled a little, but her eyes were as troubled as before.

"Something else worries you?" Ellen said.

"Yes . . . it's what worries me most. . . . It wouldn't matter so much what people say or how much they misunderstand. But the thing I can't stand is that sometimes they make me feel disloyal to Maury; and sometimes I even wonder if Maury would feel as they feel—that I'm rejecting his mother."

"Maury would know better!" Ellen reassured her firmly. An idea had begun forming in Ellen's mind and she fought it fiercely, knowing already that in the thought was born the action.

"Lee, could you not stay here?" Ellen asked.

Lee glanced around her, resisting the hold that this house had upon her. She shook her head. "I wouldn't be so alone in a place where Maury had never been!" she said.

"Why do you wait then? Why do you not make the change at once?" Ellen asked.

"It isn't so easy as that," Lee answered. "It's almost impossible to find an apartment at all. That's part of what Sara keeps saying. She makes me sound so unreasonable."

"Lee," Ellen said slowly, "it just happens I know of an apartment. I heard of it just the other day."

The spasm of hope in Lee's face was swiftly quelled. She shook her head. "It wouldn't do any good," she said. "With the defense plant, every apartment in town has a waiting list a mile long."

"This apartment I think you could get," Ellen said insistently, while the words ached in her throat. "It is very nice. I happened to see it. Small kitchen, very clean. A bedroom and a living room. The paint is new."

Lee laughed in spite of herself. "Ellen, you sound like a real-estate agent in the depression," she said. Very cautiously she moved along the perimeter of hope. Then, "What makes you think I could get it?" she said.

"You could get it," Ellen assured her. "The man who owns it is a friend of Rabbi's . . . a very good friend."

Lee took Ellen home, but Ellen did not go upstairs to her room; she could not bear to. Instead she walked. And she thought of Kurt, With an awful rage of love and disappointment and un-fulfilled hope, she thought of Kurt. And it was too hard a thing, to think of what her action had denied him.

She tried instead to think of Lee, of what the apartment meant to Lee. But she could not quite stop thinking of what it had meant to Kurt and to herself.

Ellen had come to the park. She sat on a stone bench and watched the swift darting movements of the squirrels punctuating the languor of the late July afternoon. She sat there trying not to think of all these things which the apartment had meant to her. But suddenly, to her amazement, she understood that giving it to Lee Kalman meant even more. So many ways Ellen had sought a new beginning, and in all the ways that she had tried she had experienced no real sense of beginning. But truly to care what happened to some other human being . . . perhaps that was the beginning she had sought. And she did care what happened to Lee Kalman. Giving the apartment to Lee had implanted beneath her sorrow a joy that was new.

Ellen stood up; she was suddenly in a hurry to go home, to find Kurt, to tell him. She walked very fast. Her feet almost stumbled on her own doorstep. A moment before, she could have wept for what her action denied Kurt—a chance to make life a little more gracious, a little more beautiful—but now she knew that she had something far better to give him—this sense of a new beginning.

"Kurtchen!" Ellen called, as she went running up the stairs.

It was not until the next day that the full irony of her own situation was brought home to Ellen. In the morning she went to the grocery store, and there she met Mrs. Stein, engrossed in that deep concentration which is common to pinchers of fruit. Mrs. Stein finally put a carefully selected sack of peaches into her basket and moved along to the corn which she would subject to the thumbnail test.

Ellen almost smiled. "Good morning, Mrs. Stein!" she called out breezily. Mrs. Stein looked up, squinting a little as she withdrew from her preoccupation.

"Why, Ellen . . . I had no idea you'd be shopping here."

Ellen resisted the temptation to meet this inanity with the observation that rabbis and their wives eat, too. Instead, she commented upon the exceptional quality of the honeydew melons.

But Mrs. Stein had suddenly recalled something that intrigued her even more than food. She sidled up to Ellen, squinting a little, as if this odd mannerism of eye excluded them from the casual eaves-dropping of fellow shoppers.

"Is it not a shame that poor Sara should not have a Jewish daughter-in-law to comfort her now?" she whispered hoarsely.

Suddenly Ellen could be silent no longer.

"Mrs. Stein, if Sara had a Jewish daughter-in-law, nobody would think to mention it twice if they could not agree to make their home together."

Ellen saw the shocked resentment in the old woman's face.

"I would think, Ellen, that you, of all people, would understand!" she said indignantly.

"I do understand, Mrs. Stein," Ellen assured her. "I understand that things will never be better than they are if every problem between a Jew and a Gentile is distorted into a problem of prejudice."

Mrs. Stein heaved herself up in disdain. She eyed Ellen suspiciously.

"Well, Ellen, I think it is pretty clear how Lee feels," she informed her. "And I think we should comfort poor Sara all we can!"

And so Ellen began to see. . . . The beginning she had sought to make for her husband, to assure his hopes and dreams, when finally it was made in a way that could be acknowledged by the heart, was turning out to be one that well could mean the devastation of these very hopes and dreams.

Ellen Rosen knew that what they had said about Lee Kalman would be as nothing compared to what they would saw about the rabbi's wife who championed a Gentile girl against a faithful, deserving and bereaved member of her own congregation.

223

Chapter 19

I

THE AUSTIN Building was the oldest and least efficiently maintained of Fall City's four large office buildings. But in spite of this fact, its tenants possessed a certain prestige which they partly bestowed and partly reaped.

The brass spittoons in the lobby of the Austin were more vigorously assaulted than the chrome and bakelite stands containing clean white sand which stood between the elevators of the Whit and Osage Buildings. And the antiseptic corridors of these two structures lacked the sense of something important which seemed to lurk in the smell of smoke that haunted the gloomy Austin lobby.

The Austin Building had its doctors, its lawyers, its land and cattle companies, its insurance agents, its oil companies, and its real-estate dealers; but its real distinction was in the fact that it was the stronghold of those citizens who unwaveringly clung to the importance of "coming of pioneer stock."

Bill Morrow sat at his desk behind the plate glass window which bore his name and stared out at the late afternoon activity which centered in this end of Main Street. Young Dinny was shining a pair of cowboy boots on his homemade wooden box, which meant that fifteen minutes later he'd be downstairs in the basement where the men played pool. The last of the bright young stenographers from the Plains Oil Company were returning from their afternoon coffee at Lindy's. Jim DeFor was out there, leaning on a parking meter, trying to scare up a buyer for some of the cattle he couldn't feed on his burned-out rangeland.

Bill Morrow sighed. It was a sigh which bespoke no discontent. He saw Dory Winslow coming up the street, the inevitable brief case under his arm. The door eventually opened and this rather dapper gentleman moved briskly into Bill Morrow's grimy little office.

"Hello, Bill," Dory said. He put the brief case on the desk and sat down before Bill had a chance to ask him. Briskness always discomfited Bill Morrow; he leaned back in his swivel chair a little restlessly.

"How're things, Dory? . . . How's the furniture business?" Bill asked.

"Couldn't be better," Dory answered. "Look, Bill, I want to enlist your help."

"Anything I can do, Dory."

"You know, Bill, for a couple of months I've been talking up the idea of a high class and high price men's club for Fall City. Bates wrote an editorial about it in the *Tribune*. And there's been a lot of talk."

"I know; it's a damn good idea," Bill Morrow answered. "That's the sort of thing that could pull Fall City up by the bootstraps . . . outgrow this cowtown reputation . . . this hick stuff," Bill expounded grandly. He was quoting freely from Bates' editorial, knowing in his heart that he was pretty much of a hick himself.

Dory Winslow seemed heartened by his enthusiasm.

"Well, you know, Bill, these things don't do themselves. It takes more than talk. And it takes more than one man. The way I see it we need about a dozen of the most representative businessmen in town to get together and make the plans and start the organization . . . and put in the first money, too, of course."

"I think you're absolutely right," Bill Morrow agreed.

"Well, the point is, I think you ought to be on that list of men," Dory told him.

The flush of pleasure rose in Bill Morrow's round and amiable face. Dory Winslow always made him feel a little ineffectual; but suddenly he felt grandly capable.

"Well now, Dory, that's not a thing a man would want to pass up—to be on the ground floor of organizing something like that. I'm your man, if you think I qualify."

"Good, that's fine!" Dory picked up his brief case. We'll meet tomorrow night at the country club for dinner . . . start the ball rolling! Be there about eight."

Bill Morrow leaned back in his swivel chair and laced his fingers across his vest. This was a moment for savoring. In spite of his brash and confident exterior, Bill had never outgrown a small-town boy's wonder at his own importance.

The next night, when Bill Morrow saw the men who had responded to Dory's plea for cooperation, he was even more impressed. Assembled around the table in the dining room in the Country Club's west wing were Skip Henshaw, progressive new president of the First National Bank; Guy Lawrence, head of Plains Oil; Billy Lawson, gray-haired and young, whose family once had owned most of three counties; a couple of junior executives in their neatly creased suits; dry and humorous Stony Barton, who owned grocery stores in eight towns; Dr. Tom Sanders, president of the Kiwanis Club; dour and gouty Charles Anderson, whose business acumen was legendary; and urbane Dory, himself.

At this first meeting the men consumed thick steaks and mainly congratulated themselves upon the importance of their undertaking. The second meeting, held a week later, they got down to business, to planning the sort of club house they would want, to considering proposed sites, to determining the cost of membership. But this second meeting went a little jerkily. Nobody seemed to have his mind entirely on the phase of the project under discussion at any particular moment. Gradually Bill Morrow began to have the uneasy feeling that this inattentiveness among the others had something to do with himself. Stubbornly he fought down this idea. He was very hearty and full of high spirits, and the others were almost too eager to match his *camaraderie*. At last he could not deny that something was amiss; but he did not know what.

Several days later, when Dory Winslow stopped by his office again, Bill Morrow had the sudden premonition that he would learn what the trouble had been.

"Bill, we'll meet again tomorrow night," Dory said in his crisp impersonal manner.

"I know, I'll be there," Bill answered.

"Bill, I think we'll get around to discussing rules for membership," Dory said. He hesitated significantly.

Bill, who had been tamping down tobacco into his pipe, glanced up, glanced away. The broadness of his own thumb nail tamping down the tobacco seemed suddenly to intrigue him.

With a small impatient movement Dory got a better grip on his briefcase under his arm.

"Bill, it's bound to come up at the meeting about admitting Jews. If you can't make it, we'll understand."

And when Dory Winslow had gone, Bill Morrow thought of Lee.

He thought of the silky softness of a small girl's pigtails and the way they quivered with the warm, ecstatic excitement of life. He thought of a sleepy head on his shoulder and the trip down a dark hall to bring a drink of water. . . . He tried to think of later things: of the odd, hurtful, little aloofness of an adolescent girl, and of dates, and of the years when she didn't seem to need him anymore. . . . But it was of a little girl that he thought—of knobby knees, and shoes that always looked comically big, and small artless hands, held out brimming full of love.

It wasn't possible to decide anything, not really, without thinking of Lee. Bill got up from his desk and moved restlessly about his office. He banged a file drawer open and shut, shuddering at the clanging metallic sound.

He sat down again. Bill Morrow was fond of thinking of himself as a tolerant and broadminded man. He had always been rather pleased with himself because of the way he treated his Jewish nephew-in-law "just like anybody else." For his encounters with Maury he had adopted a manner of officious raillery . . . and he had never understood Lee's tense, constrained reaction to his attempts at "friendliness."

It had been Bill Morrow's attitude that he could forgive Lee for loving Maury, even for marrying him. But the one thing he was not ready to forgive her was the feeling that she finally had allowed her loyalty to her husband to exceed her loyalty to the way of life that had nutured her. As long as she had loved Maury "in spite of his being a Jew," Bill Morrow had felt that at least a proper balance, a perspective, was maintained. But gradually he had come to the uneasy feeling that the "in spite of" was no longer a corollary of the loving. And this he did not know how to forgive Lee; this made her alien to him.

In the weeks since Lee had departed furiously out of his house he had tried and tried to understand how he had bungled so completely in presenting to her what he considered a logical and practical course of action. He had wavered between the irritated impulse to "wash his hands of her, completely," and the wistful, baffled hope "that sooner or later, she's bound to come to her senses."

Bill Morrow sat at his desk after most of the tenants of the Austin Building had gone home. He sat there after darkness had moved in through the plate-glass window, surrounding him with night. He sat there and he faced his decision—Lee on one side, the whole social structure of his life on the other.

II

Sam Levinson stood beside the sunken marble fish-pond in the lobby of the Fall City Hotel, speaking to fellow Rotarians as they filed out after their noon meeting. By two's and three's they paused to speak to each other, and most of them stopped to speak to Sam.

"How's the bond drive going, Sam?" Guy Lawrence asked him, peeling the cellophane off a cigar and stopping just short of aiming the wadded wrapper at a fat and insolent orange fish. "God! I'd hate to come in here in the middle of the night drunk," he said.

Sam laughed. "The bond drive will be over the top by the end of the week at this rate," he said.

"That's one thing, Sam; you can really put them over the top. And you always seem to do it without getting their dander up. Not me! Any drive I head, I have to shake it out of them with brute force, and before it's over the public and I are both a wreck."

Sam laughed again. He felt urbane and capable. It was good for a man to be successful at things.

Dory Winslow wandered up from another group.

"Hi, Sam!—See you tonight, Guy."

"Sure, Dory. I think I can make it."

"God, I get tired of these meetings," Guy Lawrence expostulated. "Spend half of every day conferring with a bunch of junior executives. And damned near every night somebody wants to meet about something. I'm not too sold on this club idea anyway. We're a bunch of country hicks, and we might as well know it. It's going to be too damned high-priced for my blood."

"Go to the meeting, maybe you can learn how to get it without shaking it out of them," Sam said. Sam felt a tingling along the back of his neck. There was absolutely no way that he could express how urgently important it was to him for Guy Lawrence to go to that meeting. He could only be bland and humorous and not let it be known how much it mattered.

"Yeah, maybe I could at that!" Guy said, "Well, see you, Sam. I've got to get back to the office."

Sam Levinson went across the street to where his Cadillac was parked in the parking lot. He got into the car; but he did not start the motor. He sat there, mulling over the last hour—the way they talked about the club in his presence, the way they all but included him in their conversation. Sam could not believe that they meant to exclude him. Sam first had heard the men discussing the new club at a meeting of Rotary, then at a meeting of the Chamber of Commerce, and then for weeks they had talked of little else.

Probably there was no man in Fall City capable of appreciating such a club to a greater extent than Sam Levinson. Elegance did not make Sam nervous as it did some of his midwest-born-and-bred contemporaries. He was capable of being entirely at home in a setting of contrived elegance. Sam liked to do things with a flair; he liked to do things the expensive way. But as matters stood, there was no place of distinction in Fall City where he could take an out-of-town business associate for dinner, or where he could entertain guests up from Dallas or down from Chicago. There was no place of taste and elegance, besides his own formal and ornate dining room, where he could arrange a small party.

In the whole town there was only one place which had any claim to distinction at all, and that was the Country Club; and Jews were not admitted to the Country Club. This fact had, through the years, caused Sam more secret chagrin than any embarrassment that he had ever suffered. Over the span of two decades, Sam Levinson's personality and his willingness and ability to accept civic responsibility had made it possible for him to cultivate many non-Jewish contacts. As his position became more secure and respected in the community as a whole, as more and more doors were opened to him, he felt more and more keenly his exclusion from this pinnacle of acceptance and success.

This exclusion was, of course, never mentioned between Sam and his friends who were members. Twice, during the years, there had been incidents involving Jews and the Country Club. Once, a socially prominent Gentile girl had married a Jew, thus forfeiting her membership. Another time, a new couple in town had been offered membership before it was known that they were Jews, and to the great embarrassment of everyone concerned the offer was gracelessly withdrawn.

But Sam Levinson went to great lengths to contrive explanations for these special instances. And over and over again he tried to persuade himself that the rule about Jews was an archaic one, made thirty years before, when people felt differently. Over and over again he tried to persuade himself that some day his friends would get around to changing the rule, making it conform more to this enlightened era—for, after all, Jews were no different than anybody else. He could see himself that there were lots of Jews they wouldn't want; but then, there were lots of Gentiles they didn't want, either.

However hard these rationalizations had been to sustain, Sam had sustained them. But now it was no longer a question of whether he could sustain them. In the new men's club these feeble but vital props to his ego were being put to the test. Now they would either make the rule excluding Jews all over again, or they would not make it. There could no longer be evasion or equivocation that Sam could translate into mere procrastination. They must make their decision; and Sam Levinson knew that upon their decision the whole premise upon which he had built his life would stand or fall apart. And Sam Levinson was afraid.

With a desperate interest Sam assayed each of the men who had been chosen to get the thing going. A word, a phrase, an inflection of voice could often tell a great deal about a man's feelings, his outlook and attitude. Sam searched his mind for the content of each smallest encounter he had ever had with each of these men. Carefully he weighed and evaluated. And, finally, according to his estimate, there were six who would vote "yes," to including Jews, and six who would vote "no." Heading those who would be opposed was Dory Winslow; and heading those in favor would be Guy Lawrence. And if the vote was as equally divided as he supposed, then there must be something to turn the tide one way or another. There must be some deciding factor.

One of the men Sam Levinson counted upon to vote "yes" was Bill Morrow, Lee Kalman's uncle. Upon this one man Sam Levinson placed all of his hopes. Surely, for Lee's sake, Bill Morrow would feel more than a passing and impersonal interest. Surely from Lee's point of view, Bill Morrow would understand how it was. Sam Levinson backed his car out of the parking lot. One man who really understood how it was should be able to turn the tide.

On impulse Sam Levinson decided that he would drive by to see Lee Kalman. He had seen Lee only twice since Maury's departure, but he suddenly wanted to reassure himself about Lee. As Sam stopped in front of the Kalman home, he saw a moving van drawn up in the driveway and a rawboned young man in overalls gave him a card with a scribbled address at which Mrs. Kalman could be found. Sam drove to the apartment.

It was Lee herself who quickly answered his knock at the door, and he saw at once that her face was flushed and troubled.

"Well, Lee! What's the trouble?" he demanded heartily.

"I've just found out something that distresses me very much," Lee answered honestly. She turned back into the room and Sam saw that Ellen Rosen was sitting on one end of the couch, the other end of which was piled high with books and two pictures.

"Hello, Mr. Levinson," Ellen said, her voice perhaps a note lower than it ordinarily would have been.

Sam nodded curtly. He was prepared to hear that Ellen was the cause of Lee's distress.

"What's the matter?" he asked Lee again, as if he personally were prepared to soothe away all trouble.

"It was Ellen who told me about this apartment . . . and I just found out that she and Rabbi were supposed to have had it."

"I didn't want that she know it. The owner of the apartment had only to tell her," Ellen interposed with genuine concern.

"I move out of a fine, big, comfortable house to take the apartment, and leave the Rosens in one miserable room," Lee wailed.

The unconscious reproach in these words grated unendurably on Sam Levinson's ego. He glanced more appraisingly around the apartment, ferreting out the details. His eye took in the smooth, gray carpet under foot, the attractive modern furniture, the bookcases now half filled with Lee's books, the brass planters of ivy before the tiny fire place.

"I didn't know anything about an apartment for the Rosens," he said biting the words off sharply.

"It was only a matter between Rabbi and Mr. Benson," Ellen replied with a quiet dignity that belied the look of fire that leapt to her eyes. "Mr. Benson offered the apartment to Rabbi . . ."

Sam Levinson had not missed the look of fire in Ellen's eyes. He stood there, smiling at her sardonically, trying to make the dark eyes waver before he should answer. But Ellen's eyes did not waver.

"You should have taken the apartment," he said finally. "The rest of us could have fixed Lee up somehow!"

He laughed, turning to Lee with the constrasting offer of a warm, protective geniality. But Lee rejected it, her eyes moving swiftly to Ellen, who sat still where she was, feeling the fierce bite of her nails in the palms of her hands.

Lee's glance came levelly back to Sam Levinson's florid, sensual and oddly handsome face. "I can't offer you coffee," she said, "the gas isn't turned on."

"Don't give it a thought!" Sam blustered. "I just wanted to see if we could do anything for you."

"The Rosens have done everything for me that anybody could do," Lee answered simply.

Sam Levinson twisted his hat in his hand, but Lee did not invite him to sit down. In that moment the tall, rawboned young furniture mover came loping up the hall.

"I got the furniture for the kid's room now . . . if you're ready,

Mrs. Kalman," he said with gauche politeness that infuriated Sam Levinson.

"That's fine, you can bring it right in," Lee answered. She began to push a chair aside to clear a path to the bedroom. Then she seemed to remember Sam. She hesitated.

"It was nice of you to come," she said.

And a moment later, after a curiously graceless departure, Sam Levinson, who prided himself on urbanity, found himself down in the street again.

The next morning Sam Levinson heard about the meeting where membership was discussed—he heard about the meeting that Bill Morrow did not attend. And he knew that Jews would not be admitted to the new men's club.

It took Sam a few days to allow the full sense of what had happened to be borne in upon him. And like a child who is not able to understand or accept, he searched the faces of the men he knew; he searched their faces for the look of this thing which had so devastated him. But the look of it was not in their faces. And more devastating than the exclusion itself, was the fact that it could be accomplished as a simple, unpremeditated matter of course, leaving no trace of soul-wracking decision upon the faces of those who made it.

Sam sat next to Guy Lawrence in the Grill when he went for coffee, and Guy Lawrence talked about the bond drive again and about the war, and his eyes met Sam's in the usual clear and friendly way, without embarrassment or constraint.

Sam bumped into Bill Morrow in the drugstore, and Bill shook his hand with the usual heartiness of greeting.

And Dory Winslow called on the phone to tell him that the order could be filled on the chaise longue that Myra had so admired, if she still wanted it.

To swallow rage and match casual unconcern with casual unconcern was a thing Sam Levinson was temperamentally unable to do. He was a thoroughly embittered man, ready at last to take refuge in his Jewishness. In this moment of defeat, he girded himself with a bitter racial pride to exceed the pride of those who hurt him, a racial exclusiveness to exceed their exclusiveness.

But dealing in generalities could not appease Sam Levinson. His wrath was so intense that it must pit itself against something. With grim fury he thought of how he had stood, awkwardly unwelcome in the doorway of Lee Kalman's apartment only the day before. The irony of his having counted upon her twisted in him.

And he seized upon this chance to avenge himself at the source of his present humiliation. He made Lee Kalman the object of his scorn; he pointed to her as the embodiment of Gentiles who must be shunned and scorned.

And when Sam Levinson had cast Lee Kalman in this role, he found that, as bonus to his bitterness, he had a ready-made reason for his harsh resentment against Kurt and Ellen Rosen—a contrived reason that, to his own mind, absolved him of the smallness of personal antagonism.

Already there had been gossip about the fact that Ellen Rosen had given the apartment to Lee. But there is a viciousness that accrues to idle gossip only when a chance circumstance lends itself with plausibility to malicious purpose. The circumstances lent themselves incredibly well to Sam Levinson's dual purpose of discrediting the Rosens and avenging his fierce and bitter pride. And he did not wait long to avail himself of the opportunity.

That night in the game-room in the basement of his new home, Sam was playing poker with Herman Morris, Max Shaffer and Sid Meyers. The shaded light that pulled down from the ceiling was drawn low, pitting its harsh brilliant light against the green felt of the table.

Sam shuffled the cards; he started to deal another hand; but instead he threw the cards down on the table.

" 'Nother drink?" he said. He got up and went to the liquor cabinet against the wall. He poured four more drinks. Herman Morris got up to stretch his long legs.

Sid pushed back from the table.

"Come on, let's get on with the game. I'll lose my shirt at this rate!" Max Shaffer complained. He wasn't used to playing for such stiff stakes; Sam looked at him disparagingly.

"Say, what's eating you Sam? Same old story?—mad 'cause you weren't invited?" Herman asked, his morose face taking on the look of malicious humor.

Sam shot him a cutting glance that would have quelled most such comment. But Herman was no longer impressed by Sam's officiousness.

"Or is it Davey and the rabbi again? . . ." Herman continued uninterruptedly.

"Why bring that up?" Sam asked shortly.

"You're the one who's always bringing it up," Herman said, shrugging his drooping shoulders.

"Well, who wouldn't! What kind of a Jew do I have teaching

my boy—a German Jew! And what kind of a Jew is a German Jew?" Sam shrugged his shoulders, too; but for him the gesture attained a certain elegant expressiveness. "Look at the German Jews," he said. "They were accepted by the Christian world, and that's all they cared about. They were more for Gentiles than they were for other Jews. And look what's happening to them."

"God knows it's hard to look when you think . . ." Max Shaffer began; but Sam quelled him with a glance.

"And the sad part is they don't learn," Sam said. "Just look how it's working out right here. Our own rabbi's wife sides with a Gentile in a showdown. They even gave her their own apartment when they could have lived better . . . been more of a credit to the congregation!" Sam railed indignantly.

"We should have found them a better apartment in the first place," Max interposed, a little timidly; but this remark Sam ignored entirely.

"And now what happens?" Sam asked rhetorically. "This very girl's uncle shows how he feels about the Jews. He slams another door in our faces. It's damned hard to take any time; but when your own rabbi is busy doing them favors . . . well! you know how I feel. I think I've made it pretty clear."

Chapter 20

MRS. STEIN climbed, panting up the stairs at the boarding house next to the synagogue. Under one arm she carried a warm and slightly mashed loaf of nut-banana bread for the rabbi and Ellen, and in the other hand, in a mesh shopping bag, she carried her Red Cross knitting. She had come to stay awhile.

She knocked on the door, and Ellen answered immediately.

"Why, Mrs. Stein, come in. It's nice of you to come," Ellen said, taking the paper-wrapped parcel that was promptly extended to her.

"I know you don't bake, Ellen. I thought the Rabbi might like this," Mrs. Stein said. She sighed wearily from the climb up the stairs and fanned herself with one fat hand.

"Thank you," Ellen said evenly. She caught the inside of her lip between her teeth. It had become an excruciating test of endurance to see how long she could accept Mrs. Stein's barbs without retorting in kind.

Mrs. Stein sat down in the lumpy chair and pulled out her knitting. The untidy ball of thread escaped its mesh bag and went rolling out over the floor. Mrs. Stein's considerable bulk seemed to sag dejectedly as she took up her needles in pudgy hands and set them clicking at each other viciously.

"How are you coming with your knitting, Ellen?" Mrs. Stein asked.

"Fine," Ellen replied casually. She smiled to herself, knowing that by Mrs. Stein's criteria—baking and speaking a fluent Yiddish—she was hopelessly inadept. "I'm knitting one large sweater a week now," she told her guest.

Mrs. Stein glanced up crossly. It was not an answer which pleased her, as she herself could find time for only one small sweater every two weeks.

"Ellen! . . ." Mrs. Stein dropped her knitting in her lap, unmindful of the stitches that slipped free. She leaned forward so that the chair seemed to move forward with her. "Ellen, my dear, do you and Rabbi know what Sam Levinson is saying," she whispered hoarsely, narrowing her eyes.

Ellen shook her head.

Mrs. Stein remembered the day in the grocery store; she was

slyly curious about what Ellen's reaction would be. She folded her flabby arms over her massive bosom and began her recital.

"He's speaking out against German Jews!"

"What is he saying?" Ellen demanded, her eyes impenetrable in their darkness.

"He's saying that all they wanted was to be accepted by Gentiles, that they cared nothing for other Jews; he's saying that's what's behind all that is happening to them now."

"Why is he saying it? He speaks against us, but why?"

Mrs. Stein had arrived at the part of her recital which she personally relished. Her eyelids fluttered again in a characteristic gesture.

"Well, Ellen, there were lots of us thought your first loyalty should have been to Sara, not Lee Kalman, and that's the point Sam is making."

Mrs. Stein felt herself wavering a little under the intensity of Ellen Rosen's gaze.

"Maybe we didn't like it . . . but everybody makes mistakes," she said in a mildly conciliatory tone, "and as for you being German Jews . . ."

"You'll forgive us for that, too?" Ellen demanded.

Mrs. Stein looked hurt. "Now, Ellen, there's no call for you to be angry!" she maintained.

German Jew!—To have lost an identity is to know bright, distorted moments when that identity is too powerfully superimposed again upon the heart.—When Mrs. Stein had gone these words seemed to claim Ellen again with all the nuance and complexity and deep tragedy of their meaning.

German Jew!—The very words evoked a bitter, tearing nostalgia for a world that had existed within a world that destroyed it. Life is not lived in a vacuum, Ellen thought almost hysterically. To have loved life is to have loved the place where it was lived. The pure distillate of emotion becomes defined and committed to memory through small irrelevant details: the laughing pause for breath at the landing of the stairway, the little shop where suppers could be bought late in the afternoons of busy days, the mailbox at the corner, a bench in the park—these were the native land of the heart. Ellen hated all things German with a fierce and unrelenting hatred, even the feel of the language on the tongue. But to hate all things German was a refraction of the spirit that tried the very soul.

Ellen understood that Sam Levinson's attack was an intensely personal one, against Kurt, against herself. It was as if all that had formed them, all that had brought them together was attacked. It was as if the thing that was attacked was the validity of their pride in themselves, in each other. For herself, Ellen might have borne this, but for Kurt, she could not.

Suddenly Ellen was possessed with the need to go to Kurt—to offer comfort for what he might not even know about, to seek comfort for what she could not even express. Suddenly she was running down the stairs, across the yard. She paused at the door of the synagogue. The Eternal Light burned above the pulpit; a look of quietness, almost of slumbering, lay upon the seats. But from Kurt's study she could hear the peck, peck, peck of a typewriter.

Ellen tiptoed to the door of the study.

"Kurtchen," she said softly, as if to disturb the trend of his thought only a little bit.

Kurt turned around in his chair. Quick amusement leapt to his eyes with the awareness of this special consideration. He caught up Ellen's hand and kissed it.

"One minute, Sweetheart!" he said, and briefly he turned back to the typewriter.

It was the German typewriter that had come with him from Duisburg, and in appearance it seemed to bear more relation to an old fashioned sewing machine than to the American streamlined typewriters. Ellen sat down and watched him type. It was strange, Ellen thought again, the things that survived the complete devastation of life—a typewriter, the two small Persian rugs which Ellen had put finally here in the study because they seemed so hopelessly to misfit the rented room, the few pieces of silver, and the china which would seem to be the most perishable of things, and two rings, one of which had belonged to her mother.

Suddenly Ellen was remembering the three bracelets she wore on the day they left Germany, three heavily-ornamented, copper bracelets that a friend had asked her to wear.

. . . *"the bracelets, Ellen, they're not like you."*
. . . *"Minnie gave them to me, Kurtchen, she asked me to wear them."*

In Holland, Ellen had delivered the bracelets to Minnie's father. Beneath the ornamental copper was solid gold—enough to launch an old and bewildered man and his wife upon a new life in a new world. If Ellen had been caught—but then, at the time, it had not seemed too great a thing to ask, too great a thing to do. German Jews—people who did not know how to give themselves up gracefully to annihilation . . .

"Now!" Kurt pulled the typewritten page from the machine and spun around in his chair. "What's with you, Sweetheart?"

Ellen looked into his smiling eyes without quite being able to believe the smile.

"Kurt, do you know what Sam Levinson is saying?" she asked him.

A little of the zestfulness seemed to desert his bearing, so that he looked vulnerable to a weariness that might encroach at any moment upon what was vital and almost joyful.

"Yes, Ellen, I know."

"Kurt, how could one Jew speak so of other Jews? . . . How could they not know? . . . Where is their sense of rescue?"

Kurt sat looking at Ellen for a moment. He reached out a hand and touched her hair in a small caress.

"They do not understand, Ellen. . . . Even being Jews, they do not understand."

"But what don't they understand? Why don't they?"

Kurt sighed. "To suffer within the limits of humanity is to suffer within the scope of man's imagination," he replied. But the Jews of Germany . . . they are cast off beyond the imaginations of men by a suffering that is too great . . . too great . . ."

"How is it just?—If suffering exists to become meaningful, how is it just that some men should suffer more than others can even comprehend . . . how could it be just?" Ellen's dark eyes were on Kurt's face for a moment, and then she put her hands over her face.

And Kurt watched her, strangely unable to comfort her; for in that moment he realized that, paradoxically, part of the ability to comfort depends upon a lesser awareness. But in that moment Kurt suffered the tragedy of which they spoke anew, not as a man suffers it, but as it is enfolded in the exquisite soul of a woman.

The same week that Sam Levinson began his tirade against German Jews, Kurt Rosen was thumbing through his mail at the synagogue one morning, and noticed an unfamiliar postmark. The letter was from Australia. He tore it open.

There were two sheets, one crisp and new, the other much creased and limp.

Instinctively, Kurt read the old and creased page first. The salutation was to Ellen.

"Dear Ellen. Your father died, Warsaw ghetto, May 1942. There were no shrouds. We wrapped the body in newspapers so that it would not be naked in the coffin. Every rag counts. Minnie."

Kurt read the note three times: once for himself, and once for Ellen, and once for the way that he would tell her. And then he glanced at the new sheet of paper. A man named Carl Thomas, newly arrived in Australia, had received the enclosed note from a second man, who had received it two months previously from a member of the Polish Underground which had smuggled from the Warsaw Ghetto its furtively scribbled, unanswered appeals to the world. The man named Carl Thomas concluded by expressing his sympathy in a crisp and impersonal phrase.

Kurt folded the two letters together again and put them in his pocket. If he hurried, he might catch Ellen before she left for the Red Cross. As he came out of the synagogue, he saw her already standing on the corner, waiting for the bus. She saw him, too, and waved.

Kurt was glad, suddenly, to see her there. To tell this thing outside, under the open sky, where the wind could blow the words away, would be better, somehow, than to tell it in a small tight room, where, for one suffocating moment they might be closed in with the horror of it.

"Kurtchen, do you come to town, too?" Ellen called to him. "Where is your hat?" The wind blew his hair and she smiled at him.

"No, Ellen, but walk with me for a moment," he said, and he caught her hand. Gently between them they swung hands for a moment.

"What is it, Kurt?" Ellen said.

"Ellen . . . knowing all that you know . . . would you rather think of your parents as alive or dead."

"I'd rather think of them as dead!" Ellen answered quickly, the words hardly moving on her lips.

Kurt held her hand hard against his side.

"Your father is dead," he said simply. "Come, I'll show you the letter."

That night Ellen dreamt that she was in the railroad station at Duisburg where she had been a thousand times. But the storm troopers were at the gates and about the platform and at the entrance of the boxcar. And she stood on the platform with the people of her husband's congregation . . . but she did not know

239

them, yet . . . for in the dream she was a child, searching for her father.

And suddenly she saw him; and in her child's eyes he was young and vigorous as he had been in the days when his youth and vigor and fire of imagination had been the hallowing place for a small girl's timid dreams . . . and she started to run to him . . . but in that instant he saw her, too, and he made a small staying gesture with his hand, and his eyes warned her. And she stood where she was as he unobtrusively made his way toward her. When he stood beside her, he seemed hardly to turn in her direction.

"Do not seem eager, Liebchen," he said. "They resent even our ability to comfort each other"—and briefly his eyes met hers—and she was no longer a child, but a woman with a woman's awareness. And she stood beside him as a woman, but as his daughter. And he was older, too, and stooped of shoulder. But the sun was warm and gentle on the haggard bleakness of his face, so that the glow seemed to come from within, and all that had ever been between them of love and warmth was between them now, though for a time they did not speak or look at one another. Finally, he said,

"How is America, Liebchen, you haven't told me?"

And Ellen felt in these words the acrid sharpness of presentiment which is the essence of dreaming . . . and she knew that he would go and she would not. Yet, in that instant, there seemed nothing to divide their destinies . . . and there was only the wild and throbbing anguish.

When morning came, the dream still was more real than the reality of the small drab room where Ellen sat at breakfast with her husband.

"Ellen!" Kurt leaned toward her, laying a hand over hers. She brought her eyes to his face.

"Kurt, I don't want any here to know. . . . Can you understand that?"

Kurt thought of Sam Levinson, of Mrs. Stein. "Yes, Ellen, I can understand it. But when you say the *kaddish* in the synagogue . . ."

"I'm not sure that I will say the *kaddish* in the synagogue . . . I'm not sure that I can." Earnestly Ellen studied Kurt's face for any hint of shock or reproach; but there was none, only an infinite gentleness.

"They deny us so much, . . . we must not deny each other that—the saying of the prayers," Kurt said.

Something hard and bitter flashed in Ellen's eyes. "Oh, yes,

we Jews have no choice other than depend upon each other . . .
even to pray for the dead!"

"Ellen . . ."

"It is not tragic enough! Still, ten Jews who do not know what
it is to be a German Jew . . . ten Jews who have no sense of
rescue . . . must form a *minyan* so I can say the *kaddish* for my
father."

Kurt did not try to answer her; he came and stood beside her
and put his arms around her.

"I'm sorry, Kurt. I'm sorry to say these things to you. But I
do not know if I can rise with the mourners."

When Kurt had gone to the synagogue, Ellen got up from
the breakfast table and began to clear away the dishes and to
put the room in order. But an anguished sense of guilt and disloyalty moved in her steps.

It was not God to whom she felt disloyal, but to Kurt, Ellen
realized with a strange dispair. The throbbing anguish, the wild
rebellious bitterness did not acquiesce at all to the thought of
God. Kurt thought she had learned to love God, but it was not
true. She had learned to love holiness for its perfection as a
mood, but she was not at all sure she understood the way in
which holiness bound the soul to God. She did not feel bound
to God. And it was not God upon whom she relied, but Kurt.
Ellen felt an aching sadness that this should be so, that she
could believe only in Kurt while the whole meaning of his life
was a belief in something beyond himself.

Ellen thought about God and washed the dishes, and when she
poured the sudsy water down the drain, she looked around for
other jobs to do. It was very important to keep busy . . . because
she was not sure at all whether she would be able to rise and say
the *kaddish*.

The next Friday afternoon, Ellen lit the Sabbath candles a
little before sundown, and when it was seven-thirty she went
next door to the synagogue to greet the members of the congregation as they assembled. The door of Kurt's study was closed, and
she did not go back to him. And she still did not know if she
would say the *kaddish*.

At eight o'clock Kurt came out of his study and entered the
pulpit. He looked out upon those assembled for a moment, and
then he said:

"We will begin our services, with the singing of the Sabbath
hymn to be found on page 387."

Ellen began to sing, just as on any other Friday night. The voices of the others who sang rose and fell in a curiously toneless and melancholy rumble above which her voice exulted.

And Kurt began to read: "How goodly are your tents, O Jacob, your dwelling places, O Isreal—"

And now Ellen listened to his voice, to the voice of the man who had won her from a way of life she yearned after to a way of life she could only partly follow. And she heard in his voice a love and a compassion for all humanity which fell for the most part upon ears of those unmindful of their need. Her own need was great, and she was mindful of it. And she listened and knew that the love and compassion were more for her than for any other. And that they should be thus most beautifully expressed, not to her directly, but in an entreaty to God, brought a curious and a beautiful awe to her heart.

And finally, as Kurt read the prayer before *kaddish,* Ellen listened so intently that a small blue vein throbbed in her throat.

> *As we recite Israel's hallowed prayer, we aver, despite our woe and anguish, that life is good and life's tasks must be performed. Help us, O Lord, to rise above our sorrow and face the trials of life with courage in our hearts. Give us insight in this hour of grief that from the depths of suffering may come a deepened sympathy for all who are bereaved, that we may feel the heartbreak of our fellow men and find strength in helping them. Heartened by this hymn of praise to Thee, we bear our sorrow with trustful hearts, and knowing that Thou art near, shall not despair. With faith in Thine eternal wisdom, we who mourn, rise to sanctify Thy name . . .*

And Ellen Rosen stood . . . and Kurt's voice met hers over the intervening heads . . . and these ancient and worshipful and beautiful words which each man must claim for himself, joined them anew. In these words was the strength and comfort that had accrued to them from all that they had hallowed through all the centuries that ten Jews had prayed together.

In these words, at this moment, there was released to Ellen a meaning she had not found in them before and a strength that is not known until there is need of it. And the voices of the mourners moved over the words like feet shuffling softly over the stepping stones of eternity.

Yis-ga-dal, v'yis-ka-dash shmei ra-bbo . . .

242

Chapter 21

LEE KALMAN felt very keenly the things that Sam Levinson was saying about her uncle; but however often she heard them insinuated, she could not believe they were true. Finally, on a rainy afternoon, she got in the car and drove to her uncle's house. She ran up the sidewalk, her raincoat flung over her shoulders, the drops of water caught in her hair. Almost at the same moment Bill Morrow drove into the driveway. Lee waited for him on the porch.

"Well now, Lee! This is a nice surprise. You going to stay for supper?" he asked as he joined her at the front door, big and vigorous and as blustery as the weather.

"No, Uncle Bill, I can't stay. I just had to come talk to you a minute."

"Well, come on in; it's a little wet out here." He laughed heartily, pushing the door open for her. "Hey, Myrtle, Lee's here."

There was no answer. Lee picked up the note that said Myrtle would be playing bridge until six o'clock.

"Well, come on in and sit down," Bill Morrow said, taking off his wet raincoat and standing there a little uncertainly as if he didn't know what to do with it.

Lee did not move from where she was standing.

"Uncle Bill, they're saying you stayed home from that meeting on purpose. . . . Is it true?"

He seemed on the verge of inquiring what meeting, but then he decided not to equivocate. "Now, Lee, you know how people talk," he said.

"I want to know, Uncle Bill, I want to hear it from you.—Is it true?"

Bill Morrow let the coat drop down on the floor and he sat on a spindly little ornamental hall chair that seemed about to tumble under his weight.

"Now, Lee, listen," he said intently. "Your aunt and I have always tried to make the best of the fact that you married a

243

Jew. But you have to be fair. Remember we have our lives to live, too, and among our own kind. You couldn't expect us to go out on a limb . . . not when it wouldn't make any difference anyhow."

"It would have made a difference!" Lee said. "Some things have to be accomplished only a little bit at a time, and only by people who have some reason to care enough. . . ."

"Look, Lee, I don't think I deserve your reproach," Bill Morrow said, "God knows I've treated Maury like any other man. But marrying him was your business; you told us so often enough. Well, I can't make it my business now. You ought to be able to see that."

"Yes . . . yes, I do see . . ."

"Now, Lee, every time we talk about this I hurt you. God knows I don't want to; but it's not as if you didn't know beforehand. You can't expect . . ."

"I don't expect anything, Uncle Bill. I only had to know for sure. I only had to hear it from you," Lee said.

Lee had never moved from just inside the door. Before Bill Morrow could think of a reply she had stepped outside the door and it was closed behind her, and she was gone.

In the rain Lee drove back to the apartment. It had been eight weeks since she had heard from Maury; and at times, as now, the panic would fly up in her throat and she would fiercely batten it down, or wait numbly for it to subside, so that the days might be counted off. And on this day Lee felt a great loneliness and a great need—"treated Maury like any other man," her uncle had said—Lee wept in her heart for her husband's pride in manliness, and for the sensitivity that was love of life, and for his gentleness with her. But regardless of how many ways she might bring a sense of him near to her, it seemed to Lee that she was alone in the problem that faced her now; it seemed to her that Maury was swallowed up in a vastness her need could not penetrate.

Lee got back to the apartment about five-thirty. Julian sat by the window, watching it rain, and Amy was in the tiny kitchen making a salad and singing a low, mournful melody as she worked.

"Amy, you better go now, if you want to get to your sister's in time for the party," Lee called to her.

Amy stuck her black head out of the kitchen.

"Maybe I bes' stay and make supper," she said, looking fretfully from Lee to Julian and back again, as if she didn't feel quite easy about leaving them on so dismal a day.

"I'll make the supper . . . you go and have a good time," Lee told her, smiling at the old woman's concern. Reluctantly Amy took off her apron.

"I'll take you," Lee said.

"No'm, Willie's already waitin' out back," she said a little sadly, "I'll be here bright an' early tomorrow."

When Amy had gone, Lee flipped on the light, and brightness filled the room. It was a room whose smallness and compactness offered a retreat where silence did not move away into the corners. Lee put a finger in the copper planter of ivy that Ellen had given her. The dirt was moist; Amy had watered it.

Restlessly Lee glanced about her. Julian had dumped his block box, and its contents were strewn over most of the floor. Lee sat down on the rug.

"Here, let's put them away," she said. "Come fill up my lap." She made a round hollow place in her skirt.

Julian watched her solemnly. "I don't want to," he said.

He was growing tall and his head was shaped like Maury's. The babiness that had still been about his ways in the summer had deserted him now. He stood there and a certain unconscious manliness in his stance made Lee's throat ache. She got up from the floor, feeling that she had insulted him by suggesting this picking up game which was a relic from his babyhood.

"You pick them up, while I get supper on the table," she suggested.

"I don't want to," Julian said again.

In his truculence Lee recognized more than stubbornness. She leaned down until her eyes were on a level with his.

"Julian, what do you want?" she asked him.

He looked away from her. "I want daddy," he said.

His earnest little face invited no evasions. "Yes, Sweetheart, so do I," Lee answered simply. She thought for a moment that he would cry, but he didn't. She took his hand.

"Come on, let's fix supper," she said.

In the kitchen, Julian stood on a stool and stirred the eggs for scrambling, while Lee got out the salad Amy had made and opened a can of peas. Then, while she scrambled the eggs, she let Julian set the table. By the time they sat down in the tiny dinette at one end of the living room, the little boy's mood had been entirely transformed by the importance of helping.

"Pass the peas—peas porridge hot—peas in the pod—pea

shooter!" he chanted in the whimsical vernacular of childhood, and Lee felt in him the confident gaiety of the unchallenged spirit.

"Where did you learn to talk like that?" she asked him.

"Bill talks like that," he informed her grandly. Bill was eight and lived in an apartment on the third floor.

Lee smiled; later, as she helped him undress for bed, she smiled again because it occurred to her that his knees were no longer the knees of a baby, they were the knobby and scuffed knees of a growing boy.

Always when she thought of the things that she must decide for Julian's sake, she thought about them in long vague thoughts as if there were so much time to decide. But suddenly it seemed as if there were not much time. But what exactly must she decide? She was not sure.

When Julian was in bed, Lee came back into the living room and sat down. She turned on a lamp and picked up a book; but she did not open it—Julian . . . and Maury . . . and what must she decide?

Suddenly Lee was remembering a thing that had happened when Julian was born. It had seemed then, an incident, isolated in the flow of time, but Lee recognized it now as only the first encounter with a problem they had been so adept at evading.

When Julian was born, Lee had taken it as a matter of course that he would be circumcised; but her reaction was a wildly emotional one when she learned that Maury had had a Jewish doctor, not her own doctor, to perform the operation. Lee's first knowledge of the fact came when she overheard a conversation between Maury and the two doctors in the hall outside her hospital room.

Lee could close her eyes and return to the moment, to its bitterness and hurt and fury. Even the sound of the voices came back to her with no inflection altered.

"Well, thanks Dr. Rubin . . . thanks a lot," Maury said.

"I'm glad this one was on you," Lee heard her own doctor say, "I'm afraid I wouldn't have made a proper Jew of him."

They all three laughed.

"I don't know what this schmo expects of me. I'm no *mohel*," Dr. Rubin replied.

"What's a *mohel*?" Dr. Gibson asked.

"A *mohel* is one who does circumcisions," Maury replied.

"You've heard the joke about the *mohel*?" Dr. Rubin asked.

"No."

"A new father went to the address where he was supposed to find the *mohel;* but there was a clock in the window. When the man came to the door, the father said 'Can you tell me where to find the *mohel?'*—'I'm the *mohel,'* the man told him—'Then why do you have a clock in the window?' the father inquired— 'And what should I have in the window?' the *mohel* asked him."

And they laughed. The three men laughed together there in the hall. And Lee, lying in bed on the other side of the door, heard the three voices and found in them much that she could not bear. The Gentile doctor spoke with tolerant amusement, the Jewish doctor with humorous indulgence, and Maury's tone was hearty and vaguely conciliatory and contained all the brash and half-embarrassed pride of the father of a first-born son. The tone of the three voices together seemed to infer something that must be apologized for, and Lee felt sick with resentment.

A moment later Maury came in and sat down on the side of her bed.

"How is the new mama?" he asked her, his eyes crinkling with a special amusement he was inviting her to share.

"Maury why didn't you tell me you were going to do it?"

"Do what?"

"Have a Jewish doctor circumcise the baby." Her voice was tense and Maury saw that she was angry. He took her hand in his.

"It was just one of those things that happens on the spur of the moment, Lee. I didn't even have the idea until Dr. Gibson and I were going upstairs and we happened to meet Dr. Rubin in the hall."

"But why couldn't Dr. Gibson have done it just as well. How did you know he wouldn't be angry?"

"Don't be silly, darling. He understood."

"Understood what? That's what I want to know—understood what?"

"For gosh sakes, Lee, nothing in particular. When a Jewish baby is circumcised there's a ceremony, that's all. It's something kind of special. It's called a *briss*. A specially-trained person, called a *mohel,* performs the circumcision and says special prayers. And when it's done, they touch a drop of the wine that the prayer was said over to the baby's lips, and dern if the little devil doesn't stop crying every time."

Maury smiled as he told her this, but Lee did not smile.

"And afterwards I suppose they serve refreshments!" Lee said hotly.

"Well, yes, as a matter of fact they do. It's something pretty special. The grandmamas spend a lot of time in the kitchen for a couple of days before."

"I think it's horrible!" Lee railed out at him, "I think it's a pagan thing to subject an infant to."

She turned her face away from him, and Maury knew that she was crying. He saw that he had really hurt her. At first he had been trying only to explain that the gesture had been for him nothing more than a sentimental way of acknowledging the deep nostalgia which the birth of his son roused. But suddenly he wanted to make Lee understand the real dignity and significance of this ancient rite. But he did not know the words to use; he did not know to say that it represented a covenant with God. And as he made his fumbling effort to explain, Lee felt only the humiliation of knowing that his compromised and casual gesture had only made a farce of the meaning which he seemed only vaguely to understand himself.

Remembering, Lee got up; she went in the kitchen and made fresh coffee, and she sat alone and drank it. It was so painfully easy to recall every detail of that tense and strained interlude in the hospital; but it was not so easy to recapture the exact quality of the days and weeks that came after. There was about them the strangeness of the unsolved dilemma and Lee searched them now for meaning that had eluded her at the time.

After her first outburst, Lee had not mentioned the circumcision again; but the anxiety had persisted, and the troubled feeling that Maury had, in some subconscious but deeply motivated way, marked their child for a destiny that he might, through her, escape. Lee had become possessed by the need to neutralize this gesture. She had felt a growing compulsion to have the baby baptized. But gradually she had realized that this gesture, too, would be a hollow one, a like thing to what Maury had done, but not so honest, for it would be a deliberate action, not one born of impulse.

With this new insight, Lee had come close to Maury again. She had understood the likeness of their separate dilemmas—the dreadful loneliness of knowing that, because of a lack of personal faith, neither of them possessed any way of consecrating parenthood. And the feeling that there was need to consecrate— which to each was new—was sad and reverent and beautiful and lonely.

This was the exact quality of the strangeness and loneliness

248

that hovered over the first weeks of young Julian Kalman's life—Julian Kalman . . . not a *briss* . . . not a baptism . . . but the inability of either parent to make either ritual meaningful.

Now, on this night five years later, when Lee Kalman had reconstructed with painful exactitude the mood of those poignant days, the thing that seemed strangest to her in retrospect was her own naiveté, that she could even have imagined that there was anything her child might escape through her. On this night, Lee reached a bitterly corroborated conclusion—there was nothing he could escape. Whatever he might become, he must learn to suffer what a Jew suffers. Her talk with her uncle had made Lee realize that to seem to have a choice was the profoundest irony. The choice was made by people who could be casually contemptuous. And the lot of her child would be the lot of any Jewish child. But unlike a Jewish mother, she must go through the motions of bringing him voluntarily to a life of discrimination and rebuff. And this was the thing her spirit stubbornly resisted.

The next morning Lee Kalman went to see the rabbi. She found him in his study at the synagogue. He stood up as he saw her and he came to her with outstretched hand.

"Hi, Lee!" he said, and Lee smiled because the greeting sounded so improbable coming from him.

"You're laughing," he said. "Why?"

Lee felt the strangeness of a smile upon her tense lips. "I'm not laughing very much," she said, "Rabbi, this time I'm just another person bringing you a problem."

"Come in, Lee. Sit down."

Lee sat in the chair Kurt offered her.

"Now, what's troubling you?" he said and his voice did not seem to intimate that there was any trouble which was insoluble.

Lee ran her tongue around the inside of her lips. "Rabbi . . . there's something I have to know. What does prejudice do to a child's spirit?"

Kurt Rosen looked with deep compassion at the young woman who was facing this question for the first time. And he thought of her son—a child, half Jew, half Gentile, who would be claimed by neither. Talmudic law said that he must become what his mother was; but to the Gentiles he would be a Jew. And although he might not be a Jew in his own eyes, or in the eyes of other Jews, he would be discriminated against as a Jew. To him would accrue all of the disadvantages and none of the compensations of being a Jew—not even the fellowship of those who suffered similarly.

That the passion and devotion and loyalty and tenderness of a real marriage could bequeathe to a child born of its beauty so bitter a heritage, augured, for parent and for child, a vulnerability that was hard to contemplate.

When Kurt did not answer immediately, Lee leaned forward a little in her earnestness.

"Rabbi, please try to tell me in terms of real people. How was it for you when you were a child?"

"For me it was very different from the way it will be for your son, Lee," Kurt told her.

"How do you mean?"

"Time and place alter many things. I was a child in Europe thirty years ago. There, and then, prejudice was an omnipresent thing . . ." He considered a moment, and then he added, "but not a blight on the soul. No one thought to deny that prejudice existed, or to equivocate about it. There was in this very honesty a freedom of the soul."

"But now . . . and in America?" Lee asked.

Again Kurt considered for a moment before answering. To love America as he loved it, with such awareness, with such special poignant tenderness for the imperfections of which perfections are born, was a thing no native born American could quite fathom or duplicate.

"Lee, when people try for a great and noble ideal—like democracy and equality of opportunity—they must assume success in order to have the courage to keep on trying," he began. "Here in America prejudice is denied. Minorities are invited to proceed on the assumption that it does not exist, in order that someday it may not exist."

"But now?" Lee insisted.

"But now it does exist . . . for each one it does exist, at some time, in some way. And there is always the shock to sensibilities that have been beguiled by ideals away from the actualities."

"But how can you prepare a child?" Lee asked him.

Lee's penetrating and insistent question made Kurt wonder how much of what he had learned from experience she had sensed. And the encroachment of awareness upon innocence is not an easy thing to see. With a deep warmth of human sympathy he tried to answer her question—what does prejudice do to the spirit of a child?

"A great deal depends upon how truly a child is made to feel his own worth as an individual and as a human being," he told her. "We have a saying from a wise rabbi, 'If I am not for myself, who will be for me; and if I am for myself alone, what am I?'"

Lee sat for a moment, looking into the serene face of the man who spoke to her. She had come to him with the feeling that she had nothing to offer her child but a life of frustration and bitterness; she had come to learn how such an offering is made. But suddenly she understood that the thing she might offer her child, if she could but realize it herself, was a concept of life beautiful and strong enough to make it worth the high price at which it must be bought. And so she did have a choice, after all.

"Rabbi, could I send Julian to Sunday School at the synagogue?"

"According to talmudic law, Lee, a child will take the religion of his mother."

"But his father is a Jew; he could be a Jew, couldn't he?"

"Yes, he could . . . but, Lee, it would be easier for you and for your child if he could be what you are."

"Rabbi, if I had something to offer him, that might be true. But I haven't. And when I glimpse the thing that you could offer him, I want him to have it, even if it is not mine."

Kurt looked at Lee and he thought of Ellen; he thought of how much it is possible for a woman to be hurt; he thought of how much it is possible for people to hurt each other.

"Lee," he said, "would you mind telling . . . how exactly it is that you arrive at your decision."

"I'll try to tell you, Rabbi. I'll try to be honest with you. I'm afraid it hasn't much to do with religion, actually. But it has a great deal to do with life. . . . Rabbi, if I raise him as a Gentile, they'll only teach him contempt for what he is. It seems to me the soul can survive contempt, but not self-contempt. I want you to teach him to be a Jew with his soul."

Kurt heard what Lee Kalman said with a sense of disappointment, but also with a sense of hope. Lee had not arrived at the destination, but only at one of the milestones, one of the stopping points along the arduous way of understanding.

"Lee," Kurt said, "you have been under a great emotional strain. You should not try to make final decisions now. Send the boy to us, if you like, but wait until he is older to decide."

Lee Kalman wakened to the sound of knocking, the sound seemed to have left her dream to become unanchored in space. It was an urgent impatient sound. She jumped up so quickly she felt dizzy; slipping her arms into her robe as she went, she ran to the door. This would be an end of waiting. One way or another, this would be an end of waiting!

"Telegram for Mrs. Maury Kalman," the boy said. He had the look of a boy who had delivered many such telegrams, it was not a young look any more.

"Thank you," Lee said numbly. She signed her name with a stubby pencil. She took the yellow square envelope in her hand.

To open it. The tearing of paper was a small frightening sound.

> *Mrs. Maury Kalman*
> *1521 Arch Road*
> *Fall City,*
>
> *The Army of the United States regrets to inform you that your husband, Captain Maury Kalman, must be officially listed as missing in action . . .*

Lee held the telegram in her hand. She felt the numb sense of wonder that things do not fall apart utterly, that minute follows minute in perfect order. She heard the steps of the delivery boy going down the hall. She closed the door.

Lee stood there in the living room of this small apartment which was not home. The sounds of wakening had not yet begun to creep through the walls of the building, and the stillness of dawn pressed at the windows. In this stillness was utter aloneness, and Lee Kalman stood at the center of it with the telegram in her hand.

Lee sat down on the couch, she sat there until she heard Amy let herself in by the kitchen door. Then she slipped back into her bedroom and hurriedly dressed. She paused at the door of the kitchen where Amy was grumbling a picturesque commentary on life as she made the coffee.

"Amy . . ."

"Lordy, Miss Lee! You scairt me!" Amy threw up her arms and then suddenly she leaned forward like a stooped little gnome. "Ain't nothing wrong?" she said, and her voice took on the warm softness of people who are adept at comforting.

Lee shook her head. She couldn't say it yet.

"I didn't sleep well, I want to walk a while before breakfast," she said.

Amy nodded, and Lee had the feeling that she knew. Lee turned away quickly before she might cry. She left the apartment and, in the still expectant air of early morning, she walked . . . she walked to her house. She stood beside the tall hedge, and she felt a hunger that the mere sight of the house could not appease. On the porch was a tricycle; but it was not Julian's tricycle; and the car in the driveway was not their car. And inside people soon would be waking, who dwelt in this house, but who did not call it home, as she called it home who no longer dwelt there. Lee wanted to run up the steps; she wanted to implore them to let her in; she wanted to exhort them to leave. She wanted all traces of other lives to vanish from these familiar rooms.

It was as if she might find Maury if only she could go in and walk through the rooms. She wanted to go in, to throw herself across the bed, to weep. It would be strange to weep for Maury in a place where he had never been.

Suddenly Lee felt the dryness of her lips and she drew herself up short, appalled at what seemed implicit in her thoughts. She must not go in search of him; she must wait for him to come. She must not think of him as dead, not once must she think of him as dead.

Lee glanced back at her house and it seemed to have closed her out, and she was glad. She must not go back to what of Maury dwelt there as long as there was hope that somewhere in the world he spoke and breathed and contained in a living body the essence of a living self.

Lee turned her back on the house and started up the street. The sky was bright over the buildings of town.

As she neared town, Lee stood for a moment looking up and down the familiar street. Now she must say to someone "Maury is missing in action." She must say it out loud for someone else to hear. And that would be the real beginning of a new era of her life built upon pure faith. . . . Faith in what? Lee asked herself in panic—faith that Maury would come back—but faith in what?—

But first, before she thought about that, she must speak to someone; she must say it out loud. Lee saw Jerry Phillips crossing the street at the corner. Suddenly she was possessed by the fear of seeing someone she knew. She began to walk very fast.

It was toward the house where Kurt and Ellen Rosen lived that she turned her steps. She would say to them—"Maury is missing in action! . . . "

Ellen Rosen heard the knock at the door and put down the morning paper. It would probably be the milkman, she thought, as she went to answer; but when she opened the door Lee Kalman was standing there.

"Lee! So early? Is anything wrong?"

"I got a telegram . . ." Lee began. She had the envelope in her hand in case she would not be able to say it; she could not quite say it.

Ellen took Lee's arm and drew her inside the room; she took the telegram in her own hands and read it.

"Were you alone when you got the message?" Ellen asked her quickly.

Lee nodded.

"I'm so glad that you come to us," Ellen said, "it is not good to get used to some things alone."

Lee felt the warmth and the human sympathy so eloquently expressed in Ellen's voice, in her dark eyes; and the first waves of panic began to subside.

"How long since you heard from Maury?" Ellen asked her.

"A long time . . . nine weeks."

Ellen lifted the telegram again briefly. "I think your own heart tells you how much to hope. This doesn't change anything, it's only that official notice is being taken of the waiting."

"The waiting . . ." Lee repeated, as if the word suddenly engulfed her with its awful meaning.

Ellen looked into Lee's bewildered face, and saw more clearly than she had ever seen before how sorrow is met by those who have been assiduously taught from birth that unblemished happiness is their birthright, and that catastrophe only befalls others. To Ellen, this in itself seemed a tragic thing.

"Lee, come, let me give you some coffee to drink," she said gently, noting how the color had gone from Lee's face, how rigidly she held her hands in her lap.

"Come!" Ellen said again.

Lee got up, she came and sat at the little table, and Ellen poured the coffee for her.

"Drink it black," she said.

Lee drank the coffee and watched Ellen Rosen. What was the comfort she had come seeking here. It was more than the compassion which she felt reaching out to her. It was the understanding of which this compassion was born.

Lee's voice was small and tight when she spoke.

"Ellen, I don't know what to do," she said. "I don't know how to wait. I don't know how much to hope!"

For a moment Ellen did not answer. The wisdom of the Jewish heart bought at so high a price, included a deep sense of tragedy as a part of life inseparable from every other part. And to a person who has known tragedy, Ellen knew that even tragedy carries its own connotations of invincibility. But in Lee Kalman's background the seeds of this wisdom had not been sown.

"I don't even know what sorrow is . . . not really . . . not in my own life," Lee said, her eyes on Ellen, imploring her to answer.

"The telegram does not mean sorrow . . ." Ellen began.

"But if it did . . . if it did mean that. I don't even know how people live with sorrow."

"They live with it many different ways," Ellen said, "but there is a way so that sorrow becomes more of a tribute to what is lost than a lamentation for what must be borne."

Lee shook her head; she did not understand it. Her grief was a brittle and an unyielding thing, and Ellen felt, in Lee's deep reluctance to endure, the innocence of the unchallenged.

"Lee . . ." Ellen began, but she did not go on. She looked into the face that was turned to her with such an intense appeal, and in that moment, when she did not speak, she took to her own heart some part of Lee's grief so that in this haven its rigidity might be a little eased.

"Lee, Rabbi is in his study at the Temple. This morning he reads the services for Shavus. He could say a prayer for Maury," Ellen said quietly.

Lee looked up quickly. "I wish he would . . . I wish he would."

"Come, let's go then. It's almost time for the services to start."

Lee sat in the back of the synagogue, while Ellen went to speak to Kurt in his study, and then Ellen came and sat beside her. There was hardly more than a *minyan* of the most observant Jews in the synagogue for these feast day services, their black *yarmulcas* on their heads, their prayer books in their hands. And a quietness hovered in the sanctuary. Many times since Maury had gone to war, Lee had come to the synagogue for Friday night services, and she felt here a sense of home. But suddenly she did not want to stay. She felt as if she must be up and out, walking

255

again in the streets. But the door of the study opened and Kurt Rosen walked to the pulpit. His eyes came directly to hers, acknowledging grief as lesser souls can never quite acknowledge it.

Kurt Rosen began to read from the prayer book, and Lee tried to listen to what he was saying. In his voice, as in Ellen's face, was the answer to what she sought; but here, too, the answer was a spiritual essence which must be captured and defined. Lee felt the loneliness of her own unknowing heart.

Numbly Lee read the parts of the service that were in English, and listened to the parts that were in Hebrew.

Shema Yis-ro-el A-do-noi El-o-he-nu, A-do-noi E-hod.
Hear, O Israel, the Lord our God, the Lord is one.

God . . . what was God? Lee felt the stirring of memories that ached in her. . . . What was God? . . . The innocence of a child, the yearning of an adult? There comes a time when you have to believe, not just vaguely, but with some awesome intensity; but was God only the nothingness in which one human soul must go in search of another—Maury, Maury! Lee clenched her fists until the nails dug deep into the palms of her hands.

Kurt Rosen began to speak again, and the first words did not portend to Lee the magnificence of the moment at whose brink she stood. But the first words laid a stillness upon her heart so that it did not resist.

With a quiet, pervading dignity, Kurt Rosen read:

> *Wrapt in the sacred stillness of the sanctuary and filled with the consciousness of God's presence, we turn away from things of earth to contemplate the mysterious nature of our inner being, and to capture and to hold the heavenly vision revealed to our soul. We know that not with eyes of flesh nor with power of mind can we see and grasp the sublime truths of eternity. It is given to the soul alone to find, to feel and to know the living spirit that pervades and animates all. We are floating in an immeasurable ocean of spirit; and in this house of worship, as we bow our heads in prayer with serene mind and yearning heart, the tides of the infinite come with mighty pulsations throbbing through our soul. Spirit touches spirit. We are face to face with God.*

As Kurt Rosen finished speaking, Lee did not move; she hardly breathed. It was as if she spiritually stood on tiptoe, waiting.

Lee came back to the Rosens' apartment with Ellen when the

services were over. She sat at the small table while Ellen began to prepare lunch. For a few moments her face was deeply thoughtful.

"Ellen . . . I hardly know how to say it . . ." she began. Ellen came and stood beside her, and Lee, looking into the dark and sympathetic eyes, felt once again that, if only she could fathom what she saw in Ellen's face, things would not seem so strange and so bewildering. "Ellen, you don't know what it feels like to be so unsure of things. You don't know what it feels like to want to believe, and to want to have faith . . . and not to know how!"

This anguish which was new to Lee's heart was old to Ellen Rosen's heart; and Ellen realized, almost with a sense of amazement, that the faith of her own heart, maintained at such cost to her turbulent spirit, was, in Lee Kalman's eyes, a serene and infallible thing. And as suddenly as she realized this fact, Ellen determined to preserve this feeling of serenity and infallibility as long as Lee had need of it.

Both Ellen and Lee turned quickly at the sound of the door opening.

"Hello girls! . . . Sweetheart! . . . Lee!" Kurt came forward, offering his hand once again to Lee. He sat down at the table opposite her.

"Rabbi . . ." Lee said urgently. "When I first knew that Maury was missing, I thought I could not stand it if I could not somehow have faith that he would come back. At first I was not even sure I believed in God. And then in the synagogue . . . suddenly, I knew I did believe. But still I don't have faith. How do you have faith, Rabbi?"

"How do you mean you don't have faith, Lee?" Kurt asked her quietly.

"Just think how many women there are in the world who are pinning their whole lives on the faith that their men will come back . . . and just think how many of them won't come back."

"Yes, Lee, that's true."

"Then, Rabbi, how do you have faith . . . what do you have faith in?" she asked him beseechingly.

Ellen, with an odd little surge of tenderness, stood looking across the room into her husband's serene and gentle face, intent, now, upon Lee's problem. How often she herself had crept within the shelter of that serenity. In that moment Ellen felt herself come to the brink of discovery. Was Kurt's faith maintained at so great a cost to him, too? Was its sense of infallibility preserved to comfort and to replenish her and others whose need was great? Was belief ever easy to those who really believed?

Kurt's eyes did not waver from Lee Kalman's face.

"You must have faith, Lee, not that Maury will be spared by God, but that he will not be abandoned by God," Kurt told her quietly.

Lee did not answer immediately. She turned her face a little away from them toward the window. And in her face there was a quietness. Ellen Rosen, watching her, saw the innocence that had so often touched her fast waning. To hear a much-sought answer brings a moment of comfort, but to accept it is a long and an arduous and a comfortless thing. Ellen, who had been this way before, knew that hers to give was, not the answers, but the comfort. She came and sat on the couch beside Lee.

Finally Lee turned back to the rabbi.

". . . that he will not be abandoned by God . . . no matter what happens . . . whether he lives or dies, he will not be abandoned by God . . . is that what you mean, Rabbi?"

"Yes, Lee."

Slowly Lee nodded her head. She glanced a moment at Ellen, then back again to Kurt.

"That's not what I wanted. . . . But then, I guess, it's more than what I wanted. I think I could have faith in that."

Chapter 22

THE ALARM clock whirred out its querulous tidings that a new day had begun, and Ellen awoke with a curious feeling of auspiciousness in her bones. Kurt was already out of bed and dressed; she could hear him in the kitchen making coffee. Ellen sat up on the side of the bed and reached for her slippers.

And then she identified the curious low throbbing sense of excitement.

"Kurtchen," she called, "tomorrow is the day!"

"Right!" Kurt came to the door. He caught her hands and pulled her up and kissed her eyelids, feeling still the coolness of sleep beneath his lips.

"Tomorrow we shall be real on-paper-Americans!" Ellen said, and both of them laughed, thinking of Mr. Friedman.

A few moments later, Kurt and Ellen sat down to breakfast together, sharing between them a lightness, a buoyancy, an excitement of mood. They brought to this moment no armor of worldly cynicism. They held in their hands the purity of joy; they held it up for each other to see.

"Kurtchen, do you think we will feel any different when we are officially Americans?" Ellen asked, buttering a roll and putting it on his plate.

"Oh, indeed!" Kurt said grandly. "Then we will not have to worry so much . . . Americans are very gifted non-worriers!"

"How else will we be different?" Ellen pursued, grinning at him.

"Well, there are certain emotional conflicts. We will cuss pedestrians when we are in cars, and cuss cars when we are pedestrians."

"The conflict should not be so great for us. We are mostly pedestrians," Ellen reminded him drily.

"Right!"

"Kurt, I'm glad . . . so glad . . . aren't you?"

"I'm glad, too."

For a moment they ate in silence. Kurt and Ellen Rosen knew how it was to love a country while their hearts ached for its vulnerability. Woven through the busy and hectic days of the past war months, had been the weekly lessons at the Federal Building, preparing them for their final citizenship examinations. Over and over they had listened to the academic question "What does America mean?" They had heard the matter-of-fact pedantic sentences from a textbook . . . the drone of a teacher's tired voice . . . but here a phrase or there a word to kindle the imagination . . . to reveal a glory pinioned to bright hopes. And they had known that America was outside in the street . . . and in faces: a lonesome soldier from Brooklyn waiting for a light to change; a tired old farmer leaning against a building, pensively rubbing the stubble of beard on his chin; a little girl capering from one parking meter to the other as her parents moved slowly, hand in hand, up the street. They had sat in a classroom knowing that America was out there in the street . . . in faces . . . and in a flag atop this very building that furled and rippled in the breeze . . . and in a strand of music wafted out from some neon-glorious juke box in the café at the corner . . . and in houses where people lay down to sleep and wakened to the light of the sun.

"What do you do today?" Kurt asked, the first to break the reverie into which they had fallen.

"USO this morning. Traveler's Aid this afternoon," Ellen answered. "You?"

"Two meetings. Civic Defense and Red Cross. And tonight a sermon at the Air Base because the chaplain is out of town. You come, too, and sing?"

Ellen nodded. She got up and began to clear the table. The business of the day was pressing. Tomorrow was a day for becoming Americans. But today was a day for fighting America's fight.

Six months after Pearl Harbor the war finally reached Fall City. The big air base at the edge of town was completed, and soldiers arrived by squadrons instead of the between-trains twos and threes that Fall City was used to seeing. Suddenly every restaurant, every theater, every bowling alley, every drugstore and hotel seemed to be constantly filled with a shifting hoard of soldiers with twenty-four-hour passes.

Paper plans for Red Cross Motor Corps and Canteen, for USO and Traveler's Aid were suddenly pressed into reality, and many citizens became entirely engrossed with fighting the battle of Fall City. But now at last Kurt and Ellen Rosen were able to fight their war.

Kurt Rosen became an unofficial chaplain with duties that were limitless because he must limit them himself. He assisted the

Jewish chaplain at the Fall City Air Base and several times each week he journeyed to smaller army installations within a hundred-mile radius, where there were Jewish soldiers, but not Jewish chaplains. And the tasks which he was called upon to perform kept constant pace with his willingness to perform them. His days started at dawn and sometimes did not end until midnight.

And Ellen put in a full nine-hour-day six days a week doing war work. In the morning when she and Kurt ate breakfast together in their kitchen, daylight was only a pale gray wash against the window and an electric light burned overhead. By eight o'clock Ellen had set things in order and was waiting for a bus that would take her to the Red Cross. At twelve o'clock she hurried home to fix lunch, hoping that Kurt would be there to eat with her. A little after one o'clock she would be on the bus again, heading for the Auditorium where she would spend the afternoon hours working at the USO, at the Traveler's Aid or at the Civic Center. At six o'clock she would be on the bus again, returning home to make supper. And by the light of dusk, matching the light of dawn, she and Kurt, often too weary for conversation, would eat their last meal of the day together. In the evenings Ellen knitted, determined to maintain her average of one large sweater a week to be sent overseas.

There is a degree of energy and a cast of mind that serve, and a degree of energy and a cast of mind that fight. Kurt and Ellen Rosen were fighting.

This was the only way that they had to fight for the country that had given them freedom. They were fighting for the country they loved. And they knew how it was to be old in the wisdom of the world and to love a country that was new in concept—how it was to love a country that had held so lightly and bestowed so casually the gift of freedom, depriving them, for so long, of nothing but the right to protect it. And finally, now, they were to be given the right to protect it, to expend every ounce of will and energy to protect it.

Behind the USO Snack Bar at one end of the big auditorium foyer, Ellen was making cheese sandwiches while Molly Turner, small, blonde wife of Fall City's recently inducted District Attorney, wrapped them in waxed paper.

Molly worked with the complete manual concentration of a child, Ellen thought, smiling inwardly, as she watched her. Suddenly Molly stopped, sighed, laughed.

"Ellen, you can make the sandwiches in less time than it takes me to wrap them!" she wailed.

Ellen laughed. And because the laugh had a mellow, beckoning warmth, a young corporal who had been on his way to the magazine rack, diverted his steps and stopped by the Snack Bar to ask, shyly, for a cup of coffee and two dunkers.

"Let me make now, and you wrap!" Molly said, as Ellen turned back to her. But at that moment Eve Jennings joined them.

"Ellen, let me take over for you." Eve said. "There's a young soldier in the record room, and he's all upset. I think maybe you could talk to him. He asked if there was a rabbi in town, and I told him the rabbi's wife was right out here making sandwiches." Eve smiled, pulling the strings of Ellen's apron and then fastening it around her own waist.

"Now, maybe I can keep up with Eve," Molly Turner called out grandly, winking at Ellen.

"Just see that you don't forget to put in the cheese," Ellen called back to her. She crossed the large recreation room and rapped lightly on the closed door of the record room which, at this early hour, was usually empty. The door was jerked open immediately, and framed in the doorway was a young soldier who was indeed the picture of distress. His tie was pulled askew and the collar of his khaki shirt was unbuttoned. His close cut, curly hair looked as if his fingers had been often plunged through it in despair.

"I'm Mrs. Rosen," Ellen said, "wife of Rabbi Rosen. Is there something I could do for you?"

In that instant Ellen saw beyond him sitting almost hidden in a deep leather chair, a girl with large dark eyes and lips that parted over even teeth in something only little less than a smile.

"Oh, Mrs. Rosen, please come in," the young corporal said. "Mrs. Rosen, I am Danny Neuman . . . and this is my . . . this is Julie Kohn."

Danny made a small gesture toward the girl, and she got up and came and stood beside him.

"Hello, Mrs. Rosen," she said. In her voice was the faintest hint of humor as if Ellen must understand that this situation was not so bad as Danny seemed to think.

"Let's sit down, all," Ellen said. She sat on the piano bench, and Julie sat down again in the leather chair. Danny half sat, half stood against the table on which were piles of records.

"Mrs. Rosen," Danny said, "Julie came all the way from Minnesota and we were going to be married. But . . . but now . . . it looks like I'll be shipping out any time, any day."

"That's ridiculous! Mrs. Rosen, I keep telling Danny it is. I came to marry him, and I'm going to!" Julie sat forward in her chair, an intense and graceful little creature.

Danny sighed. He crossed his arms over his chest. "Julie, you know how your family feels. If we could have had even a month together. But only days . . . hours . . ."

"Danny, I want to be married to you, that's all."

Danny looked at her helplessly for a moment, and then he turned to Ellen.

"Mrs. Rosen . . . with Julie and me . . . we don't have to be married to know we belong to each other. All day yesterday the fellows were getting married . . . about a dozen of them . . . mostly to girls here in town. Like staking a claim on something you're not sure is yours. It made me sick. I don't want it like that . . . and if I shouldn't come back . . . you have to think of those things."

Ellen looked from Danny to Julie and back again. Julie had tears in her eyes. How could people so young be so sure, Ellen wondered . . . but then, how could people any older ever be so sure again.

Ellen turned her eyes questioningly to Julie, now. Julie was a tiny thing with delicately molded bones and a small exquisite face. She looked, at once, too fragile and too durable to be true. Ellen glanced back at Danny; she felt in him the longing to hold Julie, to caress, to protect, to cherish. It was a poignant love and the ache of it was a wild beauty in this drab little room.

"Mrs. Rosen, what do you think?" Julie demanded, and her level gaze did not invite evasion.

Ellen thought of Lee Kalman and how she had stood holding a telegram in her hand. She thought of Kurt.

"Danny is right," she said quietly, hardly able to make the words leave her lips. "If people love enough, they don't have to be married to know they belong to each other."

"But if people love that much, they ought to be married," Julie answered simply.

"Julie . . . Julie!" Danny thrust his fingers back through his hair again. "I can't do it to you. To send you home to your family with a name they'd hate. When I come back I can make them like me, Julie. I know I can. But not if I did this to you."

"Danny, there's just no use talking!" Julie maintained fiercely, her voice a little higher than before.

For the first time Ellen noticed the small suitcase beside Julie's chair.

"When did you get in town?" she asked.

"A couple of hours ago. The morning train from Chicago," Julie said, wearily, and Ellen saw the blue smudges of weariness on the clear skin beneath her eyes.

She glanced at Danny almost reproachfully. "What you need is a place where you can be together and alone and quiet . . . to talk to each other and decide. I give you the key to our apartment. You go there and when I am through here at noon, I come. Then we can get in touch with Rabbi about what you want to do."

Before they could protest, Ellen went to get her purse. She came back with the key and the address written on a card. She told them which bus to take.

"Mrs. Rosen . . ." Julie stretched out her hand, "We can't thank you enough. Not ever."

Not ever . . . what lonely, aching, prophetic little words.

Ellen pressed the small hand that was extended to her, and then placed it in Danny's hand and folded his fingers around it.

"There's coffee in the percolator, and rolls in the bread box," she told them.

Ellen watched them go and then she went back to making cheese sandwiches.

At 12 o'clock, Molly Turner offered Ellen a ride home, and she was glad not to have to waste time with the bus. She felt a curious responsibility for Danny and Julie; and, as she hurried across the yard and up the steps to the apartment, her breath was coming quickly.

Julie thrust open the door even before Ellen's hand touched the knob. Her face was both serene and radiant.

"We waited for you," Julie said, "I sent Danny to the store and made some sandwiches. I hope you won't mind."

"Mind? Of course not! But there was plenty here; you didn't need to go to the store," Ellen answered, turning her smile quickly to Danny.

Danny stood with his hands thrust in his pockets. The haggardness of his young face was in startling contrast to the grin that now adorned it.

"Mrs. Rosen, we decided," he said. Hardly looking, Ellen saw the ash tray on the table beside him, and the crumpled pile of mashed out cigarettes.

"What did you decide?" she asked him gently.

Julie came to him and moved within the circle of his arm.

"We'll be married," she said, "as, of course, we should."

Ellen swallowed. She couldn't have told why she was so glad. "That's wonderful," she said softly.

And Julie's rapturous laughter was a small, bright thing on the air. "Come, let's eat lunch," she said, catching up Danny's hand and Ellen's hand together.

They sat down at the table. "I got paper plates," Julie said, "I didn't want to mess things up."

"And when is this wonderful wedding going to be?" Ellen asked.

"Right away . . . today," Danny said, the shadow of the old anxiety was in his eyes again.

"Right away, indeed," Ellen laughed. "I must get in touch with Rabbi as soon as I can."

"I have to be back at the base at seven-thirty," Danny said. "Then I'll try to get a three day pass. But I have to be back tonight at seven-thirty."

"Then how about four-thirty?" Ellen asked.

"Four-thirty is a very nice time for getting married," Julie answered dreamily. She leaned toward Danny and caught up his hand playfully and planted a small round kiss in the cupped palm.

"Julie!" he said with mock reproach.

Ellen glanced at the clock above the stove. In less than half an hour she was due at the Traveler's Aid.

"Look," she said, "we have not much time. I'll tell Rabbi you will be at the synagogue at four to speak to him. I'll be back from Traveler's Aid for the wedding. But remember, you need also, two witnesses . . . and . . ." she winked at Danny . . . "and, of course, a corsage for the bride," she teased.

Danny laughed, Julie laughed; the sounds mingled sweetly.

Ellen got up from the table. "Stay as long as you like, *meine kleinen Kinder,*" she called to them from the doorway, and then she closed the door behind her.

On the bus, riding back to town, Ellen looked out on the sun-dappled street, and felt, already, the weariness of a long day in her bones. The next stretch would contain three hours, only, she reminded herself. "Why do you do it, as though somebody were driving you!" Tita Gold had demanded petulantly when Ellen refused to come as a fourth for bridge.

Why do I do it . . .? Ellen thought. In the back of her mind were Danny and Julie. She had never seen them before this morning. She might never see them again after this afternoon. But today they were the reality and substance of her life.

It seemed to Ellen that she and Kurt were fighting at last the enemy that had dwelt too long beyond their reach. And the young soldiers they served were their link with the war. Soldiers from all parts of a great and vast America—some cocky, some thoughtful, some scared, some confused. But theirs were the hands in which rescue would lie. And for these young soldiers who would carry the fight beyond where *they* could carry it, for these who would fight for them, she and Kurt felt a love and a tenderness that was not based upon any worn clichés about "duty to our boys," but was warm and intense and personal.

To harbor, to comfort, to answer a human need when it was felt—these were the things that *they* could do. And the weaknesses and the gallantries of these human needs, *they* were able to know.

"Why do you do it . . .?" . . ."How could you not do it?" Ellen felt herself answering as she got off the bus at the corner of the Civic Center in one room of which the Traveler's Aid was housed.

Ellen went first to the telephone booth and called Kurt. She reached him, now, at his study and told him briefly about Danny and Julie. And then she went out to the big desk that Ann Barlow, tumble-haired and blithe of smile, was happily preparing to leave in a state of wild confusion.

"Ellen . . . you don't mind? I promised to take Jeanie to the show," she lamented "or I wouldn't leave things in such a mess. I fell behind on the filing. And people keep calling in, because of that story in the paper yesterday, asking for rooms. Golly! . . . well . . ." Ann paused, suddenly out of breath.

"Go, Go! I make it ready," Ellen insisted, eager, almost, for the quieting of a confusion that could not speak. She picked up a handful of cards and began to straighten them.

"I filed P's under B's last time," Ann said a little wistfully, as if sure that her worst sins were now about to come to light.

"We can only try," Ellen reassured her, "it's worth a lot to be willing to try."

Ann seemed pleased. "Gee, thanks, Mrs. Rosen . . . Ellen . . . thanks!" And away she went.

Ellen took the card indexes and began to file the cards. One Room . . . One Room with Bath . . . One Room with Kitchen Privileges . . . Garage Apartment. . . ." There were lots of new cards. It seemed, indeed, that the morning had been a busy one.

And then the telephone began to ring. And Ellen began to fill

266

out the cards. "I don't want anybody with children!" they kept saying, "but I do have a room I wouldn't mind renting to someone NICE!"

Someone 'nice' . . . at the beginning Ellen was smiling inwardly. Always it must be someone nice . . . and with no children, of course. Ellen sighed. She spent a full half hour, interspersed with telephone calls, helping a raggy little blonde woman from Alabama sort through the cards endlessly. The trouble was that the pert and blue-eyed little woman had four children, and all four of them were with her now, inspecting, respectively, the water cooler, the pencil sharpener, the lock on the bottom drawer of the desk, and a bowl of goldfish which had, heaven knows how, become a part of the furnishings of the Traveler's Aid Agency.

A little later Ellen arranged transportation for a shy, unhappy, soldier's wife who, penniless, must now make a long and lonely trek across the country. And she helped a red-faced sergeant from Colorado find a room for his mother who was coming to spend his twenty-first birthday with him.

And all the time the phone kept ringing . . . "read in the paper that you needed rooms . . ." And another card to be indexed.

A little after three o'clock, Ellen filled out perhaps the hundreth rental card of the day. A good address. A pleasant, well-mannered voice.

"I think we should all do our bit," the voice said with only a trace of condescension in its well modulated tones. "I'm more than happy to rent out this little apartment above our garage. It's lovely, too. We fixed it up for our son when he was coming back and forth from college."

"I think that's very fine," Ellen said, making quick notes on the pad of paper. "I'm sure some young couple will be very lucky to have such a nice place," Ellen was thinking of the lack of embarrassment with which some people offered hardly more than chicken coops.

"Oh, by the way," the cool voice continued, "you understand, of course, I want only a Christian soldier."

The words came rolling over the line like hard little marbles of sound, that fell, one after the other, into a great space.

Ellen put down the pencil. And she pushed the card a little away from her, so that a whole stack of cards fell off on the floor.

"You speak to Mrs. Rosen," she said, "and I am Jewish. But I would not send you any Jewish soldiers."

And then, with a terrible calmness, she waited to see if the well-modulated voice would answer. But there was only a pause containing nothing at all. And then a discreet little click of the receiver at the other end. And Ellen hung up the phone and walked around the desk to pick up the fallen cards.

Ellen sat down again; she wished that someone would call or that someone would come in. But no one did. All day long everything had been bound up with loving America, but not this moment.

"The ideal alone is perfect," she told herself, "but if I thought that perfection were even possible, I would be doing an injustice. People are only people, any time, anywhere. And it is so hard for them to realize the best in themselves."

Frantically Ellen searched her mind for some fragment of thought to make the hurt and the humiliation of the last moment pass. And, almost with a sense of contrition, she remembered a humiliation that had been even deeper. She remembered the day that Mrs. Stein had called, and luckily she herself had answered the phone.

"I take a soldier," Mrs. Stein had volunteered, "but please send me only a captive."

"A captive?" Ellen had inquired, puzzled.

"A captive . . . A captive or at least a lieutenant," Mrs. Stein had insisted grandly.

Ellen thought of Corporal Danny Neuman, and of his human need. Corporal Danny Neuman was not excluded more by the one than by the other. And with the ache of a well-modulated voice still in her ears, Ellen exhorted herself not to expend her rage at one human weakness out of proportion to another.

A little before four o'clock, Ellen walked from the Civic Center to the Bon Ton Bakery and bought a white-iced layer cake, and a little celluloid bride and groom to adorn it. She stopped in the dime store for candles and paper napkins. And when she got off the bus a block from the synagogue, she stopped in the drug store and bought two bottles of ginger ale. "The Champagne of Ginger Ales," it said on the label. She smiled.

Ellen went down into the vestry at the Temple and set the table with a white cloth. She put the wedding cake in the center, and the candles on either end. She made coffee in the big silver urn and put the ginger ale on ice in the kitchen. She stood back from the table and wished, for a moment, that she had bought flowers. She pushed the cake a little more to the center and straightened one candle. And then, because it was nearly four-thirty, she hurried up to the synagogue. The door to Kurt's study

268

was closed, but the wedding canopy was in place above the altar. Two young soldiers whom Ellen remembered having seen at the air base were sitting far to one side whispering quietly to themselves. Ellen greated them, and when the outside door opened again it was Davey Levinson who came bursting in. Under one arm he had a library book and a catcher's mitt.

"I was supposed to have a lesson," he told Ellen breathlessly. The dust of the vacant lot was still smeared across his face.

"We have a soldier wedding," she whispered back to him. "Here take this handkerchief and wipe your face. Then put on your *yarmulca* and you can sit back here and watch. Rabbi gives you the lesson when he is through."

Davey started to protest, but then he was a little curious, so he did as Ellen told him. He wiped his face and he put on a *yarmulca,* and he slipped in a back seat to watch.

Promptly at four-thirty the door of the study opened, and Kurt came and took his place behind the pulpit; a moment later, Julie and Danny, walking close together, but not quite touching hands, came out of the study and took their places under the purple velvet canopy. Each of them smiled, seeing Ellen, and the smiles were the odd, stiff, little smiles of the young and awed. And Kurt, seeing Ellen, smiled, too, and his smile was a welcome and a silent acknowledgment that he understood about Danny and Julie, that he understood how much it mattered.

"Friends," Kurt said, looking out over the empty chairs at the two young soldiers . . . and Davey Levinson . . . and Ellen . . . "We are gathered today to witness the marriage of Danny Neuman and Julia Kohn. Praying to God that He may guide and sustain this groom and bride, we say the traditional words, taken from the Holy Bible: 'Blessed be he that cometh in the name of the Lord; we bless thee from the house of the Lord.' "

When Kurt had said the opening words he nodded to Ellen. Understanding immediately, she came and stood beneath the pulpit to one side. And she began to sing, and the clear notes throbbed with an exquisite love of life which these two, standing side by side, newly understood.

> *. . . Because you come to me, with naught save love,*
> *And hold my hand, and lift mine eyes above,*
> *A wider world of hope and joy I see . . .*
> *Because . . . you come to me . . .*

While the last notes lingered, warm and loving, on the still, sun-drenched air of late afternoon and in Kurt Rosen's ears, his eyes rested with a rare and mellow compassion upon Danny Neuman and Julie Kohn. Julie's hand had crept into Danny's, and thus they face him. Quietly Kurt began to speak to them.

"Danny . . . and Julie . . . the marriage upon which you enter today is an act of faith—of faith in God . . . faith in each other . . . and faith in your country. It is an act of faith in God, because you build your first home, not in any place the eye can see, or the hands reach out to, but in God's merciful arms. It is an act of faith in each other, because by the very act of marriage in circumstances such as you face, each of you acknowledges the other to be a person of character and fortitude and dependability and understanding tenderness, capable and willing to meet the challenge of the future. And finally, your marriage is an act of faith in your country, knowing that it will preserve you for each other. You, Danny, although you must fight and brave the danger of war, will not be expendable simply because you are a Jew. And you, Julie, will wait, and Danny will not have to fear that, in the very act of going forth to protect you, he might come home and find you vanished. Young American Jews alone of young Jews in all the world at this time can part at the very hour of their joining, knowing that they leave—intact—a good life to come back to. And you alone may be sustained by the knowledge that you yourselves are allowed a part in preserving this good life . . ."

Neither of the young soldiers in the audience moved. Davey Levinson, who had crept up beside Ellen, watched with such rapt attention that three small freckles stood out vividly across his nose, and Ellen Rosen felt the hot tears in her eyes. The two silver goblets were on the pulpit before Kurt. He removed the cover from the first one, speaking, still, very gently to the young couple who stood before him.

"Danny and Julie, the moment of your marriage, far away from family and friends, could seem to you a very lonely time; and yet, in this moment, you may learn a lesson you will value through all your lives . . . and that is that a man and a woman, loving enough, can learn to be all things to each other . . ."

Kurt lifted the first of the goblets.

Bo'ruch a-tto a-do-noi E-lo-henu melech ho-olom
Bora' pree hagofen

Blessed Art Thou, O Lord, Our God, King of the Universe,
Who bringest forth, the fruit from the vine.

270

Danny and Julie sipped from the first goblet which was beautifully carved, signifying life's joys . . . and from the second which was austere and unadorned, signifying life's sorrows.

And in the last moment of the ritual Danny crushed beneath his heel the small glass goblet ". . . in anguished memory of those of our people who are beset and oppressed, and in acknowledgment that only those values in life which are eternal and indestructable must be pursued."

Then Danny Neuman kissed his bride.

Three hours later, sitting in the little frame chapel at the Air Force Base, as Kurt began to conduct the service, Ellen's eyes wandered out over the khaki-clad congregation, looking for Danny. She and Kurt had promised Julie that they would see that Danny had a ride back into town in the jeep that the commander provided for them, if he could get his three-day pass.

As Kurt read one of the psalms, he paused, glancing up, and Ellen's glance followed his. A young soldier was approaching rapidly up the aisle. Behind him, waiting just inside the door, were two MP's. An officer jumped up from the first row to inquire of the young man the reason for his intrusion in the midst of the service; but Kurt signaled the officer back, and the young man came and stood before him. It was Danny Neuman.

"Rabbi, we're being shipped out tonight. . . . Would you pray for us?" Danny said.

"Danny, we will pray with you," Kurt said, and to the congregation, "Please turn to Psalm 91."

Someone handed Danny Neuman a prayer book. He stood looking at the printed page, and when Kurt began to read, Danny's lips moved numbly over the words.

> "Dwelling in the shelter of the Most High,
> Abiding under the protection of the Almighty.
> I say of the Lord
> 'He is my refuge and my fortress,
> My God, whom I trust.'
> He will deliver you from the snare of the fowler
> And from the destructive pestilence.
> He will cover you with his pinions,
> And under his wings shall you take refuge;
> His truth is a shield, and an armour.
> You shall not be afraid of the terror by night,
> Nor of the arrow that flies by day—"

And the next day was citizenship day! Ellen tried not to think of Danny, or of Julie, a lonely little figure who had boarded an early morning plane. She tried not to think of them, because this was a day that must forever after have an importance all its own.

In the morning Ellen baked cookies, dozens of small cookies for guests who might come with good wishes. And she iced them in red, white and blue icing, smiling a little as she did it. Later in the morning she went to town and bought a large black hat which had an air of specialness about it. She wore it when she went to meet Kurt at two o'clock at the Federal Building. She saw Kurt coming and under his arm he carried a florist's box. He walked with that special swagger of a man bearing flowers.

"Kurtchen, what?"

They sat down on one of the benches where old men usually sunned themselves, and Ellen opened the box. Inside was a corsage made of red, white and blue carnations. She began to laugh, a warm low laugh.

"Kurtchen, I think we are both very foolish!" she said.

He looked at her with mock indignation. "That's a fine thing to tell a gentleman when he brings you flowers. I do not think you would have said that twelve years ago."

"The little blue flower—how did they make it blue?" Ellen asked him, unable to keep the smile out of her voice.

"I'm sure I don't know. I'm a rabbi by profession," he informed her.

"I'm sure that knowing how to make little flowers blue pays much better than being a rabbi," she teased him, "I have the feeling that you were very extravagant."

Kurt shrugged. "Who gets to be an American every day?" he asked her.

"Kurtchen," Ellen said, suddenly half serious, "I think we should celebrate this day instead of birthdays—after all, this is a kind of birthday."

"Right!"

They went upstairs to the stuffy little ante-chamber beside the court room. The others waited there—a Mexian woman with a mantilla over her head; a tall young Swede with a tense, strained look about his eyes; an Englishman who spoke with a Cockney accent, and his nervous, birdlike little wife, who spoke hardly at all. Kurt shook hands with each one of them and wished them well.

The fat clerk of the naturalization service came bounding into the room; quickly he counted to see if they were all there. In his hand he had the citizenship papers, filled out and ready for signing. He sighed a little at all the wearisome tasks that fell to him.

"Judge Keene is holding a hearing right now. I'll see if I can get permission to interrupt," he said to none of them in particular. And he bounded out again, through the door into the courtroom. He left the door ajar, they saw him go up to the dais and whisper something to the judge.

The attorney down on the floor stopped midway in a sentence of a dissertation that had been going on for quite some time. He glanced at his client, a dour, tobacco-stained farmer who refused to allow a federal highway to cross his land.

Judge Keene picked up his gavel and banged it down with a flick of his wrist.

"Court's adjourned for fifteen minutes!" he said. He looked balefully at the glum and stubborn people who were beleaguering him with their stubbornness. "Bring in the candidates for citizenship," he said to the clerk.

The clerk motioned to the doorway, and Kurt Rosen led the others into the room. The lawyer who had been expounding his views made a gesture of exasperation and sat down. The farmer stood up for a moment, stamped his feet impatiently like a horse in a stall, and then he sat down again too. The eyes of the contending parties were fixed glumly upon these candidates for citizenship who stood in a tense little line before the judge. The Mexican woman clasped nervously at her mantilla, and the tall Swede stood rigidly erect. Kurt and Ellen Rosen exchanged a smile.

Judge Keene cleared his throat. He leaned forward a little, so that his deeply lined face seemed to pull at the tendons of his skinny neck. His pale eyes had a penetrating directness as they moved from face to face.

"These men and women wish to become citizens of the United States?" he said to the clerk.

"Yes, Your Honor. They have fulfilled all the requirements."

Judge Keene nodded his head. He glanced beyond those who stood before him, to those others who waited to resume their petty quarrel. And the curt impatience of his manner seemed to bear within it the insensibilities and inadequacies with which he must contend hour by hour, day by day.

His eyes came back to the candidates for citizenship. For the briefest moment he seemed to shrug aside his preoccupations and to enter into a fleeting and undefined spiritual trysting.

"I wish to congratulate you people upon having earned the right to become citizens of the United States. All privileges, duties and responsibilities of citizenship now become yours," he paused a moment, ". . . and you can hold any public office except that of the President of the United States," he concluded, drily.

"You will please repeat now the pledge of allegiance to the United States flag," he said, and his voice croaked a little in its attempt at softness.

The six people began to say it together—Kurt and Ellen, the English couple, the old Mexican woman, and the young Swede—

"I pledge allegiance to the flag of the United States of America and to the Republic for which it stands, one nation, indivisible, with Liberty and Justice for all!"

As it was said, Kurt and Ellen turned a little to each other. There were no bands playing, no songs sung. But the moment took to itself the glow of their own mood and gave it back to them.

When the judge had dismissed them with his repeated congratulations, the official of the Naturalization Service took them again into the small ante-chamber and gave them their citizenship papers to sign. He smiled a little at their earnest pleasure.

"These papers must not be copied," he told them. "They are like money, if they are lost or destroyed, they must be reissued."

Kurt thanked him gravely. He folded the two documents and put them in the inside pocket of his coat. He and Ellen walked out again into the bright, warm afternoon.

They were Americans.

The Rosens hurried home in case members of their congregation should come. An hour passed, and the afternoon paper was delivered; and in it was a picture of Kurt and a story about the citizenship.

"Read what's on the other side, I want to cut it out for the scrapbook," Ellen said.

"The ink's hardly dry on the paper, could it not wait?" Kurt asked her.

"No, now. Nothing is official until it is in the scrapbook," Ellen told him. She got out the scrapbook, and she pasted in the story and the picture.

Still wrapped in their shining mood, Kurt and Ellen laughed a great deal, and they had a great deal to say to each other. After long months of having hardly time to eat a bite together, these moments alone and in leisure were a rich pleasure, the more so for the feeling that they might at any time be interrupted.

A little before five o'clock, Anna Meyer stopped by, but she was on her way to town, and she had only a moment to give her good wishes. She ate one of the cookies Ellen had baked, but she refused a cup of coffee, insisting breathlessly that she simply couldn't spare the time.

When she was gone, Ellen didn't look at Kurt. Very solemnly she began to set the table with the best linen and silver and china. She prepared the dinner, and she served it with candles on the table. And they drank toasts to each other with the best wine.

When they had finished eating, and the candles were burning low, Kurt pushed back from the table, smiling his pleasure.

"I think that American husbands help their wives with the dishes," he said tentatively, cocking one brow in disapproval of this custom.

"Please, Kurtchen, don't change too much, I couldn't bear it," Ellen answered laughing.

"You mean my offer of assistance is refused?"

She looked at him knowingly. "If it was an offer, it is refused," she told him. "You go put on records. I clean the dishes."

The evening passed as the afternoon had passed, made warm and beautiful by their love for each other.

But there was a turning point, a point when expectancy turned to dread, a point at which Ellen began intensely to resist the thought of a knock at the door, when every nerve resisted the thought of an intrusion. But there was no knock.

And when it was time for bed, Ellen went into the kitchen and took the red and white and blue cookies off the plates and packed them away in tins.

The next evening Kurt and Ellen sat down together to a hurried dinner after a long day of varied tasks. Kurt felt Ellen's subdued mood, and he waited patiently for the lilt that would come to her voice when the mood lightened. But the lilt did not come, and her face was grave and pensive. Finally, Kurt said: "Ellen, it's hard always to realize that other people can take for granted a thing that means so much to you. They didn't stay away on purpose. If they had understood what it meant to us they would have come."

Ellen merely nodded. He studied her face thoughtfully for a moment.

"Sweetheart, will you never be happy here?" he asked her gently.

"How can you be happy in a place where people care so little?" she asked him. And now it was he who nodded.

Kurt ate in silence for a time, and then he said, "Tonight, we will write the letter to the Rabbinical Organization. We will ask for an assignment somewhere else."

After dinner they went together to Kurt's study at the synagogue. Kurt sat down at the typewriter; he took a piece of paper and rolled it into the machine. He thought a moment and then he began to write. When he had finished, he glanced over the letter, signed it and handed it to Ellen to read.

She handed it back to him a little questioningly.

"Well, that's it," he said. He folded the letter and put it in the envelope, and Ellen put on the stamp.

They walked a while in the calm warm night before they went back up to their room. When they returned home, Kurt took the letter from his pocket and propped it up on the bookcase.

"Kurtchen, are you sure?" Ellen asked him suddenly.

"We've written the letter, Ellen. We'll leave it here . . . for three days. Then if we still want to mail it, we will."

"Do you think something might happen in the next three days to make us change our minds?" Ellen asked, almost smiling, a piquant mixture of exasperation and indulgence lightening her mood.

Kurt shrugged his shoulders and smiled back at her.

"Who knows?" he said.

Chapter 23

THE RED CROSS was housed in one of Fall City's mansions of an earlier day, a somewhat dilapidated, much-partitioned structure, now staring dolefully out its windows at a liquor store across one street, and a used-car lot across the other.

On a Monday afternoon, Lee Kalman and Ellen Rosen, in company with half a dozen other women, sat folding bandages at a long table in the big sunny room that once had been a nursery.

Ellen worked quickly, but it seemed to Lee that the gauze caught on a hangnail with each bandage she folded, and the whiteness was a blur before her eyes. Most of the women were chattering, but Lee did not speak, and only Ellen's occasional quiet-toned comment steadied her.

Margory Hilton, looking dignified and austere in her gray uniform, came bustling in to inquire:

"How many stump sops do we have?" The phrase, which in other times and other places might have had an outraged gentility, sounded only harsh and flippant on a socialite's tongue. Lee did not want to be the one to answer, although the bandages were stacked right in front of her. Ellen made the count and called out the number, while Lee went right on folding.

When Margery Hilton was gone, she glanced up a little apologetically.

"Take you home," she said to Ellen, "We could stop by the store if you need anything."

"That would be fine," Ellen answered, matter-of-factly.

When the gauze and the bandages and the surgical scissors had been locked away in the big old cabinet at the end of the room, Lee and Ellen walked out together, into the languorous afternoon. A delivery boy's motorcycle spewed up a raucous cloud of sound in the slow-moving stream of traffic, and from the college of music above the liquor store a weary trumpet solo was wafted out the open window to blend with the cadence of early summer.

Lee felt her senses reaching out incredulously to the feel, the temper of this day.

"What are you thinking?" Ellen asked her, noting the bemused expression on her face.

"Just that here . . . war seems very far away," Lee answered gravely.

"It does indeed," Ellen replied, sighing.

They got into Lee's car and drove to the grocery store, and when they had finished shopping and were riding once more down a sunny, peaceful street, where children ran and shouted and doused each other with a hose, Ellen felt again Lee's curious sense of remoteness.

"Lee, how is everything?" Ellen asked her.

Lee smiled a quick reply. "Pretty good. Since Maury's mother went to Minnesota to see her brother, I don't even have to feel guilty any more." The words were punctuated with a nervous little laugh.

Ellen did not reply, but Lee felt the discerning dark eyes upon her with a warmth of sympathy and fondness. Suddenly she abandoned all pretense. She wanted to speak.

"Ellen, sometimes I feel as if it is not Maury who's lost, but I. Sometimes I have the feeling that Maury can come back . . . but that I can't . . . not to the person I used to be. And I wonder if Maury will even like the person that I've become."

"I think he should be very proud," Ellen told her.

Lee did not answer, her face was perturbed. She drove up in front of the big house beside the synagogue and stopped the car.

"Come in a while?" Ellen asked her.

Lee shook her head. "Julian's waiting for me."

"Lee, how do you feel that you've changed so much," Ellen asked her.

Lee considered how she would answer. "When I was young . . . and fell in love with Maury . . . I thought people were either good or bad; and I thought you rely on a person's estimate of himself. I've discovered none of those things are true. I'm one of the disenchanted . . ." Lee said, beginning to smile, "and I think men don't like their women to be disenchanted."

Ellen ignored the attempt at whimsey and considered the deeply serious uncertainties that lay beneath it.

"I don't think a man minds if his wife grows up," she answered.

"Honestly, Ellen . . . you always hear . . . if two people love each other enough, they can go through anything together. But nobody tells you what people who love each other should do about the things that happen to them when they're apart."

"That's true," Ellen agreed simply.

"Sometimes I think that during the whole generation we live

278

in, men and women will be trying to protect each other from what they've learned alone. Maybe we'd be a whole century ahead if they could just . . . somehow . . . share the meaning of things with each other."

Ellen looked with keen sympathy into the troubled young face. "Lee, if you understand that much, you will find a way of sharing it all with Maury . . . and to help him share it with you," Ellen told her.

"I hope so. . . . I only hope so," Lee said.

A sense of wanting to help, and not knowing how, took firm hold of Ellen's mood as a few moments later she climbed the steps to her apartment.

"Kurtchen," she called, pushing open the door with her knee. She hurried through the front room to put down her bundles— bread and cheese from the grocery store, yarn from the Red Cross knitting room—on the kitchen cabinet.

"Here," Kurt called, straightening up in front of the ice box where he had been surveying the contents.

Ellen closed the ice box door. "I make something for you," she said. "How long have you been home?"

"An hour. And I just finished a sandwich," he told her.

"Ah . . . that's fine." Back in the living room, Ellen kicked off her shoe and massaged one aching foot, a rich relief coming slowly to her face.

Kurt laughed at her. "What did you do today?" he asked.

"USO this morning. Red Cross bandages this afternoon. . . . Here, sit down, please. You can hold the yarn for me while I roll the balls." Her eyes chided him for the ineptness of men.

She looped a skein of olive drab yarn over Kurt's hands, and began to roll.

"I saw Lee Kalman," she said.

"Fine!"

Ellen glanced up. "Everything is not so fine," she said; her face was thoughtful as she continued to roll. Kurt saw that, in her preoccupation, she had all but forgotten him. Smiling a little, he disentangled himself from the thread and hung it over the back of a chair. He wandered off to the bookcase to look for a missing volume.

"Kurt, I wish we could make it easier for Lee!"

Kurt quickly turned back to her, surprising the look of concern in her eyes. In his hand he held an envelope that had been propped against the books.

"Ellen, this letter asking for a new assignment . . . shall we mail it?" he said.

Suddenly Ellen smiled at him, a knowing smile that conceded fate's uncanny subservience to his earnest desires.

"No, Kurtchen, not just yet. I think we might be needed here," she told him.

Leaving Ellen, Lee felt unable, yet, to face the confining limits of four walls, and so she made errands for herself, stopping by the library to pick up a book, stopping by the cleaners to get her linen suit. The warm haze of late afternoon was creeping down the sky, as she turned her car toward home.

Julian, hearing her step in the hall, came prancing and capering to meet her; and Amy, taking the grocery sack in her arms, looked up to announce reproachfully.

"Miss Lee, you forgot the bread!"

Lee laughed. "Tell you what! I'll set the table while you and Julian run down to the store," she said.

"Let's go. Let's go!" Julian shouted, tugging at Amy's hand. And with her mixture of mumbling, grumbling and laughing, Amy allowed herself to be pulled off toward the door.

Lee, glad of a few more moments alone, spread the cloth on the table. The doorbell rang and, a little petulantly, she went to answer it.

Lee opened the door. There in the hall stood Maury. He was stooped over, intently scrutinizing the engraved card that bore her name above the doorbell—"Mrs. Maury Kalman"—and below the engraving, in a five-year-old scrawl, "Julian"—

Maury straightened up as she opened the door. And they stood looking at each other for a second, and they did not speak.

"He can write?" Maury asked, glancing wrily back at the card.

"Maury . . . Maury!" Lee laughed. The sound bubbled up in her throat so that it hurt a little.

Lee came into Maury's arms. Holding her still, he lifted her and set her down again inside the apartment, and he closed the door. And then he kissed her. Her soft lips responded to his wild hunger, and his passion became an excruciating tenderness, as he held her, loving her.

Finally, he held her back, looking into her face.

"Happy homecoming!" he said softly.

"Oh, Maury . . ."

Standing there together neither of them could lay firm grasp upon the moment, so rigidly schooled were their very senses in denial. Lee pressed her face against Maury's tunic and he held her, and she felt her heart releasing the tears it had contained so long.

"Where's Julian?" Maury whispered against her hair.

"He went with Amy to get bread for supper," Lee told him.

"My wife, she still forgets to get the bread for supper," Maury said wonderingly, as if this were the first tangible link with the past.

"Come, sit down!" Lee said. She let go his hand for an instant, and then took it again, laying her cheek against the open palm that she cradled in her own two hands. "Maury, I have to touch you. I have to feel your being real. Maury, they said you were missing . . ."

"Later," Maury said, "later we'll speak of it." And he lifted her face again to his kiss. "Tell me about you . . . and about Julian."

At that moment a clatter in the hall announced Julian's arrival, and Amy opened the door shushing him determinedly.

Maury stood up, the little boy looked at him uncertainly, and took a step toward his mother.

"Julian . . ." Maury said, there was not quite an entreaty in his voice.

Julian hesitated a second more, and the flicker of memory quivered in his small face.

And suddenly he ran to Maury. And in a blending of motion that is the language of the heart, the man stooped down, and the child was gathered up, and they stood, father and son, a small body pressed against a tall one, their heads together, and no word spoken.

"My Lawdy, Miss Lee . . . My Lawdy . . . My Lawdy . . ." Amy began to chirp and she jumped excitedly from one foot to the other.

Much later, the Kalmans sat at dinner; and Maury, his long legs half in and half out of the tiny dining nook, balanced the telephone on his knee as he completed a long-distance call to his mother. The telephone rang again as he lifted it up, and when he answered he spoke in clipped, formal tones, while Lee looked on quizzically.

"Who was that?" she asked when the conversation had ended.

"A reporter from the *Tribune* . . ."

"But how . . .?"

"Billy Jennings drove me home in the cab; I guess he called the paper. . . . Damn it, Lee. I don't want to be interviewed," Maury said, getting up suddenly, rubbing his hand down the back of his head in a gesture of annoyance that Lee remembered so well.

Lee tried to laugh away his reluctance. "But my dear Captain, you're a hero!" she teased, catching up his hands to waltz him around the floor with her. But the mood was not so quickly banished. Maury sat down on the couch, drawing her down beside him.

"Lee, I'm not a boy scout that got lost in the woods. Anything that's important I can't tell them. I haven't any stomach for all that tripe about survival behind enemy lines. I wish to hell they'd leave me alone."

Lee sat up straighter and looked at Maury.

"Maury . . ."

Maury's eyes, haunted by some distance she did not know, came back to her face and he saw that he had frightened her.

"Don't worry, Lee!" he laughed suddenly. I'll give the young lad a thrilling story. . . . "Truth is stranger than fiction, and all that!" he winked at her, but Lee was not reassured. This was an attempt at the type of repartee at which Maury had been so adept; but Lee could not quite look at him, at the hard line of his jaw that seemed so incongruous with his bantering tone.

Maury stood up as if the walls of this small room bound him too tightly. And then, sensing that his movement had been abrupt, he smiled again, stretched his arms above his head.

"At least here there's not room to get lost," he said, winking at Lee.

"Maury, I wish we were home!" Lee said, and she could not keep the wistfulness from her voice.

Long before Lee was ready to admit it, Kurt and Ellen Rosen recognized that Maury was gripped by a taut and relentless perplexity. They sensed it in their first visit to the Kalmans' on Maury's second night home. And Kurt, having heard Maury express his reluctance to be interviewed, watched with alarm during the next few days as a single interview was expanded into a running commentary on Maury's activities during his stay at home.

"In his own home town Maury is a hero," Ellen said, as she cut out another clipping to paste in the scrapbook, which was becoming an informal chronicle of the entire congregation.

"I don't think Maury feels like a hero," Kurt answered.

"Did he speak to you?"

"No, but I have the feeling he will."

"What do you suppose is the matter?"

Kurt shrugged. "War isn't easy for anybody," he said. "It could be so many things."

"I don't think Lee knows either . . . and it troubles her," Ellen replied, her brow creasing thoughtfully. She was remembering the visit to the Kalmans and how it had seemed that Lee bent every effort toward creating small moments that her husband might cherish in memory.

There had been, Ellen knew, the art of loving in the way that Lee poured coffee from the silver pot, in the way she bent forward to hold a lighter to Maury's cigarette, in the way she drew the shades against the encroachment of night. There had been the art of loving in the way she held out her hands to hands that would hold them; and when Maury caught up her hands it was as if he accepted these small and precious gifts of her love knowingly, with a humility that was somehow hard to witness, in gratitude for such tiny things.

"Kurt . . . I hope it can be all right for them, before he has to go away again. It has to be!" Ellen said fiercely, turning her eyes to him as if he must hold the answer.

"I'm sure it will be," Kurt replied with a confidence he did not feel.

Kurt was even less sure three days later, when he sat at a banquet table and watched Lee watching her husband as he addressed a Parent-Teacher's group. Kurt sensed that, for Lee, all of these functions which centered around Maury had surrounded him with an aura of strangeness, so that time and again a moment which might have been made sweet by some gesture, some quick caress, contained only the strangled, yearning thought of it.

An hour later Kurt stood beside Lee as Maury accepted the good wishes and congratulations of all who pressed around him. And once Kurt saw their eyes meet above the intervening heads.

"It isn't easy for either of you," he said to Lee.

"If they would only leave him alone!" Lee answered quickly. "There's so little time . . . and so much to . . ." she didn't go on. She saw Maury elbowing his way through the last stragglers to join them. And she smiled at him.

"Hi, Rabbi . . . Hi, Lee!" there was something almost boyish in his words; and Kurt saw that his smile followed the old pattern, although the quality of it was somehow altered. Maury tucked Lee's arm under his.

"Ready?" he said to them, placing his visored cap on his head.

And in that moment a plump and determined little woman seemed to swoop down on them from nowhere.

She held out her dimpled hand and Maury, a little slowly, accepted it.

"Captain Kalman, I think you're mighty nice to give us all this time when I know you'd rather be home with your charming wife," she fluttered.

Lee smiled. Maury did not reply, he waited impatiently, and Kurt saw the familiar tightening of his jaw.

The little woman laughed nervously. "Captain Kalman, there's just one favor I'd like to ask you. I'm program chairman for our circle at the Baptist Church, and I'd be a big success if you'd come talk to us for even fifteen little minutes."

"When do you want me to come?" Maury asked, the fine edge of irritation just beneath his voice.

"This Thursday afternoon at three. And Captain Kalman, I think it would be so nice if you'd talk to us about Brotherhood in the Armed Forces."

For an instant a grimness froze in Maury's face. "I'll speak if you like, but I have nothing to say on the subject of Brotherhood in the Armed Forces!" Maury told her, his manner brusque, almost surly.

Kurt saw the color drain from Lee's face, as she laid a hand on Maury's arm. And glancing at the frumpy little woman, he saw bewilderment come into the face which had held flagrantly sentimental admiration. Her flowered hat quivered for an instant as if it personally had been affronted, and then the quiver almost seemed to reach her pink rouged lips. But at the same time something was beginning to harden in her guileless, blue eyes.

"Maybe we're all taking too much of your time, Captain Kalman. You don't need to come unless you want to!" she said on a rush of breath, and turning, she all but ran away, her high heels clattering on the floor.

"Maury!" Lee said.

Maury put his hand on her hand where it lay on her arm. He smiled at her, his manner forbidding mention of the incident just past.

"Come on, Rabbi, let's go," he said; and, as he spoke to Kurt, there was only a flicker of apology in his voice.

284

At the end of that first hectic week, Maury went downtown alone one day to visit some of his old haunts, to see some of his old friends. While he was gone, Lee draped herself in a big apron and went into the kitchen to make the spaghetti which had been one of his favorite dishes.

Maury came back a little before supper time to find her flushed with heat and exertion.

He kissed her, embracing flour-splattered apron and all.

"The harder you work, the more your hair curls," he said, pulling out one blonde curl and watching it spring back into place.

"It's the sweat of my brow that does it," Lee retorted, wiping the back of her hand across her forehead. "You must not forget to be an appreciative husband when you eat this concoction."

Maury laughed, and Lee turned back to the stove for some final stirring.

"Whom did you see?" she asked, tasting from the spoon.

"In the army a cook would be court-martialed for that," Maury teased.

Lee shot him a subduing glance. "Whom did you see?" she repeated.

"Oh . . . Sam . . . Benny . . . a few people."

"Sam Levinson?"

"Yes. He's all worked up as usual."

"About what?"

"When the board elects a rabbi, he's got a man he wants for the job," Maury said, almost angrily.

Lee put down the spoon. She turned around from the stove wiping her hands savagely on the apron in a gesture of protest.

"He makes me furious!" she said. "He's unfair and unkind, and I don't see why anybody listens to him. Sometimes I just hate him, that's all!"

Maury looked at her in astonishment.

"Lee, Sweetheart, why is it so important to you?"

"Kurt Rosen is such a good rabbi," she maintained fiercely, and for a moment Maury thought that she was close to tears. He smiled at her, a little wryly.

"Seems to me, Mrs. Kalman, you'll have to let the Jews pick their own rabbi," he said.

"Maury, the Rosens are my friends," Lee said, "and Sam Levinson has been so unfair."

Maury, loving the look of Lee's flushed and angry face, began suddenly to grin at her indulgently, secretly amused that Lee, thinking him lost, should have sought a sense of his being in the things which had begotten him but which he himself so little understood.

"Lee, you're getting to be more of a Jew than I am!" he told her.

Lee was looking at him solemnly.

"Maury, I don't think you're glad," she said simply.

Maury had been sitting on the high kitchen stool. He got up; he put his hands in his pockets; he took them out again.

"Lee, I never tried to make you think I wanted it," he said a little helplessly.

Maury saw that he had hurt her. He stood there for a moment, not knowing what to do.

"Lee . . ." he wanted to go to her, but he had the feeling that she did not want him to come. And Lee found to her own amazement that she could not speak to Maury of the things she had so longed to tell him, things that had become somehow interwoven into her feeling for him so that, by not speaking of them, she felt almost as if she were withholding a part of her love.

And now, across a tiny cluttered kitchen, they looked at each other and they smiled a little. And they both knew that they would try desperately to be as they once had been for each other. And each felt a foretaste of that utter loneliness of spirit that would be engendered by such a pretense.

The next day Maury went to see the rabbi. He stopped by the Rosen apartment late in the afternoon, and he was glad when Ellen told him that Kurt was in his study. He entered the synagogue quietly and raised a hand in greeting when Kurt glanced up from his work.

"Well, Maury! It's good to see you. Come in." Kurt called to him.

"Hi, Rabbi," Maury said, his determination seeming to waver a little under the warmth of greeting. Kurt understood this.

"Maury, I'm glad you've come," he said, shaking hands, and the tone of his words seemed to relieve Maury of the necessity of contriving an explanation.

"Thanks, Rabbi," Maury took the chair Kurt offered him. He sat there for a moment without speaking, and Kurt did not rush him or begin a trivial conversation. He merely waited.

"Rabbi, Lee tells me Julian is going to Sunday School at the

Temple now," Maury said tentatively, leaning forward a little in his chair, pounding one fist softly into the palm of his other hand.

Kurt had wondered how Maury would begin; this was an overture he had not anticipated. "That's true. I explained to Lee that the Jewish religion assumes that the child takes the religion of the mother; but she seemed very earnest in her wish that he come to us . . ."

"She is very earnest, Rabbi. I don't quite understand it." Maury made a small, baffled gesture with his hand. "Rabbi, I hope you won't think I'm crazy. I can't quite sort out my feelings. Lee thinks she's done something that's very wonderful. And the awful, terrible part is that I don't know. I don't even know if I'm glad."

Kurt nodded. His discerning gray eyes met Maury's and he did not interrupt.

"Rabbi, that sounds like an awful thing to say . . . like a strange thing to come here and say to you."

"Maury, what is it that troubles you?" Kurt asked.

"Rabbi, I just can't figure out what's happened to Lee. I come home and find out that she hardly even speaks to her own uncle . . . why, he raised her from a baby. She was crazy about him! And the friends she used to have . . . she doesn't call them any more. I can't go off again knowing she's living on an island by herself with nothing . . . with just a bunch of wonderful ideas!"

"What wonderful ideas, Maury?"

Maury looked at Kurt helplessly for a moment. "Rabbi, we talk about the Jewish heritage being so glorious . . . so wonderful! We talk about it in the synagogue. And it's as if all of that has caught fire in Lee's mind . . . as something that she can give to Julian. Something she can do for him. It's as if she's perfectly content just to live in the shadow of it . . . on the fringe of it."

In Maury's voice was the deep, anguished knowledge of estrangement, and the paradox that he suffered it not for himself, but for Lee.

"Maury," Kurt said, "I know you worry about Lee, but I don't think you need to worry so much. Lee has gone a long way toward achieving an understanding. And understanding protects people against many things from which others cannot protect them."

Maury faced Kurt squarely. "That's just it, Rabbi. I don't

think she understands at all . . . not how it really is. And I keep thinking that some day something may happen to make her so sorry . . . to make her hate everything she thought she loved."

"Maury," Kurt said quietly. "You made Lee your wife, and that was a chance you took . . . a chance you both took. But now you do her an injustice to deny for her what is true for yourself."

For a moment Maury did not reply. He sat very still looking at the titles of books stacked on the desk, then slowly his eyes came back to Kurt.

"Rabbi, I never asked Lee to submerge her whole identity in mine. I never even wanted her to," he said finally.

Kurt, looking upon this quiet despair, understood the contrition that a man can feel when, by his very love, he must bring his wife to a way of life in which the stealthy winds of humiliation can blight the very heart.

"I never wanted it," Maury said again.

And Kurt knew that only by thus holding Lee at a distance could Maury Kalman feel that he had guaranteed that she would never have to endure more than she felt able to endure . . . only thus could he keep open to her an avenue of escape, even one that would take her from him. And yet Kurt knew that it was not escape that Lee Kalman sought.

"Maury, it seems to you that Lee is lonely and alone, and it hurts you to see it. But you must realize, Maury . . . some people are destined to journey far afield from their beginnings. And those who make the journey must always pass through areas that they can only traverse alone. You, too, must be patient . . . and try to understand."

Maury stood up. "Rabbi, thank you . . . thank you for letting me talk to you," he said and he held out his hand to Kurt.

Maury's need of compassion weighed heavily on Kurt's spirit. When Maury had gone and Kurt turned back to his books, he had lost savor for the theme he had chosen for his sermon. It seemed to lack the deep wells of strength and understanding from which this compassion might flow out to Maury and to others like him whose need was great. He sat for a moment, quietly looking out of the window, and then he took up the prayer book and turned to a favorite passage in Jeremiah:

Fear not, O Jacob, My Servant
Neither be dismayed, O Israel

For lo, I will save you from afar.
And your children from lands of captivity.
O Israel you shall again be quiet and at ease.
And none shall make you afraid . . .

And he could not help balancing it with a line from Isaiah:

For a brief moment I have forsaken you
But with great compassion will I gather you . . .

. . . *And with great compassion will I gather you.* . . . The promise waited to be fulfilled.

Chapter 24

WHEN KURT had finished outlining his sermon, he no longer consciously thought of Maury Kalman; but he found himself wondering, instead, how much a man ever really understands the meaning things may have for the woman he loves.

His mind wandered back to the un-mailed letter that he had written to the Rabbinical Organization. Ellen had not let him mail it; but how much, he suddenly asked himself, had she wanted him to mail it. He truly did not know.

Kurt sighed. He could not help smiling, a little, at the ironic twist his thoughts had taken. He was thinking that an ordinary man asks the woman he loves to share his life, but a minister must ask the woman he loves to share the lives of others.

He thought of telling this to Ellen, and he thought of how she would smile. But in his mind's very act of creating the image of her face, he was struck by the poignance of so blithe a spirit being obliged, always, to exist at the suffrance of other people. . . . A congregation? . . . What could a congregation possibly mean in her life?

Suddenly Kurt's thoughts were carrying him a long way back to how it had been at the very beginning. He was remembering Duisburg . . . and the first day that he and Ellen had set out together to pay visits to members of the congregation.

The first visit had been to a successful young industrialist and his bride; and Kurt had but to close his eyes to recall the flush of breathless wonder in Ellen's face as they approached, by way of a stately and many-laned private park, the brooding, haughty, stone mansion whose stained-glass windows, like some exquisitely imagined kaleidoscope, created an ever-changing fantasy of light and color.

In a richly exotic salon as large as the whole synagogue in which he now sat, Kurt and Ellen had been greeted by their vigorous young host and his fashionably pale wife who held out her hand for shaking.

Ellen caught up the limp hand eagerly. "It's beautiful here!

Beautiful!" she exclaimed. "How nice for two people to begin their life together in such a lovely home!"

The last remark, rendered in suddenly sedate tones, was made, Kurt knew, out of deference to his position as visiting rabbi. He was ready to smile, but his host was smiling already, a knowing, wordly smile. And as Ellen reached out to beauty with the curiously uncorrodible innocence of the life-loving, Kurt saw in the eyes of their host an admiration that was not innocent. And about the lips of their hostess he saw the forming of a tight little line.

Watching Ellen almost with dismay, Kurt felt the next two moments lifted out of their stiff and formal context to become imbued with a sense of something rich and sensual and *verboten.* And the talk was, all the while, very polite and correct. But in a sudden laughing gesture, their host snatched up an oriental shawl of exquisite color and design, that hung over the end of the handsome couch, and flung it around Ellen's shoulders.

"Rabbi, your wife enhances such a setting beautifully!" he called out, his white teeth showing in a flash of smile.

Ellen, her dark hair tossed back over the muted colors of the shawl, laughed; and her laughter, throbbing and muted, too, created a like fabric of sound.

And Kurt, confronted in that instant by a longing beyond his means to appease, felt a fierce compulsion to take Ellen away . . . to take her away and to show her their real lot in life—not beauty and the caress of luxury, but pain . . . the pain that belonged to other people.

From the mansion Kurt drove with Ellen across the city to a tall house in a decaying neighborhood, where a shout in the street might well be a curse and where grimy wash was hung to dry in narrow courtyards. As they went, Kurt told her that they would visit now a great-aunt of the young industrialist whose house they had just left.

They climbed five steep flights of stairs and knocked upon a doorway in the dim hall, to be admitted, at last, by a skewered and wispy little woman who went scuttling off as soon as she had let them in.

Ellen, turning into the room, was startled to see the gaunt, unmoving figure of a woman propped up amidst soiled pillows in a wheelchair beneath the small window. And with a sense almost of fright Ellen realized that the large, staring, blue eyes had been fastened upon her from the second she entered the door.

Kurt took Ellen's hand and drew her with him to the side of the woman. When Kurt smiled at her, Ellen sensed in this drawn face the impulse to a smile which wooden lips would not obey.

"Frau Essinger, I bring my wife to visit you," Kurt said, bending a little nearer as if she might otherwise not hear. The staring blue eyes took on a new intensity, which the muscles would not accept. And Ellen, feeling suddenly the awesome responsibility of being a rabbi's wife, sat down in the straight chair that was close beside the wheel chair.

"I'm glad I could come," Ellen said with a frightening sense of the inadequacy of words.

Looking for a more tangible expression of her sympathy and concern, Ellen saw that the shawl which had covered the woman's knees had slipped down to the floor, and she stooped to pick it up. With its rough texture clasped in her hands, she lifted it and smoothed it around the shrunken legs, and in her fingers was the memory of another shawl, and for one anguished moment her eyes met Kurt's. As she turned back to Frau Essinger, there was in Ellen's face the stark understanding that within the narrow prison of this paralyzed body a living being dwelt.

Frau Essinger did not take her eyes from Ellen. Ellen Rosen, young, beautiful, had come into this dreary room with the flush of the recently beguiled on her cheeks; and this frail shell of a woman had seen, and a femininity, long dormant, had been stirred by some half forgotten memory of herself.

Frau Essinger tried to speak. Her lips twisted and the sounds came as gasps from her lips. Kurt bent nearer to try to hear what she would say.

"Kurtchen, ask her if there is anything we can do," Ellen implored him.

Kurt looked at Ellen dubiously, some hidden protest in his face.

"'I think . . . she wants to know if you would brush her hair . . . for her," he whispered.

Ellen made herself go to the dresser; she took up the ivory-handled brush in her hand; she turned and her eyes moved swiftly past Kurt. She came back and stood beside Frau Essinger; and she took out the three large hair pins and the untidy hair tumbled down.

Ellen began to brush. The hair was long . . . and black . . . and streaked with gray and silver . . . and in the light of the sun it came alive as Ellen brushed. But in the gaunt, passive mask of Frau Essinger's face there was no longer any flicker of life's lost hopes, or of its bitter, searing sorrow.

Kurt, standing by helplessly, watched Ellen wield the brush with long, sweeping, rhythmic strokes. It hurt him to see her ability to understand too well. And with something almost like remorse, he longed to create for her . . . and to harbor and protect . . . that which some deep knowledge of life had impelled him to destroy—the bright, unblemished ecstasy which contains no hint of pain. . . .

When Kurt went home to supper he was still in the thrall of memories that moved with a clear poignance across his mind; and Ellen saw that he sat with the paper before him, not reading it.

"Kurt, I love you," she said with the tones of one who trespasses knowingly into some secret domain of thought.

"Of course, you do," he answered.

"Of course, I do! . . . The incredible ego of men!" Ellen chided, laughing at him.

Kurt laughed, too. "Of course, you do, or you wouldn't have shared everything that's come my way."

"Kurt, what were you thinking about a moment ago?" Ellen asked.

"I was thinking of the time in Duisburg . . . the visit to the rich young man . . . and to his poor sick aunt. . . ."

Kurt saw in Ellen's face that the memory had a strange pull upon her senses, too. "Kurt, why did you take me there that day?" Ellen asked.

Kurt shook his head. "I don't know. I was trying to think of it myself."

"Were you trying to show me how mean and heartless people can be?"

"No . . . not that. . . . Maybe I was trying to show you how very little people can imagine what it's like to be someone else."

"How very little Sam Levinson can realize what it's like to be the Rosens?" Ellen said, beginning to smile.

"Yes, and how very little the Rosens can realize what it's like to be Sam Levinson," Kurt said, smiling in reply.

Ellen brought out the bowl of fruit and set it on the table. Her eyes searched Kurt's face as he calmly peeled a pear and cut it into slices.

"Kurtchen?"

He smiled, knowing that she had been debating what to say. "Yes, Ellen?"

"Kurt, I wish that you would not go . . . I wish you would not go through with the *bar mitzvah*."

"Ellen, it's Davey, not his father, who is going to be *bar mitzvah*," Kurt told her, his smile now trying to insinuate a little of its humor into her serious mood.

"Yes, Kurt, but it's his father who will get up at a meeting and try to take away your job."

Kurt shrugged his shoulders and continued to eat the pear.

"What do you do now?" Ellen asked him.

"The Levinsons come with Davey; we go through the whole thing."

"In three days will be the board meeting when they elect the rabbi for the next two years; and, two days after that, the *bar mitzvah*. Kurtchen, you should not be required to do it!"

Kurt wiped his fingers on the napkin, then took off the *yarmulca* he wore while eating and put it in his hip pocket. He stood up and kissed Ellen on the forehead.

"You do it?" she said.

Kurt pretended not to have heard the question. "It's seven o'clock and I promised to meet the Levinsons at the temple at seven. Will you join us?"

"No, I'll stay here," Ellen said.

Kurt kissed her again. "I'll be back as soon as I can," he told her.

When Kurt had gone, when Ellen had watched him as he crossed the yard to the synagogue, when she had seen the light go on in his study, she turned back into the gloom that had crept with evening into the room. And she too flicked on the light.

She cleared the supper dishes away, washed them and dried them and put them into the cabinet. She took the broom and swept up the crumbs from the old and worn rug. And with broom in hand, she began to think of the first day in Fall City, and the first cleaning of this room. All that had been strange then, was familiar now—the creak of the floor board just three steps inside the door, the lumpy cushions of the couch, the window that would not stay up. Acting upon some curious compulsion, Ellen continued to sweep the floor; she took out the dust cloth and dusted the furniture. She rubbed up a shine on a table-top that once had drunk polish into its thirsty pores. These things

294

were not hers, but they had absorbed something of her life . . .
and of Kurt's. And Ellen was suddenly loathe to give them up.

Feeling, almost, the sting of tears in her eyes, Ellen looked
around her. This room was only a place . . . and the city spreading out around this house was only a place . . . and what is
the meaning of a place to the heart? Ellen felt the strangeness
of wanting so much to cling to something that had often been
disappointing. What, she wondered, does the heart find to love
in places that have been unlovable? Places are made up of people,
yet their identity is their own, separate from people. Duisburg,
Koenigsberg, Berlin — these were places as Fall City was a
place.

"Place . . . place . . . place!" Ellen said aloud. The word intrigued her. "A place of our own . . . a place in the sun . . . a
place to strike root."

What was this yearning and what did the heart derive from
a place, Ellen wondered. A place, she knew, could be loved after
the people who inhabited it were hated. A place could be loved
for the way that life itself was loved there. And in whatever
place she went with Kurt, she could love life, itself, Ellen told
herself fiercely.

Ellen stood in the center of the floor and thought these
thoughts and then she put away the broom and dust cloth. She
went back to the window. The lights were lit in the synagogue
now, and she could glimpse Sam Levinson's light-colored Cadillac parked at the curb. Ellen drew the shade. She put a symphony on the record player and sat down on the couch and closed
her eyes to listen.

The wrenching loose . . . the beginning again . . . would be
hard. But this time Ellen understood, it was only a place she
would be leaving behind, not life itself.

Sam Levinson stood at the pulpit with Kurt, mumbling through
the Hebrew that he would have to read at his son's *bar mitzvah*.
Davey sat beside his mother in the front row. Myra Levinson
kept glancing at her diamond watch; she kept playing with it,
turning it a little on her wrist. Davey slumped down in the
seat until he was balanced on the end of his spine. He closed
his eyes and tried to visualize his father in a prayer shawl. He
couldn't.

"Shall we go through it again?" Kurt asked Sam when he had
stumbled to the end of the reading.

"Oh Heavens, Sam, we don't have time. Rabbi can write it

out for you. You can run through it a couple of times at home," Myra interposed impatiently.

"That's right, Rabbi. You just see that Davey here is letter perfect. Nobody gives a damn about whether I can read Hebrew or not," Sam replied.

Davey's eyes popped open, he sat up straight. He wondered how Rabbi felt about hearing his father say damn in the sanctuary.

"Davey is ready, he has only to write his speech," Kurt said.

"Oh, that won't be anything," Myra said, "he can do that tonight when he gets home."

"I don't want to write a speech," Davey said abruptly.

Davey knew that in his speech he was supposed to thank his parents for the priceless heritage they passed on to him; he was supposed to promise to uphold its precepts as his parents upheld them before him. Suddenly he rebelled.

"Oh, Davey, don't be silly," Myra said. "If you can't write it you can get Mervin to write it for you, he's good at themes. But you could write it if you just would. . . . Maybe Rabbi could write it for you," she suggested brightly, twisting the watch on her wrist. And Kurt noticed there was something both baffled and defiant beneath the surface brightness.

Sam Levinson came down from the pulpit. He reached over and gave Davey's ear a playful tweak.

"Well, what else, Rabbi?" he said.

"Oh, I know something I wanted to tell Rabbi," Myra interrupted nervously. "When the scrolls are taken out of the Ark, I don't want any of that kissing of the Torah."

"Oh, Myra, for God's sake!" Sam said impatiently, starting off up the aisle.

"I mean it!" Myra maintained. "I don't care if it is an ancient custom. It looks so silly to outsiders. And I don't want it."

Kurt Rosen still stood beside the pulpit. He looked from Sam Levinson to his wife and back again. He did not intend to exhort them to respect, for in his own heart was a degree of love and respect of holiness which would render even the exhortation a gross insensibility.

But abruptly, Davey was on his feet. He took one look at Kurt Rosen and then he turned away as if he could not bear to look at him.

"I want it!" he shouted at his mother, "I want them to kiss the Torah. That's part of it and I want it!"

Myra Levinson looked at her son in astonishment.

"Davey, be quiet!" Sam said brusquely. "What could you possibly know about it. I think your mother surely ought to have more idea about the fitness of things."

Davey Levinson could not look at the rabbi. He felt suddenly that he would cry—and for a boy to cry the week before his thirteenth birthday!—Davey started toward the door with his head down. He hurried up the aisle not looking at his father or his mother. And with a baffled shrug Myra turned and followed after him.

Kurt stood watching Davey Levinson's swaggering young figure, thrusting forward, out through the door and into the night.

And when the door had closed behind his parents, too, Kurt stepped down from the pulpit and turned off the lights in the synagogue. He went into his study and checked off the list of names that Sam Levinson wanted called to the Torah when his son was *bar mitzvah*. When he had set the list in order, he began to divide the readings.

As he worked, Kurt was wondering how it was possible that the young ever survive the insensibility of their elders. The thought seemed to suggest Maury Kalman to him again. With such a terrible yearning Maury had talked about understanding. Davey Levinson was loved, but he was not understood. Maury loved Lee, but he did not understand her. Love, without understanding, it occurred to Kurt, was a reproach to the spirit exceeding all others.

It all seemed, in some curious way, to have to do with courage. It seemed that in life people would gamble on anything in the world before they would gamble on the courage of one they loved. It seemed . . . sometimes . . . that they would deny life's greatest blessings rather than see courage put to the test. Sam Levinson did not trust his son to have courage to face life on its own terms. And Maury Kalman did not have the courage to allow his wife to follow the dictates of her own heart. People believed in a great many things, Kurt thought—they believed in joy and despair, in love and in hate—but they did not believe in courage! . . .

It was after 11 o'clock that night when Kurt came home from his study. No light shone under the door, and so he let himself into the apartment quietly. He came through the darkened living room, and into the bedroom. And he paused in the doorway. The soft, even sound of Ellen's breathing came to him; and the summer moonlight, streaming in through the wide-open window, enveloped her in its light, creating from her beauty its own bewitchment.

In the graceful abandon of sleep, Ellen had flung one arm over her eyes against the wooing moonglow. Kurt took the arm gently down from her eyes. He sat beside her, looking into this face that contained in sleep some haunting essence of its waking vibrance. Kurt looked around him at the dim outlines of familiar objects, and it seemed to him the shadowy silence of the room held everywhere the hint of her being.

"My own . . . my own!!!" Kurt did not speak the words aloud.

He was thinking that, when too long and searching a look at life had painfully opened up new spaces in the heart, there seemed always to be just that much more room for loving.

Fleetingly, Kurt thought again about courage. Looking into Ellen's sleeping face, he was thinking how it was to have discovered the courage of one who is loved. And he knew, in that moment, that to have faced finally the fact that to love is not to protect . . . is to come differently with the gifts of love.

Kurt laid a hand against the cheek that lay so smooth in the moonlight. Ellen's eyelids flickered, they opened. And in her eyes were the profound and beckoning depths of the moondrenched night.

"Kurt!"

"Sweetheart!"

Chapter 25

THE NEXT afternoon, Davey Levinson left a scout meeting and walked to the synagogue. The door was locked. He sat on the step for a moment and then went next door and upstairs and knocked at the Rosens' apartment. Ellen answered.

"Davey!—You weren't supposed to have a lesson today, were you?"

Davey shook his head. "I have to see Rabbi," he said.

"He'll be back soon, come in," Ellen answered. She saw the flush of determination in the boy's face. "Davey, are you hungry? Would you like some cookies and milk?" she asked him.

Davey nodded his head with a jerky little movement.

"Here, sit down, I fix it for you," Ellen said. Ellen got out a tin of cookies and put some on a plate; she poured a glass of milk. "How was the scout meeting? What did you do today?" she asked him.

Davey brightened and Ellen realized he had been dreading that she might ask why he wished to see Kurt.

"Our scout troop went on an excursion—we went to a farm where they do diversified farming. We got to see everything. I even rode on a tractor," Davey said.

"And the farmer, was he glad to have you?" Ellen asked, smiling a little to herself.

"Oh, yes! He said we caught on fast. He said if any of the boys ever wanted a job! . . . I was the only one he let drive the tractor. I drove it clear down the row; and he said I drove it straight as an arrow!"

Davey was speaking excitedly, cramming the cookies into his mouth each time that he paused to elaborate, and when he could hardly speak he gulped down the milk. Ellen watched him and understood how his young heart was troubled; and she was thinking how agilely the very young can escape into the realm of imagination.

The telephone rang, and Ellen went to answer it. In a moment she came back to Davey, who was still eating the cookies, a bemused expression on his face.

"That was Rabbi," she said. "He's out at the Air Base, and he won't be able to come in for quite a while yet."

299

Davey stood up, spilling crumbs out of his lap. The last vestiges of the day-dream which he was so intently spinning deserted him.

"Oh—" he said. For a moment he was engulfed again in the shame and humiliation he had come to bear to the rabbi. He looked at the rabbi's wife whose warm eyes were on him gently, and he considered trying to explain it to her. But he did not know how.

"I guess I better go," he said. He picked up his school books.

Davey did not go straight home; when he did get home, his father had already returned from town and it was nearly time for dinner. His parents were in the den talking about the *bar mitzvah* just as they had been talking about it for weeks. They were arguing about whether or not the turkeys they would get for the celebration should be kosher.

Davey sat down in the roomy corner of the couch. He sat there and waited, as he had been waiting for weeks, for someone to have a little time for him, for someone to give any indication that the event would be more than a social occasion.

"Where is my Hebrew book?" he asked suddenly, jumping up.

His mother glanced at him impatiently. "Oh, Davey for goodness sake. It wouldn't be in your father's den. Go look in your room."

Davey stood there a moment and then wandered out into the hall. This had been only one of several small tentative overtures he had made, hoping that some one would show an interest in what all of this meant to him. And this overture, like all the others, had netted only a mild impatience—as if he had merely learned to spell words or to do equations.

Davey had wanted to tell the rabbi that he would not go through with the *bar mitzvah*. But he thought of his mother's intent preoccupied face, and he doubted if now, in the last moments, he would have had the courage to refuse. It seemed to Davey, as he thought about it, that all the work and study to which he had applied himself during the past year had been merely a means to an end. And the end, he was startled to discover, was the ceremony itself, the ritual, the occasion—not what it signified, but what it was itself—a *bar mitzvah!*

Davey wandered down the hall to his room. He dreaded the moment when he would have to come back in to supper.

The next morning, when Davey did not come to breakfast, Myra Levinson went to call him.

She rapped on his door, "Davey!" she called. There was no answer. She pushed the door open and even before the room came fully into view she had the feeling that Davey was not there.

"Davey!" she said again sharply.

"For God's sake, Myra, the eggs are getting cold. Can't he get to breakfast on time?" Sam called from the end of the hall.

"Sam, he isn't here," Myra said.

Sam threw down his napkin on the hall table as he passed through. "What do you mean, he isn't here?"

Sam peered in Davey's room. The bed had been slept in; it was, in fact, wildly rumpled; clothes were hanging half out of drawers, as they often were when Davey dressed in a hurry.

"Well, don't stand there and look like you think he's run away," Sam said impatiently. He spent the night here, that's for sure. And then he got dressed and took off somewhere. He's pouting and I don't know about what. But I'll have a talk with him all right."

"Sam, go call outside," Myra said.

Sam went to the front door and called. There was no answer.

Somehow, Sam didn't feel like going to the store. He stayed at home and hours passed, and irritation turned to anger, and anger to anxiety. Reluctantly, Sam called to confirm the fact that Davey was not at the home of his best friend.

"Well, where can he be?" Sam demanded of his wife.

"I don't know . . . I just don't know. We haven't got a relative in a thousand miles of here. He wouldn't just start out . . . and why?"

Sam Levinson sensed why. It had something to do with a stubborn integrity which he himself did not possess, and which, because he did not possess it, baffled him.

"It's easy enough to see why!" Sam retorted. "Davey was a different boy till he started these confirmation lessons. Now he's got his mind all full of a lot of high-flown ideas that haven't a thing to do with reality. All the rabbi needed to do was to teach him to read his portion in Hebrew. It damn sure ought to be up to a father to teach his son how to feel about life."

Myra did not reply. She had begun to do needle point and it nearly drove Sam crazy. Noon came and went and there was no word from Davey. Sam got in the car and drove around to some of the places he could think of where a twelve-year-old boy might go. But he did not find Davey. He came back home.

"Sam, why don't you call the rabbi?" Myra suggested tentatively.

"God damn the rabbi!" Sam flung back at her. Sam had the

galling suspicion that if Davey communicated with anybody it would be with the rabbi. He couldn't stand it.

"Call him!" Myra said. Her eyes flashed a hard brilliance that Sam had encountered but few times. He got up and went to the telephone and called the rabbi.

When Kurt had talked to Sam Levinson he could not settle down to work again. He left his study and went home to speak to Ellen; he told her what Sam had told him.

"Ellen, when Davey came to speak to me yesterday, did he tell you what he wanted to talk about?"

"No, Kurt. I only had the feeling he wanted to tell you he wouldn't go through with the *bar mitzvah*."

Kurt nodded; his eyes were thoughtful.

"What did Sam Levinson say to you when he called?" Ellen asked.

"He's very angry. He feels that it's my fault that Davey has run away."

"Your fault!"

"He thinks I influenced him too much."

"Kurt, where do you go now?" Ellen asked, as he put on his hat.

"I look for the boy," Kurt said.

Ellen did not protest. She knew how much Davey Levinson meant to Kurt, apart from all other things that might be considered. And she thought of Davey and the look in his eyes of some half-realized shame and the need to expiate it.

When Kurt had gone, Ellen continued to stand where she was, thinking about Davey Levinson, about how he had sat eating cookies and talking very fast and very excitedly without ever changing that look in his eyes. And in the next moment Ellen felt a curious tensing of her nerves before she was hardly aware of the trend her thoughts had taken.

. . . The farmer . . . the farmer who had said 'if any of you boys ever want a job!'

Ellen went to the telephone; she called scout headquarters and asked the name of the farmer the troop had visited. She scribbled his name on a piece of paper and the directions for finding the farm. And then, hardly hesitating a moment, she called Lee Kalman and asked it she could spare an hour or so. Ellen was waiting on the sidewalk, fifteen minutes later, when Lee drove up.

Ellen got into the car and handed Lee the paper with the directions to the farm written on it.

"Could you find this place?" she asked.

"The Philbrook farm? I know where it is. Out on the River Road. It's the place where the barn looks about three times the size of the house."

"Would you be so kind . . . take me there," Ellen asked.

Lee glanced quizzically at Ellen, "This is a most mysterious errand," she said as she turned the car around and started back through town.

"They can't find Davey Levinson," Ellen offered, "I have a feeling he might be there."

"Did he run away?" Lee asked.

"I don't know for sure."

"Does anybody know it yet?"

"Not many."

Lee glanced at Ellen again. "That's pretty good. You, of all people, find Davey and persuade him to come back . . . and save face for Sam Levinson."

"I wasn't thinking of saving face for Sam Levinson," Ellen said a little bitterly.

"No, I don't imagine you were. It's just funny how things work out," Lee replied.

Ten miles out on the highway, Lee turned the car into a dirt road that wound erractically through a pasture, then divided into forks that went to the house and to the barn.

"We'll try the barn, it's closest," Lee said. She stopped the car in front of the hulking structure and tooted the horn. A lean, spotted dog wandered from inside the doorway. Ellen got out of the car, and an overalled man with freckled arms, curly hair and a quick shy smile, waved a greeting to her as he came around the side of the barn.

"Mr. Philbrook?" Ellen inquired.

"Jimmy—Jimmy Philbrook," he said.

"Mr. Philbrook, I am Mrs. Rosen. I come looking for . . ."

"You're looking for Davey," he said, and his eyes began to twinkle.

Ellen nodded, reproachfully.

"I was going into town later on and call his dad," Jimmy Philbrook said. "You know, Mrs. Rosen, nearly every boy has to run away once or twice before he's grown. But you could have knocked me over with a feather this morning when he came pounding on my door. Reminded me I said if any of the boys ever needed a job . . ."

It was difficult to be angry with Jimmy Philbrook; he seemed to take for granted that a certain amount of anxiety on the part of Davey's parents must be deserved to have evolved such a situation.

"Where is Davey?" she asked.

"He's riding the tractor. You wait here, I'll get him."

A few moments later, when Ellen saw Davey coming toward her, striding along with a boy's earnest bravado, she felt very sharply the irony of her own presence here, and for a fleeting second that frightening sense of disorientation in time and space threatened her. In this new country the hardest thing for Ellen had not been the discrimination of the Gentiles, but the fact that Jews, who were bound together by a common suffering, should be able to turn upon each other. There had persisted the feeling that, having suffered at the hands of others, they should know what suffering meant and spare it to each other as far as they were able. This was the feeling that had brought Ellen to Davey Levinson; but, as she confronted him, she felt sharply and bitterly in her heart the thing that Davey's father was doing to Kurt.

"Hi, Mrs. Rosen," Davey said, without quite looking at her.

"Hi, Davey." With the palms of her hands, Ellen boosted herself up onto the bed of an old wagon that stood in the shade of the barn. Nimbly Davey clambered up beside her. He was sweating and sunburned and his breath came quickly but evenly.

Davey glanced at Ellen. He was so lonely, and he was so glad that she had found him that he felt like crying. Ellen Rosen somehow always made him feel warmly glad to be alive. But he did not feel that way now and he kept looking at her and waiting for the feeling to come, and when it did begin to come he was almost shy in her presence.

"Davey, why did you run away?" Ellen asked him.

"I don't know, Mrs. Rosen. I just wanted to be by myself, that's all."

"Davey, don't you want to be *bar mitzvah?*"

"It isn't that," Davey said quickly. "But when something doesn't turn out like it's supposed to be you just don't feel like going through with it."

"Davey, what troubles you most?" Ellen asked him.

"I don't know; nobody seems to understand things. The rabbi has been so good to me . . . and my father . . . well, he doesn't seem to understand it."

Davey looked at Ellen and wondered if she, of all people, wouldn't understand how he felt about the rabbi. It seemed to Davey that Ellen and the rabbi spoke together as if they knew some wonderful secrets. And in the presence of either of them, he could feel a little of the specialness of what they knew together. He tried to see in Ellen's face if she understood him now.

"Davey," Ellen said tentatively, "your father . . . he's been a good father to you, has he not?"

"Yes, yes, he has," Davey replied.

"And you hate what you're doing to him by running away?"

"Yes. But I don't think he likes me anymore." Davey had begun to kick his toe against the tongue of the wagon. Very intently he watched his sneaker bounce off the sun-bleached wood.

Suddenly Ellen could have wept. She had been trying to think of some way to explain Davey's father to him. But what Davey needed was not a philosophic explanation of the contrarieties and paradoxes and incongruities of life. He was a human being and the sense of those things was in his soul, troubling him, baffling him, goading him to seek his own answers. What he needed was the warmth of some human heart in which to anchor these things to reality. That's what human beings required of each other, really—the warmth to make the soul's individual searching a less lonely thing.

When Ellen did not speak, Davey turned his head and looked into the dark eyes that were so intently upon him. Without quite knowing why he did it, he sidled a little nearer to her, and she reached over and took his hand.

"Davey, of course your father likes you. He loves you very much," Ellen told him.

"Then why doesn't he know what I'm like inside?" Davey demanded. His eyes, dark and troubled, were full on her face, searching for his answer.

Ellen wished for Kurt. She did not know how to explain things to people, things that mattered so much.

"Davey, how does your father treat you when you disappoint him?" she asked.

"He gives me another chance."

"Why does he give you another chance?"

Davey considered. "Because he knows I would have done better if I could."

Ellen nodded; she waited for Davey to think about what he had said. And Davey did think about it. He felt the rush of an aching love for his father, and fleetingly he perceived his father's confusion which was both a bitterness and a yearning. Suddenly he felt the fierce need to help his father maintain the pretenses of his pride until he could, in his own time, dissolve them.

"Davey, don't you think you could give your father another chance?" Ellen asked him finally.

Davey kept concentrating on the toe of his shoe. Didn't she realize what giving another chance would mean? It would mean that he could not forsake his father again no matter how his heart yearned after the way the rabbi had pointed to him. If he went back, it would be to a *bar mitzvah* according to his father's definition, a *bar mitzvah* in which he stood before those assembled and promised to uphold, as his parents had upheld, the heritage they passed on to him. Davey thought of saying this to Ellen, but he did not know how to say it.

"I don't know," he said. "I'd have to think about it a little bit. I want to go in the barn by myself and think about it," he said. He jumped down off the wagon bed.

Ellen added no further plea, she only smiled at him and he paused a moment, drinking in the warmth of the smile like the warmth of the sun. And then he turned and went off into the barn alone.

Ellen sat there for a few moments, and then she got down and went to the car and sat with Lee. But she did not feel like speaking; she sat with her hands clasped in her lap, watching the door of the barn.

"You want him to come back very much, don't you?"

Ellen nodded.

"Why?"

Ellen did not know how to explain it. She only knew that in trying to comfort Davey she had felt oddly comforted herself.

She turned to Lee to try to explain, but instead she said: "What are you thinking?"

"I was thinking about kindness."

"What about kindness?"

Lee thought of how it had somehow ached in her throat a little to watch Ellen Rosen and Davey Levinson sitting there talking together. The exquisite, earnest, artless, delicate, wonderful thing between them which was almost hurtful to see, was something that could not have been captured between committees or delegations.

"I was thinking," Lee said, "how funny it is that we expect kindness to be in the air like part of the climate."

"It isn't though, is it?" Ellen said.

Lee shook her head.

"It begins and ends with one human being speaking to another human being," Lee said meditatively, and she was thinking that here perhaps was the final guarantee that, however group might be arraigned against group, there would always be one human heart that might speak to another human heart—to forge a new beginning, or another tiny link—in the long, long, striving toward understanding.

"Ellen, do you really want to stay in Fall City?" Lee asked her suddenly.

The question startled Ellen; a day earlier she would have known the answer, but now she was not sure. She began to think of the members of her congregation. Considering them individually she was able to perceive the need and the vulnerability of each. It was only when she thought of them as a group that they seemed formidable and cold. Even in the most trying moments, confronted by them en masse, there had always been some small individual gesture that saved a little. Into her mind flashed the memory of Esther Morris, pregnant, carrying a big basket of groceries up the stairs, the sweat standing in tiny drops on her lip and brow.

"Why speak of it?" Ellen said quietly. Suddenly she did know what it meant to want to stay, but with the joy of realization came a sharp sense of futility, the feeling that this insight had come too late. And now she waited for Davey.

"Here he comes," Lee said.

Davey came striding across the hard-packed earth in front of the barn, with a nonchalant air of unconcern, exactly as if he had only stopped in to buy some eggs.

"Hi, Mrs. Kalman," he said. He opened the back door of the car and climbed in.

Ellen turned in the seat to face him; her eyes met his.

"Ready, Davey?" she asked him.

"I'm ready," he told her, but Ellen saw that something still troubled him.

"What is it, Davey?"

"When we get back, you could just let me off downtown," Davey said earnestly. "I could call my father from downtown."

Ellen nodded. "Davey, will you go through with the *bar mitzvah?*" she asked him.

"Yes," Davey answered. The syllable made only a slight sound on his lips, and this time he didn't look at her. His eyes traveled the blur of the land that moved past the car window. And he did not speak again.

Chapter 26

THE SUN was low in the sky, laying a soft, caressing luminousness over the tired surfaces of the city, as Ellen got out of Lee Kalman's car and waved good-bye to her.

Ellen paused, undecided whether she would most likely find Kurt at home or in his study. She took a chance on the study, entering the Temple quietly by the front way. The door to Kurt's study was open and she glimpsed him, *yarmulca* on head, apparently deeply absorbed in the books on his desk.

"Kurt, he's gone home," Ellen said from the doorway.

"You found him? . . . Where?" The look of relief sprang so quickly to Kurt's eyes that Ellen knew he had been thinking of Davey.

"Where was he?"

"On a farm. He told me about going there with his scout troop. I had only a *Vermutung,* a hunch."

"What did he say?"

"Kurt, I don't know exactly. He can't seem to make things come out even. You open up a new world for him. And his father tries to close the door again."

"What did you tell him, Ellen?"

"I didn't know what to tell him. I said that when people fail each other it isn't usually because they want to."

Ellen saw in Kurt's face the deep awareness of a boy's aching, inarticulate need.

"Kurt, have you talked any more to Sam Levinson?" she asked him.

Kurt nodded. "He is very angry. He says Davey has changed so much he hardly knows his own son."

"And he blames you?"

"Yes, I'm afraid he does."

Ellen thought of Davey Levinson sitting on the old wagon bed, some curious integrity stiffening his young back. "Kurt, there was a moment when I couldn't stand the way he looked at me . . . as if I, of all people, were somehow asking him to betray you."

Kurt reached out a hand and took Ellen's hand.

"Kurt, he couldn't have picked a worse time to run away . . . one day before the congregation meeting."

"It doesn't matter."

"But Sam Levinson is so angry."

Kurt smiled, trying to coax a little humor into Ellen's serious face. "It isn't new that Sam Levinson wants a different rabbi. Only now he thinks he has ample reason for wanting to get even with me."

"For teaching his son to be a good Jew?" Ellen demanded furiously.

"For taking his son away from him," Kurt amended.

"Kurt, maybe I did an awful thing to Davey . . . bringing him back," Ellen said thoughtfully.

Kurt shook his head. "No, Ellen, perhaps you have taught him the most important lesson of all—that he can't run away. There are a great many people who must learn that being a Jew isn't something you can run away from. But the more sensitive, they have to learn that it isn't something you can run away with. Whatever it can mean it has to mean in the here, and the now."

For a moment they were both silent. Kurt began to set the papers on his desk in order. Ellen looked out of the window into the yard next door, filled now with the soft and fluid shadows of late afternoon.

"Kurt, there was something else I wanted to tell you," she said so quietly that the words seemed hardly to disturb the air between them.

"What, Sweetheart?"

"Kurt . . . maybe it's too late . . . but I wanted you to know that now I understand how it is to know when people need you . . . and to want with all your heart to measure up to that need."

"Ellen, I love you," Kurt said.

II

When Davey Levinson got out of Lee Kalman's car, he didn't call his father, as he had intended, but, instead, he caught a bus. And the trudging steps of the home-farers, as they boarded the bus at every street corner, measured out his own return home into jerky stops and starts. And there was, in this artificial and diminishing reprieve, a certain comfort.

Finally, as he walked the half block from the bus stop to his own front door, Davey felt his shoulders sagging dejectedly and his steps drag heavily along the sidewalk. It was not exactly a matter of being tired, although the muscles of his shoulders ached a little from his labors of the morning. He began to whistle, a thin, straggling, little tune, as he came up on his own front porch.

"Mom! . . ." the word seemed to grow after it left his lips. But it was his father whose stern and angry face he saw first. Sam Levinson came out of the living room into the entrance hall. He stood for a moment, regarding Davey with cold and unrelenting eyes. And then he turned and walked brusquely back into the living room. Davey knew that he was to follow.

Then he saw his mother, and she stood very still and very tense by the fire place. And he knew that he had hurt her. He felt suddenly hot and sweaty and smudged and young, and he wished that she would come and throw her arms around him.

Sam sat down and lit a cigarette.

"Maybe this young man wouldn't mind telling us . . . where were you?"

"I was out on the Philbrook farm."

"And what made you decide to come back?"

Davey felt a sudden impulse to truth, a sudden fierce urge to pit himself against his father. "Mrs. Rosen persuaded me to," he said.

"Oh . . . Mrs. Rosen! How did she know where you were?"

"She just knew!" Davey's shrill young voice carried all the ache of his parents' not knowing. Ellen Rosen just guessed, but his parents didn't know how to guess.

Some grim, fine-edged, sardonic thing had come into Sam Levinson's face, giving it, perversely, an almost aesthetic look.

"Isn't it funny," he said. "I had the feeling that if we looked hard enough we'd find you hidden away somewhere in the Temple. It would be ironic, wouldn't it, if this generation of Jews produced another Jesus! You know the Christians have a story about Jesus. They say when he was twelve he disappeared. When his poor, distraught parents found him, he was in the Temple. And what do you suppose he told them? Calm as you please . . . like this young man here . . . he told them that he was about his father's business."

"You're my father," Davey said stubbornly. His eyes were cast down. Something in him twisted away from understanding his father's words.

"It seems I only thought so," Sam replied.

Myra Levinson's face had turned very white; "And how would you know so much about the Christians?" she demanded derisively.

Sam Levinson's eyes flew to her face, noting the two red spots that came quickly to her cheeks and the brightness of her eyes.

"That's easy!" he retorted. "I used to go with a little *goyishe* gal before I met you! She took me to church sometimes. I learned not to take myself so seriously!"

Davey could not stand to look at his mother; with a choking sob in his throat he turned and ran from the room.

"Sam, how could you!" Myra sat down, suddenly, on the ornate French sofa.

Sam looked at her. The sound of her last words had seemed to call him from a long way. He saw anguish flicker in her face, and for an instant it was as if, what he had done to Davey, he had done instead to the girl he had seen fifteen years before walking across a stage in a way to entice and enrage the heart with a joy that was innocent of its own vulnerability. Sam took a deep breath. In that instant he realized that, within the woman his will and taste had created, the warm, ecstatic creature of former days existed still. He felt a terrible longing; suddenly his face was drawn and old and he sat down at the opposite end of the couch.

"I don't know," he said. "I don't know how I could!"

Myra stood up; she came and laid a hand against his cheek, a slender cool hand that belonged, not to the Myra he had created, but to the Myra he had destroyed. She seemed to understand what he did not even let himself understand.

"Sam, go to him," she said.

He didn't tell her how grateful he was to her; he made no move to hold the hand as it fluttered away from him. He stood up, hesitated, and then he turned and went to find Davey.

Sam Levinson went to Davey's room, but Davey was not there. He walked down the hall and paused by the closed bathroom door.

"Davey?"

There was no answer. Sam put out a hand and tried the knob, which did not give to his touch.

"Davey, open the door I want to talk to you," Sam said. His voice was gruff.

There was no answer.

Sam felt foolish and inept, standing there behind a locked door through which he must shout out the things he could hardly bring himself to say.

"Davey! . . ." He tried the door again, he listened for some noise a boy might make. "Davey . . . we used to be friends . . ."

In Sam's own ears his voice was querulous. He hated the feel of it. He felt the sweat breaking out in the palms of his hands.

And then he heard the sound that was like a sob, muffled, strangled, buried, forcing itself out, betraying the boy who had made it, slipping out away from him, through the closed door.

"Davey! . . . "Sam's hand rattled the knob impatiently. "Stop being stubborn. And let me talk to you. I want to apologize for what I said."

And then he heard it. One faucet turned on, two faucets turned on. And then the tub faucets . . . three and four. Four water faucets turned on full force, to drown out the words. He could hear the torrent of water rushing forth in the bathroom, hitting the porcelain, gurgling in the drains, bouncing. There was only this and no sound that a boy would make.

Sam Levinson felt the heat, the rage rising in his face. His blood seemed to pound with the violence of the running water.

"Davey!" he called out. And his voice was stark, and loud. It echoed through the house. He could hear the sound of his own voice moving through the rooms . . . moving past Myra somewhere in the house, moving in the emptiness.

The water still splashed and bounced and gurgled beyond the door. Beyond the door his own son stood, shutting him out, refusing him, denying him.

Sam Levinson turned on his heels and walked away.

The next morning, when the Levinsons sat at breakfast, Myra wore the mandarin-red, silk hostess coat with the big sleeeves that always got in the way of pouring coffee.

Sam noted this fact with a vague sense of irritation, as he watched her filling the cups, holding the sleeve back with one tense hand.

His eyes moved on to Davey. Davey's T-shirt was stretched out at the neck and around the tail.

"Are those the best clothes he has?" Sam demanded, finding something tangible against which to pit his rancor.

"They are his favorite clothes," Myra replied.

"Then by all means! . . ." Sam felt the rising sarcasm in his voice. He swallowed. Davey just sat there; it was a defiance so subtle it infuriated him. But Sam didn't say anything. Whenever he started to say anything there flew up in his throat the taste of the bitter words he had spoken the night before . . . the bitter taste of the words, and the memory of how Davey had shut him out.

"Myra, don't make any plans for tonight," Sam said with slow emphasis, his eyes fastening significantly on his son. "You know we meet tonight to elect a rabbi."

Davey did not raise his head; and Myra did not reply.

"Davey, sit up and eat," Myra said. Her voice contained its own note of impatience, but it was a companionable impatience. It was something Davey accepted. He sat up a little straighter, feeding himself cereal with an intent rhythm. Myra smiled at him; it was a smile the warmth of which Sam had long ago ceased to earn. And for one dreadful moment he thought Davey was going to cry; he knew he would hate Davey if he cried.

"Now what's all this?" he demanded.

Myra still did not reply; Davey did not reply.

Sam threw down his napkin. "Damn it! What's going on here! The soft looks! The sad looks! Is somebody dead? Have I done something so terrible?"

For an instant, a mixture of hope and despair flickered in Davey's passive but unrelenting young face. The spoon was poised in mid-air. He seemed to consider if he would blurt it all out, the heartache, and the bitter disappointment, and the yearning for what was lost and what was not yet quite gained. For the first time in many days he let his eyes meet his father's squarely. And Sam quelled the hope with a glance.

Myra watched. A little nerve twitched at the corner of her lip.

"The voice, Sam, remember the voice! The *tour de force* is accomplished only with a soft voice. Don't forget it, Sam," she said contemptuously.

Slowly Sam Levinson's eyes left his son and, with some stark, forbidding thing still mirrored in their depths, came to rest on his wife.

"I won't forget it, Myra. I'm an old hand at this sort of thing!"

Sam Levinson got up, he walked out of the room, and he went to work as on any other day.

III

Later that morning, Kurt sat in his study at the Temple and considered how he would deal with the question of Sam Levinson. Finally, a little ruefully, he picked up the telephone and dialed the number of the Levinsons and asked Sam to come to talk to him.

An hour later Sam Levinson came into the synagogue with the brisk air of a man of many affairs.

"Good morning, Rabbi," he called out brusquely. He took off his hat and sat down opposite Kurt's desk.

313

Kurt did not allow himself to be hurried. He regarded his guest in silence for a moment, and then he said:

"Mr. Levinson, your son comes for the first time to the Torah in a couple of days. It should be one of the proudest days of your life."

Sam's scornful and angry eyes met Kurt's for a moment. "Look, Rabbi, nobody needs to tell me when to be proud of my son. I was proud of him when he took his first step. I was proud of him when he made his first straight "A" in school. I know what things to be proud of."

"That's very important," Kurt answered, ". . . knowing what things to be proud of."

"Rabbi," Sam Levinson leaned forward, breathing heavily, "as I told you once before—preach to me from the pulpit all you like. But don't preach to me from across a desk."

"I don't preach to you at all," Kurt said quietly. "I want only that you consider this, Mr. Levinson. Our religion demands respect for our parents as one of the most important duties of life. But that places a tremendous responsibility upon the parents to deserve respect."

Sam Levinson stood up angrily. A fiery red had replaced the pallor of his face. His eyes had narrowed; scorn was more deeply etched into the lines around his mouth.

"And does it make Davey Levinson's father less worthy of respect because he desires a new rabbi?" he demanded hoarsely.

"Please sit down," Kurt said patiently. "You are more than welcome to your opinion of the rabbi . . . although I must say that I wish that I might change it. But this much I am contending: your son has earned a dignified entry into his sacred obligations of Jewish manhood . . . one that is not marred by his own father's scorn."

"Now the rabbi coaches me how I must act," Sam said, his laugh a bitter rasp on the air.

Kurt ignored both the remark and the laugh.

"Mr. Levinson," he said, "I do not think that we differ so greatly. Neither of us would deny the importance of facing the future with courage . . . but how? You see it in terms of cutting loose from the past. I see it in terms of bearing witness to the eternal challenge of the past. This is a choice no man can make for another. But if . . . between us . . . we have taught Davey the need of courage itself, we have done well."

Sam Levinson's face was grim, his next words slow and deliberate. "Rabbi, I claim no partnership with you in Davey's

314

training. I trained him to be an individual capable of living in the world which he must—of necessity—inhabit. You trained him to believe that ideas are a commodity he can use instead of courage. This time you won. In the next instance I hope to win."

"You speak of the congregational meeting?"

"I do."

For a moment Kurt almost laughed. "Your frankness, at least, is admirable."

"And for you, Rabbi, I must say, at least, that you're game. If I were a rabbi, I would refuse a *bar mitzvah* to the son of a man who was determined to have my job."

"It is Davey who is my chief concern . . . not his father. And Davey has given me no reason to deny him a *bar mitzvah*," Kurt answered.

For a moment Sam Levinson's eyes met Kurt's. "Good afternoon, Rabbi," he said brusquely, and a moment later the outside door clanged shut to cut off the sound of his departing steps.

IV

In the afternoon Lee Kalman waited for Maury to come home from town. When he came, he brought a mechanical racing car for Julian and got down on the floor to demonstrate it.

"Plastic!" Maury said in disgust. "Imagine that, nothing but plastic toys." Already one of the wheels had come off and he was trying to put it back.

"It's been like that for quite a while now," Lee said drily. "You've been away . . . maybe you hadn't heard . . ."

"A war?" Maury said in mock consternation. He looked ridiculous sitting there on the floor with a toy racer in his hand. Lee began to laugh. She nodded.

"Yes, a war," she said.

Clucking his tongue and shaking his head, Maury sent the racer spinning under the desk, while a wildly excited Julian went scooting after it.

Lee helped him retrieve it. She bent down and looked into her son's eager, intent little face. "Why don't you go show it to Bobby?" she asked. Julian went bounding off and Lee turned thoughtfully to Maury. He reached out a hand and pulled her down on the floor beside him.

"There's something romantic about sitting on the floor," Maury said, nuzzling his chin against the softness of her cheek. But Lee's somber mood was no longer able to sustain the note of whimsey.

"Maury, did you hear anything in town?" she asked him.

Maury stretched and clasped his hands around his knees. He looked at Lee and didn't want to answer.

"It doesn't look good," he said finally.

"Why?"

"Sam's like a mad bull. It's leaked out about Davey running away; and he's going around telling everybody it's the Rabbi's fault . . . making a big *tsimas*."

"And what about the others?"

"Sam's money went a long way toward building the synagogue. And he has prestige."

"Nobody will buck him?"

Maury reached out a hand and touched Lee's hair, in a small caress.

"It looks that way," he said.

"Maury, it isn't fair!"

"I know it isn't, Lee. But that's the way things nearly always turn out."

Lee sat quite still, and in her eyes was a shadowy look Maury had seldom seen. He moved his head a little, in a faint unconscious gesture to reclaim her.

"Maury," Lee said, "There's something I want you to do for me."

"What?"

"I want you to go to the meeting tonight and speak out against Sam Levinson."

"Lee, I have to go to the meeting . . . but . . ."

Maury stood up. He rammed his hands down in his pockets and moved around the room as if it were suddenly too small to contain his bitter self-dissatisfaction. Lee felt his impatience keenly.

"Maury, what's happened to you. What's come over you . . . sometimes I don't even know you!"

For a moment Maury looked at Lee. He sat down on the couch and lit a cicarette. And the smoke was a haze before a face that had become, in a matter of moments, deeply haggard. Maury was thinking again of Jules Kohen.

He was thinking of Jules' lonely grave, and of the bitter, seeping cold on the day the coffin was lowered into it . . . and the clods that were piled in a mound on the grave . . . clods like boys used to throw at each other . . .

Jules—Jules Kohen, Private First Class. He bought the corporal stripes at the PX, but he never made corporal.

"Yes, Captain!" Jules always said, snapping smartly to attention. He never quite smiled; but the Captain business was something funny between them.

"I met a colonel who was a drummer . . . he sold ties in Nebraska," Jules would say, and he never laughed; but they both knew that it was funny.

"And you, Jules, what were you in private life?" Maury would ask him.

"In private life?" Jules would say, shrugging his shoulders dejectedly in a gesture that was sadly comic.

"Come on. In civilian life, what were you?"

Maury was thinking how the dread of the soul was somehow like the monotony of whiteness that had lain upon those hills. And after a while there was something in the men that resisted, not so much the enemy, as the demands of authority.

Oh, yes, the men were rigorously submissive to the authority of Captain Kalman . . . but they denied a private named Jules Kohen not only companionship but peace.

Maury thought of that bitter, cold, violent, waitful winter when some human companionship was a prerequisite for sanity. Sometimes he had looked out of the flap of the command tent to glimpse a lonely, hunched figure hurrying in a wide perimeter around the clearing where the men sat huddled about a campfire. And the figure had seemed more one with the cold and lonely trees than with these human beings who warmed their fingers in which blood ran blue in the veins. . . . And Jules Kohen had had a book he read by the lamplight in his tent. But the leather cover of the book was cold and clammy to the touch, and the pages turned with a small rasp in ears that hungered so ceaselessly for the sound of a voice that might speak numbly and awkwardly the bitterness, and futility, and fatigue, and longing that his heart also knew.

"Maury," Lee said finally, a little apprehensively.

Maury did not answer immediately. He was thinking how startling a single shot can be when the surrounding silence is intensified by the quiver of many distant guns. The single shot fractured the stillness, and Captain Maury Kalman, studying maps in his tent, had felt along his spine that forewarning of personal disaster. In three strides he had stepped into the cold night. Figures were dim, hardly distinguishable in the moonless darkness. But voices carried, sharpened on the cold still air.

317

"Goddam little Jew bastard. What was he trying to do anyway!"

"Trying to get back into camp. Skipped out and then didn't have the guts to go AWOL," the sentry said.

"That's a hell of a way to get shot down—repenting for your sins!" the third man laughed.

And Maury Kalman had known before he went to them that Jules Kohen would be dead.

"Maury," Lee said again.

Maury's eyes came slowly to her face. "Lee, a man simply doesn't have in him . . . what it takes to champion a lost cause."

"A lost cause? . . ."

"Lee, I feel anger and indignation . . . and regret. But I honestly don't feel that anything in the world I might say or do would keep Sam Levinson from having his way."

"So you wouldn't try?"

Maury began to pace back and forth. He thought of that meeting and of trying to get up before those men . . . and he thought of Kurt Rosen sitting behind a desk quietly speaking to him. He felt some awful wrath with himself and with the frailties and evasions of human behavior.

"Lee, a man has got to believe he can do some good before he is able to risk making a presumptuous fool of himself. It isn't something you can do for the sake of a hollow gesture."

Maury faced Lee imploringly, awaiting her answer.

"Sit down, Maury. Please stop pacing up and down!"

Maury sat down on the couch again. Lee got up from the floor. She took another cigarette from the pack on the coffee table and gave it to Maury and lit it for him.

"Maury, there's something I have to know—would you stop being a Jew if you could?"

Maury looked at her with angry protest. "For God's sake, Lee, what has that got to do with . . ."

"It hasn't got anything to do with anything. I simply have to know, that's all. I have to know. Would you stop being a Jew if you could?"

Maury sat smoking. His only movement was the movement of hand to cigarette and back again. Finally he said:

"That's something I don't even know myself."

Lee did not answer. She knew of nothing to say.

Chapter 27

ALL DURING dinner Maury and Lee spoke hardly at all, each very studiously watching for moments to help Julian —Maury to mash his potato, Lee to pour his milk and butter his bread.

Finally, as Maury prepared to leave for the congregational meeting, their glances met briefly and evasively, and Maury's kiss on Lee's forehead was quick and cool.

"Bye," he said.

"Bye," Lee answered. She watched him go; and with something like a nostalgia, her heart forced a reluctant awareness of the way that hair grew at the back of his neck, of the familiar rhythm of his movements, of the gesture of a hand reaching out to draw a door shut behind him.

Lee's hand shook a little as she lifted her coffee cup, and she felt a sharp longing and regret that seemed to fuse within her. Every nerve impelled her to follow Maury, to call to him. But she sat still. She heard the outside door close; a moment later she heard the car drive away. And then she was left alone with a terrible sense of how she and Maury had failed each other.

Suddenly, unable to stand it any longer, Lee was on her feet. She went into the kitchen where Amy was finishing the supper dishes.

"Amy, could you stay with Julian for a while?" she asked.

"Yes'm, I sho' could," Amy said in her delighted little way of responding to all requests.

Lee only smiled at her as she turned away. She would have to hurry, hurry. To walk the eight blocks to the synagogue would take time. Everything seemed to be defined in terms of time. She had only minutes to get to the synagogue, only days left to spend with Maury out of, perhaps, a lifetime.

Lee walked so fast her lungs hurt, and the hurt was of contrition, of self reproach. Caught up in the agonizing sense of time's passing was the burden of misunderstanding. She had failed Maury by demanding too much, by naively assuming that the feeling of one heart could be translated into action by another heart. And Maury had failed her by understanding so little what her heart's feeling was.

319

When Lee got to the synagogue, the door of the vestry was closed. Now and again the sound of mingling voices was wafted out from the building to be swallowed up, faint and indistinguishable, in the darkness. The meeting had begun. Numbly accepting the fact that she was too late, Lee stood there on the sidewalk and watched the feathery design that the tree branches made in the puddles of light cast by the corner street-lamp. It seemed to Lee that so much which was human and vulnerable crowded in upon this moment. She could not make amends to Maury, and now she felt returning the dreadful anxiety for the Rosens. Lee stood there for a long while, until she felt a chill in the warm summer night. And then, unable to make herself go home, she climbed the broad steps to the darkened and empty sanctuary. She opened the door and almost timidly hesitated just inside the doorway. The room lay in the slumbering quiet of the glow from the Eternal Light.

The Light imparted an even deeper stillness to the room. Its glow bathed in a soft radiance the empty pulpit and laid a sheen upon the velvet curtain of the Ark. Its touch and its silence were upon the front rows of seats. Its boundaries were not defined by walls, they blended into darkness before walls were met, and the windows let in a swift-moving hint of passing light from the street below; they were dark with a smooth, cold yearning for the Light that the room contained at his heart, the Light that moved out toward them.

Lee Kalman sat down on one of the back rows of seats. She felt strangely stirred. In her mind there welled up the familiar question, urgent and unanswered. What was Judaism? . . . A belief in God? . . . a belief in God which confronts the invincible spirit with its own vincibility . . . a belief in God which is aware, and sometime anguished, and often exultant . . . and profound.

Judaism was this . . . and more . . . much more. It was a way of feeling about life. Lee thought of Kurt Rosen and of how each time he sent her away it had been to reach a deeper level of understanding. So stern and demanding a thing it was, which, at the same time, held such a gentleness for human fallibility. And then Lee thought of Maury. She and Maury had failed each other; but their failings did not amount to failure. It seemed to Lee that this idea allowed Maury his confusion while granting her her realization. And why did they strive at all? This much was demanded of them. It was a concept that confronted the limited imaginations of men with the sense of their own immortality so that the goal of their striving was ever contained within themselves, their living link with God.

Lee closed her eyes. She closed her eyes and felt for a moment a curious peace in which she moved as a stranger.

Sitting there alone she wept for misunderstanding what Maury did not comprehend.

II

That night Maury Kalman had felt an almost insurmountable reluctance at the thought of going to the congregational meeting, and Lee's quietness as they sat at supper had been a reproach he almost welcomed as deserved. Maury delayed as long as possible and went to the meeting late, but the business session had not yet begun.

The lights in the vestry were bright. The men were gathering in small groups. The sound of the discussion was noisy and erratic, and there was the tenseness of impending struggle in the air.

Moving from group to group, Maury could hardly swallow the taste of a fierce impatience with the men in this room, with the way that men in general come together to decide a question. Maury acknowledged to himself that almost invariably side issues are allowed to become the deciding factors. Here, tonight, the election of Kurt Rosen would be decided, not upon his own merits, but on the basis of whether this man or that liked him or found him amenable to his whims. But what was the real question, the real basis for decision—Maury was not sure that he knew.

Benny Gold had gone up on the stage, he was banging on the table with a gavel. The other officers wandered up and took their places around the table, and the members of the congregation reluctantly abandoned their small private conversations and took seats before the stage. Maury sat down to wait.

There was a feeling of impatience in the room as Benny Gold called the meeting to order and the routine was begun. No one listened to the reading of the minutes, or responded to the request for old business.

"Is there any new business?" Benny Gold asked laconically.

Herman Morris was immediately on his feet. "I move we elect Kurt Rosen rabbi for another two years!" he said, casting a sly glance in Sam Levinson's direction.

"I have a motion that we elect Kurt Rosen rabbi for another two years. Do I hear any discussion?" Benny said. Relish for a

321

good fight was in his voice; all eyes in the room had turned toward Sam Levinson.

Sam stood up; instead of remaining beside his chair, he came to the front of the room.

"Gentlemen, I would like to lead off on this discussion, if you don't mind." Brisk, urban, genial, worldly, Sam Levinson stood before them, exerting every fraction of personal magnetism which he had at his command. "'I personally am of the opinion that we should change rabbis," he said. "I know of a man we can get who is ideally suited to our needs. I think all of you will admit that when we took Kurt Rosen it was as a last resort. We had to have a rabbi and he was available. There may have been a little patriotism mixed in it too. He was a refugee and we wanted to help. Well, we've broken the ice for him now, we've given him his start—and I think we have our own interests to think of."

"Look, Sam, what're you selling us?" Herman demanded. "Kurt Rosen came here with the best recommendations of any rabbi we ever had. In Europe he was a big shot."

"We are not European Jewry. We need a man who understands American Jewry," Sam Levinson said succinctly. "I would like to tell you a little about the qualifications of the man I have in mind . . ." he began.

Old Mr. Jacobson got to his feet. He stood for a moment, blinking a little, his hands were thrust down in his pockets. He had a curious old-young look, a blending of many things.

"Sam," he said almost reproachfully. "We're not interested in hearing the qualities of any other rabbis. . . . I ask you, who has ever brought us all together under one roof before? In this congregation nothing happens that doesn't happen to Rabbi Rosen. Who's there in the middle of the night if you need him? Who reminds those who can't even remember their own *Yahrzeits*? And was there ever a man less interested in the insides of our purses . . .?"

"No one is mentioning our purses, Mr. Jake," Sam said condescendingly. "All I'm saying is . . . we ought to have a young American-born rabbi who understands the important things . . . who can help us blend into the American culture. It's all just a matter of emphasis, anyway. You can emphasize how you're different, or you can emphasize how you are alike. I just want a young American-born rabbi who understands what things to emphasize. . . . Now tell me, don't you think that's reasonable enough?"

Joe Friedman popped up, taking courage from Mr. Jacobson's

322

words. For an instant his mustache twitched in agitation. "Is some in this room is thinking they elect the president of the country club!" he shouted, in a high falsetto voice, like a mouse bearding a lion in its den.

Sam Levinson's face flushed an ugly red. His lips curved in contempt. Mr. Friedman gasped at his own audacity, but he hurriedly pressed on.

"For us who is *frumm* the Rabbi is fine. Is a *talmid chochom!*"

Sam Levinson's sardonic gaze rested squarely on his rather absurd little antagonist.

"And are there enough of the pious to make a *minyan?*" he demanded.

"And if there aren't, Sam, is that something to brag about?" old Mr. Jacobson called out.

Abruptly Sam Levinson laughed. "The eternal Jew! He answers a question with a question." In the words there was a biting scorn.

Dr. Ben Klein, with the fine instincts of the peacemaker, rose quietly to his feet. Benny pounded the gavel for quiet.

"Okay, Doc, what do you say?" he called.

Ben Klein smiled a little, almost whimsically.

"Look at us here in this room," he said. "Here in our synagogue, in the middle of America, are Jews who have come from Poland, from Austria, and Russia and Lithuania. And Jews who were born and bred under the soda pop and hot dog—nonkosher hot dog—insignia of the good old U.S.A. We're divided on questions that range all the way from whether to have music in the synagogue, to whether Moses received the Ten Commandments directly from God. Maybe we ought to ask ourselves if the mere fact of our Jewishness could ever unite us. If we don't want to ask that, we damn sure better ask ourselves what is really at stake."

Ben Klein hesitated. There was a flurry of whispered remarks in the room. Sam Levinson smiled knowingly.

"I'd say our future as a congregation is at stake. What would you say is at stake, Dr. Klein?" he said. But it was not Ben Klein who answered.

Isadore Jacobson's gaze met Sam's levelly. "I would say that spiritual survival itself is at stake," he said.

Urbane and suave, Sam regarded Mr. Jacobson for a moment, then his glance dismissed him.

"Friends," Sam said, "all of us are stirred by words like spiritual survival. It has a challenging sound. You might even say a one-day-a-year sound. But why kid ourselves. The important thing is how we are able to live from day to day . . . how we are able to get along with the rest of the world. I'll tell you damn well, I'm not a hero. I want to get along with the rest of the world. Just think of it this way. The best things in the Jewish religion we've already given to all the other great religions. They claim them just as much as we do—the Ten Commandments, the psalms, things like that. My feeling is that to be a good Jew doesn't have to forever and eternally separate us from the rest of mankind. But do you think anybody else is ever going to realize this if we don't realize it ourselves?" Sam hesitated. He waited for them to be drawn by his persuasiveness along the route that he had indicated. His tone was almost gentle as he continued.

"Gentlemen," Sam said, "I do not see how we can even hesitate, or how we can hang back on the grounds of sentiment, when we now have an opportunity to get a man who is exactly suited to our needs. Kurt Rosen still has what Herman calls his excellent qualifications. He would have no difficulty in finding a congregation elsewhere," Sam concluded.

Sam sat down on the first row of seats, with the air of one who has accomplished his mission. He did not glance around at the men behind him.

"Is there any further discussion?" Benny asked nervously.

There was an indecisive twitter in the room, and suddenly without knowing he intended it, Maury Kalman was on his feet.

"Mr. President, may I say something?" he asked.

"Well, I should say so! Captain Maury Kalman, our returning hero. Come on up here, Maury, so we can see how you look in that uniform." Benny was trying to be cordial. He was glad that someone had moved into this tense moment so that he did not have to dissolve it himself.

Maury made his way to the front of the room. . . . Returning hero, indeed! The word was bitter in his ears; the mockery of it dogged his steps. He stood before the assemblage and he did not know exactly what he wanted to say.

"I haven't any right to try to influence your decision, because right now I have other business than congregation business to attend to. . . ."

"Speak right up young man, your dues are paid," Benny said in another attempt at levity, when Maury paused and did not quite know how to go on.

"I was only thinking . . ." Maury said, "I've seen all of this happen so many times before. In eighteen years we've had fifteen rabbis. . . . What are we looking for?" The words came from Maury's lips with the sound of their true groping. He was not thinking of the man who would fling back an answer at him, he was thinking of Kurt Rosen. But the answer was flung back.

"We are looking for the right rabbi," Sam Levinson replied blandly.

"And what makes you think Kurt Rosen is not the right rabbi?" Maury demanded, still not knowing where his words would lead.

"Look, Maury," Sam said smoothly. "You haven't been around here, there are things you don't know. We appreciate your interest . . . but . . ."

Sam's suavity infuriated Maury. Without even realizing that he did it he reached up and loosened his tie.

"You're right! I haven't been around here. I went a long way off . . . and I took a long look back. Fall City is a nice, quiet little town where everybody can afford to be alike. But I saw a kid from another nice, quiet little town get his guts shot out, and when he died somebody called him a little Jew bastard. He hadn't told them he was a Jew . . . they told him!"

A tense quietness fell on those assembled. Sam Levinson began to realize that he must proceed with caution.

"Maury . . . you've been to war . . . you've had a bad time . . . you've come through with flying colors. And we're proud of you. But you've got to realize that certain things don't have anything to do with other things."

"Oh but they do . . . they do," Maury said. He did not know himself. He did not know the self that was speaking. He was thinking how Kurt Rosen had said to him "understanding protects people from things from which no one else can protect them." Suddenly Maury knew that he must fight for understanding. He took a deep breath and no one quite dared to break the tension of it.

"Sam . . . think about this . . . when I was thirteen, I wasn't *bar mitzvah*. When I was thirteen, we were changing rabbis." Maury's voice was deceptively calm.

Sam moved restively in his chair. "Mr. President, I think the Captain ought to come to the point," he said to Benny.

"We got time . . ." Benny replied.

Maury stood looking at Sam Levinson; he let the full impact of Sam's scorn and sarcasm bite deeply into his spirit. And then he replied:

"Sam, could the point be that, with Kurt Rosen as rabbi,

you're afraid your son will learn to be proud he's a Jew? Are you afraid he'll be too quick to admit it!"

Sam Levinson leapt to his feet. The heat of anger moved in the air about him.

"Look here, Maury, you're way out of bounds!" His voice was menacing in its quietness. "But now that you ask, I'll tell you. I intend for my son to realize he's an American first, last, and always. That's what I don't want him to forget. He's not a Jew, citizen of Diaspora. He's Davey Levinson, citizen of the U.S.A."

Sam's eyes had narrowed. He spoke of a boy named Davey Levinson. But Maury was thinking, also, of a boy named Julian Kalman. And in Sam Levinson's face he saw his own fear and uncertainty and confusion. And he hated the sight of them.

"Sam . . ." Maury said, his voice hoarse with an emotion he did not understand, "Sam, do you think he can be a better American for not knowing what he believes in? Do you think he'll be a better anything by not knowing what he is?"

There was a curious hush in the room. The bitterness in Sam Levinson's face was framing itself for a reply. But a babel of voices, loud and excited, rushed into the silence. And Maury did not wait to hear what Sam Levinson would say. He was running down off the stage. He had the answer, now, for Lee. And time was so short, so very short!

As Maury hurried down the aisle a spurt of applause greeted his departing steps.

"Speech! . . . Maury . . . Speech!" someone shouted.

But Maury only waved his hand. He could not wait to see what happened, to see what they would, finally, do. He opened the outside door and the fresh, cool night air hit his hot face.

"Question, question!" he heard Sam Levinson shouting furiously. "There's a question before the house!"

As Maury came out into the night he noticed, standing beneath a tree at the side of the building, a woman's slim figure blending only partly with the shadows. She stood there a moment, as if waiting, and then turned to walk away.

"Lee!"

Suddenly Maury was running across the yard. "Lee!"

She whirled around at the sound of his voice, and Maury knew that she had not seen him leave the building.

As Maury came to her, he saw the soft blur of her face in the moonlight turned to him questingly. There, beneath the damp, murmuring, summer-smelling limbs of the trees, he took her in his arms. She moved within the circle of his arms and he kissed

326

her—her lips, cool and wild, her eyes with the sweet salt taste of
unshed tears, the edges of her hair haunted by the fragrance of
her being.

"Lee . . . Lee!"

"Maury! . . . What . . . what happened!"

"I don't know . . . I couldn't wait to see. I had to find you."

Her laugh was fragile and without weight on the air. "Where
did you think I'd be?"

"Lee, I lost you. And you waited for me. And I found you."

"Maury . . ."

"Lee . . . hush! Only this I have to tell you. I know, now, all
the things you knew already. Nothing . . . nothing in all the
world . . . can keep us from having a good life. We're ready for
it now. And it's ready for us."

Lee sensed the bitter irony of this moment even as she became
aware of a brass army button cutting into her cheek where she had
pressed her face against Maury's chest. And for an instant the
protest ached in her throat.

Maury seemed to know what she was thinking. He lifted her
face again to his kiss, and in that instant Lee understood that
whatever in life is fully realized, achieves, in the instant of its
realization, its own eternity.

"Maury . . . let's go home," Lee said.

With his arm around her, Maury lead her to the car.

Ellen Rosen sat with the half finished Red Cross sweater in
her lap, and her knitting needles moved only fitfully. She glanced
at Kurt and he seemed absorbed in the book he was reading.
And her mind wandered back to the way that the evening of
waiting had begun.

. . . As she cleared away the evening dishes Ellen had paused
now and again beside the window to look down upon the Temple
yard where the members of the board were assembling. She saw
Sam Levinson as he walked up the steps . . . a moment later she
glimpsed Mr. Jacobson hobbling across the yard with his curiously agile gait. And she saw Maury Kalman stop for a moment
to speak to Benny Gold and Herman Morris.

When Ellen paused for a final moment in front of the window, Kurt smiled as he watched her. He was thinking that he had
seen her, first, standing beside a window, just so still. But the
light that enveloped her now was not the brilliance of midday,
but the soft warmth of a setting sun. And her dark beauty
seemed already to hint at the coming night.

"Is it a good view?" Kurt asked her.

Laughing, she turned to him quickly, as a child would realizing that it is observed. "A nice sunset. Not so good a view," she answered, and she came for a moment and sat on the arm of his chair.

"Kurtchen, we could go to the movies," she said half seriously.

"I think better the rabbi has to see if he is elected," Kurt replied.

For an instant the last glow of a waning day seemed to back up into the room, leaving the world beyond the window pale and quiet. And the moment was breathless and beautiful and quickly past.

Ellen sighed. "You know, Kurtchen, I think the rabbis are very wise to insist that the day ends at sundown. It means you can go to bed with a clear conscience. A new day already is begun." In her voice there was drollery and her eyes were teasing him a little.

"Is your conscience not clear?" Kurt demanded sternly.

"Not so very clear. . . . Do you not know that if I could I would bring down fire from Heaven to destroy anyone who ever says a word against you."

"Aha!" Kurt laughed. "A fine scriptural flair she has, the wife of the rabbi!" And pulling her down suddenly from her precarious perch on the arm of the chair, he kissed her.

"Kurtchen! *O lass mich in Ruh!* . . . Did you forget that I must knit! Think of some poor shivering soldier!"

"You think of the shivering soldier; I think of my sermon. And no more of this flirtation now!" Kurt answered, laughing still.

But now, an hour later, Ellen tried to think how this mood of whimsey had deserted her. And she explored, a little reluctantly, the sense of an immense solemnity that seemed to be claiming her.

For some key to her feelings Ellen studied Kurt's face, keen and intent, which seemed to draw the lamp's glow into its own mood. He felt her eyes and looked up, smiling.

"That's enough of that!" he said, closing the book, with his usual quickness of perception. He got up and, in his stocking feet, walked across the room and sat down beside the phonograph. He began pulling the albums one by one out of the shelf.

"What do you want to hear?" he asked.

Ellen shook her head. "You decide." Her voice was husky; she did not entirely trust it. She knitted a few stitches, only for an excuse to cast down her eyes.

"Come . . . come! What do you want to be reminded of ?" Kurt insisted, "Mozart's *Jupiter Symphony* for the year we went to the festival in Salzburg; Beethoven's *Eroica* for the concert we attended on our honeymoon; Mendelssohn's *Concerto* for the first concert we heard in America?"

"Let's be reminded of the honeymoon," Ellen said, releasing her mood a little to his mood.

"Fine!" Kurt began to take the records out of the folders.

Ellen watched him, loving the odd little zest for living that welled up in the simplest thing he did. The first rich, full notes of the *Eroica* swelled out into the room, and Kurt came and sat beside her on the couch. He put his arm around her, and she leaned her head against his shoulder, closing her eyes so that they would not reveal too much.

It seemed to Ellen that only in moments when their entire future was in other hands than theirs, did she and Kurt know, any more, their true selves, the hard, tight core of self that does not surrender to the demands of duty, yet may be truly known only when the reins of duty are slack. In a moment such as this they could be, again, the man and the woman who once had wandered hand in hand by the sea.

Ellen felt in her spirit the shimmer of the sea on that distant day and the wild yearning lure of the future. And inwardly she wept for the girl who had not suspected the cost of devotion. Inwardly she wept for Kurt who had wanted to give so much, and who had not known, ever, the price of his love to her. She glanced up into the face which, in repose, showed the strain of the past weeks.

. . . Duty . . . she had been thinking about duty. And now she thought about Sam Levinson. And about the *bar mitzvah* day after tomorrow.

"Kurtchen," she said suddenly. "Do you ever feel that we are only what other people expect of us?"

Kurt smiled. "No. To me you are all things beautiful and good."

"I am other things besides."

"Maybe so. But goodness and beauty encompass all the things you are."

"Kurt, they don't. They don't at all! In my heart I'm vengeful. I hate Sam Levinson. I hate him in the fiercest way I can."

Kurt did not answer, he only held her.

"Kurt, you used to be able to get so angry. And you learned to be so patient . . . so very patient!" Ellen felt the hot tears spring to her eyes, and she turned her face away.

329

All of the variables and improbables of life seemed to crowd in upon this moment.

"Kurt, I don't like times like this! I don't like not knowing what's going to happen."

"Ellen . . . please!"

Ellen was very still in his arms. The waiting had grown too long. And waiting moments seemed always, as they were outlived, to move backward into the shadowy realm of "might-have-been." For Ellen the world of "might-have-been" was inhabited by a million half-remembered choices and, above all, by terror and the specter of death and annihilation. And now, she found that to consign any new part of her life to any new "might-have-been" was a painful, anguished thing. Ellen felt her hands grow cold, she felt that she would dream it all again.

"Ellen, don't be afraid," Kurt said to her. He had her hand in his; he felt its coldness.

And then he took the face that was turned from him between his two hands, he looked into the dark eyes which had offered him so much but whose depths he had never fully fathomed. Ellen did not move; her stillness was an exquisite stillness, and her black lashes briefly swept her cheeks. And Kurt's lips came slowly to her lips whose gentle curve was the deepest yearning of the spirit, and he drank from these lips the very fullness of life. And Ellen was not afraid.

The telephone rang, and it was Kurt who moved to answer it. Ellen tried not to listen, she tried not to hear what was said.

"Ellen . . ." Kurt said, hanging up the phone, "they ask that I join the meeting to hear good news. It was Mr. Jake."

"We're . . . going to stay?" Ellen asked.

"We're going to stay."

"Kurtchen! . . ."

"Will you come with me, now?"

Ellen shook her head. "I wait for you here." she said. "Kurt, they don't deserve you. But I'm glad!"

Kurt's laugh was warm on the air. "Ellen, I love you!" he called out to her.

And Ellen watched him go.

Chapter 28

The Lord spoke unto Moses saying: Speak unto the children of Israel and bid them to make fringes in the corners of their garments throughout their generations, putting upon the fringe of each corner a thread of blue. And it shall be unto you for a fringe, that ye may look upon it and remember all the commandments of your Lord, and do them; and that ye go not about after your own heart and your own eyes, after which ye use to go astray.

That ye remember to do all my commandments, and be holy unto your God. I am the Lord your God, who brought you out of the land of Egypt to be your God. I am the Lord your God.

DAVEY LEVINSON sat in the carved wooden chair on the platform and listened to the rabbi reading these words with a quiet solemnity that laid a hush upon the congregation. Davey felt around his shoulders the soft caress of the silk *tallit*. When he inclined his head only a little, he could see its stripes of blue. He stuck his fingers through its fringes and felt the threads, smooth and silken, against the damp palm of his hand.

This was the day of his *bar mitzvah*. This was the day he had worked for and wanted. Almost impatiently he waited for the awe to descend upon him, but he could not quite escape the sense of himself, of being only Davey before the very throne of God.

As the rabbi read from the prayer book, Davey looked out over the congregation. With manly disdain he noted that all the little boys had their hair neatly combed; and their *yarmulcas* made their ears seem to stick out apprehensively. The little girls sat in clusters, side by side, putting their heads together to whisper. All the women seemed to be holding their prayer books in gloved hands.

And the men wore *tallitim* about their shoulders. But the look of their business selves clung to them, the look of their everyday selves, Davey noted with a curious little ache in his heart. Only the old men looked different when the put on their prayer shawls . . . only Mr. Jake . . . and Mr. Friedman . . . and Mr. Weber.

What would it be like if there were no old men, Davey found himself wondering, as the congregation rose to read the silent prayers. Davey searched the silence in which pages were turned quietly. At the core of the silence were the murmurs and the sighs of the old men, murmurs and sighs that seemed to be borne up irrepressibly from some deep, hidden recesses of the spirit.

For a long time I will not be an old man, Davey thought, but I have a Sabbath self . . . I have a Sabbath self just as they do.

Davey, feeling somehow that movement was undignified, sat so still that his foot was beginning to go to sleep. He shifted a little in his seat. He knew that, by turning his head only a little, he could see both his mother and his father sitting in the second row. Slowly he let his eyes look, swallowing up in his throat the sense of being lost—lost beyond the looks of their faces, beyond the sound of their voices.

Davey looked first at the stiff, proud face of his father, closed up in its outside manners. He was strangely unmoved; to look did not make him afraid inside. And then he glanced at his mother. For one frightened moment he began trying to make his mind form the first words of his speech. And when the terrible, vast inner silence began to dissolve itself, Davey knew that it hurt him to look at his mother.

He moved back in his chair so that he couldn't see his parents any longer. Once again he waited. This was the day of his *bar mitzvah,* this was the day when something very important must happen within himself. Davey waited for the sense of awe. He tried to start a feeling that would begin deep down inside of him somewhere so that he could feel it grow. But to try to start the feeling was like pressing on a spot that is numb.

Almost with dismay, Davey concentrated his attention once more upon the rabbi, needing desperately the look, the glance, the word that had so often set him right. For a moment it seemed to Davey that the rabbi's vestments endowed him with a dignity, an aloofness, to close a boy out. Here was a moment when rapport must stand the test of strangeness, and, as Davey focused all the awareness of his questing heart upon Kurt Rosen, he could feel within the rabbi's manner the thought of himself. He was not forgotten. He listened very hard to what the rabbi was reading from the scriptures.

The rabbi's voice moved out above the heads of the congregants with calmness and dignity. And the answering voices surged up to him, searching and lost and somehow sad, containing the mingled sound of a great longing . . . but for what? Very intently Davey listened.

Oh Lord, thou has searched me, and knowest me.
Thou knowest my every step;
Thou understandest my thought from afar.
Thou measurest my going about and my lying down,
And art acquainted with all my ways.
For if there be a word on my tongue
Thou O Lord knowest it altogether.
Wither shall I go from Thy Spirit?
Or wither shall I flee from Thy Presence?
If I ascend up into heaven, Thou art there:
If I make my bed in the nether world, behold, Thou art there.
If I take the wings of the morning,
And dwell in the uttermost parts of the sea,
Even there would Thy hand lead me,
And Thy right hand would hold me.
And if I said, "Surely the darkness shall envelope me,
And the night shall shut me in,"
Even the darkness is not too dark for Thee,
Yes, the night shineth as the day;
The darkness is even as the light.
I will give thanks unto Thee,
For I am marvelously made;
Wonderful are Thy works;
My soul knoweth it right well.
Before my days were fashioned,
In Thy book were they all written down.
How mysterious are Thy purposes, O Lord,
How vast is their number.
Search me, O God, and know my heart,
Try me, and know my thoughts.
And see if there be any guile in me,
And lead me in Thy way forever.

Davey Levinson hardly breathed. It was beginning to happen. In some silent, nebulous way, it was beginning to happen, the knowing of it. The words of the psalm stirred in him some deep wish of the heart which he could not articulate.

Almost breathlessly Davey waited for a sense of God to fill the room; he waited to feel the spirit of God descending. But what he felt was not a descending of the spirit of God . . . it was an ascending of the spirit of man that seemed, finally to rise up in this room. God did not seem to come, but there was the reaching up

333

of the human heart, and an insupportable yearning. And Davey did not know whether it was the same thing, and the not knowing was the ache of being young.

The moment was at hand for the opening of the Ark. The rabbi was calling out names of men in the congregation; names which, when said in Hebrew, had a strange and awesome sound upon the air.

Sam Levinson . . . Benny Gold . . . Herman Morris . . .

Davey stole a glance at his father; but in his father's face was nothing of what he himself had been feeling.

Herman Morris, coming up behind Sam Levinson, was tall and thin and morose as always. And Benny Gold, who stubbed his toe on the step to the platform, looked only self-conscious.

As he stood up and took his place beside these men, Davey Levinson felt a fierce impatience with his elders. Where, his spirit implored, was the thing they had to give to him; how had they not laid firm grasp upon it? The sense of it was in this room; the sense of it was upon them; but they did not seem to know it fully. Davey's young heart cried out in protest that he would not receive the gift from hands which knew its worth. It was not right that only the rabbi should know it. His eyes for a moment were on Kurt Rosen, who briefly answered his questioning glance with a smile.

Maybe I am supposed to be a rabbi; maybe anyone who feels like this is supposed to, Davey thought. . . . Maybe that's what it means to know. But then he didn't want to be a rabbi. So many things in life called to him which were not a part of goodness.

Near to his father Davey Levinson stood, with the wall of strangeness between them.

The congregation rose. The men turned their faces toward the Ark. The rabbi paused, then, and Davey Levinson saw his father reach out and pull the tasseled cord. Slowly the heavy, velvet curtains were drawn back to reveal the ancient, precious scrolls with their jeweled velvet and satin covers.

Before the Torah, Davey Levinson stood awed and proud and filled with a sense of his own smallness.

The congregation sang:

> And it came to pass that when the Ark moved forward,
> Moses said: "Rise up, O Lord, and let Thine enemies be
> scattered; and let them that hate Thee flee before Thee. For
> out of Zion shall go forth the Torah, and the word of the

Lord from Jerusalem. Blessed be He Who, in His Holiness gave the Torah to His people Israel.'

And Kurt Rosen began to read:

"Almighty God, reverently we stand before Thy Law, the Torah, Thy most precious gift to man—the Holy Writ our fathers learned and taught and preserved for us, a heritage unto all generations. May we, their children's children, ponder every word and find, as they, new evidence of Thee in every precept, each eternal truth. O Light of the ages, Thou art still our light, our guide and fortress. May Thy Torah ever be our Tree of Life, our shield and stay, that we may take its teachings to our heart, and thus draw near to Thee. Amen."

II

As Sam Levinson reached out the hand that drew back the curtain of the Ark, he felt some curious tensing of his muscles, some incredible impulse to weep, some wild flight from self. In this moment there was something that impelled the spirit, something that cried out for recognition. And for an instant, Sam Levinson felt the realness of God. And in the same instant he knew himself as a Jew . . . not the Jew who can be like anybody else in the world, but the Jew, by his history and destiny unique among God's creatures, eternal, self-damning and holy.

And the moment passed. Shaken, Sam looked around him. . . . To have glimpsed truth and to know that he would immediately abandon it was frightening. Sam looked at the men he knew—at Benny Gold . . . and old Mr. Jacobson . . . and Ben Klein. He looked at them and he sensed in them what he had felt in himself. The fact, subtle, final and irrefutable. Was it true that there was, in essence, a Jewish Character, and that in all the millenniums it had not changed? The thought frightened Sam even more. His son was *bar mitzvah,* and he heard his name called third to the Torah.

Sam Levinson took the fringe of his *tallit,* with his fingers pressed the silken cords against the yellowed parchment of the Torah before him, and lifted them to his lips. And in that moment he knew his own hypocrisy. He did not look at his son, or at his wife; but he understood that Myra, in her outbreak against kissing the Torah, had shown an integrity that far exceeded his own. He looked at the Torah, and its Hebrew characters were incomprehensible to him. He began to read from the small card where Kurt Rosen had written out the words for him. And the ancient, gloried, resounding Hebrew words came numb from his lips.

When he had finished, Sam Levinson avoided his son's eyes. Showing a careful nonchalance, he walked down off the platform and took his seat again beside Myra. With an impulse he could not have understood, he took her hand for a moment and released it awkwardly. Her eyes did not waver to his own, and he listened as the others read.

> Blessed art Thou, O Lord our God, King of the Universe, Who in giving us a Torah of truth, hast implanted ever-lasting life within us. Blessed art Thou, O Lord, Giver of the Torah.

On this Sabbath, seven men were called to the Torah and seven times this blessing was said. Harry Greenglass read in a murmur that had not tone or color. Benny Gold read with the Yiddish of his childhood haunting the phrases and giving them here and there a piquance, a charm. Herman Morris recited by rote. Mr. Weber, his face unmoving, read in the very intonations that had molded his first speech at the side of a stern and pious father. And there were those who read with the compulsion of some dim and half-forgotten *heder* pressing them on.

. . . At Sinai they broke the tablets, Sam Levinson was thinking. They first refused the heritage before they accepted it. And it is always so; however we cleave to it, we also refuse it. But the breaking is never a final breaking, and the denying is never a final denying.

Am I different from the first Jew who denied it, Sam Levinson asked himself, and there was fear in his heart for having asked it. The sense of his own will, of life's immediacy, its urgency, were too great. He knew that he would not cease to deny.

But with a terrible yearning he looked at Davey sitting there on the platform with the *tallit* around his shoulders. He thought of Davey as a small child. He thought of the little boy with the great dark eyes and the quiver of eagerness in his small, bright face when he said: "My Pop can do it; he can do anything!"

"Davey . . . Davey look at me," Sam Levinson felt himself imploring. "Look at me now!"

He knew that somehow all the things which were happening inside himself must show in his face. And he wanted Davey to see, to look in his eyes and see it before it was too late—because Sam Levinson knew in his heart that his pride would assert itself again. That he would not be better, perhaps only worse, because of the moments just passed. There was so little time when Davey might ever know, and Davey would not look at him.

> Blessed art Thou, O Lord our God, King of the Universe, Who in giving us a Torah of truth, hast implanted everlasting life within us. Blessed art Thou, O Lord our God, Giver of the Torah!

The eighth one called to the Torah was Davey Levinson. Davey came forward; he stood beside Kurt, exchanging with his mentor one small, confident glance. And then he began to read. With the curious, irrefutable dignity of the perceptive young, he spoke, unstumbling, unfaltering; and his confident tones reached out, clear and ringing, to impel the ears of those assembled. And they listened . . . and they were reminded . . . and each drew into the frame of separate memory the unyielding sense of their oneness. And Sam Levinson felt it happening.

When Davey had finished reading, he straightened his shoulders and stood for a moment regarding the congregation.

Is he afraid, Sam thought wildly. And although he could not actually see them, he knew how vividly the three small freckles across the bridge of Davey's nose must stand out. Sam felt Myra begin to weep beside him, and the sense of an old loving moved painfully in the newly-chafed places of the spirit.

Davey made a small, boyish gesture with his hand. For an instant, his eyes steadied themselves on Kurt Rosen's compassionate face. And then he began to speak:

"Friends! . . . In the first chapter of Jeremiah we read that, when Jeremiah was called by God to be a prophet, he was afraid and he replied that he was too young. But the Lord said to him: 'Don't say that you are too young.' I, too, am young. But that is a condition that the passing of time will quickly correct." Davey paused and the congregation laughed and then he went on with new confidence. "And I am sure, that even now, with the word of our God as revealed in the Torah to guide me in my dealings with my fellow human beings and in the conduct of my personal life, I can begin to take my place in the life of our community . . ."

With amazement Sam Levinson listened to his son's words. He had read the speech; it hadn't impressed him. He had not realized how well Davey understood what he was saying. Frantically, Sam Levinson wondered, how does a father see his son approach manhood? And what of those things that can never be remedied which have not been remedied before this moment is unexpectedly at hand? Sam felt his face closing up. He no longer waited for Davey to look into his eyes. Davey went on speaking, and Sam tensed himself for the words that would come next.

"Because I have this wonderful heritage to guide me, I want to thank my mother and my father for their loving care of me, and for their example before me. . . ."

Davey's dark eyes came directly to his mother, and with a curious tenderness he accepted her silent tears. He did not look at his father. He turned now to Kurt Rosen.

"And I want to thank the Rabbi because he has worked hard and been patient . . . and he's taught me things that I so much wanted to know. . . ."

Kurt Rosen looked up in surprise. These words were not in the speech that Davey had so painstakingly rehearsed. And so genuine was the gratitude that passed from teacher to pupil and back again that, for an awful moment, it seemed doubtful that Davey could get back within the frame of those carefully formed words. Davey paused, he swallowed, and his Adams apple moved up convulsively. Sam Levinson saw Davey discover that he was not afraid to pause. Davey smiled a little at all the people whose warmth and love seemed to reach up to him in this, the hour of his *bar mitzvah,* and he went on with his speech.

When he could no longer listen to his son; Sam Levinson drew upon a bitter fact to heal his heart. That he had been forced to look upon himself with loathing was, he knew, the final thing for which he would hate Kurt Rosen.

III

By the rivers of Babylon
There we sat down, yea we wept,
When we remembered Zion.
There, upon the willows, we hung up our harps.
Our captors demanded a song,
And our tormentors bade us be merry:
"Sing us a song of Zion."
But how could we sing a song of the Lord
Here in a foreign land!

If I forget thee, O Jerusalem,
Let my right hand forget its cunning,
Let my tongue cleave to my mouth,
If I remember thee not,
If I set not Jerusalem above my chiefest joy.

Kurt Rosen thought of these words. And he thought of Davey Levinson. He thought of the boy who had come day after day for almost a year . . . the boy who wore blue jeans and T-shirts and sneakers . . . who hummed a song called *Dipsy Doodle* . . . and loved to ride in a jalopy that had "men working" printed all over the sides . . . who grinned if you mentioned a shy, blue-eyed young lady named Peggy Smith. . . . He thought of the boy who came to a quiet synagogue and learned to read Hebrew, and sat sometimes with his eyes beguiled by a daydream, while his mind now and then grasped some truth, some fleeting sense of himself. . . . sense of himself . . . somewhere, between jean-clad boy and the ancient psalm with its throbbing heartache, existed the Davey Levinson who stood now, a slight, erect figure, in the pulpit, and in clear, ringing tones addressed the congregation. For a moment it hurt Kurt to see Davey standing there, so straight, so fine, so solemn, and so separate from the whims, the cockiness, the moods, the sensibility and the puckish small-boy humor that he had come to know so well.

Bar mitzvah . . . with each *bar mitzvah* boy it seemed to Kurt that he stood anew at the threshold of all meaning, sharing with a fledgling spirit a moment ultimate and absolute, in which past flowed into present and the current was, for a moment, stilled.

Here, before him, was a human being and upon him the blurred imprint of the centuries, waiting for the touch of his own spirit to illumine it. Here, a Jew, standing at the very brink of his own destiny . . . with the light to guide his way . . . and the passions and the loves and the hates of life contained within him . . . and the horizons stretching far beyond him. *Bar mitzvah* . . . I am the Lord your God who brought you out of the land of Egypt, out of the house of bondage!

Kurt looked at Davey Levinson and he asked himself the question that he could never escape—What have I given him?

> *Thy word is a lamp unto my feet*
> *And a light unto my path.*
> *Teach me to do Thy will,*
> *For Thou art my God*
> *Thy teachings ever make for righteousness;*
> *Give me understanding, and I shall live.*

For some there could be this simplicity of belief . . . but for others? . . . For Davey?

O Lord, how can we know Thee? Where can we find Thee?

339

Thou art as close to us as breathing and yet farther than the farthermost star. Thou art as mysterious as the vast solitudes of the night and yet art as familiar to us as the light of the sun . . .

Kurt heard Davey approaching the end of his speech. He had read from the Torah. He had addressed the congregation. He was ready, almost, to hear from his rabbi the words of God-speed that would send him out into the wide expanse of his tomorrows . . . into the bright, wide expanse of his tomorrows . . .

There was here a profundity that must be acknowledged . . . the profundity of an ever-new joy in life arising from the ashes of an ever-renewed martyrdom. This was a moment which could not, in truth, exist apart from the sense of a martyrdom too great in dimension for the soul to grasp.

Bar mitzvah! . . . A Jew standing for the first time before the Torah . . . and all within him that will not assimilate, that will not blend and will not acquiesce, burns brightly for one moment, kindled by the light of a million souls . . . and he is separated irrevocably from the basest wish of his heart to vanish . . . and he is united fleetingly with the supreme reality of his true self . . . which he must come to know . . . or search forever over the face of the earth.

Davey was turning to Kurt Rosen. In his eyes was the quest . . . and the confidence. It was time for the rabbi to speak. Kurt Rosen arose, he went to the pulpit. For a moment his eyes met Davey's candidly.

"My dear, young friend, today you are, for the first time in your life, standing before the Torah—which means that the book of the Torah should become your book. How, in the life of the Jew does something become his own? . . . By saying a blessing? The Torah does not become yours when you keep it in your library among your other books. It does not become your own when it is kept here in the Ark and you do not attend services. The Torah can become your book only if you study it, if you follow its teachings. If our religion were to you only a book in the closet, you would lack the living Jewish spirit.

"From today you are counted for a *minyan,* and you belong to the congregation. This fact signifies that our congregation's house of worship is your house of worship, that its honor is your honor. In America I often heard people tell a *bar mitzvah* boy that he now is a man. That is not true. Your life, for many years to come will go on as it did in the past. Loving parents will protect you as they have up to now. But from this day a new phase in

340

your life begins, that of religious responsibility for what you are doing.

"This Sabbath is called *Shabbos Pinchos;* it is named after a man who, at a critical moment in the life of Moses, stood up to guide his people to the right path, to the path of virtue. What is virtue? The great Greek philosopher Aristotle said that virtue is the golden mean, the ability to keep away from all extremes. From the viewpoint of the Torah we cannot agree with Aristotle. The Bible demands that we, as did Pinchos, stand for the good with all our heart, with all our soul and with all our might. But there is something correct in Aristotle's point of view. Exaggerated thrift leads to stinginess; indulgence may become a sign of weakness; adhering to your own ideas may lead to stubbornness. In all these cases, it is good to observe the golden mean. The man who does so is called 'a good person.' But here, too, lies a danger. A so-called good person is one who wants to be on good terms with all people. In order not to be at odds with anyone he keeps quiet where he should speak and take a stand. Today our Jewish brethren overseas suffer so much, because so many of the so-called good people do not have the courage that characterized Pinchos. They do not want to take a stand, though they know that innocent Jews are mercilessly killed and abused only because they are Jews.

"You once told me that you read a story describing the sad fate of slaves, and that a shudder went through you when you read how the poor slaves were not treated as human beings. When the same thing happened from antiquity to modern times, the so-called good people kept quiet. Deep in their hearts they pitied the slaves. But they would not with all their hearts, with all their souls and with all their might, fight for the right of the slaves to be treated as decent human beings. Because they were silent and did not protest against injustice, slavery has been able to endure so long and to raise its ugly head today again.

"We Jews regard peace as the greatest blessing and the greatest good for which men should strive—not the peace of comfort and smugness, but peace, based on justice and freedom for all the children of man. Of Pinchos it is said he was zealous for God, which means that with all his heart, with all his soul and with all his might, he stood for virtue. Therefore the rabbis compare him with Elijah, for whose coming we pray so that hatred and war may disappear from this earth. Because Pinchos stood for virtue with all his heart, God said to him: 'Behold I give him my covenant of peace.' He finds true peace who knows that he has ful-

341

filled his duty. We wish for you, Davey, that you become a faithful Jew and a good citizen of our beloved country, and that you stand for the right and hate evil, and work for the success of virtue with all your heart, with all your soul. And it is our prayer and the prayer of your parents and relatives and friends that the peace of God and the peace of a good conscience be yours all the days of your life. Amen.

"And now in the name of our Temple Sisterhood I give you this book of the Bible, our holiest possession. In it you will find the sentence that has become the profession of our faith. What it is?"

Davey Levinson stood a little straighter.

Shema Yisroel, Adonoi Elohenu, Adonoi Ehod.
Hear, O Israel, the Lord our God, the Lord is one.

Davey Levinson's glance then flickered out for a moment over the audience seeking out his mother, passing fleetingly over his father, and coming again to rest on the rabbi before him.

His young face was solemn, his eyes bright, his lips silent. He waited. Kurt Rosen raised his hands above the boy's head.

"Lord God, as Thou hast proclaimed in Thy Holy Torah saying: 'Whenever I hear my name called, I shall come to thee and bless thee' . . . we pray Thee, be nigh unto us, accept this boy's profession of faith, and let him share in the blessing of Thy Holy Scriptures: May the good Lord bless thee and keep thee, may the Lord let His countenance shine upon thee, and be gracious unto thee, may the Lord lift up His countenance upon thee and give thee peace. Amen."

Chapter 29

WITH a spurt of gravel under its wheels, the last car pulled away from the curb before the Temple, and the small sounds of its departing were swallowed up in a vast hot, Saturday afternoon languor.

And inside the Temple the final echo of voices raised in good wishes and congratulations to Davey Levinson had sunk into the Sabbath stillness. The Temple was empty now, except for the Rosens.

Ellen, standing in the doorway of Kurt's study, watched him folding his *tallit*. He looked up to smile at her and in his gray eyes there was the acknowledgment that life is good.

"Kurt, it was beautiful."

"Thank you!"

Ellen wanted to say more; she wanted to tell him how a thing of beauty, born of turmoil and bitterness and dissent, has a special power in the heart. But she did not know the words to use.

"It was truly, truly beautiful," she said again. "It was a wonderful ending to a year of hard work."

Kurt glanced at Ellen. There had been a moment during the service, as he stood trying to instill into the spirit of the boy before him a sense of human dignity and destiny and repose, when he had looked out over the congregation to glimpse in Ellen's upturned face the broader inheritance of the human spirit—the protest and the struggle and the flight.

"Was it not a good beginning, too?" Kurt said finally, his eyes coming to rest with a curious gentleness upon the face whose exquisite variations of mood he knew so well.

Ellen's eyes did not meet his. She felt the old upsurge of panic. The staying . . . the going . . . had become so confused in values, so mixed with human vulnerability and fallibility . . . and the choices were so new and strange and unwoven into the fabric of the heart. So often victory and defeat had seemed to wear the same guise, had seemed each to contain the other. But Ellen knew that Kurt was asking her if they had, after all, begun again. Ellen swallowed and Kurt saw the small flutter of motion in her throat. Slowly her eyes came to his.

343

"A good beginning, too!" she said huskily.

Kurt took her hand; they walked out from the study into the vestry. From the *kiddush* cup, Kurt poured two tiny goblets of wine and placed one in Ellen's hand.

He lifted his glass.

"*Le'hayyim!*"

"*Le'hayyim!*" Ellen's voice answered with the warm vibrance of life coming new to this moment.

And Kurt watched the lips he loved touch the crystal rim of the glass.

"Ellen, I think the moment has come when we can truly say the blessing that belongs to those whose labors have been rewarded by God," Kurt said quietly, and he began to recite the blessing:

> *Praised art Thou O Lord, Our King of the Universe, who has kept us alive, sustained us, and enabled us to reach this season!*

In Kurt's words Ellen's inner ear heard the profound gratitude for their own togetherness which had withstood all the vicissitudes of life, growing with each new trial more blessed.

She felt the hot tears spring to her eyes. As she looked into the face of her husband, serene and compassionate and without reproach, she longed to bring to this moment of consecration and renewal and hope, some prayer that might be, to God, the offering of her own tempestuous spirit. She longed to acknowledge to God not only the thankfulness, but the anguish out of which true joy is born. Her dark eyes were intent upon the face of the one she loved and silently the words of the psalmist came to her lips broadening their aching, lonely, exultant meaning to embrace her heart's own travail:

> *Our soul is escaped, out of the snare of the fowlers;*
> *The snare is broken, and we are escaped.*

344